Praise for the

Alone

E. J. Noyes is easily one of the most gifted writers pulling us into whatever world she creates making us live and feel every emotion with her characters. Definitely, loudly, vehemently recommended.
- Reviewer@Large, *NetGalley*

Alone is an absolutely stunning book. This book is not a 5 star, it is well above that. You don't see books like this one very often. Truly a treasure and one that will stay with you long after the final page.
- Tiff's Reviews, *goodreads*

For being one of my most anticipated want to read books to read in 2019, this one sure had a lot of expectations to live up to! I can say with full authority, that it met or exceeded every single hope that I had. Noyes has done it again, cementing her place as a "must-read" author. *Alone* lived up to all the hype, and is easily one of the best books of 2019!
- Bethany K., *NetGalley*

There are only a handful of authors that I will drop everything to read as soon as a new book comes out, and Noyes is at the top of that list. It seems no matter what Noyes writes she doesn't disappoint. I will eagerly be waiting for whatever she writes next.
- Lex Kent's Reviews, *goodreads*

There are only a few books out there so compelling they seem to take control of you and force you to read them as quickly as possible. You can't put them down. You just want the world to go away and leave you alone until you can finish this story. *Alone* by E.J. Noyes is that book for me. This novel is absolutely wonderful.
- Betty H., *NetGalley*

Not only is this easily one of the best books of 2019, but it has worked its way onto my personal all-time top 10 list. There is not one formulaic thing going on, and it's "unputdownable".
- Karen C., *NetGalley*

I cannot give this anything more than five stars, but damn I wish I could. I would give it 15.

- Carolyn M., NetGalley

Ask, Tell

"This is a book with everything I love about top quality lesbian fiction: a fantastic romance between two wonderful women I can relate to, a location that really made me think again about something I thought I knew well, and brilliant pacing and scene-setting. I cannot recommend this novel highly enough."

- Rainbow Book Reviews

"Noyes totally blew my mind from the first sentence. I went in timidly, and I came away awaiting her next release with baited breath. I really love how Noyes is able to get below the surface of the DADT legislation. She really captures the longing, the heart-break, and especially the isolation that LGBTQ soldiers had to endure because the alternative was being deemed unfit to serve by their own government. I applaud Noyes for getting to the heart of the matter and giving a very important representation of what living and serving under this legislation truly meant for LGBTQ men and women of service."

- The Lesbian Review

"EJ Noyes was able to deliver on so many levels... This book is going to take you on a roller coaster ride of ups and downs that you won't expect but it's so unbelievably worth it."

- Les Rêveur Reviews

"Noyes clearly undertook a mammoth amount of research. I was totally engrossed. I'm not usually a reader of romance novels, but this one gripped me. The personal growth of the main character, the rich development of her fabulous best friend, Mitch, and the well-handled tension between Sabine and her love interest were all fantastic. This one definitely deserves five stars."

- ceLEStial books Reviews

Turbulence

"Wow… and when I say 'wow' I mean… WOW. After the author's debut novel *Ask, Tell* got to my list of best books of 2017, I was wondering if that was just a fluke. Fortunately for us lesfic readers, now it's confirmed: E.J. Noyes CAN write. Not only that, she can write different genres…Written in first person from Isabelle's point of view, the reader gets into her headspace with all her insecurities, struggles and character traits. Alongside Isabelle, we discover Audrey's personality, her life story and, most importantly, her feelings. Throughout the book, Ms. Noyes pushes us down a rollercoaster of emotions as we accompany Isabelle in her journey of self-discovery. In the process, we laugh, suffer and enjoy the ride."

- Gaby, *goodreads*

"This was hot, steamy, even a little emotional… and I loved every second of it. This book is in first person. I know some don't care for that, but it works for this book, really. Always being in Isabella's head, not knowing for sure what Audrey was thinking, gave me almost a little suspense. I just love the way Noyes writes. I know I am fan-girling out a bit here, but her books make me happy. All other romance fans, I easily recommend this. I just hope I don't have to wait too long for another Noyes book."

- Lex Kent, *goodreads*

"The entire story just flowed from the first page! E. J. Noyes did a superb job of bringing out Isabelle and Audrey's personalities, faults, erratic emotions and the burning passion they shared. The chemistry between both women was so palpable! I felt as though the writer drizzled every word she wrote with love, combustible desire and intense longing."

- *The Lesbian Review*

Gold

This is Noyes third book, and her writing just keeps getting better and better with each release. She gives us such amazing characters that are easy for anyone to relate to. And she makes them so endearing that you can't help but want them to overcome the past and move forward toward their happily ever after.

- *The Lesbian Review*

"This book is exactly the way I wish romance authors would get back to writing romance. This is what I want to read. If you are a Noyes fan, get this book. If you are a romance fan, get this book. I didn't even talk about the skiing... if you are a skiing fan, get this book."

- Lex Kent, *goodreads*

Pin's Reviews—"I love everything about it—the setting, the protagonists, sweet and convincing romance, a nice bunch of secondary characters, the skiing...The writing is excellent with great dialogue and pacing. There is some well-placed angst along with a really believable conflict. On top of all that, the ending (the entire last chapter) is truly great. I love when the author knows how to write a really satisfying ending."

- Pin, *goodreads*

If the
Shoe Fits

Other Bella Books by E. J. Noyes

Ask, Tell
Turbulence
Gold
Ask Me Again
Alone

About the Author

E. J. Noyes lives in Australia with her wife, a needy cat, aloof chickens and too many horses. When not indulging in her love of reading and writing, E. J. argues with her hair and pretends to be good at things.

If the
Shoe Fits

E. J. Noyes

BELLA
BOOKS
2019

Bella Books, Inc.
P.O. Box 10543
Tallahassee, FL 32302

Printed in the United States of America on acid-free paper.

First Bella Books Edition 2019

Editor: Cath Walker
Cover Designer: Kayla Mancuso

ISBN: 978-1-64247-056-7

Acknowledgments

I owe a massive thank you to my D.C. and beer guru, Christina for taking on research for me with such enthusiasm. And by extension, thanks to all the pals you annoyed for me. I think I know more about your city now than I do about mine…

American Kate, your cheerleading, constant support and well-timed GIFs saved me. Thanks for looking at wedding dresses and hairstyles with me, and being one of my 'Hey, American, what would you call this?' people.

BFF Kate… Too bad, I'm saying thanks. You helped a lot. Deal with it.

Thanks to the usual suspects at Bella. You guys are awesomesauce. And sorry about the last-minute cover nub fiasco…

Cath, it was a quick game indeed. Thank you for being such a good scorekeeper.

Pheebs, I know some of Brooke's "faults" are your (ahem, adorable) quirks but I promise they don't annoy me. This one is for you. Out of all the gals you could have gone gay for, I'm kind of pleased you chose me. I'm still so sorry for laughing during my wedding vows.

CHAPTER ONE

The picture of my sister and me had a huge smudge mark right across Sabine's face, which made her look as warped as one of Picasso's Cubist portraits. I kept a lid on my laughter and focused my attention back on Joseph Weisman who was still trying to *make me see reason*, as he kept putting it. Jamming the phone between cheek and shoulder, I stretched across the antique solid walnut desk I'd inherited from my mentor and plucked a tissue from the box kept there for clients.

As I wiped the smudge from the glass, I finally interrupted with my best take-no-shit-schoolmistress tone. "Joseph, let's lose the bullshit. We both know your client won't get sole custody, so for the hundredth time, whyyyy are you still pushing for it?"

"Jana," he purred like the sleaze he was. We'd been out a few times before I realized that the arrogant prick attorney façade was no façade. The bastard still thought he could charm me, and he *still* mispronounced my name. "What can I do to help you see our point of view?"

I cut him off with a flat declaration. "Nothing. Frankly, you're being sexist and insulting to both my client, and to me because as I've told you repeatedly, my name is pronounced *Yah-nah*. But back to the matter at hand. Aside from the fact he travels constantly for his job,

Bradley Denham has anger management issues. He can't provide a stable or safe environment for his daughters. Honestly, you should consider yourself lucky that visitation is even on the table."

"And your client's a lesbian," Joseph fired back. "Do you *really* think she's going to be awarded sole custody?"

A flash of anger heated my neck. Actually, and not that it mattered in the slightest, Michelle Denham was bisexual. But pointing that out wasn't going to help my case at the moment, though I wanted nothing more than to rant and rave and tell Weisman where to shove his homophobic misogynist views—namely so far up his ass they'd wither and die. Instead, I tamped down my annoyance and smothered him with calm realism. "Oh, the alleged same-sex relationship? That's flimsy and you know it. There's been absolutely no proof. I wish you'd give up on this pointless avenue and stop trying to deflect from the facts."

The word *alleged* had stuck in my throat. My client's sexuality had absolutely nothing to do with her excellent parenting ability, but her soon-to-be-ex husband was an asshole and grabbing at anything he could to discredit her. Because that was pretty much the only card he had to play. Every time I cautioned Michelle that she should keep her sexual preferences quiet—at least until I'd wrung everything I could from her husband, and her kids were safely in her custody—I felt like an all-round horrible person. And a fraud.

I knew what keeping secrets like that did to people, having witnessed my sister spend a chunk of her Army career suffering under Don't Ask, Don't Tell, even as she was falling in love with her fiancée slash ex-commanding officer. I saw what hiding Sabine's sexuality did to her, and there I was telling someone else to hide an essential part of themselves too.

Joseph answered with a grunted, "Whatever." Such an ineloquent shithead.

Despite his rugged good looks, he had multiple unattractive traits and I mentally slapped my forehead for ever agreeing to go on a date with him. I consoled myself with the reminder that it'd been the nice thing to do because he'd been new in town, and if nothing else—I was a fucking nice person.

I set the now-clean photo back on my desk. "Let's get back on track here. As outlined, we're asking for sole custody with generous visitation for your client, providing he keeps up with his child support payments and attends anger management counseling. My client is not at fault here. Among other things, your client committed adultery." With his twenty-year-old secretary of all things. What an unimaginative cliché. "If it wasn't for Bradley's…indiscretion I highly doubt my client would wish to have their marriage annulled." A sidestep. On our second meeting Michelle had whispered, around her tears, that she was relieved and grateful he'd been caught in his latest affair, giving her an excuse to finally end sixteen years of emotionally abusive married non-bliss.

Joseph's response was another grunt. Neanderthal. This time I gave myself a mental pat on the back to congratulate myself for never sleeping with or even kissing him. I swung side to side on my chair and executed a perfect slam dunk of tissue into wastebasket. "As I've stated numerous times, Michelle Denham wants to keep this out of court and would rather resolve it through mediation because *she* cares about the effects this divorce is having on her daughters. You're just wasting everyone's time and lining your pockets while doing so." A text from Sabine drew my attention away from his response.

Dinner ordered for 7 under your name x

I glanced at my watch. Shit, almost six thirty. Time to get the hell out of the office for the night. One-handed, I closed my laptop and started packing files into my briefcase. Joseph picked up his droning, until eventually I had to cut him off. Again. "Look. You know I'm right. Think of what losing this case will do for your reputation, and convince your client that mediation is the best way to proceed."

He sighed. "Fine. But he's set on having his day in court and I still don't know why. I'll put it to him and get back to you." Just as quickly he executed an about-face back to smarmy prick. "What are you doing now? Want to get a drink?"

"No. Even if it wasn't a conflict because of our current clients, I really just don't want to see you socially. Also, I have to help my sister plan her wedding. To another woman. Goodbye, Joseph." I hung up without waiting for his response.

And if the bastard tried to use something from my personal life, like my sister's sexuality, against my client? I'd hang him out to dry.

I used my key to unlock the front door of Sabine and Rebecca's house, calling out their names as I made my way through to the kitchen. Sabine jogged down the stairs, jumped over the last two and landed lightly on the polished wooden floor. "Hey, Jannie."

"Hey." I unloaded my briefcase and laptop bag onto the kitchen table and set takeout bags on the counter. "Where's Bec?"

"Texted twenty minutes ago to tell me she'd just left the hospital. Should be home any time now." Even if I hadn't been able to tell from the creases and dark smudges under her eyes, just by listening to her I'd have known she was tired. Her normally husky voice was an octave lower than usual and the wrong side of gravelly. "How was your day?" Before I answered, Sabine pulled me in for a hug. My big sister gave the best hugs, hugging hard with her whole body until she was satisfied, or felt I was, and then with a final extra squeeze she'd release me.

I wrapped my arms around her waist and let my forehead rest against her shoulder. In her embrace, as always, a little of my tension drained away. "Long and frustrating. Judge Lowan hates me and Joseph Weisman is being a complete prick. I'm considering billing *Weisman Hours* just to make up for the heartburn he gives me every time I have to speak to him. I need the money to pay for peppermints to get rid of the puke taste every time I think about him. Stupid misogynistic, homophobic asshole."

Sabine released me from the hug but held on to my shoulders. Her eyebrows were raised, a look I knew well. It was the "Are you done?" expression. When I remained silent, the eyebrows dropped, as did the edges of her mouth. "Weisman… Didn't you date him a few months ago?"

"Before I realized what a douchebag he was, and what a bad idea it was to socialize with someone who might be my opposing counsel, we went out twice because I was feeling charitable," I clarified, toeing off my pumps. "It wasn't dating. In fact I wouldn't even call them dates. Just drinks and bad, boring conversation."

"Mhmm." It came out with a look. A look of *yeah, right.*

"Go away." I tried to sound menacing, but Sabine's face made me laugh after the first word was out of my mouth. "Joseph Weisman and I didn't date because as you know, I don't date. I *go on* dates. The distinction is important, Sabs."

"Yeah yeah." She grinned, twisting her engagement ring around and around on her finger. Sabine had always been a fidgeter, but I'd noticed that since Bec gave her that ring she'd amped up the fidgets, constantly spinning the ring and moving it along her finger as though reassuring herself it was there.

I shrugged out of my suit jacket and draped it over the back of a chair. "How's work, Major Pain?" My overachieving Army-surgeon sister had just been promoted, and because it was required of me by sibling law, I used every opportunity to be facetious about it.

In less than eighteen months, Sabs would be done with her contracted seven-year stint in the armed forces and move into a civilian surgeon job, like Bec. Though I'd never say it to her, I was counting down the days until she was done. It was possible, but highly unlikely she'd be recalled to active duty from the Reserves, which meant I could stop spending my life worrying about her deploying again.

I quenched the memory of the weeks I spent with her in this house while she recovered from what we collectively referred to as The Incident. Sabine never shared the full details of what had happened, and probably never would. All I knew was that a vehicle she was in got hit by an exploding rocket-something, a man was killed and my sister was shot. Those details were more than enough for me.

Sabine nodded, still turning the ring. "Same same. I'll grab you something to wear so you can get out of that suit." She squeezed my shoulder and strode away, her posture Army-stiff straight.

The garage door began rolling up less than thirty seconds after Sabs went upstairs. She raced back down, tossed a bundle of clothes at me and rushed to meet Rebecca at the door connecting their laundry to the garage. I pulled on the clothes she'd thrown my way, turning up the pant legs. Though Sabine and I looked very much alike—dark eyes, darker hair—she was a good three inches taller.

I left my skirt and silk blouse draped neatly over the chair with my suit jacket. For the past couple of years, I'd been meaning to leave a few changes of clothes in their house but had never gotten around to it. I even had my own bedroom here, in case I ever drank too much to drive home, but something always stopped me from moving in clothing and other essentials. Though I knew neither of them thought it, sometimes I already felt like I imposed enough. The annoying little sister.

I busied myself with the important task of opening a bottle of white as the sound of Sabs and Bec in the laundry talking about their respective days carried through the house. They emerged with their hands brushing each other's, then split off wordlessly. Bec smiled a warm greeting at me and headed upstairs to shower away her day of trauma surgeries. Yuck.

Sabine came back to the kitchen to pour the wine. "So you had court today?" She poured a full glass for me, then barely a half for herself. With the medication she took to help with the things that lived inside her head, she didn't like drinking too much.

"Yep and again tomorrow at ten."

"What's up with Weisman?" She passed me the overfilled glass.

I drank a grateful mouthful and filled her in while we waited for Bec. Five minutes later, blond hair lying in wet curls against her neck, and still pulling her shirt down over her stomach, Bec brushed past Sabine with a quick cheek kiss and came for me. "Hello, lovely." She hugged me tight then pulled back, smiling at me. I loved her smile, always bright and genuine, with mischievous dimples.

Rebecca Keane was one of the sweetest people I knew, but underneath lay a person with a steely core, fiercely loyal and very protective of Sabine. Bec was also the only person I'd known who could tame my sister. Not in the way someone tames a wild animal but the way someone knows how to calm an agitated beast, while still allowing them to be themselves. And for that, I would love her forever.

"I missed lunch and I'm dying for a drink," Bec declared, stealing a sip of Sabine's wine while she waited for her glass to be filled.

Down the street, a car backfired and Sabine jerked awkwardly, turning toward the window. When she was tired, she was extra jumpy around sudden loud noises. Rebecca subtly placed her hand on my sister's back, steadying her with the contact. "Ready to eat, sweetheart?" she asked in a low voice.

Sabine closed her eyes and squared her shoulders. I could almost count along with her as she brought herself back to the present. After a few seconds, she rasped, "Mhmm, yeah."

Bec stretched up to kiss her and gently pulled Sabs to the table. The three of us were quiet for a couple of minutes, sorting out who wanted what and passing containers around. "They lowered my PTSD meds again," Sabine offered out of nowhere, her voice entirely steady. I knew she'd mentioned it because of what had happened minutes before. She wanted to tell me she was okay without coming out and saying as much.

I exchanged a look with Rebecca, whose expression was impassive, indicating she already knew. "Yeah? How're you feeling about it?"

"Really good." Lowering a dosage of meds was probably not a big deal for most, but was a huge one for my sister who set herself impossibly high standards. I often felt like I'd spent my life trying, and failing, to measure myself against her.

"That's great, Sabbie."

Bec drank a healthy gulp of wine and sighed, her lips curving into a smile of pure satisfaction before she looked to me. "What's new, Jana? How's work?"

"The usual, busy but good. Sometimes annoying. You?"

"Same." She watched Sabine serve salad onto a plate for her, murmuring her thanks before turning her focus back to me. "How'd that date go last night? An artist wasn't he?"

Hastily, I swallowed my mouthful and corrected her, "Stage actor. The artist was last month."

"Are you seeing him again?"

"Nope. Among other things he chews with his mouth open. But I have a second date with the software guy on Friday."

Sabine snorted, but hastily plastered an interested look on her face when Bec swatted her and told her to behave. I smiled beatifically at my soon-to-be sister-in-law. "Bec, I'm so glad you're officially going to be my sister." I jerked a thumb in Sabine's direction. "I'm thinking of sending this one back for a refund, citing defective sistering."

Sabs pointed her fork at me. "Hey, don't blame me for putting the truth in your face. You're the one who breaks out in hives at the thought of anything approaching double-digits for dating a guy."

She was right. Almost. I never quite got to hives but I did get antsy after a couple of dates. Even if I liked the guy, there was always *something* that moved him from my maybe list to my no list. It hadn't always been like this. Somewhere along the way, looking for Mr. Forever in a never-ending sea of Mr. No Thanks, I seemed to have become a bit commitment phobic. I'd been a champion of casual dating, and sex if the guy was right, for a number of years now. With my busy work life, it suited me just fine.

We chatted about nothing important over dinner, then settled in the den to run through some final details for their end-of-September wedding in just under seven weeks. *Wedding* wasn't exactly correct but it was the term we all used. Though same-sex marriage was legal here in D.C., it wasn't yet legal in Ohio where we'd grown up, and where the ceremony was to be held. Mind boggling that in 2012 we still didn't have nationwide marriage equality.

Of course, Sabine being Sabine, couldn't just do the easy thing of getting married here and being done with it. Our aging paternal grandparents weren't up to traveling, so Sabs and Bec decided to have a garden ceremony at our parents' place in Ohio so Oma and Opa could be involved, see dresses and all that shit. Then Sabine and Bec would make it legal with a quickie, courthouse marriage as soon as they got back from their not-wedding.

I settled myself on the floor, leaning against the easy chair so I could face them sitting on the couch. Sabine opened her planning notebook. Invites were out and RSVPs returned. All the furniture, marquees, canapés and booze were ordered after numerous back-and-forth with our parents. Flights to Ohio were booked. Everything was pretty much set. Except my dress and matching tie and pocket square for Mitch, Sabine's best friend and their shared best man.

Sabs tapped her pen against the notebook. "Jannie, you need to go for a final fitting to make sure everything is right."

"Yeah, okay, I'll go in a few weeks when things settle at work."

"We're W minus forty-seven days. In a few weeks is too late. Especially if it needs altering."

Bec wisely stayed quiet while my sister and I nitpicked back and forth. Sabine was so anally retentive that sometimes I just liked to antagonize her for the sake of it. In this case, it was harmless because I knew it wouldn't take long to alter a dress, assuming it even needed it after the last fitting. Which it shouldn't. I mentally sucked in my stomach. "I know how much time we have. A shitload. There is so much time I could have ten dresses organized by then. And it won't need altering. It'll be fine," I said with affected nonchalance.

Her lips set firmly and I braced myself for an outburst. Instead, I got a quiet, "I'm sorry. I just want it to be perfect." Sabine held my gaze and her dark eyes, exact copies of my own, were so sweet and earnest that my resolve to be annoying broke away.

"I know, Sabs, and it will be. I promise I'll go ASAP and get a tie and pocket thing for Mitch too while I'm out."

"That'd be great, thanks. Now that Mike's bakery is established, he's finally stopped working almost twenty-four-seven and Mitch has that goofy *don't want to leave my boyfriend* look pretty much all the time."

Bec laughed softly. "Ah, love."

Sabine's mouth lifted into an indolent grin as her eyes settled on me. "Speaking of—"

I cut her off with a sharp, "Nope."

Rebecca patted Sabine's knee then stood. "Bathroom," she explained.

Sabs tilted her head onto the back of the couch to watch her fiancée walk away, a ridiculously happy smile on her lips. Once Bec was out of sight, Sabine moved to top up my wine but I placed my hand over my glass. "You're not staying tonight?" she asked.

"No, I need to go home and make sure I'm on fire for court tomorrow."

She filled Bec's glass instead, then set the empty bottle down on the coffee table. "I don't mean to be pushy. I just want you to be happy, Jannie. That's all. I don't want you to wither away under a pile of work."

"You're not pushy. Much." I stretched out a leg and nudged her calf with my toes. "And I know you just want everyone to be as happy as you are, but I'm content with my harem of casual men." Even as I said them, those words seemed hollow and I couldn't quite figure out why.

CHAPTER TWO

Our office in one of D.C.'s older Second Empire-style buildings was a ten-minute walk to the courthouse, and unless it was hot enough to make me sweat, or raining enough to be annoying, I generally took advantage of the proximity and walked. After gathering my handbag and briefcase, I popped my head into the filing room. "Belinda! Are you ready to go?"

Belinda, a few months into her summer internship, jumped and spun quickly to face me. She grimaced. "Sorry, Ms. Fleischer, but I can't. Mr. Weston needs me to find notes from a custody ruling on a case of his from ninety-eight. It's, uh…urgent?"

I let out an exaggerated groan. "Next time, Gadget."

"Sure." Belinda's return smile was uncertain, and her lack of understanding to my *Inspector Gadget* cartoon reference made my thirty-five suddenly feel very old. When had that happened?

"When I get back, we'll do some prep for Denham versus Denham, okay? Try not to drown under boxes in the meantime."

This time, she nodded vigorously, and I understood her apparent relief at getting a break from trawling through boxes of files. On my way out of the office, I stopped to knock on my associate's open door. "Will! Can you please stop boring the intern? She's supposed to sit in on my case and learn some actual court stuff today and you've got her digging through boxes of shit from fourteen years ago."

Will Weston—a tall, salt-and-pepper-haired guy with a smile that could sway the surliest judge—raised both hands. "I know, I'm sorry but I have to get this done before I go away. Unless you want to step in and take it over for me?" Though teasing, his smile still had a touch of charm in it, as though he thought he might persuade me to work on a case for him while he spent a week on a beach in Belize with endless booze and bimbos keeping him company.

"Pass, but thanks," I said, backing away. "I have more than enough work to keep me busy." And to intrude into my feeble attempts to have some sort of social life.

"It was worth a shot," he called after me.

Once the elevator doors closed I studied myself in the mirror. Everything appeared to be in order. Still, I smoothed my bangs, wiped the corner of my mouth with my thumb and pressed nonexistent wrinkles from my skirt and jacket. The small flutter of nerves I always experienced before court arrived right on schedule, and I banished them by reminding myself that not only was I impeccably attired, but also well-prepared and basically just an all-round kickass attorney.

Ego boost success! The nerves had abated by the time the elevator announced its arrival on the ground floor. Still early in the morning, the lobby was only half-filled with other professionals milling around with their coffees and conversations. Walking briskly to the front doors I mentally ran through the case I was about to win for my client, though as my mentor once said—nobody really wins in family law. Except the lawyers.

When I was midway across the marble lobby floor, a woman walking backward and waving at a young suit-clad guy in the coffee shop crossed my path, clearly with no idea that she was about to collide with me. And collide she did, despite my attempt to get out of her way. I scrabbled at her arm, squeaking as my right foot turned over and I almost went down.

The woman spun around, gained control of her about-to-spill coffee—an extra shot nonfat latte judging by the barista's scrawl—and clasped my bicep to steady me. "Shit! I'm so sorry. Totally my fault." Her grip tightened, holding me upright while I hopped and tried not to drop my briefcase and handbag.

Straightening, I realized right away that I'd, or rather *she'd*, just snapped the heel on one of my barely two-week-old shoes. "You broke my heel!" The accusation was louder and bitchier than I'd intended and more than a few people turned to us to see what the fuss was about.

Her face went blank for a moment before panic flashed across her features. Her posture was rigid, as though she wanted to flee and was forcibly holding herself in place. The woman released my arm, clearing her throat before she said, "I did? I'm very sorry."

I brushed past her second apology with a fuming, "I have a court appearance this morning and now I don't have any shoes." Spare blouse and skirt suit in my office closet for those inevitable days when I spilled lunch on myself, but no shoes because who needs spare shoes? Sick of hopping and leaning lopsidedly, I bent down and tugged my heels off, letting them clatter to the floor. "Clearly you don't have eyes in the back of your head. You should really watch where you're walking," I huffed.

"As I said, I'm very sorry," she repeated. "It was an accident." The widening of her milk-chocolate eyes enhanced the contriteness of her apology.

Sans three inches of Ferragamo heels, my eyes were level with the woman's chin and it made me feel at a distinct disadvantage, adding to my discomfort and inability to really push my argument. No point in starting one anyway because as I'd just pointed out, I had to get to court.

I squared my shoulders and thought about the people in my office upstairs who could provide emergency footwear. One man and three women. I immediately ruled Will out, leaving me with Kelly our receptionist-slash-general errands person who was five-foot-nine and probably size ten; Erin our paralegal who was stylish as hell but with tastes leaning toward masculine and therefore not quite what I needed; and Belinda who barely scraped five-two with tiny foot size to match. And there weren't any suitable shoe stores nearby. I was screwed.

After another quick mental trawl, I decided my only option was to snap the heel from the second shoe and hope for the best. A choked, sighing grunt escaped my mouth. "Absolutely fucking perfect."

The woman took her time looking me up and down. "What size are you? Shoes," she amended quickly.

"Eight."

She exhaled. "Great, me too." The woman slipped out of her two-inch black satin heels and pushed them closer with stocking-clad toes. "Here."

"I can't wear your shoes, " I spluttered. Wearing a stranger's shoes was way too weird and more than a little gross. Still looking down, I noticed her toenails were a delicate shade of pink to match her fingernails. The color was quite pretty and at another time I might have commented on how nice it was.

The woman bent daintily at the knees and scooped up my heels, hooking her fingers in the backs to let them hang. The broken heel dangled mockingly. "Sure you can, unless you want to appear in court barefoot or hobbling. No athlete's foot, I swear. I've got flats under my desk, so it's all good." She was already walking away, backward again. Obviously she wasn't the type to learn from experience. "Just return those when you're done…Cinderella."

I glanced down at the shoes she'd discarded by my feet, then back to her. No choice really. "Where do you work?"

"Third floor. Office directly in front of the elevator. Ask for Brooke." With that she slipped into the elevator, waving at me with my own shoes.

I stared at her until the elevator doors closed, then snapped into action, slipped into the borrowed heels and rushed out of the building. I'd never been late to court, and I wasn't about to sully my record because of a ditzy latte-lover who couldn't watch where she was going.

* * *

Midafternoon, after finishing with court and holding a post-appearance victory meeting with my client, Elise No-Longer-Using-Her-Now-Ex-Husband's-Surname-of-Harris, I made my way to the third floor to return the admittedly very comfortable borrowed shoes. The office directly in front of the elevators appeared to be a property development firm by the name of Donnelly & Donnelly. The receptionist looked up expectantly at me when I stopped in front of the chest-high counter, resting my hands lightly on the surface.

"Hi, I'm here to see Brooke."

"Of course, and who may I say is asking for her?"

Shit, she didn't even know my name. I flashed a sheepish grin. "Cinderella."

To her credit, the receptionist gave no indication that she was bothered by my cryptic response. She rose from behind the desk, professional smile fixed in place. "Of course, one moment please, and I'll see where she is."

I glanced around while she wandered off to find the rightful owner of my current footwear. Behind the reception area, the office was a modernly appointed open plan with offices or conference rooms around the outside. I quickly counted nine doors, three of them open to give me a view of the occupants all working hard, or pretending to.

After thirty seconds the receptionist returned, gesturing that I should follow her. Walking across the plush carpet I had a strange and irrational thought that the employees were all staring at me, like strangers weren't a common occurrence here. As I stepped into the large corner office, Brooke rose from behind a glass and steel desk that sat at a right angle to a white drafting table and came around to meet me. The door closed behind me with a soft click.

In my annoyance this morning, I hadn't noticed much aside from her painted toenails, but now she stood before me I took a moment to study her. She wore a dark gray pencil skirt showing off the kind of legs that suggested she was a runner. A long-sleeved pale green blouse complemented her coloring, which was lighter in hair and eyes than me, and whereas I was olive-skinned thanks to Mom's genes, Brooke was darkly tanned. Apparently she spent time in the sun—the faint highlights in her slightly wavy, shoulder-length cinnamon-brown hair certainly seemed natural. That or she had a very skilled stylist.

Her ears stuck out ever so slightly, but it suited her, and for a moment I was reminded of an actress, though I couldn't quite put my finger on which one. The pretty face with well-balanced features became even prettier when she smiled at me. It was an attractive smile, warm and genuine and any residual annoyance I'd had about the circumstances of our meeting melted away. She offered her hand. "I suppose I should introduce myself properly instead of with a tackle. I'm Brooke Donnelly."

I took the outstretched hand, smiling at her joke. "Jana Fleischer."

Brooke held my hand for a fraction longer than necessary, but instead of feeling like a power play, it felt a little like reluctance to let go. "It's a pleasure to meet you for real."

"Likewise." I gestured to the sign on the wall above the receptionist's desk, visible through the glass that made up two of the four walls of Brooke's office. How on earth did she stand working in a fishbowl like this? "So, which Donnelly are you?"

"The second one. Number one Donnelly is my father." Her eyebrows knitted together for a moment before her face took on an altogether neutral expression.

"Ah, so you're in the family business."

"Something like that," she said airily before she made a quick subject change. "How did your case go this morning?"

"It went very well," I said and glanced down at my feet. "I think your comfortable shoes really helped." Very well was an understatement. Financially, the other party had come to the table and I'd secured a custody arrangement that worked in my client's, and her children's, best interests. Tonight would definitely be a *Jana Celebrates* night.

She laughed softly. "I'm pleased to hear it. Feel free to borrow them any time."

"I might take you up on that whenever I'm not sure if the judgment is going to go my way and I need a little boost."

Brooke stepped back until she was leaning against her desk, hands curled casually over the edge. Her gaze was measured, almost shrewd. "I get the feeling you don't have many days of uncertainty, Jana."

"What gives you that impression?"

"Just a hunch," she said, smiling secretively.

Suddenly embarrassed, I brushed my palm over the back of my neck. "It's just the image you know, ball-busting divorce attorney and all that."

"Ah, well from the brief glimpse I had this morning, the image works." The edge of her mouth quirked again.

Unsure as to how to answer in a way that wasn't too personal or egotistical for a woman I'd just met, I chose to say nothing and acknowledged her with a tilt of my head. We stared at each other in silence for a few moments and as I looked at her, I remembered my reason for being there and bent down to remove her shoes. When I started to slip out of the heels, Brooke held out a hand to stop me. "Keep them and bring them back tomorrow. You've got nothing to wear home."

God I was single-minded sometimes. I nodded, conceding far more easily than I had earlier when she told me to wear her shoes. "All right, thank you. I swear, I'm not usually this scatterbrained."

Brooke's smile grew warm, her eyes creased at the edges. "It's fine. I'd imagine losing your shoes threw you off balance for the whole day." She pushed off her desk and stepped closer.

I laughed. "Literally and figuratively."

We'd begun to move toward the door of her office, a natural sort of progression as the conversation wound down. I took some time to study the various degrees and awards lined up on her walls, along with a few paintings, one of which made me pause. A small shack nestled among sand dunes with a dark stormy sky swirling around it, whipping up waves. Here and there, shafts of light broke through to illuminate the house. The vibe of the painting was dark and foreboding but the shack felt like a warm, safe place. I glanced back at her. "This is fabulous. Who's the artist?"

"I am." Brooke seemed shy about the admission. "I don't just draw real buildings."

"Wow. You have some serious talent."

"Thanks," she said softly. As soon as she'd said it, that discomfort seemed to come over her again and her expression changed to intense but not obnoxious scrutiny of me. "You work up on the fifth floor, right?"

I faltered before answering, "Yes, how'd you know?"

Brooke tapped her temple with a forefinger. "I have excellent powers of deduction."

"Oh? Care to elaborate?"

She raised her thumb. "This morning you said you were due in court, so I'd already figured you for an attorney, but you confirmed it for me." A forefinger joined the thumb. "There's only two law firms in this building." Finally, a third finger extended. "The Kendrick, Weston and Fleischer I've seen next to the number five in the lobby since I started here eight years ago gives you away."

I raised both hands in surrender. "You got me. Sure you're not a detective?"

She laughed again, this time low and with a touch of glee. "Unfortunately not. I only ask because I sent your heel to be repaired. I'm sorry but the only place I could find that had a good reputation for taking care of Ferragamos won't have it done until early next week. I'll bring it up to you when it's repaired."

"Oh. Well, thank you. You didn't need to do that." I'd planned on either throwing them in the back of the closet until I could find the motivation to look for a repair place. Or failing that, I'd just buy a new pair.

"Sure I did. As you so clearly told me, I broke it, remember?" There was a teasing sparkle in her brown eyes.

I couldn't help grimacing. "I'm so sorry, I'm kind of a monster before court appearances. Excitement and nerves and laser-sharp focus and all that. I didn't mean to be a bitch about it."

Brooke shrugged. "Sure you did but it's fine, really. I totally get it."

Great, now she thought I was a bitch. For some reason I couldn't figure out, I didn't want her to think that of me. "How about I buy you a coffee one morning to make up for the bitchiness? Regular nonfat latte with an extra shot, right?"

Brooke paused, her mouth slightly open before she said, "Well that's a little creepy."

I felt the tips of my ears grow warm, and hastened to explain, "I saw your cup as I was flailing. And besides, I'll still need to return your shoes."

"And I yours, so we're even on that front. But I never turn down coffee, so I accept."

After a quick mental trawl through my schedule, I suggested, "I have an early meeting tomorrow, could we do Thursday?"

"Sure. What time suits you?"

"How's eight a.m. downstairs?"

"Sounds great." She reached around me to open her office door. "Now, if you'll excuse me, Jana. I have a team meeting starting soon and I need to get a few things organized." Brooke stepped aside and held out her arm as though she was going to escort me through to the elevators.

"Of course. I can see myself out. I'll see you Thursday morning."

This smile was warm and genuine. "I look forward to it."

A *Jana Celebrates* night really wasn't as exciting as it sounded. I made sure to leave the office at a reasonable hour and without any work in my briefcase, then opened a nice bottle the moment I'd shed my coat and laptop, and left my shoes, or rather *her* shoes, by the door instead of in the closet. Twenty minutes into my bubble bath with a glass of red for company, I called for dinner and after another fifteen minutes reluctantly dragged myself from the bath to put on some clothes, lest I give the delivery driver an extra tip that was not monetary.

While I ate pizza, I checked my two online dating profiles. Exciting, right? There were a few nudges, a couple of unimaginative probing messages, and one message that was both articulate and charming. Dare I hope? I checked the guy's page. Six-foot-one, African American, an interesting and chiseled face. Shirtless pics—oh my. Yes. Scrolling down I checked interests. Similar to mine. That's a yes. Corporate accountant. Yes. Kids, none. Pets, two cats and a tank full of goldfish. Cute. Non-smoker and social drinker. My fingers almost cramped with the speed of my response to his private message.

I'd finished half the pizza, left the rest in the fridge to eat cold tomorrow, and cut myself off after three glasses of red when my laptop sounded an email alert. Message from *KittyLover78*. Okay, so he was hot as hell, loved animals, had a good job and ticked a lot of other boxes but his username left a lot to be desired. Either he really loved his cats, or he really loved…women. Either way, what did I have to lose? Accept instant messaging request?

Yes.

CHAPTER THREE

Thursday morning I drove into the underground parking garage just before quarter to eight. As usual, the prick with the racing green Porsche 911 sporting the tag **R1CH1E** had parked just over the line of my allocated space. Every single goddamned day. I backed in slightly crooked, hoping that one day he'd scrape his hundred-thousand-dollar vanity wagon on my not-even-a-year-old Mercedes. Giving him a lesson in parking etiquette would be worth the annoyance of having to take my car to the body shop. This was my latest tactic. Ranging from passive-aggressive to scathing, I'd left multiple notes on his windshield about his parking ability, all to no avail. Next step—tire slashing.

After a quick stop in my office to dump laptop, briefcase, and coat, I took the elevator down to the lobby to meet Brooke for our coffee date. No, God no it was *not* a date. Where the hell did that come from? Meeting. No, not a meeting, too formal and she wasn't a client. Meet up? Yes, that fit.

The moment I exited the elevator I spotted Brooke reading a newspaper by one of the coffee shop's glass walls. An honest-to-goodness newspaper. Who did that nowadays, with tablets and phones available to give twenty-four-seven news? I stopped beside her elbow. "You look like a spy, hiding behind that paper and secretly watching all the comings and goings." Suddenly it hit me. A spy, of course! Brooke was a dead ringer for the actress Jennifer Garner.

Brooke lowered the paper. "Well clearly I'm not a very good one because I didn't see or hear you coming." She folded the newspaper carefully and tucked it under her arm.

I tilted my head to see what she was reading. The Washington Post's *Express*. "I can be very quiet and sneaky. When I want to be, which isn't often," I clarified.

Brooke grinned. "I'm sure you can." She tipped her head toward the door on her right. "Ready for coffee?"

"Always." As we made our way through the open glass doors, I realized an easiness had settled over me the moment I'd walked up to her, almost like we were already friends. I'd always considered myself a good judge of character, and Brooke had made me feel comfortable almost from the get-go—if you excluded our introduction—so I decided to roll with my gut feeling.

As usual, the coffee shop taking up an entire front quarter of the lobby bustled with patrons seated at tables with their morning caffeine fix, making calls and reading from tablets or books. Brooke and I lined up, standing silently but with no awkwardness. When we reached the front of the line I gestured that she should order, so I could finish deciding. Sabine called me a coffee disloyalist, because unlike most people who rarely changed their order, my coffee preference changed frequently and sometimes I didn't even know what I wanted and made other people choose for me. After quick internal musing, I decided it was a day for a nonfat caramel latte.

The cashier smiled widely at me, and even wider at Brooke. "Take a seat, ladies and we'll bring those over."

Brooke set her paper on the edge of the table so that the *Weekend Pass* section, detailing the shows and concerts and exhibits on for the coming weekend, was visible. I indicated the folded paper. "You looking for something to do this weekend?"

"Oh, no…not really. Just trying to appear like I'm into the arts scene." The smirk made it clear she was kidding.

"Ha! I saw that artwork on your office wall, I think you can safely say you're into the scene. What other sorts of things are you *into* aside from painting?"

"Team sports, being outside, disliking my job, other forms of creating art."

The disliking her job quip made me smile, until I recalled her general discomfort and adeptness at redirecting when I'd asked her about work. So I chose to steer clear. "Other forms of art like what?"

"Mostly I do small sculptures in metal, uh…knickknacks someone once called them. Also scrap material sculpture when I'm inspired and have time to go to the junkyards to ferret out bigger pieces. And if I'm in the mood I work with clay or paint."

"Wow. That's a really wide range. Not that I know much about art," I hastened to clarify. Then I pointed out the obvious, because that's what I did. "You don't really seem the type to be doing, uh… dirty kind of art things like that. You're too elegant," I added. "If you'll excuse my bluntness."

"Your bluntness is excused." Brooke smiled again as she gestured to her outfit—black, loose-leg pants paired with a pale-blue long balloon-sleeve blouse. "This is just my disguise. The moment I go home it's usually straight into coveralls and welding masks, or old clay-and-paint-spattered clothing. Making art is just a secret hobby, really." Her voice lowered, became almost sensual. "I do it for relaxation, pleasure, a sense of accomplishment. All those good things."

I swallowed, aware of the slow turn of my stomach, an unconscious and unwilling response to her tone. My question came out a little hoarsely. "So you have a studio, or something?"

"Mhmm, I have a room in the house I use as a studio when I'm painting, plus a workshop shed in my backyard that's big enough to hold all my equipment and whatever I'm working on that's loud and messy." She leaned in. "The neighbors only complain every few weeks but I keep them sweet by baking cookies and mowing their lawns."

"A backyard? As in you live in a house?"

Her eyebrows shot up. "Yes? Is that weird?"

"No no, of course not. Not at all. I guess I'd just already had you in my head as the living-in-a-condo-in-the-city type. Not the cozy-family-home-with-two-point-five-kids-and-a-dog-and-a-station-wagon type."

Brooke snorted. "Well neither of those are really me, but the second one probably fits better than the high-end city apartment. Not quite there with kids and a dog or a station wagon at the moment but someday, sure, I'd love those things. For now, all I have is an ex and a mortgage." Her smile was wry.

"You've never considered making it a career? The art thing, not the two-point-five kids and an ex and a mortgage."

She grinned, then seemed to catch herself and the amusement faltered until her smile seemed fixed in place rather than genuine. "Not really." She pointed a forefinger skyward. "My *career* is upstairs. With my father." And there was that expression again, one I recognized well, having seen it countless times on the faces of clients. Unhappy, trying to hide it, and thinking the current situation was immovable.

The server chose that moment to appear with our coffees, set mine down, and with a megawatt smile slid Brooke's order in front of her. "Didn't come to see me this morning, Brooke. Shame," she said teasingly.

Brooke pulled her coffee closer. "Thanks, Renee. Tomorrow, I promise."

"You'd better. I need to tell you about last night." Renee spared me a smile, then with a wink for Brooke, walked away.

I pulled the top from my cup to let my coffee cool. "I think that's the fastest I've ever been served coffee here. It's obviously your influence. Tell me your secret."

Her cheeks pinked ever so slightly. "Ah, it's nothing. Renee just likes to talk and we've been having chat sessions for…" Brooke's eyebrows came together. "Shit, almost three years now. It's just a little meaningless banter to start the day."

"You know I don't think I've ever seen you before and I get coffee here every morning when I come into the office. Plus with both of us moving around the building and stuff, it's weird we haven't, uh, bumped into each other before we, you know, bumped into each other."

Brooke laughed. "True. I'm usually here at six forty-five, up in my office by seven-fifteen. I come down during the day whenever the urge for caffeine overwhelms me or I need a break from my desk. I guess we've just been missing each other or doing the ignoring-a-stranger thing."

"You're probably right. And that explains it. I don't mind getting up early for the gym or whatever, but I loathe coming in before eight. But I'm usually here until seven or so at night, or working at home so I guess on balance it shouldn't matter when I get in."

Brooke laughed. "I'm the opposite. I like to get started early, then I can wrap up early and go home to do the things I actually want to."

"Oh, I'm sorry if I'm keeping you from getting to work so you can bail early."

"You're not keeping me from anything, Jana. I wanted to have coffee with you this morning."

"Well, okay then." Suddenly and inexplicably shy, and unsure what to say next, I leaned over and pushed the bag with her heels in it across the floor. "Before I forget, here's your shoes. Thanks again for the loan, I was half-tempted to keep them."

Brooke hooked a foot around the bag and dragged it under the table. "You're welcome and like I said before, you can borrow them any time." There was an amused glint in her eyes. "Look, again I'm really sorry about charging into you like that. Honestly, I don't make a habit of walking into people."

"Totally get it, saying goodbye to boyfriends can be tricky." I sipped my coffee, noting right away that it tasted better than any I'd bought from the café previously. Clearly Brooke held some sort of sway with the employees, and I needed to have morning coffee with her more often.

Brooke's eyebrows shot up and she laughed shortly. "Boyfriend? Oh no, that's my little brother."

"Ah well, saying goodbye to siblings is just as hard. Actually, I think even more so."

She smiled fondly. "Yeah, I didn't see much of him while he was a teenager and now we're kind of making up for all that time. Just some weird family stuff that's totally not appropriate for me to talk about to someone I hardly know. I'm not sure why I even brought it up. Sorry." She waved to dismiss the subject. "How about you? Siblings?"

"Just one, an older sister. Sabine's a surgeon, a major in the Army." Contrary to Brooke skirting around family dynamics, I had no qualms telling anyone about Sabine, or what she did, because not only did I love my sister fiercely but I was intensely proud of her. And not just because of what she did, but because of who she was.

"A surgeon and an attorney in the family. Impressive." Brooke whistled through her teeth. "A pair of high achievers."

I fiddled with my coffee cup. "Yeah, you could say that. My father is first-generation American and he's always been driven to prove himself. Our parents were never pushy, but I think we both unconsciously got the whole do your very best thing from him. Though definitely Sabine more than me."

"First generation?" A tiny crease appeared between her brows. "Fleischer, that's…"

"German."

"Ah, of course." Brooke leaned back in the chair. "So, this *doing your very best*, did you always want to be a lawyer?"

"Mhmm." I couldn't help grinning. "My family would say it's because I love to argue, which I absolutely do, but it's really because I like helping people."

Brooke laughed. "Oh yes, I caught a little of the arguing vibe the other morning." Before I could come up with another response to try to dim some of my less attractive qualities, she asked, "So what sort of law do you all practice up there on the top floor?" She reached for her coffee, took a sip and ran her tongue along her upper lip to wipe away a trace of latte foam.

"Family law. Like I said, I like helping people and family is really important to me." Almost unconsciously my voice lowered, softened. "I want to help people with theirs as much as I can, even if it's falling apart."

Her gaze was steady, focused, and for a moment I felt as though she could see all my deep dark secrets. "You know, I think I see it. Hardass when you need to be, but really you're soft and squishy like a marshmallow inside." She flushed, and almost immediately mumbled, "Sorry."

"What for?"

"That was rude of me." Her cheeks reddened further and Brooke touched her fingertips to both cheeks. "And now I'm seriously embarrassed."

"Don't be, it's totally fine." And also totally true.

But her blush didn't fade. She sipped her coffee, set it down and turned it around and around, all without saying a word.

I leaned closer, my elbows on the table. "Did you know when you blush, the lining of your stomach does too? Well, I'm not sure if it's blushing because it's embarrassed or whatever because I'm sure stomachs don't get embarrassed, but it turns red."

Brooke looked up, surprise and what I hoped was amusement turning her expression from almost reserved to open. "Well that's random. And also a little gross." The pink of her cheeks began to fade, but she still looked a little like a kid who'd just been scolded.

Laughing, I admitted, "It is gross, now that I think about it. Just something my sister once told me. So, how about you, Second Donnelly?" I turned sideways in the chair and crossed my legs. "How did you go from artist to developer?"

"Actually, I'm an architect. I suppose you could say I'm following in my father's footsteps. Or following his expectations would be more accurate." That undercurrent of dissatisfaction was still there, a thread I wanted to pick at and unravel. But this woman was practically a stranger and it wasn't my place to ask her to clarify or for me to even comment. Thankfully Brooke saved me from scrambling for something to break the tension. "I should probably get going. One of my team is out sick this week, and I need to delegate some work." Her regret was clear, and I empathized because I'd much rather hang out in a café and talk than deal with the inevitable shitstorm that awaited me upstairs.

I glanced at my watch. Almost eight forty. "Me too. The office has only been open for ten minutes and I'm sure I have eleventy billion phone-call notes awaiting me already."

Brooke snorted out a laugh, and in a swift motion gathered the paper, her coffee, and her bag of shoes before I could even stand. Smooth. Together we made our way toward the elevators, and though we were of similar height I had to stretch my legs to keep up. We stepped into an elevator car together, the only occupants, and pushed the buttons for our respective floors. Brooke fished in the pocket of her pants and passed me a card. "Here. If you ever need a pair of shoes, I'm your gal. Or…call me if you want to get together some time."

Holding the card up between two fingers I sketched a salute. "Will do. Thank you."

The elevator chimed its arrival on the third floor, and she turned and began to back out. "Hope you have a nice day, Jana. Try not to bust too many balls."

I mock-sighed. "You're asking a lot. And you too, make some great architect stuff until it's time to pretend you're Jennifer Beals welding in *Flashdance*."

The doors closed on her grin.

CHAPTER FOUR

Friday night, I stood naked in my walk-in closet trying to pick out a second date outfit. I needed something that said "I'm enjoying getting to know you but I'm still not sure this is going to work and you have this date, and this date only, to change my mind." First step, underwear. He wouldn't be seeing it tonight so I went with my favorite push-up bra, and panties that were less *sexy* and more *my diet to gym ratio has been a little skewed this week and I need some assistance with my body image*.

Humming The Beatles' "We Can Work it Out" I pawed through dresses. Too boring, too suggestive for a second date, too cold, too hot, makes me look washed out—note to self, get rid of that one. Eventually I settled on a sleeveless royal-blue sheath from a small boutique in Georgetown. The dress hugged my body comfortably, fell just below my knees and showed enough cleavage to remind me that such cleavage was obtained with a little extra help.

As I drove to the restaurant I reviewed some of the things I'd learned about my date, Simon—an ex-college football hero turned software designer—on our last date which was a three hour-long drinks and tapas session. The conversation had been easy, and we'd shared enough mutual interests in movies, television, and music to make the date pleasant, though not one I'd put on my list of most memorable evenings ever. My gut told me this one would bring more of the same and likely nothing more, including a third date, because frankly I didn't have time to waste on things or people that weren't going to fulfill me physically or emotionally.

Maybe a little harsh, but it'd worked for me for the past too many years to consider. My work life kept me busy enough, as did spending enough time with family and my few friends to keep me from feeling like a hermit. Going on eight dates and dithering over a guy when, if I'd been honest with myself in the beginning I would have known he was a dead end, was taking up time that I could be using to find someone who wasn't a dead end. Because surely there was *someone* out there who was a one-way, one-hundred-mile-an-hour, never-ending highway made just for me?

Simon was waiting in front of the restaurant when I arrived a very respectable almost-ten-minutes late. He bent to give my cheek a brief, barely there kiss. "Jana, you look lovely. It's great to see you again."

"You too." I raised my head to study his right eye which sported a purplish bruise spreading to the top of his cheekbone. "Yikes, did you get into a fight?"

Gingerly, he touched his fingertips to the skin just below his eye. "Not quite. Just caught an elbow to the face."

"Basketball last night?" He'd mentioned that he played every Thursday night after work with some college friends.

"That's it." Laughing, he added, "And I'm told it was totally accidental." Simon pulled the door open and with his hand lightly on my back, we went inside. The gentleman act continued as he pulled my seat out for me, waited until I was settled then sat opposite. Though I'd probably never confess it to anyone, I liked it when people did that for me. I was all for independence and feminism or whatever, but I liked feeling taken care of and appreciated and worthy of someone's best manners.

We made second-date small talk, still sending out feelers for likes and dislikes, and discovering personalities. Simon was sweet, funny, and self-deprecatingly charming. He was also attentive and kind, and appreciative without seeming like a creep. But there was absolutely no spark.

Once we'd both ordered, he pushed his water glass aside, dragged his beer closer and said, "Tell me more about your family. Last week you said you have a sister?"

"Yes, I do. Older than me by three years."

"What's it like?" He pointed to his chest. "Only child."

"It's great. We're very close."

"Is she back in, um…Utah?"

"Ohio," I corrected. "And no, she's based here in D.C."

"Oh, of course, that's right. And what's she do again? A dentist wasn't it?"

"She's a surgeon, in the Army." Though it was only our second date, I was still mildly annoyed that he couldn't remember basic details about my family—something I was quite clear about being important to me—especially when I always went to great lengths to recall personal details shared by my dates.

"Wow. Your parents raised a surgeon and an attorney. High achievers." Despite how amicable he'd seemed until now, the way he said this felt almost accusatory, like it was wrong to want the best for your kids, or for me and my sister to have aimed high and worked hard for and at our careers.

I also thought it odd that this was the second time in as many days that someone had said pretty much the same thing. The difference was when Brooke said it, she seemed impressed rather than critical. I knew which reaction I preferred. Simon's almost disparaging dismissal of my, and my sister's chosen professions turned mild annoyance to actual annoyance. I swept my hair back over my shoulder as he fixed me with a half smile, apparently wondering what my expression meant. Thankfully our starters arrived.

The rest of the evening was pleasant enough. But *pleasant enough* didn't give me insomnia, or make me think about a person constantly, or have me waking up in a sweaty throbbing mess after a very *very* nice dream. Pleasant was nice, and nice was not what I was looking for. It wasn't even nine p.m. when Simon settled the bill and escorted me outside and toward my car.

We walked. We talked. Simon held my car door while I leaned in to place my handbag on the passenger seat. I straightened, half-expecting him to have closed the gap between us for a goodnight kiss as we'd ended our first date. That kiss had also been *nice*, short, and completely unremarkable. The fact he hadn't moved and was still standing in the same place, holding the edge of my car door, strengthened my suspicion that either we were on the same wavelength, or my brief bout of annoyance had scared him off. Either way, whatever.

I rested my hand on top of his, gently squeezed his warm fingers, and smiled. "Thanks for dinner, I had a nice night."

"You too. Yes, it was nice." He cleared his throat. "So, uh…"

I jumped in where he'd dropped off, seeing no point in beating around the bush when I knew my stance and also how it seemed he wasn't particularly enthusiastic about a potential *us*. "I'll be honest with you, Simon, and it's going to sound like a total line. I really like you, but I'm not sure there's anything beyond that."

His shoulders dropped at the instant his mouth lifted into a smile. "Oh, Jana, thank goodness. Me too, I feel exactly the same. God, you're hot and funny and great to talk to but I'm sorry—there's no tingle of excitement that I usually get when there's going to be something more."

"Right? Exactly!" The relief was instantaneous. Oh, thank you thank you for men who could not only take honesty, but were honest in return.

Simon grinned. "Awesome. Thanks for being up front, and like I said it's been nice spending time with you. So uh, good luck I guess? And take care."

"You too." I stretched up to kiss him, but this time it was nothing more than a soft brush of lips against his smooth cheek. "Watch out for accidental elbows."

He laughed. "I will." He closed my car door, waited until I'd given him a quick wave and then he turned and strode away.

I blew out a relieved breath. Another one struck off the list. Who's next?

* * *

When I arrived at Sabine and Bec's for Saturday brunch, Sabs was at the kitchen counter slicing vegetables, a carton of eggs and assorted breakfasting miscellanea neatly structured around her.

"Where's Bec?"

"Still sleeping. Rough couple of days at work."

"Ah." I unloaded my contribution—champagne and orange juice for mimosas, and fresh croissants. "Everything okay?"

"Yeah, she's fine. Just tired."

When I got close, she leaned toward me and I wrapped my arm around her waist as she carefully sliced mushrooms. Resting my head on her shoulder, I asked, "You making frittata?" My sister was a fabulous cook, but had a limited repertoire, as though she didn't want to dilute her skills by spreading them across a wide range of dishes.

"You know it." Sabs indicated the fridge with a tilt of her chin. "Can you put together a fruit salad please?"

I stowed my cold things, removed other cold things and set to work as ordered. Uh, requested. After pouring coffee, of course. We worked in silence for about twenty seconds before the inevitable conversation started up with its usual flurry. Sabs used the knife to push her pile of mushroom into a bowl. "Did you sort out that work shit with Weisman?"

"Not yet, he's ignoring my calls. Actually, no. According to his secretary—he's been sick with the flu. I think he's sick with the little tidbit I dropped about my sister being a lesbian, because I learned he's not only an arrogant asshole, he's a homophobic asshole. This week's been utterly fucking insane. Oh! And did I tell you about my shoes?"

"What about them? And what about me?"

"Weisman was being a prick about a bisexual client of mine who of course I can't say is bisexual because her soon-to-be ex is also a prick, and it may have slipped out accidentally on purpose that I couldn't meet with him partly because he's an ass and partly because I had to go to a wedding planning session for my sister." I gulped coffee. "And my shoe, I think it was the morning after I came around for dinner, this woman broke my shoe in the lobby."

"How'd she break your shoe?" Sabs studied her bowls, a forefinger moving over them as if counting.

"By charging into me and pushing me over. I twisted my foot and broke the heel of my shoe."

"But that's you breaking it, not her."

"Well it wouldn't have been broken if she hadn't shoved me and made me lose my balance."

"Yeah but she didn't grab your shoe and snap it, did she?"

"Fine, for fuck's sake. It was a mutual breaking of my shoe. Better?" At her smug confirmatory nod, I continued, "What I was trying to say is after the shoe became broken, we had coffee before work."

Both eyebrows hiked up. "That's...really great, Jannie. Good for you drinking coffee."

I flicked the dishtowel at her. "If you'd listen for three seconds instead of interrupting, then I'd be able to tell you that I think I made a friend. Sort of."

Sabine nodded, almost absently moving pieces of red pepper from a bowl to her mouth. "A friend! How exciting!" Grinning, she moved to the side, anticipating my second dishtowel strike.

"Bitch. I thought you'd be happy for me, that's all. I'm out making new friends instead of…withering away buried under a pile of work, wasn't that the phrasing you used earlier this week?"

"I may have said something to that effect, yes. But I was talking about relationships, not friendships."

"Oh. Whatever. Look, my point is that it was weird because I wanted to throttle her that morning but when I saw her in the afternoon it was this feeling of almost instant comfort, like we'd been friends for ages. And it's weird, but also nice."

She made a hmming sound of agreement. "Some people are just like that, like Mitch. How was your date last night?" Even after all this time, she always asked about my dates if I didn't bring them up, which I didn't unless they were sensational.

"Meh." I directed strawberries into the bowl. "Great guy, but for someone else. Just no spark. And he has straight hair so that kind of struck him off the list anyway even if there had been any real attraction." Sabine and I both had thick, ultra-straight hair, and as a kid I'd hated it. Thankfully in my late teens, I'd discovered great haircuts and styling, but why would I want to inflict unwanted coiffure upset on my potential offspring?

"You are fucking unbelievable. Seriously? Even if you'd liked him you would have canned him because of his hair?"

"What? Is it wrong to want good genes for my hypothetical children?"

She gawped, letting out a choked kind of splutter. "What do you think would have happened if our parents had done that? Like Dad decided he wanted his *hypothetical* daughters to have bigger breasts, and Mom was worried about early onset gray hair in her kids? We wouldn't be here. Seriously. I've never met anyone as picky as you. Actually, this is beyond picky, Jana."

But was it really *picky*? "Honestly, I'm not sure I would complain if my hypothetical not-mom gave me her genetic C's instead of these A's. And as for the early onset gray? Ain't no gray in these luscious locks. That's all you, Sabs, not me."

She grunted, and I chose not to push because I had the sudden awareness that the timing of her gray hair after The Incident was likely more stress than science. Sabs opened the egg carton. "Proves my point. Even with genetics, nothing is assured. You're taking a possibility and turning it into a certainty. This whole thing goes *way* beyond not finding a person physically attractive."

I huffed. "Whatever. If it was the right person, then these little things wouldn't matter."

"Sure, but sometimes you have to compromise to get to the right person instead of writing everyone off so early. You don't give some of these guys a chance *at all*."

I raised both hands. "I know, and I agree with you there. But if you compromise in the early stages, you're giving up the fundamental things that you know will make you happy or fulfilled or whatever before you've even started a relationship. That just leaves you with shitty foundations."

Sabs started cracking eggs into yet another bowl. Cooking with her was a study in excessive washing up. "Remind me again why I debate things with you?"

"Because you always seem to forget that I get paid to argue and negotiate for what I want, and I get paid to win. And I've always been fabulous at it." I nudged Sabs in the ribs. "And maybe, just maaaybe you like letting me be better than you at something." Smiling, I popped a piece of melon into my mouth. "Seriously though, doesn't Bec do shit that drives you absolutely insane? Does she not have *things* that if they were anyone else's then it'd make you tick the no-fucking-way box? But because on the whole, Bec is Bec and she's awesome, it doesn't matter."

"Ehh, yeah, she does," my sister conceded. "And yes, she is awesome." The smile was automatic as always when she talked about Rebecca.

"Right, so you ignore those things, because you love her. Because she's the one for you. Why is it so wrong when *I'm* looking for something like that?"

"It's not wrong, Jannie. I just want you to find your awesome person."

"What's an awesome person?" came the sleepy mumble from behind us.

"You are," me and Sabs answered together.

Bec rubbed her neck, rolling her shoulders. "I appreciate the vote of confidence. Good morning, Jana. Morning, darling." She settled her glasses on her nose then crossed to Sabs, pulling my sister's face down so she could kiss her. "What are you two talking about?"

Sabine got in before me. Mmmph, shithead. "Just the usual. Jana being so picky she could hire herself out as quality control manager for the Queen of England."

Rise above, rise above. I turned slowly and shot her my best withering stare. Then stuck my tongue out and added double raised middle fingers for good measure. This refrain felt as old as me, and I secretly adored knowing I could push her buttons with something as innocuous as being ultra-choosy about relationships.

Sabs laughed and Bec joined in with a low chuckle. My older sister strode over and scooped me up into a hug. "God I love you. Now make us some mimosas please."

CHAPTER FIVE

After dumping my things in my office, saying hellos and catching up with my office staff on their weekend activities and getting an update on what had already happened work-wise that morning, I made my way to the elevators. Time for a hit of sanity-reviving coffee. I slipped into the café and was immediately enveloped by the wonderful combination of the aroma of coffee, pastries, and cooked breakfasts, and a crowd big enough to recharge my extrovert batteries until the afternoon. Near the counter was Brooke, who spotted me a few seconds after I'd recognized her.

Though her smile was instant, bright and appealing, her wave was strangely tentative. My own smile was automatic as my reaction of pleased to see her registered. "We've got to stop meeting like this," I blurted.

Her eyes widened, mouth working open and closed until she mumbled, "Oh, really? Sorry, I just, uh, you know…" She took a step backward, and everything from her body language to her expression made me think of a dog who'd just been punished for being too friendly.

I grabbed her hand to halt her retreat, wondering if my joking tone hadn't been as clear as I'd thought. "Shit, Brooke, I'm sorry. It was a stupid joke, like you know how in every romance movie ever, they bump into each other randomly and it's always that coy thing of ha-ha of course this is totally a coincidence…not. Never mind, ignore me, sometimes my funnies are funnier in my brain than they are out in the world and I forget that not everyone has a weird sense of humor." I sucked in a breath, smiled and made another, less idiotic attempt. "Let me try again. Hi, Brooke, it's really great to see you."

Her stiffness dissipated along with that kicked-puppy expression. "Hi, great to see you too. In this totally coincidentally, non-planned, non-stalkerish kind of way," she added dryly.

I couldn't help laughing at the deadpan comeback. "Of course. So are you late for your first coffee or early for your second?" I extracted cash and my loyalty card from my purse and joined the back of the line, pleased when Brooke followed.

She raised her cup. "Early for my second. Monday," she said, as if that explained it.

It did. "Amen," I muttered. "How was your weekend?"

"Busy, good. You?"

"Also busy, and also good."

My phone rang and I considered ignoring it until I saw the office number. "Sorry, have to grab this." I swiped and answered, "Jana Fleischer."

"Ms. Fleischer, it's Kelly. Just a quick one, Michelle Denham called to say she's been caught up with a childcare snafu, and she's going to be fifteen minutes or so late for your nine-thirty meeting. Massive apologies, and also tears."

"Sure, no problem." I didn't even need to ask if our receptionist had assured my going-to-be-late client that everything was fine and I'd be ready when she made it in.

Kendrick, Weston and Fleischer prided itself on being what my mentor, Ollie Kendrick, had referred to as *client-oriented*. Mostly it just meant we weren't assholes to those already going through what would be one of the toughest periods of their life. I always scheduled client meetings with a buffer to give me time to consolidate our discussion. If need be I'd absorb any run-over time by shortening my lunch break, as I'd done numerous times for clients who'd been caught by the demands of motherhood, fatherhood, or working parent duties.

I offered Brooke another apology for taking a work call during a personal conversation, and picked up where we'd left off. "So, your busy weekend. Did you get any arty stuff done?" We shuffled forward a few steps in line.

"Actually, yeah I did. I even started a new piece, which I'm really excited about. A metalwork sculpture," she elaborated as if she knew me opening my mouth meant I was about to ask.

"Sounds amazing. I'd like to see more of your work sometime if you ever feel like sharing."

Her eyes grew comically wide. "I uh, yeah I don't mind sharing, but it's probably not um, not the sort of stuff I think you'd be interested in." After clearing her throat, Brooke deftly changed the subject. "How's your day looking?"

"Well my morning just gained an extra fifteen minutes, so…yay for me I guess?"

"Nice. Use those minutes wisely," was her sage advice.

"I intend to. How about you? Or shouldn't I ask given the need for your second coffee so soon?"

She raised a shoulder, the shrug seeming more forced than casual. "Came in this morning to an abusive email from a fresh-out-of-school engineer who is adamant the design for the new apartment building my father's planning in Laurel won't work, but unfortunately he's adamant because he's totally misread the drawings. Now I'm going to have to find time to either go to his office or have him come to mine so I can teach him how to do his job. I have a thousand super urgent things to deal with, and a call with a construction foreman scheduled right when I should be eating lunch, because my father who should be dealing with it is off scouting development sites. So…yeah, not great so far." She looked so forlorn that I almost hugged her, but before I could, she raised her coffee to her mouth, which negated any hugging.

I decided on a gentle, supportive forearm squeeze. "Ouch. I'm sorry. That's a fucked-up way to start a week."

"Yeah." Brooke glanced down at my hand as I withdrew it. "I think today is going to be a drink five coffees, eat chocolate constantly and do the very childish thing of ignoring as much of my work shit for as long as I can kind of day."

I nodded my approval of her coping mechanism. "Good plan. So, this artwork? Is it a big or little sculpture?"

She paused, blushed, and after brushing flyaway hair from her cheek answered, "Uh, life-sized-ish. I've had some materials lying around just begging for inspiration, which finally hit me last week." Brooke nudged my arm gently and indicated that it was time to move forward in the line.

"Does it usually happen that way? Like a bolt of ideas out of the blue? Or is it more meticulous planning before you start?" I wasn't surprised to find that I cared about how she made her art. Artists fascinated me, mostly because my creative streak was limited to decorating my condo and repainting walls whenever I grew sick of the color.

"Bit of both, probably mostly planning in advance. Actually I think this is the first time I've just tripped over an idea like this and gone straight to work on it and had it come together."

"Well, I hope you can get home early to get to work on it some more."

"Me too." Brooke gestured to the counter. "On that note, you're almost up. I'll leave you to it, and I'd better get back to staring aimlessly at my drafting table and monitor, and metaphorically tearing my hair out. Enjoy your day, Jana."

"I will. And hopefully yours…doesn't get any worse?"

At that she laughed. "Thanks." Then she backed up a few steps, turned and walked off.

I watched her departing, aware of a sudden strange sense in the pit of my stomach and knowing right away what caused it. Brooke had been friendly and funny, but there was also an undercurrent of weariness and what seemed like dissatisfaction that went beyond a usual *work is shitty at the moment* vibe. Oddly enough, the thought of her unhappiness bothered me. Benevolent Jana is in the building.

"Ma'am? Can I help you?"

"Hmm? Sorry? Oh. Right, coffee. Uh, I'll grab a, um…grande double-shot hazelnut latte thanks." I glanced over my shoulder across the lobby to the bank of elevators. But Brooke was gone.

As anticipated, my meeting with Michelle Denham ran over time, and after I'd escorted her out to the elevator, I sat down with my meeting notes to work out how we were going to tackle this one. She still wanted to avoid court if at all possible, which was fine by me, but her estranged husband was pushing for the whole shebang—court, drawn-out arguments, custody hearings and bunches of upset and annoyance and a whole lot of money. His insistence on being a stubborn ass was making it very challenging to keep the matter easy for my client. My gut told me the only reason he was doing it was to be a bastard to his soon-to-be-ex-wife.

I made a note to call Joseph Weisman yet again to see if together we couldn't push Mr. Denham in the right direction. I rated my chance of success at about seventy percent. My thoughts drifted all over the place like a driverless car. Mostly they kept running up onto the Brooke-curb. During our short friendship—was it friendship yet?—every one of our interactions had been easy, fun, and slightly teasing. This morning had been that, but it'd also been laced with that weird upset vibe. The only time she'd seemed truly enthusiastic was when she'd first spotted me, and then talking about her sculpture.

Unsure as to why I even cared and then deciding I didn't care why, I thought about what I could do to make her day a little easier. Oma had drilled into Sabine and me repeatedly as kids—you don't need an excuse to be kind. I couldn't spring Brooke from work so she could go home to art, but I could prop her up with a chocolate stash.

Our receptionist had passed my door less than thirty seconds ago, and I took a chance she was still in earshot. "Kelly!"

A few moments later she appeared, a hand on the doorframe as she leaned in. "Yes?"

"If you're not busy, can you please duck out to the French bakery and pick up a few things for me?"

"Sure. What am I getting?"

"My lunch please and also some tasty, mood-boosting stuff. Something decadent and chocolate, éclairs or truffles, chocolate tarts or maybe even brownies?"

"No worries. And how many people need this mood boost?"

I grinned, and told her truthfully, "Everyone probably, but can you get one box of a few fabulous things just for one person, and then grab a bunch of somethings for the office staff? Cupcakes, cookies, pastries, whatever you think. I trust your choco-judgment." I rummaged in my purse and pulled out a fifty for her.

"Can do. And just your usual for lunch?"

"Please. Thank you." I tried to bring lunch with me most days, but every now and then I caved and sent Kelly for a fresh salad or sandwich or greasy soul-pleasing takeout. "Oh, and can you please ask Erin to come in when she's got a free moment? I need her to draft something for me. If Belinda's around, have her tag along too and learn from the best writer in the biz."

"Will do. Back soon." She saluted me with the cash then left me to my notes.

A knock on my partially closed door startled me from work, and it was only when I glanced at the time that I realized it was well past one. Score a point for getting so absorbed in work that the day races by. Kelly carefully set a small white bakery box on my desk, along with a sandwich and plastic cup of what was probably iced tea. Bless her.

"The rest of the bakery treats are in the break room but I don't think they're going to last long. Mr. Weston spotted them as I came in."

"Ah, well then they're probably history already." Will's sweet tooth was legendary, and he'd been known to come groveling to me midafternoon in the hope I had some chocolate or candy stashed in my drawer. I usually did, kept there just for him because it'd only taken me a few months at the firm to learn how unbearable low-blood-sugar Will was.

I opened the box holding Brooke's dessert rescue, and carefully wrote on the inner surface of the lid.

Brooke, fear not–the cavalry has arrived! Hope you're surviving. Jana.

After a moment's thought, I penned an x after my name. Though it was only a written form of the hug I'd wanted to give her earlier, it'd have to do. I closed the lid and held the parcel out to Kelly. She was utterly trustworthy and I knew she'd never open the box to look at what I'd just written inside. "Last errand and I promise I'll leave you alone. Can you please take this down to the third floor and deliver it to Brooke at Donnelly and Donnelly?"

"Am I waiting for a response to bring back?" She took the box, holding it to her chest as though it were a newborn.

"Nope. Stop, drop and run."

"You got it."

"Thanks." The moment she was out of sight, I unwrapped my lunch and turned my attention back to the issue at hand. How my gift of a gooey brownie and a coffee éclair would be received. No, that's not it. The issue at hand is…a soon to be ex-husband who would regret pushing my client to court. Goodbye, Benevolent Jana. Hello, Hardass Jana.

* * *

I'd expected to see Brooke again in the café during the week, but not as soon as the morning after the choco-delivery. She sat at a table just inside the door, situated so she could see through the glass walls into the lobby, and as I stepped into the café she stood, already smiling. My mood lifted to match her seemingly exuberant one. She seemed to do that, like she had some weird influence that instantly made me feel better when I was around her.

I didn't bother hiding my pleasure at seeing her, and seeing her looking a whole lot less frazzled than the day before. "Why, Ms. Donnelly. Two days in a row? I do believe this is becoming a habit."

Grinning madly, she held up both hands. "Nothing more than a coincidence of the totally orchestrated kind. I realized that I don't have your number, and it seemed a little too forward to come up to your office or look your firm up to call you on a business line for ah…a, um personal type thing. So, here I am. Casually stalking you."

"I see," I mused. "And why exactly are you stalking me?"

The grin faded slightly and was replaced by a look of earnest, eyebrows-raised seriousness. "To give you my eternal gratitude for your sweet gift yesterday. Seriously, you saved my ass."

"You're very welcome, and I'm glad it helped."

She gripped my forearm, firmly enough to keep me in place, but not enough to make me feel uncomfortable. Her voice lowered and I had to lean in to hear her properly. "I mean it, Jana. Yesterday absolutely fucking sucked, like one of the worst workdays I've ever had and then your box arrived and it completely changed my day. It wasn't just about the treats—which were fabulous by the way—it was the *thought*. That you'd heard something I said and then gone and done something like that. Just a really nice unexpected thing, and it made me feel good." By the time she was done explaining, Brooke's cheeks were bright pink. "It was really kind," she added quietly.

Her gratitude was lovely, of course, but what really sent warmth coursing through my body was that she'd found something in what I'd done beside a basic "here's a treat to cheer you up." I was surprised to find my throat tightening, and I forced a smile, trying to seem nonchalant and like I didn't want to cry or hug her or something. "Well, honestly, I can't take all the credit. I sent our receptionist out to buy something for you."

"Do you always try to deflect when you do something nice? It's the thought that counts and all that, and the thought was so sweet." Brooke released my arm. "Anyway, I was going to buy you coffee to thank you, but I discovered I don't even know what you drink. Then I was going to just pay for it so it'd be done when you made it down here, but that seemed kind of impersonal. In the end, I decided to wait for you and here I am." By the time she'd finished her explanation, she was almost out of breath.

I was about to tell her that she didn't need to buy me a reciprocal thing, that sending her something I'd hoped would lift her mood had made me feel good too. But she looked so damned excited, plus her rambling explanation mirrored my own rambling tendencies, and I enjoyed being with her and talking to her. "I drink everything, and coffee sounds great, thanks."

We lined up, I chose something at random and we moved off to the side to wait for our takeout orders to be ready. "So, yesterday. Did you get everything done in the end?"

"Mhmm. And with only five thousand, two hundred and eighty-one swear words."

"Shit, mustn't have been as bad as you had me believe." I winked to make sure she got that this one was a joke.

Brooke grinned. "I know, I'm such a drama queen." She flicked her hair back, huffing a dramatic sigh.

Leaning close, I murmured, "I must be rubbing off on you then."

Her mouth fell open, then twisted into a smile. She managed to get out an indeterminate sound before the barista interrupted with a call of, "Order for Brooke!"

Brooke strode over and collected our coffees, leaving me to wonder what exactly she'd been about to say. She handed mine over with a gracious, "Madam, coffee for you."

"Thank you." I collected a couple of fake sugars and together we made our way to the elevators.

Brooke punched the call button with her elbow. "So I guess I'll see you down here at another random time this week?" The statement was casual and matched by an almost slouched posture. The whole thing reminded me of how I used to try and act super cool around boys when I was a teenager.

I decided to take a chance that not only she enjoyed our banter as much as I did, but that she even wanted to hang around me. "Listen. Why don't we just make this coffee and conversation before work a regular, every morning thing? If one of us can't make it, then no harm no foul, but we may as well accept it's becoming a habit."

She paused for only a moment, before hastily agreeing, "Sure, great, fabulous. I'd like that."

"Me too," I said, meaning it wholeheartedly. "How's seven thirty work for you?"

"Perfect, but isn't that early for you?"

"Not by much, and the conversation is worth it." I held up my cup. "And so is the high-quality coffee you seem to inspire in the baristas here. I swear it's better when you're around." We stepped into the elevator together, and Brooke leaned across me to press the buttons for both our floors.

"Really? I've always found the coffee universally great." She grinned. "Maybe it's just my presence making it taste better for you."

"Maybe it is," I shot back without thinking. "Shit, will us meeting every morning mess up your daily gossip sessions with the server?"

"Nah, I make multiple trips downstairs, and I'm sure we can catch up for gossip during the day."

"Phew. I'd hate to interrupt such an important part of the day."

"You'd be worth it." The elevator chimed, and Brooke stepped out, her smile wider than I'd ever seen. "Have a good day. See you in the morning."

"You too." Left alone, I rode up to my floor, smiling the whole way. Worth it. Yeah, I totally was.

CHAPTER SIX

Mom had gone full organizational fiend, and top of her list was the fact I hadn't had the final fitting of my maid-of-honor dress. Second on the list was that I didn't have a dress for the party she was throwing the night before the ceremony. A party. The day before the wedding. I felt like I was ten steps behind everyone, still wondering why we needed a party the day before the ceremony when there would be an after-ceremony party.

When I'd asked Mom, she'd said—as though it were the most obvious thing—that we needed a party so all of the people who'd watched Sabs and me grow up could mingle and give Sabs and Bec their best wishes. And if I knew my mother, so she could show off the house and her family as she loved to do. Ergo, I needed to have a new dress. The fact I had a closet brimming with dresses was a moot point because according to Mom, none of them suited. How the hell she knew which of my outfits suited and which didn't was beyond me, unless she'd installed cameras in my walk-in closet. Her insistence on buying a new *really nice dress* strengthened my suspicion that she was trying to set me up with someone.

Yippee…

Pacing slowly in front of my office windows that gave me a view of the glass monstrosity across the street that'd recently risen up to ruin my view, I gently rebutted everything she said, and closed with, "I barely have time to pee at the moment, and I'm going to go Saturday, okay? I'm sure everyone can wait another few days for a final fitting and quality check for the dress. I've already spoken to Sabbie and Bec about it, and they're totally okay with the timing." A small lie. The little vein in Sabine's forehead had bulged. "And I promise I'll find something nice for the garden party."

Mom fretted, "Who will make sure the dressmaker has it right? And who will make sure you've found a nice dress for yourself? Don't think I don't know you pay someone to buy you clothes."

Apparently my entire family thought I was incapable of performing eighty percent of basic adult activities. It was true that I found intensive clothes shopping both tedious and stressful, so once a month a personal shopping service did the legwork for me. "Shit, Mom. I'm sure the dressmaker knows what she's doing. And I'm not *incapable* of buying clothing for myself. Remember my earlier statement about barely having time to pee? I'm busy, you know, working. And I'm fairly certain I can stand there while she runs a tape measure—" The sound of a knock on my open office door interrupted me. "…over my boobs," I finished as I turned around.

Right away, I realized that I probably should have checked who was knocking before I blurted about my breasts. The people I worked with were used to my lack of filters, but Brooke, who Kelly had just delivered, probably not so much. I'd have been embarrassed if it wasn't for Brooke trying and failing to hide a smirk.

Mom tsked me. "Fine. But I want photographs of every dress option. From all angles."

I smiled my thanks at Kelly and motioned that Brooke should come in. She did so, then closed the door quietly behind her and stood waiting. I mouthed an apology, adding an eye roll for good measure and indicated that she should take a seat. I resumed my pacing as Brooke settled on the black leather couch against the far wall of my office. "Yes fine, Mom. I'll text you pictures." Like hell. I wasn't a teenager needing my mother's approval for an outfit.

"Are you bringing a date?" she asked.

I almost snorted at the absurdity of her question, but managed to rein myself in to answer with a simple, uninflected, "No." Before she could ask why, I jumped in. "I don't know anyone I'd want to bring, and anyone I might happen to meet between now and then will be too new to be subjected to yours and Dad's special brand of parental interrogation." My parents were fabulous, and I loved them more than I could ever express. But my family took great delight in torturing and teasing me when it came to my love life. Or lack thereof. Lust life was probably a better fit. Actually even that was stretching it at the moment. How depressing.

Mom hmmphed.

I cut off any potential response with, "I have to go. A client just arrived and then I have a mountain of work to do and I, uh…need to prep for court tomorrow." My *clients* always seemed to arrive during phone calls with my mother. Very inconvenient. Brooke just managed to muffle her snort.

Mom conceded, albeit reluctantly. "Fine, go and be a legal hotshot, but call me tomorrow. We're not through with this conversation. Love you, Jana Banana."

Wonderful. I cringed as if Brooke had heard Mom calling me my childhood nickname, which she probably had given the volume of my mother's voice. Brooke and I had met up twice for morning coffee this week and shared a few semi-personal things. But *Jana Banana* was a step too far at this stage in our friendship. "Love you too. And sure, will do." Or not. I needed at least a day to regroup and prepare myself for Mom's next verbal advance.

I hung up and dropped the phone onto my desk before making my way to the couch where Brooke sat with one leg crossed over the other, a large white paper bag resting in her lap. I stared at the expanse of calf for a moment, trying to decide if I was envious or simply admiring her legs. After a few moments I decided it was both. Finally, I recalled my manners and greeted Brooke. "Hi. Sorry, my mother," I said by way of explanation for keeping her waiting.

She stood, a broad smile lighting her face. "Let me guess, you should be living your life differently to the way you are, and you're incapable of doing anything right?"

"Bingo. Very perceptive." I grinned. "In this case it's me not yet attending the final fitting for the maid-of-honor dress for my sister's wedding, and because I use a personal shopper I'm apparently incapable of buying a new dress for a party too. And you know, still single and not producing grandkids. All-round failure as a daughter," I deadpanned.

"I highly doubt that." Then, despite everything I'd just said, the thing Brooke zoned in on was, "Wait, you use a personal shopper?"

"Mhmm. It's just...I mean, I don't like wasting time wandering around stores. I'm waaay too impatient for that. I'd rather pay someone to bring me things and I can go yes, no, maybe, thanks very much and send me the invoice. But in Mom Land, a lack of time apparently translates to lack of fashion sense."

Brooke's up and down inspection of my outfit was slow. "I'll vouch that you certainly don't lack that. Prada suits you. Even if you didn't pick it yourself," she added cheekily.

"Thank you." I gave a small curtsy. "I think she's just pressing my buttons even more than usual because I have a suspicion she's trying to set me up with the son of someone from her baking group. Or sewing group. Or card game circle. Or one of the twenty other social groups she's a part of." My brain looped back. "Sorry, did you want coffee? Tea, water, something else? Did Kelly offer you something?"

"She did offer, but I'm fine thanks. So when is this wedding and alleged set-up party?"

"Six-ish weeks away. End of September. I mean, it's a wedding but not really a legal wedding. Just something for my grandparents to be involved with. We'll wear fabulous dresses and my sister's best friend and his boyfriend will stand around looking hunky in suits. Everyone will cry. Then we'll indulge in too much food, drink and fun afterward."

Brooke's left eyebrow arched curiously. "Your sister doesn't really want to get married but...thinks a pretend wedding will make your grandparents happy?"

I grinned at the leap she'd made. "No, she desperately wants to get married but she's a lesbian. Long story short, my paternal grandparents are pushing ninety and aren't up to traveling, so Sabine and her fiancée decided to have a wedding ceremony union type thing in Ohio before...you know. But same-sex marriage isn't legal there yet. Hence, the wedding that isn't. I have to do the witness duty, mini bridesmaid thing again when we get back to D.C. a few days after to make it official."

Brooke's eyebrows came together briefly before her forehead relaxed again. "Oh. I see," she said neutrally. "Sounds great."

Instantly my hackles rose, and I felt the familiar defensive indignance rise up. "Is that an issue for you?" The question came out cold and with an edge of anger.

"You being a bridesmaid twice? Not unless you're going to wear the same dress both times. That's lazy."

"Funny," I said dryly. "I meant, is it an issue for you that my sister is marrying another woman?" Even as I asked the question, I couldn't pin down why I cared about what *this* woman, who stood somewhere between acquaintance and friend, thought. Maybe because she seemed so…great, so normal and funny and kind and for her to be a homophobe was just fucked up. "Because, honestly, that would be kind of shitty of you."

Brooke's mouth fell open and she expelled a choked splutter. "Oh, hell no! It's not an issue, Jana. *Really*." She leaned closer, lowering her voice to a stage whisper. "That would be rather hypocritical of me."

It took a moment for me to realize what she was saying. "Ohhhh, you're…oh, right. Good. That's great. Fantastic!"

"Yes. It can be. Very great. Incredibly fantastic." Her smile turned conspiratorial, then she suddenly seemed to remember the reason for her visit and thrust the paper bag at me. "Sorry, totally got off track as usual. Here are your shoes, mended and in full working order. Sorry, they were only just delivered or I'd have given them to you this morning when we had coffee."

"Ah, thanks for that. I appreciate you going to the effort." I set the bag down behind my desk.

"No problem. You don't want to check they're in one piece?"

"Nope, I trust you and by extension whichever repair place you trusted."

"Good to know. Hey, listen, if you need someone to help you out with buying a dress for this party, I'm more than happy to offer my assistance."

I leaned against my desk, crossing my arms. "Really? And do you think you're qualified to assist according to the exacting standards of Mrs. Carolyn Fleischer?"

Brooke gestured to her outfit. "Well, look at me," she said. "Clearly I am."

Laughing, I agreed, "Yes, you are." My up-and-down inspection was quicker than hers had been. She wore a high-waisted, form-fitting charcoal skirt over a pale pink silk blouse with subtle ruffling at the neck, matched with nude shoes. It screamed tasteful elegance. She probably didn't need a personal shopper. "All right then. I gratefully accept, and I'm sure my mom, my sister, and my almost-legal sister-in-law will be over the moon."

"Excellent, glad I can help. When're you planning on going?"

"Saturday morning." After a beat I added, "Maybe we could grab something to eat after? My treat, as thanks for enduring the tedium of finding a dress that lives up to Mom's expectations."

"It's not exactly a hardship, Jana. But thank you, that'd be nice. We can organize details tomorrow morning over coffee?"

"Sounds like a plan."

"Great. Now I should have checked before offering to help, but… if you hate shopping, you're not going to turn full-on five-year-old throwing a tantrum because you have to try on clothes when all you want to do is hang out in the toy department, are you?"

The teasing was so easy and enjoyable, it almost felt like the back-and-forth I indulged in with my family. "No way. I was always the one sneaking off to the pet store not the toy department."

Her expression was perfectly serious. "I'm going to have to stop you from coming home with a puppy, aren't I?"

"Why can't I have a puppy?" I mock-pouted, adding some widened eyes to the mix.

"Well, maybe you can. If you behave."

Snorting, I confessed, "Well, that sucks because I rarely behave."

Her grin was slow and just a little cheeky. "Oh, Jana. I can believe that…"

* * *

The next day, Thursday, I had my first—and final—date with KittyLover78, AKA Chad. Friday was dinner with Sabs and Bec and they were both home when I arrived just after seven. I unloaded dessert onto the counter, hugged both of them and poured myself a glass of red from the open bottle on the kitchen table.

Sabine pounced. "How'd your date go last night?"

"No go. Ugh, he was so promising too. I thought all my stars were aligning until they most definitely did not."

"Ah. So why'd you ditch this one?"

"Firstly, he took me out for Mexican and ordered all my food without consulting me."

"Yeah, okay, that's gross and also totally early nineteen-hundreds misogynist," Sabs conceded.

Bec, stirring something that smelled incredible on the stovetop, glanced over her shoulder. "Who even does that? I don't even think we've done that, have we, darling?"

"No we have," Sabine quietly disagreed. "But only because one of us has been caught up at work and it's an 'I need to eat as soon as I get to the restaurant or I'm going to pass out' situation."

Bec murmured her agreement, while I nabbed a cracker and cheese from the pre-dinner snacking plate. "And! As if that wasn't bad enough, he ordered everything super spicy. Like burn your mouth until you can't feel it anymore spicy." A cardinal sin. It was there on both of my dating-site profiles under Dislikes for all to see, right underneath cruelty to animals and homophobia. Spicy food. "*And* Thursdays are an alcohol-free day, so I couldn't even chug beers to get past it."

Sabs grimaced, well aware of my spice-wimpiness. "Okay, you get a free pass on this guy, I'm not even going to tease you. That's a really dickish thing to do. Also, how many times do I have to tell you that the only way to stop your mouth burning isn't drinking but eating something not spicy, like bread or dairy."

"Oh geez, thank you for the support and your advice. There was nothing else, even the tortilla chips were covered in hot stuff. I *suffered*, Sabs! And after all that, he's still married, but separated, and spent half an hour complaining about his soon-to-be-ex and her bitch of a divorce lawyer, until he finally asked what kind of a lawyer I was. Then he went very, very quiet." Needless to say, despite the high hopes I'd had on my first contact with him, there would be no further dates.

"Well, shit."

"I knowww," I whined. "Guys, I haven't been laid in over five months. I'm developing some serious Popeye Arm here."

Bec glanced up, alarm painted on her face. "You have what now?"

"Popeye Arm," Sabs said helpfully. "You know, your dominant arm muscles get so big because you're self-servicing constantly."

Bec's grin was full-dimpled. "Ah. That's a good one."

"I know, right? I thought of it."

"That's because you were a horny shit," I mumbled.

"Yeah," Sabs agreed, leaning over to kiss Bec. She lowered her voice, but I could still hear her murmur, "Just so you know, babe, I haven't had Popeye Arm in a *very* long time."

"I'd hope not." Bec grinned, reaching up to pull my sister close for another kiss.

Sabs leaned her elbows on the counter, staring at me. "Did Mom talk to you about the party she's throwing the night before the wedding? Like we don't have enough shit to organize *and* a ceremony rehearsal that day, then she has to have a party so everyone who isn't coming to the wedding can give us their best wishes. And admire the new fence color or whatever the fuck she's trying to show off this time."

"She did, and also insisted I get a new dress for it. It reeks of a setup," I grumbled.

Sabine grimaced. "Ah, yeah, um, she mentioned Marcus Adamson."

"Who?"

"You know the Adamsons. They live at the end of the road, and their son Marcus got his shirtsleeve caught in the hay baler when he was thirteen. Me and Dad were fixing the fence after your horse busted through it, yet again, when Mrs. Adamson came screaming across the fields that border ours that they needed help."

It sounded vaguely familiar and I delved into the ol' memory bank. "Oh right. Didn't he chop his finger off?"

"Yeah, two. Right ring finger and pinky, and degloved his middle finger. It was so awesome. And horrible for him of course," she added, almost as an afterthought.

"How do you know it was those exact fingers?"

"Because I'm the one who found those exact fingers in the baling machine and put them on ice after I'd done some epic first aid on his hand," she pointed out cheerfully.

Bec laughed, while I suppressed a gag. Once I'd pushed the thought of mangled hands from my head, I told Sabs, "You're *so* gross." Still, I wasn't surprised. She had wanted to be a surgeon for as long as I could recall and had always run headfirst into every situation where someone was injured so she could help them.

"What? I did such a good job that they were able to reattach the ring finger without issues. The pinky was too mangled. Shame."

"Lovely."

"Hey, thanks to me he still has nine perfectly functional fingers." She bounced her eyebrows, grinning wickedly.

"Again, thanks for that visual. Moving on, I'm going tomorrow to check the fit of my dress and collect it if everything's fine which I'm certain it will be. I'll also get that tie for Mitch and this damned setup party dress."

Sabine's bouncing eyebrows turned to dubiously raised ones. "Will you be okay with all of that?"

"Jesus, why does everyone suddenly doubt my ability to buy clothes? Have I randomly started appearing in burlap sacks paired with checkered flip-flops and a flower garland?"

I wouldn't have thought it possible, but Sabs's eyebrows went even higher. "Uh, Jannie…you *pay* someone to shop for you."

Even Sabs didn't know, but along with the lack of time problem, I also found outfit and shoe coordination tricky. Given my job required me to look capable and confident and somewhat stylish, it was an issue. "Well, yeah but I still have to approve what she's chosen. I don't lack style, Sabbie." Small lie. "I lack time and motivation." Big truth. "Mom jumped on me about this a few days ago. Are you two colluding?"

Bec, bless her, spoke up. "Calm down, sweetheart. I'm sure Jana's got everything under control." She turned wide blue eyes to me, and I read everything in the expression. Please tell her you've got it under control or she's going to go full Bridezilla on us and I don't think I can talk her down.

"Everything's under control, Sabs. Chill, all right? And I have someone coming with me to make sure everything's as it should be, and *help* me buy another dress."

"Who?"

"Just a woman I met last week who works in our building. She's super stylish. It'll be great, I promise." I snapped my fingers. "It's the shoe breaker."

"You're trusting someone you barely know?" Sabs asked, not even bothering to disguise her incredulity or alarm.

Bec, bless her doubly, spoke up again. "I'm sure it's all fine. Just relax." She stroked Sabine's back.

My sister flashed Bec a look I knew well—anxious and trying to act like she wasn't—then turned her focus, now a pleading look, back to me. "Seriously, Jannie, please don't come home with a fucked-up dress. Please. I'll never be able to get you back there to have it fixed."

Fuck, she was pushing my goddamned buttons. Just breathe, think of calm blue oceans and Brad Pitt shirtless in *Fight Club*. It *was* her special day and all that, so I swallowed my childish retort, smiled my best smile for her and promised, "I won't. It'll be perfect, I promise. For the record, I'm not a complete idiot. And like I said, this woman knows what she's doing." I kept my smile fixed in place and hoped Brooke was as good as I thought she was.

CHAPTER SEVEN

The dress store was empty of customers when we arrived just on nine thirty a.m. The dressmaker clasped her hands together and offered me a practiced smile. "Ms. Fleischer, I've been expecting you. Your sister called earlier this week to inquire about the dress, actually. She seemed quite...concerned but I assured her everything is under control and the dress completed as discussed."

"Of course she did," I said under my breath, before plastering a practiced smile of my own on my face and responding more appropriately, "Thank you, I'm certain everything is fine. She's just anxious, as I'm sure you're used to."

"Mmmm, yes, absolutely." The dressmaker was the antithesis of every stereotype I held about seamstresses which was sixties, short, glasses, and a wrist pincushion—not early thirties, tall, auburn-haired, and looking like she should be modeling her dresses. She gestured that I should follow her to the fitting rooms.

After a glance at Brooke, already settled on one of the plush seats in the waiting area, legs crossed and phone in hand ready to pass time while I did the dress thing, I nodded. Before I disappeared around back, I said with more than a hint of fake drama, "Wish me luck..."

Brooke's smile was anything but practiced. It was warm, genuine, and adorably encouraging. "You don't need it."

It only took ten minutes for me to strip down to my underwear, be remeasured, receive a barely audible murmur of approval or thanks that I'd apparently stayed the same size, and then shimmy into the dress for a final check. The seamstress asked if I was satisfied.

I twisted to look at myself in the mirror. "Uh…I guess?" I stared some more, taking in the flowing midi skirt, the fitted bodice, and not-too-plunging V-neck with cap sleeves. The dress fit, it looked good, what else did I need? Sabine's *Please don't come home with a fucked-up dress because I'll never get you back there to have it fixed* echoed through my head. Sigh. "Just a moment, I'll have my friend check it or my sister is going to have a meltdown."

I hopped down off the box and slipped out to the waiting area where Brooke was still alone. The dressmaker followed at a respectable distance, silent while I asked Brooke, "Could I get an opinion? I think it looks great, but do you think the dress fits properly and all the rest?"

Brooke glanced up from her phone, her mouth dropping open for a moment before she snapped it shut again. Her eyes, however, remained wide open. "Shit, that's fabulous. You look incredible. Um, mhmm, everything seems, uh…yeah I think it fits. That color is… wow."

The dress was a darkish seafoam green, a compromise between blue and green for both Sabs and Bec. I fiddled with a sleeve. "Mm, thanks. I told Sabs I'd retract my agreement to be her maid of honor if she made me wear something pink, frilly, too short or generally unflattering." Which of course, had set off a round of *Jana's picky* teasing. Fleischer status quo. "I'm still a little concerned I'm going to fade into the green pasture background and be a disembodied head."

"You'd never fade into anything, Jana." Brooke cleared her throat. "What are the brides wearing?"

"Both dresses, both white." They were keeping their dresses a secret from each other, but I'd seen both gowns, and they were exquisite. "Sabs was wavering between dress and fitted tux and heels but I think her childhood fantasy of a white gown won out in the end."

Brooke stood and walked over, indicating that I should turn around. I did so, slowly, and once I'd completed a full three-sixty she gave me a thumbs-up. "I can't see any weird stitching or missing bits. I'd say you're good to go."

From behind me, I heard an exhalation and what sounded like a mumbled *Thank God.*

I reached for Brooke's hand and gave it a grateful squeeze. "Thank you. I think she'd have killed me if I didn't get this one right."

"No worries, Jana. It's my pleasure."

After I'd taken possession of the dress, Brooke and I wandered through the mall to find The Other Dress. The garment bag slung over my arm was getting in the way as I looked through racks of clothes and after my twelfth exasperated huff and shuffle, Brooke carefully extracted it from me to carry it. "For the sake of your sister. If you ruin it now…"

She bought a few blouses for work and a gorgeous A-line skirt that I was tempted by myself before I realized I'd never be able to wear it at work in case I bumped into her the day when she wore it too. We'd wandered through almost half the mall, found nothing suitable for Mom's party, and I was beginning to get hangry. Not a good mood while doing something I already found annoying. I decided I'd try one more dress and then it was time to break for lunch and recharge my shopping batteries.

I spotted yet another well-dressed mannequin in a window and ducked into yet another store with long-suffering Brooke in tow. After apologizing to her again for how boring dress shopping was, and receiving another don't-worry-about-it response, I slipped into the change rooms to repeat the strip down, dress on, ask Brooke's opinion routine. Turning sideways, I studied myself in the mirror. The cut was great and did fantastic things for my cleavage but the color was all wrong, and made me look almost sinister. Sighing, I admitted, "I think it's a little too dark for me. You could get away with it though."

"Maybe." Brooke tilted her head, tapping her lower lip with her forefinger. "I saw something I thought would look good on you. Do you mind if I grab it?"

"Go nuts." I slipped back into the fitting room to take off the dress while Brooke hunted. In nothing but my underwear, I jiggled in the overly air-conditioned cubicle, responding to texts—a frantic, lengthy missive from Mom and a calmly questioning but still panic-laced one from Sabine. A light knock on the fitting-room door made me toss my phone onto the chair in the corner.

"Just me," Brooke's slightly muffled voice assured me.

I opened the door, using it to shield myself from the other women milling about outside. "Find what you were looking for?"

Wordlessly, she held up a light blue, mid-length halter-neck dress. She seemed exceedingly pleased with herself, a smug smile tilting the edges of her mouth.

"I never even saw this. Shit, it's great." I snuck an arm out to take possession of her offering. "Thanks."

"You're welcome." Brooke leaned closer, lowering her voice to a conspiratorial whisper. "I have a gift for ferreting out clothes."

A quick check confirmed it was my size too. "That you do. Want a job as a personal shopper?" I was only ninety percent kidding.

She rubbed her chin thoughtfully, face contorted as though she was considering a life-changing decision. "Hmmm…plenty of benefits come to mind, the least of which it would mean I could quit my current stressful, soul-sucking job. I'll get back to you." Grinning, Brooke gently pulled the door closed, the soft click echoing through the small cubicle.

I left my bra on a hook and stepped into the dress. Sliding the zip up my ribs, I stared at my reflection. She had a gift indeed. The dress was *made* for me, a fitted bodice with a slightly flared skirt that fell just below my knees. And the hidden helpers inside the bust left the cleavage enhancement of the previous dress for dead. Winner.

I flung the door open, startling Brooke leaning against the opposite wall. All she said was an appreciative, "Nice." When I beckoned, she stepped into the cubicle, leaving the door open.

"What do you think?" Standing on tiptoes, I turned my back to her so I could check the hemline in the mirror.

Behind me, her eyebrows made a slow trip north. "I think you look fantastic but, uh you need a small adjustment." Brooke pointed to my collarbone, moving in as though she was going to twitch the halter strap to the side.

Moving the fabric along the inside of my left breast, I agreed, "Oh, yeah I think it might need tightening. Back there." I held the strap off my neck, pulling the dress a little tighter but it still didn't quite sit right.

"Do you want me to hold it?"

"Could you please? I can't quite get the angle right."

Brooke carefully took over, her fingers grazing my skin as she moved the fabric and held the strap away from my neck. "I think about there."

"Yeah that looks good." I raised my eyes to meet hers in the mirror but couldn't find them because they were languorously moving over my body. Her overt appraisal didn't bother me, in fact I felt a flash of excitement in the pit of my stomach that was both pleasant and unexpected. I waited until her eyes came back to mine in the mirror and was surprised by the barely disguised desire in them.

Brooke shrugged and flashed me the cutest *caught me* grin. I wouldn't have been bothered by her checking me out regardless, but something about her appreciation had gotten under my skin. And not in a bad way. After a charged moment, she murmured, "I think this is the one."

I had to swallow before I could answer in a voice that felt hoarse and far more unsteady than it should have been, "Yes. I think it is."

She stepped back, her eyes still locked with mine in the mirror, and said, "I'll leave you to get changed."

The moment I was alone again, I had to lean against the wall of the cubicle and fan my suddenly hot face. What the hell was that about?

On our way to the food court, I discovered Brooke also had an insanely good eye for color matching when she ducked into a men's store and picked a tie for Mitch after what seemed like barely ten seconds of running her finger over rows of silk before holding up a box. "This one." Then she shuffled over to another display and repeated the act, snagging a patterned pocket square in a slightly lighter but complementary shade.

Pulling the maid-of-honor dress from its bag confirmed it was an exact color match for the tie. "How'd you do that?" I demanded.

"Do what?" She held out the boxes, shaking them when I didn't take them right away. "Pick a matching square?" She grinned an entirely self-satisfied grin. "I've dressed my little brother for events and job interviews."

"No, well, yes but also how'd you choose the correct color tie right away without the dress for comparison. You looked at the dress for five minutes before, if it was even that long."

"I've got a good color brain." Her smile was fixed in place and her voice now slightly flat. "I did a fine arts degree as well as architecture, then spent a few years in Paris enjoying the starving artiste gig before coming back to the family business like a good girl."

"Oh…" So her art thing wasn't just a hobby. In that case, I really couldn't understand why someone who apparently enjoyed art as much as she did would study and do art in their free time but not as a job. "Why? Did you come back to the developer business I mean?"

"Architecture is a compromise. The only way I could incorporate an art degree was if I agreed to the whole work-for-Dad thing when I'd, uh, gotten being an artist out of my system." She gently herded me toward the cashier.

"But, it's not out of your system."

"No it's not, but my dad thinks it's a waste of time and not an actual career someone can make money from."

"What do you think?"

"I think…I don't like arguing with my dad."

I'd spent enough time with reticent clients and their even more reticent soon-to-be-ex spouses to know when to push and when to back away. So I nodded, and moved the topic to something innocuous. "Ready for something to eat?"

"Yes." After a beat and a slow smile she added, "I'm hungry."

Brooke and I hunted and gathered some lunch, then settled into a relatively unoccupied corner of the food court. The theme song to *M*A*S*H* interrupted as I was milliseconds away from my first bite of sandwich. Sabine's ringtone. Oh for the love of—

I jumped right in. "Hi. I've been remeasured for the dress and nothing's changed, and I still look amazing so I collected it. Brooke found me a great dress for Mom's setup and I look amazing in that too. I have Mitch's tie and a pocket square, which Brooke also found. Please stop harassing me."

"Whoa. Okay, that's really great. Thanks for letting me know. But I was just calling to tell you I'm going to cook Tuesday night and check if there was anything you felt like."

"Oh. No, anything's fine."

"Awesome." A pause. A subtle clearing of her throat. "So…um the dress is really okay?"

"Byyyye, Sabs. Love you." Smiling, I hung up on her.

Brooke shuffled her fork through her salad, the edge of her mouth turned up. "She's pretty persistent, isn't she."

"Mhmm." After a quick bite, I added, "I get it, this is important and all that but give me *some* fucking credit. She's worse than a helicopter parent at the moment."

"Understandable. But you looked fabulous in both dresses so I'm sure she'll settle down once she sees them."

"I hope so." I resumed attacking my lunch as a group of teens passed close to our table.

Brooke tensed perceptibly. Head down, she stared at her lunch like she was trying to find the meaning of life in the salad leaves and dressing.

I tapped the table to grab her attention. "You okay?"

Her head snapped up, eyes wide. "Oh, yeah. I, uh, just…I'm not great with a lot of people being close to me." She indicated with a vague gesture at the now-departed group. "This is kind of moving into anxiety territory for me. Even worse than meeting new people."

I set down my sandwich. "We can move or go if you want. I'm sorry, I didn't know this sort of thing made you uncomfortable." Now some of her reactions made more sense. Before I'd assumed it was just a response to my weirdness, but now I realized she was uncomfortable in the crowded café and lobby, and I felt a pang of sympathy.

"No no," she insisted. "It's fine, honestly. Once we start moving around and my brain remembers it can get away from the scary masses whenever it wants to it'll shut up. Just that being still lets it sit and think about how much it doesn't like people."

"People hey? All people?" Distraction sometimes helped Sabs's anxiety and I hoped it would help Brooke too.

Her shoulders dropped fractionally. "Most people."

"Mmm. You seemed okay when you first met me." The statement came out oddly tentative, as though testing the theory and hoping it was true.

"I was, mostly." Her face relaxed into a smile. "To be fair, our first meeting was less of an actual meeting and more of a precursor to a wrestling match. You didn't give me much time to feel too nervous or anxious."

"Noted. To alleviate anxiety, be grumpy and nasty," I teased.

Her laugh seemed genuine, and I relaxed a little. Still smiling, Brooke shook her head. "You weren't nasty. Grumpy, yeah but not nasty." Finally she looked up and caught my eye. "I didn't mind it."

Seconds passed and I had the strangest urge to reach out and take her hands, to make some sort of connection with her. Before I could, or even mull over why I wanted that, she indicated my lunch with a tilt of her head. "You should eat that. You look like you're so hungry you're about to take a bite out of the next person who walks past."

It was on the tip of my tongue to ask her again if she was really all right, but when I considered she'd already confirmed it once and that she seemed okay if not slightly on edge, I decided to let it go. "What're your plans for the rest of the day, now you're done babysitting me?"

She glanced at her watch. "Meeting my ultimate friends in a few hours for a game. Then it's probably going to be a beer plus couch plus trashy show reruns kind of night."

"Ultimate friends? You…rank your friends?"

Brooke's laugh was loud, amused, and ended in a hilarious snort. "No. They're friends with whom I play Ultimate, as in Ultimate Frisbee."

Slow clap for Jana. "Ohhh. Well fuck, don't I feel dumb right now."

"Don't, it was cute." Her cheeks pinked and she hastily added, "And easily mistaken for friendship levels instead of a sport."

"Yeah, sorry I'm not huge on different sports. So, uh, when do you guys play?"

"Training Wednesday night, games late Saturday afternoons." A grin quirked the edge of her mouth. "You could always come and watch. Or keep me company on the field. We're always looking for extras to sub in when life gets in the way."

"Oh, yeah, no…I'm good with yoga, a couple of gym classes and sporadic running, thanks. I can just about handle a week of extra spin classes when my skirts get tight, but I'm not great with anything that involves catching or throwing. Whenever I try to do sports stuff, it always lands me on my ass."

A shadow moved through her eyes and I fancied I could see her holding back an innuendo-laden comment. "Well that sucks. What about hiking or cycling?"

"I've never really done any hiking, and my cycling is limited to the stationary kind. I'm terrified of cycling in traffic."

Brooke brought both elbows up to rest on the table. "Not city cycling but out in nature and shit."

"I've never tried. I'm an indoors exercise kind of gal. Air-conditioning is one of the greatest inventions."

"Really? Give me outdoors team sports or hiking or trail running any day."

"Hmm. Maybe I should try that out some time. Fresh air and all that."

Brooke picked through her salad. "I'd be happy to take you out whenever you want to try. Or, if you ever change your mind about Ultimate or want to get together for a hike or something, just give me a call."

"I think I'd like that," I said, unsurprised that I really meant it.

CHAPTER EIGHT

I rubbed my temple, hoping it would help ease the tight tense feeling building behind my eyes. "Yes, I'm aware that you're upset, you'd been drinking and your friends egged you on. But, Patrick, may I respectfully remind you that your friends, as a whole, did not attend law school, do not spend their life working to achieve the best results for their clients—and succeeding, might I add—and have not been doing the above for almost ten years."

"But when you consider it, what's one Facebook post in the scheme of things?" he asked, the question tinged with hope.

Save me from shortsighted clients. Fighting to hold my annoyance in check, I agreed, "Sure, I'll consider what it means in the scheme of things." After a beat, I said, "There, consider it considered, and what I realized from my consideration is that posting nasty things about your spouse, even if she's soon to be your ex-spouse, on Facebook looks *really* bad. Please delete the post right now and *please* don't do it again."

He went very quiet and eventually uttered a simple, "Oh."

"Patrick, I understand how you're feeling right now, really I do. This is a stressful time for you, you're upset and angry, but please trust and listen to me when I tell you what you should and shouldn't be doing during this difficult time. My job is to make sure you're well taken care of and I take that job very seriously." The speech was second nature by now and I could probably recite it in my sleep. Then I uttered my most cringe-worthy but proven-to-be-stirring sentence. "We're going to get through this together, okay?" I held my breath, waiting for his response. Come on, come onnnn.

Patrick let out a long breath. "You're right. I'm sorry, Jana. I just want it to be over, you know?"

"I do know. Trust me, Patrick, I understand completely. I'll call as soon as I have the paperwork back from Linda's attorney." After a few more of my trusty phrases, having assured myself that I'd quashed his latest round of anxiety and that there'd be no more Facebook outbursts to jeopardize our case, we said cordial goodbyes.

Ugh. I needed a computer program that blocked people from putting offensive posts about their estranged spouses on social media. I slumped against the backrest of my chair. I still had twenty minutes until my next meeting, all my prep was done and there wasn't enough time to work on anything else because I wouldn't be able to concentrate knowing I'd have to stop again so soon. No time to inhale lunch, a fact my stomach protested with a quiet grumble. Brainless handbag cleaning to clear my mind before my next client it was.

My handbag tended to be a catchall for everything, and I tried to make time every few weeks to sort through it before things got to overflowing volcano of crap stage. In addition to my usual necessary junk like my spare phone charger and cable, emergency granola bars, hairbrush and ties, and a handful of loose just-in-case tampons that'd escaped my toiletries bag, I found a crumpled flyer for an animal rescue fundraiser, an unused straw, two packets of gum, and a squashed and browned yellow rose that Brooke had nabbed for me outside a perfume store during our shopping trip over the weekend.

As I stared at the flower, something niggled at the back of my subconscious. Brooke's offhanded comment of *if you want to get together for something give me a call* pushed its way to the forefront. Over our morning coffees I'd decided she was someone I'd like to get to know and the dress outing had strengthened the idea.

Between working at home some nights, I socialized occasionally, went for drinks with Will and our office staff the first Friday of every month for *bonding* purposes, had a meal with Sabs and Bec at least once a week and made myself go on a minimum of three dates a month. Sometimes even with the same guy.

Though I leaned toward the extrovert end of the scale, I didn't have close friends—Sabs and Bec excluded. Brooke was smart, funny, and easy to talk to, and someone I could see myself spending more time with. What the hell. One possible friendship coming right up.

I dialed the personal number she'd carefully written on the back of her business card, and she answered with a slightly cautious, "Hello?"

"Brooke? It's Jana Fleischer. How are you?"

I heard her exhalation and then all the caution disappeared from her voice, replaced by undeniable pleasure. "Oh, hi. I'm good, yourself?"

"I'm great." Ignoring the strange and unexpected flutter of nerves, I decided a joke was the best way to go. "Listen, sorry to bother you, but I need a pair of ruby red heels and I was wondering if you've got anything for me?"

"Ruby red." She clicked her tongue a few times. "I'm afraid not. In a pinch I could do a kind of candy-apple red?"

"No good, has to be ruby. Ah well, it was a long shot. Frankly, I'm disappointed that you didn't intuit what I might need."

"Very sorry to let you down," she said, laying on the mock-sincerity. Then her voice lowered, became a soft drawl. "Maybe I can make it up to you?"

The flutter of nerves turned into a weird heart stutter-step. "I'm listening."

"A round of drinks on me after work tomorrow night. I know it's late notice for a Friday, but if you're free…"

I was free and didn't even have to think before I answered. "Deal."

"Fantastic." She sounded extremely pleased. "Why don't you text when you're done with saving the familial units of D.C. and surrounds, and we'll go from there."

"Perfect, and I shouldn't be too late saving the familial units of D.C. and surrounds. Actually, that has a nice ring to it. Maybe it's time to look into that superhero outfit thing. So do I need to change or can I come straight from work?" After a few long moments of her silence, I realized that as was often the case, what came out of my mouth was little more than disjointed babble. Probably why she hadn't answered. "Sorry, my brain is a ping pong ball, and my mouth tends to follow. Did you get all of that?"

She laughed. "I'd already gathered that about you. I like it, and sorry, it just takes me a few seconds to catch up and sort one of your thoughts from the previous one. Whatever you want to wear is fine, even if it's a superhero costume. I doubt we'll go anywhere fancy, probably just hold up the bar somewhere nearby for a few hours?"

"Sounds fabulous."

"Excellent." She paused, her voice lowering again. "I'm really glad you called."

So was I.

* * *

Sabs and Bec arrived for a late dinner at eight thirty, still dressed in team uniforms from their weekly game of flag football. "Win or lose?" I asked as soon as we'd distributed hugs.

"Bec won, I lost," ever-competitive Sabs grumbled as she bent down to unlace her sneakers. She'd joined the same league as Bec a few months ago and had been unable to get a spot on Bec's team. Now they were competitors, as they had been on occasion back when they worked together in an Army posting in Afghanistan. A fact which resulted in much good-natured teasing.

Bec reached up to caress the back of Sabine's neck. "But I saw you make some wonderful plays, darling, and at least we weren't playing each other tonight."

"Yeah." Sabs huffed and dropped onto the couch, putting her sock-clad feet up onto my coffee table. She made a vague gesture toward the kitchen. "I'm starving. Whatever you made for dinner smells fucking fantastic. Is it nearly done?"

"Yep, ready when you are, and it's just chicken pasta primavera. Literally the most boring and easy meal, sorry. Long day." I could have just ordered in but had craved the relaxation cooking brought after a stressful client-filled day.

Bec stood beside me, leaning into me and wrapping an arm around my waist. "Don't be silly, sweetie. Everything you cook is wonderful. Except that time you experimented with carpaccio…" After a grin and a squeeze, she let me go to fetch plates and cutlery.

"Well, raw meat dishes aren't technically cooking," I mumbled, rummaging in the fridge. I held up a bottle of Magic Hat #9. "Did you guys want a cold beer?"

"God yes," Bec said instantly. "Thanks."

I passed her one but held off grabbing a second. Leaning around the fridge, I caught my sister's eye. "Sabs, beer? Or water or soda or non-alcoholic beer if you want?"

Sabine's eyebrows scrunched close together, one of her cheeks sucked in as she chewed and thought. I readied myself to wait while she carefully weighed the pros and cons and ramifications of the enjoyment of having a beer after exercise versus potential effects on her medication. A long moment passed before she nodded. "I'll take a real beer please."

I popped the top off a bottle and set it down in her usual spot, then poured water for myself as Bec finished setting the table.

Halfway through her dinner, Sabs exhaled a long contented sigh. "This is really good, Jannie. I needed a mega dose of carbs." She washed down a mouthful of pasta with a long swig of beer. Then she raised her fork as though to scoop up more pasta but instead, she paused and set her fork down again. Her gaze was on the table, the intense focus suggesting she was having a *moment* and trying to work through it.

Bec stopped eating, watching Sabine with a calm, yet fiercely protective expression. After a few seconds she quietly asked, "Darling?"

Sabs cleared her throat and held up an *I'm okay* hand to Bec. Then her laser-sharp focus turned to me. "Jannie, can I *please* see your maid-of-honor dress now?" The question came out with such desperation that I wondered how she'd managed to hold off asking for this long.

Laughter burst out of my mouth so quickly, I had to cover it to stop myself from spraying the table with water. Once I could breathe and talk, I agreed, "Fine, come on. Our dinner can get cold while we do this very important thing." There was a time and place for holding out on her just to annoy, but doing it when I knew delaying would genuinely intensify her anxiety was cruel.

Sabine rocketed out of the chair so fast it wobbled. "You coming, Bec?"

"I'll finish my meal and come see in a few minutes," she said calmly.

"Okay!" Sabs called over her shoulder, already three-quarters of the way up the hall.

Smiling, Bec shook her head. "Sorry, she's been antsy all week about it."

"It's fine. I know what she's like."

Sabine's voice bounced off the hallway walls. "Jana! I'm here! Come *on*!"

Sighing, I backed toward the hallway. "Fair warning, I might strangle her before the ceremony."

Bec's dimples made an appearance. "Please don't, we've already paid for everything." She chuckled and turned back to her dinner, and I dutifully made my way into the spare room after a quick stop to wash my hands lest I soil The Dress.

The dress I'd bought at Mom's insistence was laid flat on the bed, waiting to be taken for alterations. Sabs, practically vibrating with excitement, pointed at the bed. "Is that your party dress?"

"Mhmm."

"It's nice, you'll look gorgeous."

"Yeah." I bent down to smooth the fabric. "Brooke found it, right about when I was ready to throw in the towel."

"Apparently this Brooke is an angel in disguise." She hopped back a step, away from my swatting hand. With a quick, sly grin she accepted her victory before her face relaxed back to her previous desperate expression. "Ceremony dress now, please. I've been stressing about it all week."

"Stay right there, and *no* peeking in this closet." My spare room closet held both wedding gowns to keep them safe from accidental fiancée exposure. Though both dresses were safely contained in black garment bags, I had a sudden and irrational fear that she'd somehow see Bec's dress.

Sabs hummingbirded around the room. "Is it fine? It looks good, right? It's the same as your first fitting and stuff?" She'd seen the bare-bones version of the dress when we'd gone to choose color and style but hadn't made it to any other fittings I'd had since.

"As I said the four times in the last four days since collecting it, yes yes yes yes." I slipped the dress from the closet and quickly closed the door. "I have to put it on, don't I."

She nodded so vigorously I was surprised she didn't give herself whiplash. "Mhmm, yep, please."

I bit back a sigh and quickly stripped out of my ultra-comfortable sweats and tee and stepped carefully into the dress. Moving my hair out of the way, I told her, "Zip me up, please. Watch my skin," I added quickly when she half-lunged at me in her haste to finish dressing me.

Before I could turn around, Sabs grabbed me by the shoulders and spun me to face her. She blinked hard a couple of times and when she spoke, her voice was rough and choked. "Oh wow, you look so beautiful."

"Eh, I know." I leaned closer, studying her widened eyes and the trembling lower lip she held firmly between her teeth. "Are you crying?"

"Geez, what do you take me for? Some kind of sap?" She sniffed, paused and gave me her lopsided grin. "Of course I'm fucking crying. You look so amazing." Sabs gave my cheek a fond caress and turned to yell out the door, "Honey, can you come in here please?" She palmed under her eyes, still sniffling, and I had to clench my teeth to stop my tear ducts joining in with her happy crying.

Bec appeared thirty seconds later, beer bottle in hand. She leaned against the door, nodding in appreciation. "Hey, that looks fantastic."

My sister turned me to face her fiancée, and I went limp, allowing myself be moved around like a puppet. Sabine shook me side to side. "The color's great, isn't it great?"

"Yes, darling," Bec agreed. "It's great. Just what we'd thought it would be."

"And isn't the cut perfect?"

Bec shot me an apologetic look, then agreed again, "Mhmm, perfect. Jana, you look wonderful." She offered a hand to Sabs. "Are you going to come out and finish your dinner now?"

"Yeah." Sabs swiftly unzipped me and yanked me in for a hug, whispering in my ear, "You look gorgeous. Thank you, Jannie, *thank you*. I feel so much better now." She finished her hug with a rib-crushing squeeze then practically skipped out of the room. Bec's eyes met mine briefly to share a knowing look, then she turned to follow, leaving me to change.

Sabine's obvious relief was worth my annoyance but still, I could not wait until I had my regular, Type-A and slightly anxious sister back instead of this mega-panicked nitpicky micro-Bridezilla.

After dinner, Bec ducked into my bedroom to take a work call while Sabs and I settled on the couch. She stuck her feet up on my coffee table again, her toes curling and then relaxing rhythmically a few times. "What are you doing this weekend? Hot Friday night date tomorrow?"

"Actually no, I'm going out for drinks with Brooke." I leaned back and curled my legs under my butt.

"Oh. So she's a good friend then? I thought she was just a work acquaintance."

"Not yet, but I think she could be. We've been meeting up in the mornings for coffee and mindless chitchat."

"I see. Well if there's one thing us Fleischers are good at, it's mindless chitchat."

I had to squash the sudden urge to fidget. "Maybe you know her? She's a lesbian," I added when Sabine shot me a confused look.

"What's her last name?"

"Donnelly."

Sabs snapped her fingers. "Oh! Yeah, of course! Brooke Donnelly!"

"Really?"

"No," she said flatly, her eye roll overly exaggerated. "What do you think, Jannie? That all lesbians are card-carrying members of the Lez

Club and that we spend our whole lives making sure we know every lesbian on the planet?"

"Okay then, obviously not. Shit, you could have just said no."

But she was on a roll. "It's like when you tell someone you're part German, and they immediately think you know some German person they sat next to on a bus ten years ago, or their great-uncle so-and-so from fucking Wolfsberg that even they haven't met."

I lifted my hands to stop her rambling. "Fine, Christ. I'm sorry I asked." After a beat I added, "Well, do we know the great-uncle so-and-so from Wolfsberg?"

She grinned. "Shut up, you."

I poked her hard in the stomach. "Brooke also plays that Frisbee game you were talking about a few months back. She's invited me to come watch a game."

"Ohhhh, yeah, I'd forgotten about that. Cool."

"Mmm. So yeah, we've been hanging out a bit."

"Good, you need more friends."

"I do?" I straightened up on the couch, suddenly suspicious. She'd never been pushy about my social life. Love life, yeah—that was fair game. But aside from defending me against mean kids in school, she'd never seemed to care who I hung around with.

"Yeah, you do. Bec and I aren't always going to be around, you know."

Irrational panic rose up and I leaned forward, grasping her arm. "What do you mean? What's going on? Are you moving? Are you sick?"

"No, of course not." She stroked my hair comfortingly, then pulled me in for a quick hug. "But you know, we have jobs and lives and vacations and shit. And maybe one day we *will* move, if there's a job opportunity somewhere that's too good to pass up. Sometimes I worry about you being lonely, that's all."

Bec's reappearance put an abrupt end to our rapidly-turning-sad conversation. She dropped her phone into her handbag and made her way toward us. "Sorry, paperwork issue." She settled on the couch, pressed against Sabine and pushed her hand under the hem of Sabs's jersey. I saw the movement as she scratched my sister's belly and the change in Sabine was immediate, as though someone had released a pressure valve. For the trillionth time I sent a silent thank-you to whatever force had brought Bec into Sabs's life. And maybe for the thousandth time, I hoped one day I'd have something like what they shared.

Sabs slung one arm over the back of the couch. "Maybe I'll tag along to watch one of those games with you. I've been thinking about Ultimate Frisbee as another team sport."

"Sure," I agreed. "I want to see how someone can make Frisbee into a competitive sport."

One of her eyebrows rose with comical slowness. "Anything can be competitive, Jana."

"Darling," Bec interjected. "How exactly are you going to fit another activity into your schedule?"

Sabs shrugged. "I'll manage. Besides, now is the perfect time before I finish my contract and change to a civvie job, and my hours are really, *really* fucked up instead of just really fucked up."

Rebecca did nothing but give Sabs, what seemed to me, a regular innocuous smile.

Sabine's nose wrinkled. "Don't think I don't know what that look means, babe."

Bec affected an innocent look. "What? I was agreeing with you."

"Nuh-uh. That was the *I'm not sure it's a good idea, darling* look." Sabs's fingers played against Bec's ribs until she squirmed and begged for mercy. When she went limp, Sabine leaned in and kissed her.

The kiss went on for long enough for me to have to clear my throat, and Sabs pulled away after murmuring something to Bec that made her smile again. My sister leaned back against the couch, an arm sliding around Bec's shoulders. "So, Mom said she went to the florist to check the bouquet orders and they showed her a demo." She flashed me a cheeky grin. "Wanna see the pictures?"

Oh, for the love of—

CHAPTER NINE

Friday morning, in anticipation of my evening at the bar, I took an Uber instead of driving. Work blurred steadily until all my meetings, briefs, drafts, phone calls, and nitty-gritty things were done. Brooke had texted me just after lunch with the details of a bar a few blocks from our building, and at five p.m. I responded to let her know I was just finishing up work and would meet her there in twenty minutes.

Wide smiley emoji response. Cute.

When I arrived thirty-five minutes later, I spotted her sitting at the bar nursing a half-empty glass of white and wove through the thin crowd of Friday post-work drinkers to slip onto the seat beside her. "Sorry I'm late," I said, which was my version of a normal person's *hello*.

Brooke turned sideways on her barstool to face me. "Hey, no problem at all." She glanced down.

I twitched my ridden-up skirt back down to mid thigh. "Just to give you fair warning, for future meetups, I'm always late unless it's work. Then I'm ridiculously, borderline OCD punctual."

She laughed. "Surely not."

"Surely yes. My family call it Jana Time. The time I'm told to be at family events is always earlier than everyone else and I usually still get there late. For some reason, something super important like redoing my eyeliner or checking YouTube and social media always comes up." I leaned over the bar, smiled at the cute bartender to catch his attention then turned back to Brooke. "My therapist says I'm subconsciously balancing out all my time spent waiting while early for court and clients. I think it's her way of being polite when she's really saying I'm just a total time flake with no respect for other people's schedules."

She laughed again, shaking her head as though she couldn't quite believe what I'd said was true. It was. One hundred percent. The bartender paused in front of us, and I pointed at Brooke's wineglass. "Two of what she's having, thank you."

Brooke protested mildly, "Hey now, I'm already ahead."

"Well I'll just have to catch up." I pulled out my credit card and placed it on the bar.

"And also, I thought the deal was a round of drinks on me."

Oh, right. "No matter, you can get the next round then, or *rounds* in future drinking sessions."

Her lips quirked. "So there will be future drinking sessions?"

"Well I'd assumed so. Unless you reveal something abhorrent tonight." I clutched her arm, mouth open in feigned horror. "You're not a Republican, are you?"

She gasped. "What do you take me for? Of course I'm not."

"Phewww. Secret lover of Britney Spears?"

She shook her head slowly, adopting a serious expression. "Nope. Not that there's anything wrong with her or her fans, of course."

"Of course. How do you feel about Ryan Reynolds?"

"Well, I'm a sucker for a good rom-com, so yeah, *The Proposal* was pretty good, though that might have been Sandra Bullock influencing my decision. But if we're going to dig into it, then I'm going to have to say *Two Guys, a Girl and a Pizza Place* has been his best work so far."

"Okay. You pass."

Brooke sagged, pretending to wipe sweat from her forehead. "Ohmygoodness. I'm so glad I studied for this get-together."

"Study is the key to success, or so my mom always said." At Brooke's questioning look, I explained, "She was a high school teacher at our school. English and history. Now she works part-time at the school's admin and subs in teaching when needed."

"Did she ever teach you?"

"Thankfully no. My sister was such a teacher's pet, she would have melted in panic if Mom taught her, and I was...uh, kind of naughty in school." And outside it too.

She deadpanned, "I don't believe it." Her expression slipped midway through her teasing, giving way to a grin. "Do your parents live in D.C.?" Brooke downed the last quarter inch of her wine.

"No, they're still in Ohio. They settled there once my dad was done in the Army and haven't moved from that house since."

Both her eyebrows shot up. "Ahhh, so Sabine followed in your father's footsteps with the Army then?"

I was both surprised and pleased that she'd remembered both Sabine's name and part of her occupation. "She did. And my grandfather and great-grandfather's too."

"Nice. How about you? Never considered joining the military?"

"Ugh, no, not for me. And not even ten seasons of *JAG* could convince me to become a military lawyer."

"Well if those smokin' hot uniforms can't change your mind, then nothing can," she said dryly. Two more glasses of wine arrived. I pounced on mine and clinked it against hers.

"Cheers." Brooke sipped, making a low rumbling sound of enjoyment. "God that's good."

I drank a large mouthful, enjoying the mild fruitiness playing over my tongue. Brooke had good taste in wine. "Very." After a quick glance around the space, I turned my attention back to her. "Are you okay here or did you want to move to a corner or something?" Though the bar wasn't crowded by any stretch, there were still people moving around and standing close-ish to order.

"Nope, it's fine. I come here fairly regularly and know it's usually quiet, even on a Friday. Plus the staff are semi-familiar so it's fine." She smiled shyly. "But thank you for thinking of me."

"You're welcome," I murmured.

She swiveled on her stool, staring intently at me, and I thought she was going to say something deep. Instead she asked, "You hungry?"

"Starving. I just remembered I skipped lunch."

"Are you adverse to something greasy? A glass of wine on an empty stomach, and I'm afraid I'm going to start talking shit. Well, even more shit than I already have."

"I think I'd enjoy listening to you talking shit but I rarely turn down something greasy."

Grinning, she turned away to lean over the bar, trying to catch the attention of one of the bartenders. The way the pose showed off her enviable cleavage, I wasn't surprised that it took less than ten seconds for one of them to come over again. I also wasn't surprised when he jumped at the chance to help the moment her voice dropped to something low and sultry as she ordered.

Brooke dropped back onto her stool, crossed her legs and spun back to face me. "Nachos, cheese sticks, and fries. Sorry, I'm a hungry drinker and I missed lunch too."

"Oh dear God, don't apologize. I feel like you've tapped into my secret eating fantasies."

She bit her lower lip, the corners of her mouth turning up in little twitches. Then it seemed she couldn't hold it back any longer, and said with more than a hint of amusement, "Mm, well of course those things I ordered are great, but they don't top my list of, uh…eating fantasies."

Laughing, I swatted at her. "Why, Ms. Donnelly, are you flirting with me?"

The flush, which was becoming familiar, appeared on her cheeks and neck. She didn't answer but looked like she was mentally sorting through possible responses and coming up short with every option as she turned her wineglass around and around on the bar.

I jumped in. "Sorry, I kind of feel like I'm always putting my foot in my mouth and making you uncomfortable."

"No problem. I sometimes miss social cues, so…" She paused coyly, then with a wink added, "And yes, I might be flirting with you. Or maybe the wine is."

The thought sent a warm thrill through my body. Interesting. I stared into my glass, searching for something neutral to rein my wayward thoughts back. "So uh, your younger brother. Does he live in D.C. or just visiting that morning we met?"

The corners of her mouth were now lifted in what looked suspiciously like a knowing smile. "Marshall lives here. He finished his journalism degree last year and is interning at *The Hill* thanks to a helpful professor who thought the sun shone out of Marshall's butt. He's aiming high, wants to get into the White House press corps, and of course he'll get there because he's one of those annoying people who always gets what they want because they work so hard."

"Ah, yeah, my sister is like that. Assholes," I added with a laugh. "Are you guys close?"

Her nose wrinkled. "Not really. I mean I love him but uh, we were kind of…I suppose estranged would be the best way to describe it. I'm pretty sure my mom got in his ear about me, was worried I'd corrupt him with my gayness I guess, and he was kind of distant physically and emotionally until recently." She smiled, though it was thoughtful rather than pleased. "Thankfully Marshall learned to think for himself when he left for college and turns out he's pretty liberal."

Quietly I asked, "So, would it be safe for me to assume that you don't get along with your mom then?"

"No, I don't. At all." Brooke pushed her wineglass a few inches away, then apparently reconsidering, picked it up and drank a long mouthful. "My mother is…in the Hamptons at the moment I think. I haven't seen her for, shit, almost twelve years? She sends me a card and money every birthday and Christmas like a good absent parent, complete with a passive-aggressive message about how she loves me but doesn't condone my *lifestyle*." Brooke smiled sweetly. "So I spend the money on things to make art involving naked women which I know would piss her off."

A server balancing multiple plates interjected before I could respond. Brooke nabbed a cheese stick, dunked it in the dipping sauce and bit off a mouthful. "Ah, shit that's hot." She set it down and swallowed a gulp of wine.

I scooped up a perfectly balanced portion of nachos, dangled it over my mouth for a second and ate the whole thing in one mouthful.

Brooke blinked a few times. "Wow, mad nacho skills. I always end up wearing half of them on my uh—never mind."

I poked her arm. "Breasts? It's okay, I'm definitely not offended by that word. I even have two of them myself."

"Mmm, uh, yes. You do." She took a small portion of nachos. "What other skills do you have that I should know about?"

"I have many, and most of them are utterly useless. Like, I know all the words to pretty much every Madonna song. I can dance MC Hammer's *U Can't Touch This* better than he did. I can do backflips off a horse, and for a while Sabine and I were even dabbling in putting together a horseback circus act."

"And how did that work out?"

"Not very well…" I moved closer, pointing to the scar just under my lower lip where my teeth had gone right through when I'd fallen and landed on my face. "We tried a western gunslinger type double hang off each side. The horse didn't like it."

"Ouch." Brooke leaned in, forehead furrowed as she studied my mouth. Her eyes flicked up to mine and for a moment I saw an unexpected flash of heat in them before she cleared her throat. "So, the MC Hammer dance."

The look in her eyes had caused an answering surge of heat to run slowly down my spine, like warm massage oil trickling along my skin. My answer came out hoarsely. "Mhmm, like a pro."

"I'd like to see that some time."

I flailed for safe ground. "Well if you can find someone who has the song on their phone then you might get lucky."

"You know that guarantees I'm going to download it myself."

I caught her eye, and the only thing I could say to that was, "Shit."

Brooke snorted out a laugh. "Don't worry, you're safe for now. But I'd like to see your moves sometime." She paused, eyebrows drawing together. "Sounds like you and Sabine are really close."

"We are. My whole family is really, but Sabs and I have always been joined at the hip. Same wavelength, same weird sense of humor." I smiled, suddenly feeling shy about admitting, "I know it's lame but my sister has always been my best friend."

"It's not lame at all, it's sweet. Does she go away on deployments and stuff for her job?"

"She did. But she's stationed here until she finishes her contract in just over a year so no more deployments thankfully."

The brush of Brooke's fingers against the back of my hand was brief, but still comforting. "That must have been really hard for you guys."

"It was. Every time she went was like torture." I debated whether or not to mention The Incident but decided against it. "Anyway, it's all over now unless the Reserves call her back once she's finished with the Army, but apparently that's a one in a zillion chance. I hope they don't, I mean danger and missing her aside, I hate thinking of her being away from her fiancée. Or wife by then."

"True. That must really suck." She fidgeted with the small bowl of ranch. "Um, so I didn't push in on a potential date or anything tonight, did I?"

Glass halfway to my mouth, I assured her, "Not at all. I think the dating thing is slipping back into a downward cycle. I feel like it's been dud after dud these past six months or so." Tongue loosened by wine I added, "I haven't had sex in so long I've almost forgotten what it's like."

Brooke raised a cheese stick as if in salute. "I'm with you there. It's been..." Her nose wrinkled adorably. "Actually, I don't want to think about how long it's been. I'm considering applying to have my virginity reinstated."

"Then there's not some girlfriend waiting for you at home who's going to come after me for keeping you out late?"

"Not at all. Happily single." She snorted, covered her mouth. "Well, not happily, more like resigned."

My brain raced ahead, mercifully leaving my mouth behind before I could counter with a teasing *I'd date you* or similar as I would say, and actually had jokingly said, to other friends in the same situation. The fact she was a woman wasn't what stilled my tongue. It was that having quickly run a mental marathon through that very scenario—dating *her*—I realized though while it was teasing, it also wasn't entirely teasing. The unbidden thought both terrified, alarmed and excited me.

I carefully pushed my hair back, ignored the frantic racing of my heart and said as brightly as I could, "Happens to the best of us. Including me, obviously." I reached for a cheese stick.

"Careful, they're hot," she cautioned and seemed pleased when I broke my morsel open and set it on a napkin to cool. "So where's the issue? Seriously, and I know this is so crass, but a woman like you being single just seems wrong."

"Likewise." I raised my glass and when she clinked it, said cheerfully, "To the shouldn't be singles!" Once I'd swallowed a mouthful of wine, I admitted, "I'm picky. Or, to hear my sister describe me, really fucking picky, like the pickiest person on the planet."

"Define picky."

I stared at the cheese stick, which was surely cool enough after twenty seconds, then dunked both halves in ranch and stuffed them in my mouth. "For starters, I have this thing I call the six-inch rule."

Brooke set her glass down, spluttering her wine in laughter. "Six inches? So…that's your minimum?"

Well aware of the innuendo, because it'd been a running joke with pretty much everyone since I'd inadvertently said it a decade earlier without thinking about the actual words, I just nodded cheerfully and confirmed, "Yep, has to be six inches taller than me."

She reached for a napkin and carefully wiped her mouth. After clearing her throat, her voice was clearer when she asked, "So what, five-eleven or more?"

"Mhmm, thereabouts."

Still laughing, she said, "You really are something else, Jana Fleischer."

Graciously, I inclined my head. "I'm going to take that as a compliment."

"You should. It was."

I recognized the subtle undertone of flirting and wondered if she was even aware she was doing it again. Ego aside, she wasn't the first woman to flirt with me. Some of Sabine's friends did it and it'd become an enjoyable game between us. I didn't mind and the way Brooke did it wasn't aggressive or predatory. It was interesting, flattering, and I found myself unconsciously moving forward to meet her, then catching myself.

Wine, you are so fucking sneaky.

After carefully selecting a clump of nachos, Brooke stared at it as though looking for the meaning of life before eating it with a contented sigh. She wiped her fingers on the napkin. "What's wrong with them then? Where's the roadblock? What do you want from a relationship?"

Shrugging, I admitted, "Just little things wrong mostly, but they're still big enough that I can't get past them." I didn't want to dredge up my long list of why I didn't want to pursue past relationships, and thankfully she didn't push.

"And...what do you want?" she prompted me again.

It felt silly to say it, but at the same time I had the strangest feeling of wanting her to know some of my inner thoughts. I stalled by eating a laden corn chip and swallowing a mouthful of wine. "I guess I want what my parents and sister have. Love, understanding, respect. I want someone I can laugh with every day, but also someone who gets that sometimes work sucks and I'll be stressed and short with them but it's not personal and I'm sorry. Someone who'll be with me through the bad shit, and who'll let me help them when they're going through bad shit. Someone who knows what I need without me having to constantly spell it out. I want *connection*."

Brooke nodded thoughtfully, not saying anything and I felt compelled to keep running through my wants. "You know, Bec, my almost sister-in-law, fishes Sabine's tees from the dirty laundry and sleeps in them if she's home alone while Sabs is working. They make each other work lunches all the time. My dad makes my mom tea every morning and delivers it to her, and she leaves little love notes for him around the house. It's all stupidly cute." I had the sudden sensation that I might cry, and I blinked back the feeling. "They've all found ways to enhance what they have, and compromise on other things for harmony, but never seem resentful. I want someone who gets that family is the most important thing to me, mine and the one we'd create together. I need good communication because I spend so much of my life trying to fix things that would be so much simpler if real, honest communication was involved. Oh. And fantastic sex of course. So, I don't want much really..."

She smiled at my vast understatement. "Not much at all."

"Mmm. But I've had so many duds, and I feel like I don't have whatever it is that lets you have a relationship, the ability to look past those small things I always get stuck on. Like...an ability to compromise would be the best way to describe it."

"Really? Is it that, or just that you might not have found *the* person yet? The one who's worth compromising for."

I took a few moments to think about it and came up with no answer. "I'm not sure, maybe it's a bit of both?" I smiled and took my first real breath in what felt like five minutes. "Sorry, that was really long and kind of intense. What about you?"

Brooke straightened on the barstool. "Listening to what you just said, I think I want pretty much the same thing. Or, I know I did want that. I thought I might have it with my ex but that didn't work, so now I think I'm a bit cautious about it all. I mostly want trust, and someone I can laugh with. I haven't had many girlfriends, but I've never felt like my previous partners really *got me*, you know? Well there was one during my stint in Paris but that was never going to work."

I leaned in. "Tell me more about your time in Paris. How long were you there?"

"Three years, and there's not much to tell really. I studied and made art, slept with a bunch of very lovely liberated French women, engaged in a consuming love affair with eighties British punk music, styled my hair into a Mohawk every morning and went around with way too much eyeliner and black lipstick." She smiled into her wine, voice dropping to a murmur. "Best few years of my life."

"Mohawk? No way. That's fucking incredible. How big?"

Brooke glanced up and raised a hand with forefinger and thumb a few inches apart. "Not shaved but I did have peroxide tips. It *was* incredible, but it also made me look like a teacup." She grinned and put a finger behind each ear, pushing them forward.

I couldn't help laughing. "Nooo."

"Oh yes. Totally. I had to let it grow out before coming back to the States." The grin faded to more of a tight-lipped smile. "I finished my art studies, and then my architectural degree, and started working for my dad." She seemed to shake off a thought, collect herself again as though putting on a mask.

It was a mask I wanted to carefully peel away and show her she could trust me to say whatever she needed to. But I couldn't think of anything to say that didn't sound inane, or pushy. So I offered up the only thing I could think of. "Another round?"

CHAPTER TEN

We left the bar just after eleven fifteen and made our way down the street away from the crowds of people smoking, talking and hooking up outside. I was on the drunker side of tipsy, wonderfully so, and more than a little pleased at the easiness of the entire evening. I'd been right about Brooke being a comfortable sort of person to spend time with. Yet as pleased as I was, my pleasure was being smothered by an old worry—the one exacerbated by years of annoyed friends and withered friendships—that I was a bad friend because I couldn't prioritize friendships over other things in my life.

I grabbed her hand, tugging her to a stop and pulling her away from the curb. "Brooke, listen. I don't…have many friends, close friends that is."

She frowned. "Okay? That's hard for me to believe for someone like you." After a beat she hurried to add, "Someone extroverted and uh, vivacious."

"No, it's true. I find it hard to fit friendships in around work and trying to go on dates. And most people get upset with me when I have to cancel something because I'm stressed as fuck about a court appearance or a difficult case, or a last minute something that I need to do for a client." I shrugged and let go of her hand, regretting the action immediately when the loss of comfort registered. "So I've kind of let most of my friends fall away over the past decade or so. Like I said, my sister and her fiancée are basically my friend circle. Or friend duo. The rest are just acquaintances really."

Brooke's smile was cautious. "Oh. Well I don't have any friendship expectations, Jana, if that's what you're getting at. And even though I enjoy our morning coffee and chats, I'm not so clingy that I need to socialize with someone every day. I'm a quality over quantity kind of gal, so don't even worry about it."

"Great, I'm glad. And sorry to throw that at you out of the blue. I like spending time with you, I really do. I'm just worried if I suddenly bail on something you might think I don't want to spend time with you, when the reality is probably just something boring, like work."

"No worries at all, I'm glad you clarified. Come on, let's get you to this pick-up place." She laughed, shaking her head. "The place where the car is going to collect you I mean."

I doubted the innuendo was intentional, but my brain still screamed at me to react in kind. If it was someone *else* as charming, fun and funny as Brooke, I probably would have. But judging by my reactions during the evening, it was dangerous to play along with her flirting. "What about you? Did you call for a ride?"

"I'm taking the bus." She pointed down the street. "Stop's right there."

"The bus? Why not a cab?"

"Because I like the bus."

For me, who loathed public transport and would rather spend an hour driving in traffic every day than deal with strangers touching me, being loud in my space, coughing and sneezing over me, the concept was foreign. It took me a moment to form thoughts and even then all I could say was an incredulous, "Seriously?"

"Mhmm. I can't stand D.C. traffic so I rarely drive in, and being on the bus gives me almost an hour of quality reading time every day."

"You could read in a cab," I pointed out.

"I could, if the driver is one of those lovely silent ones, which so few of them are, and unlike on the bus, it's kind of rude to have headphones in to block out the cab driver. Plus, by the time the bus winds around and makes its stops, I get ten more minutes than I would driving even with shit traffic. You really can't beat public transport. Bus, train, plane even. All of them give so much wonderful free time."

What a novel concept, reading instead of working during transit time. "Wow, I don't think I've ever done anything on a flight except work, or sleep. Do you live far from the bus stop?"

"Nope, a three-minute walk, well-lit." She reached for my hand, squeezed it. "It's fine, I've done it thousands of times."

My fingers closed automatically in response, trapping her hand in mine. "Can you text me when you get home? Or else I'm going to worry about you."

Nodding, she agreed, "Sure." Then she carefully extricated her hand and motioned toward the street where a car had just pulled up. "I think this is you."

I checked the license plate against my phone app and made sure I had my purse and assorted crap. "Thanks for tonight. It's been a while since I had such an enjoyable night out. I think you may have just saved me from cracking up over my shitty week."

"It was my pleasure, and likewise. I'm always glad to save your sanity if ever needed."

"I'll remember that." My automatic next step was to reach out for a hug, but I stopped myself at the last moment, unsure if we were yet in that *hugging when parting* territory. So I settled for a smile and a bicep squeeze, tried not to be envious of her understated muscle tone, and murmured another, "Thanks." I climbed into the backseat and waved until I was around the corner and out of sight.

During the ride home, I restrained myself from checking emails—such things were never a good idea after alcohol, and also had to stop myself from texting Brooke to check if she was home yet. Chill out, Jana. She said she did this walk all the time and the trip was almost half an hour long. Still, I found myself unable to shake the antsy unease and checking my phone every few minutes between staring out the window at scenery that blurred by, and not entirely due to the speed of the driver.

I'd just finished drying off after a shower when her message landed. *Home safe. Even got a whole chapter read. Thanks again, I had a really great night.*

A whole chapter, you speed reader! Glad to hear it and so did I x

I wasn't prone to spouting platitudes like *I had a great time* or *thanks for a lovely evening*, but as I stared at my words I knew I really did mean it. I *had* had a great time with Brooke and it'd been effortless. I'd never found talking to strangers or acquaintances problematic but small talk often required effort to keep a conversation moving. With her, I felt comfortable and had from our first meeting after the shoe incident. Our conversation was natural and unforced, even with slightly awkward topics. She was just easy to be around.

There was enough stress and annoyance and not-easy in my conflict-ridden life, and the prospect of an easy friendship was incredibly appealing. There was also something else about her that I couldn't quite pin down. Something…more. My brain was too tired and wine-fogged to properly mull over what exactly *more* was.

I readied for bed quickly and made myself drink a few glasses of water before sliding naked between cold satin sheets and pulling the duvet up over my head. My eyes fell closed and as I drifted, snippets of conversation from the evening looped lazily around my head. It had been a good night.

I fiddled with the strap of my handbag, the words sticking when all I wanted to do was force them out. After swallowing a little of my doubt, I managed a soft, "I'd date you."

"Would you now?" Brooke's eyebrows slowly rose, her mouth lifting into an amused smile. Arms crossed over her breasts, she tapped her chin thoughtfully. "Well, you know, part of dating is kissing."

"I know. I want that."

"Hmm. Really? You want…this?" When I didn't answer, she leaned closer, giving me time to move away. For the tiniest fraction of a second I considered doing just that, pulling back and telling her that I really wanted to kiss her but I'd never been interested in girls. But I said nothing.

Her lips met mine, warm and soft and tasting faintly of wine and strawberries. She opened her mouth and ever so softly stroked her tongue along my lower lip before pressing inside. Her tongue wasn't a forceful intrusion, rather a gentle question and I answered immediately. The kiss was unhurried, languorous yet at the same time frantic and needy.

Brooke kissed the edge of my mouth, my jaw, my neck, as I held on to her lest I fall to the pavement. "Come home with me," she whispered in my ear before her lips found my neck again. "I want you naked underneath me," she murmured against my skin.

Someone down the street slammed their car door.

And I woke up. My heart thudded with the shock of being pulled from a dream, *and* the contents of said dream. "What the fuck?" I mumbled to myself. Well, that was surprising.

I drew in a few deep breaths to settle myself, and once the thudding of my heart eased, a new sensation took over. Excitement. My skin hummed from the dream-kiss, a pleasant warmth spreading through my body. I inhaled quickly, let it out slowly. It was just a dream. Dreams don't mean anything. Do they? I mean, *of course* I'd had dreams about making out with women before. Celebrities, sportswomen and the like but never someone I actually *knew*. A tingling feeling settled at the base of my neck which I dismissed as the after effects of being dragged sharply and reluctantly from such a dream.

And maybe, just maybe, the feeling was a little bit of excitement or confusion because I wasn't at all bothered by the dream. From the short time we'd spent together, it was easy to see that Brooke and I could be a good match…except for one glaring detail. She was a woman, and I'd never dated a woman. Never thought about dating a woman.

I sat up, pushed my hair out of my eyes and tried to focus on something other than my drink-dry mouth. First things first, get rid of the dry horrors. I stumbled from bed and to my bathroom where I cupped my hands under the stream and bent to swallow the water. When I straightened, I noted the eyeliner and mascara I hadn't managed to fully wash off in my drunk-ish haze had smeared. Add that to the bed head and water dripping down my chin, well…

Mhmm, looking so hot right now, Jana. Ugh. Even if you weren't totally deluded and confused, why the hell would Brooke want you when you're a total wreck who can barely make it past the third date with anyone? Get your ass back to bed and sleep off this wine and whatever it's doing to your brain.

* * *

Monday morning, by the time I'd gone through my usual dumping of stuff and heading back down to the lobby, Brooke was waiting for our regular coffee date. Jesus, no, we've already been through this— it's not a damned date. I tried to act like I hadn't had, and enjoyed, a kissing dream about her. But with brain and body still humming from the memory, I felt more than a little unbalanced when she strode up to me. Did she always walk like that, with that subtle hip swing? Or was I only just noticing it now because of…that dream thing.

Brooke stepped in beside me, smiling like she'd just received some fabulous news. "Hey, happy Monday!"

"Mm. I think our definitions of happy are a bit different."

She laughed. "Rough weekend?"

"Well, once I'd gotten over Friday's wine, it wasn't so bad, but I was definitely reminded that I'm getting too old for long drinking sessions. Sunday, I met Sabs and Bec for lunch in the city, did some housework to get ready for my cleaner to come this week, spent some quality time with *Grey's Anatomy*. The usual." Oh hey, and by the way you're a fabulous kisser.

"Ah, so just stuck in a regular Monday funk."

"Something like that. You ready to get—" Kissy. Shut up, brain. "Coffee?"

"Am I ever." She indicated that I should go ahead, but paused when a tall, silver-haired gentleman strode over from the elevators, a briefcase in one hand and an umbrella in the other.

He acknowledged me with a glance and a polite smile but zeroed his attention to Brooke. "I have a meeting with my lawyer. I'll be back in a few hours. Can you make sure you have that initial plan for the Henley project finished by the time I get back, and I need you to talk to Kim about her vacation time."

I noticed a change in Brooke as he spoke with her. She'd withdrawn, shoulders slumped as though she was trying to involute. She nodded, and agreed with a quick, "Mhmm, yes, of course." She then gestured to me. "Dad, this is Jana Fleischer. Jana, this is my father, Richard Donnelly."

I shuffled my handbag into the crook of my left elbow and offered my right hand. "Hello, Mr. Donnelly, it's a pleasure to meet you."

"Fleischer...familiar name," he mused, taking my hand for an ultra-firm shake. "You must have worked with Oliver Kendrick before he passed away?"

"Yes, I did. He was my mentor."

"Hmm." His stare was measured, almost shrewd, as if he knew something I didn't. "Is Will Weston still a partner?"

"Yes he is. It's just the two of us now."

"Oliver handled my divorce a good, oh it must be...close to twenty years ago now." At my apparent confusion he chuckled. "I've been in this building a very long time. Oliver was a great guy, even if he charged me through the nose the way you all do."

Ah yes, the money-grubbing attorney fallacy. Of course it wasn't a complete fallacy—some of my contemporaries really were avaricious shitheads. But I worked my ass off for every minute I billed my clients and gave them every ounce of my skill and compassion. I flashed Richard my best smile. "Well, you know, we need to make sure we can keep up our bi-monthly vacations to Europe and add to our stable of luxury cars every three months. Not to mention keep the kids in private schools, pay an au pair for every one of them, and consume caviar and champagne at every meal."

Richard stared at me for a few seconds, his expression so blank that I had a twinge of panic. Maybe I'd gone a little too far. Great, now I'd offended Brooke's dad and she was going to ditch me as her almost-friend.

But his mouth split into a smile a moment before a deep belly laugh burst forth. "A lawyer with a sense of humor—will wonders never cease."

Graciously, I inclined my head. "I try."

Brooke laughed softly. Phew.

"Well, if I ever happen to get divorced again, I know who I'll want on my side." He leaned in. "Of course, that'd mean I'd have to marry again and honestly, the first one nearly killed me." He patted Brooke's shoulder. "I'll see you back in the office. Also, our meeting on Thursday at three, you haven't confirmed it."

"I'll be there," she said quietly.

"Good." Then he continued across the lobby floor and out the door, after throwing me an absent, "Pleasure meeting you, Ms. Fleischer."

Brooke watched him leave, the muscles in her jaw bunching. Then she straightened up, visibly squared her shoulders and smiled. Or pretended to. The lines around her eyes made it clear the smile was forced. I was about to ask if she was okay, when she curled her fingers around my wrist and pulled me along with her. "I'd kill for coffee, let's go."

* * *

The rest of my week was a typical blur of court appearances, client and staff meetings, explaining how it all worked to Belinda and generally trying to do ten things at once, interspersed with meeting Brooke every morning for coffee, and dinner with Sabs and Bec on Wednesday. Six thirty p.m. came and went on Thursday, and I was still at my desk working through a pre-nup when my phone vibrated with a message. Though I'd muted my phone, seeing Brooke's name had me reaching for it.

Hey, sorry for the late notice—would you happen to be free tonight?

I am. Or will be once I'm done in the office.

Still working close to 7? That's heinous. Mind if I drop by when you're done?

Course not. I'm pretty much finished. Give me half an hour to wind up, get home and shower etc.

I'm still in my office too. I'll be up there in 5 minutes. If that's okay?

It's okay. Also, didn't you just tell me working late was heinous? Front office door's unlocked.

There was no reply and I set my phone aside to save my work and close down my laptop. After a few minutes I heard the main door open and rushed out of my office to greet Brooke. "Why hello, Working Hypocrite."

She raised both hands. "You got me." Though her tone was light, her expression most certainly was not. "Sorry, I didn't mean to intrude on your after-hours stuff, I just didn't feel like sitting in the office by myself staring at cost estimates anymore and thought you might be free."

"You're not intruding at all. Come on through." I led her into my office and indicated a seat.

But she didn't sit, just stood with hands balled into soft fists by her sides. She seemed quiet, wan and vacant, yet at the same time coiled and edgy like she was about to cry or yell. She glanced around, peering out the door. "You know, I didn't realize until my dad mentioned it that there were only two of you up here. I always got the feeling you guys were a cadre of attorneys stalking around saving the world."

"Nope, just the two of us and a small team of excellent offsiders. The Kendrick in the firm's name is a bit sneaky. Ollie was a bit of a bigwig in D.C. family law circles and his estate stipulated we were allowed to keep his name attached to the firm, because he wanted people to remember him. Having Kendrick helps us but honestly, I just like feeling like he's still around by having his name close to mine. He really was a good guy."

"Must be why he chose you to join his firm then." Brooke cleared her throat, rubbed her eyes.

"You okay?"

Brooke shrugged. "Yes, no." She pointed behind me. "Do you have any booze in that nice antique credenza? Television shows always have lawyers with a stash of booze and cigars in their office. Is that real or has TV lied to me again?"

I backed toward the credenza—a gift from Oma and Opa when I made partner of the firm. "Geez, what do you take me for? Some kind of boozy, shady, under-the-table-deal attorney?" I asked as I deftly opened a door and pressed the switch that made a panel slide out. My favorite, though admittedly rarely used panel. The panel that held a Waterford Crystal decanter half-full of eighteen-year-old Glenlivet and a set of matching glasses given to me by my maternal grandparents when I passed my bar exam.

"Right now, I take you for an angel," she breathed. "Bless you."

I bowed, pouring her a half-inch and leaving the decanter out so she could administer more as necessary. Then I reached into the bottom drawer of my desk and dropped a handful of Hershey's Kisses on the desk in front of her.

Brooke's shoulders sagged. "Oh God, I could marry you, you fucking saint." Her stare moved between the scotch and the chocolate. Chocolate won, and she plucked up a Kiss, fumbling with the wrapper. She'd barely chewed and swallowed before she raised the glass and drained the liquid in a long swallow, shuddering when she was done. "Sorry, that was really rude." She sniffed hard and blinked, her eyes watering.

The more I watched her, the easier it became to see her watering eyes weren't from chugging hard liquor, but because she was crying.

"Hey," I said quietly. "Seriously, are you all right?"

"Yep, I'm all right." She sniffed again, the empty glass shaking in her hand.

"Brooke…" I stepped close, took the glass from her and set it on the desk. Then without thinking, I enfolded her in a hug.

Brooke's arms came around me instantly, she buried her face in my shoulder and the watering eyes quickly turned into full-blown, body-shaking crying. Around hiccupping sobs, she choked out, "Sorry, I lied. Not really all right."

I held her as she cried, rubbing her back. There was nothing I could say, all I could do was soothe her with my hug and gentle sweeps of my hand between her shoulder blades. Brooke's face remained pressed to my shoulder, fingers clutching my blouse tightly at the small of my back. I had no idea why she was upset, but I did know that holding her and comforting her felt so good. I tightened my hold on her, gently massaged the back of her neck.

Brooke drew in a few ragged breaths, shuddering as she pulled back and disengaged from our embrace. She wiped her palms under her eyes. "I'm sorry, I just didn't know who else to talk to. I didn't mean to unleash on you like that."

"Not at all. I'm always here if you need me." I reached for the tissues. "Do you want to talk about it?"

She shrugged, looking so utterly defeated and helpless that I wanted to gather her in my arms again. She tossed the used tissue into my wastebasket. "Just the most predictable story on the planet. I fucking hate my job. I feel sick every morning thinking about having to come in here and to work. It's stressful as hell and I don't want to be designing malls and apartment buildings, but my dad just doesn't get it. And the kicker is he wants to retire and me to take over, and

I just can't find the guts to tell him no. I don't want to be a fucking property developer and I *don't* want to run the company. That's what that meeting today was about. Me stepping up and taking over." She pressed her hands to her diaphragm, drew in a few slow breaths. "I just feel so stuck and suffocated, and I don't know what to do."

"Oh, Brooke. I'm so sorry, sweetheart. That must be incredibly hard." What else could I offer her? I had no solution, no magic wand. But…I did have myself. "Do you want to come home with me, I'll make us some dinner and drive you back to your place after. I don't want you to be alone. I mean, unless you want to be alone of course."

Brooke stared into the empty tumbler. "No, I don't think I want to be alone." She poured a second, smaller measure then pressed the stopper back into the decanter. Instead of chugging this time, she took a smaller sip of scotch and exhaled. After a long, taut moment she looked up, her eyes telegraphing her emotion, and what seemed like desperation that my offer of company was a genuine one. "If you don't mind."

"Of course I don't mind." Relieved that she seemed to have relaxed, if only a fraction, I began to pack up. "Give me a few minutes to close up shop here."

Her eyes brimmed with fresh tears. "Thanks. You're a really good friend, Jana."

CHAPTER ELEVEN

Brooke declined my offer of another alcoholic drink, declaring with a wry smile that she'd probably get even more weepy and mopey. So I left her with a glass of water and instructions to make herself at home while I changed into my favorite threadbare jeans and an old Army PT shirt of Sabine's I'd borrowed after staying there for an all-night movie session. Brooke had moved to the other side of the living room to study my photos and the few paintings on the walls.

I stood behind her and noticed right away that she'd shrunk a few inches and was now just taller than me. She'd also rolled up the sleeves on her button-up blouse to her elbows, this show of comfort and relaxation in my home pleasing me more than I'd have thought something so simple could. I spotted her heels standing side by side next to my couch and a sudden thought hit me. "Have you worn those heels you lent me since I returned them?"

Brooke stared down at her toes, which curled against my plush cream carpet. A familiar flush rose to her cheeks and neck and her reply was hasty. "Oh, no. I kind of just put the bag into the closet and forgot about them. I have plenty of black heels so I haven't really missed them."

"Pity, they're incredibly comfortable."

"That they are." Brooke cleared her throat, turning slightly away. She pointed to a photo of Sabine and me, doubling astride Errol, her first pony. "You and Sabine?"

"Mhmm. I think she's about ten there, so I'd be seven."

Brooke leaned closer to the pictures, looking between that photo and a more recent one of me and Sabs. "Goodness you two look alike."

"Thanks. She's the smarter and better-looking sibling, or so she'll tell you any chance she gets."

Brooke side-eyed me. "I'm not sure about that. Do you still ride?"

Incredibly aware of her proximity and the offhanded compliment she'd just given me, I had to work at not sounding like a squeaky excited teen when I answered, "No, not for about fifteen years I guess. We both sold our horses a few years into college." I picked up the picture, studying the image of Sabs and me on Errol. She sat in front, utterly straight and looking fearless while I sat behind her, as close as I could with my arms around her waist and my cheek against her back. "Honestly, I only took it up because Sabine did. She used to compete in English riding and was really good, but I always preferred just bumming around on the trails and doing a little jumping here and there."

"Ah, a regular cowgirl."

I laughed and set the frame back down on the dresser. "Something like that." I touched her back. "Are you hungry? Is pasta okay?" My fridge and pantry could always be relied upon to hold enough ingredients for a decent impromptu meal.

"Pasta's great. Can I do anything to help out?"

I slipped by her and into the kitchen. "Absolutely not. But I might grab you when it's time to clean up." I smiled over my shoulder. "Take a seat, shouldn't be too long. Any allergies or food hatreds?"

"Anchovies. Eggplant. Both hatred, not allergy."

"Noted. You're safe in my house, from anchovies at least." I pulled out cherry tomatoes, marinated feta and a deli container of mixed olives. While the water came to a boil, I quickly halved the tomatoes and set to work removing pits from the olives.

Brooke sat at one of the high stools that lined the other side of my kitchen counter, slowly turning her water glass in circles. "Do you usually go to this much trouble when you have a friend over for a spur-of-the-moment dinner?"

"Cooking isn't trouble for me, especially not a quick and easy meal like this." I glanced at her before resuming my careful slicing. "Actually, cooking is probably one of the most relaxing things in my life, especially extravagant recipes. Gives me something to focus on, makes my brain be quiet for a while. I like to make batches of meals and leave them for Sabs and Bec so when they get home at some fucked-up hour after having to deal with fuck knows what all day or night, they've got a decent meal."

"You are incredibly sweet, you know that?"

"You do remember our first meeting, right? The snapping and annoyance and bitchiness?"

She laughed. "I do. I think I remember telling you that I thought you were all bluster and bravado with a marshmallow core."

"Yes, I remember that too." And I remembered liking it. I bent my head to concentrate before I sliced off half my finger.

I'd hastily pulled my hair up into a clip, and now my haste was making me pay. I blew strands from my face over and over again and let out another exasperated huff. Brooke laughed and came around the counter into the kitchen. "Here, let me help."

"Thanks." I turned my head toward her.

She was right behind me, so close her hip brushed mine. "You have great hair, so thick and straight." Brooke's fingers brushed my neck as she carefully collected my hair in a bundle and restrained it in the clasp again.

The sensation was like someone was lightly sliding their tongue along my spine. Jesus. What was wrong with me? Clearly she exuded some pheromone that was going straight to my...whatever body part picked up on pheromones. I squirmed, trying to get rid of the admittedly pleasant feeling trickling over my skin. "I guess, except for the fact it's got a mind of its own and I have to layer the hell out of it to make it look decent." I motioned with my chin at her glossy brown hair, which she'd let down and was now curling softly at her collar. "I'd much prefer hair like yours."

She grinned. "Yeah, until it goes completely crazy the moment there's any moisture in the air." Her voice dropped a few decibels. "I think we always want that thing we don't, or *can't* have."

"Very true." I twitched my ear toward my shoulder, trying to indicate my repaired hairstyle. "Thanks for that."

"No problem." She moved back a couple of steps but remained close enough that it felt like she was still touching me. "Sure I can't help at all?"

I turned slightly to the side so I could cook and look at her when I talked. And so I could create a little distance between us. "Nope. Everything's totally under control."

"Oh I can see that." She leaned against the counter, careful to avoid the assorted cooking debris, and folded her arms. "Do you always have to be in control of everything?" There was no accusation or malice in the question, simply a quiet curiosity.

"Not always, but it's kind of my default state in case you hadn't noticed. But, believe it or not, sometimes I enjoy someone else taking control of me." A smile stuck itself on my lips and refused to leave.

Her answering smile was bright, warm, and more than a touch cheeky. "I'm not sure I believe you but okay, whatever you say."

"It's true!" I held up the middle three fingers on my right hand in salute. "Girl Scout's honor."

She raised a dubious eyebrow. "You were a Girl Scout?"

"Mhmm. For about four months until my troop leader indicated that maybe I wasn't suited to the team aspect of scouting."

"Why?"

"Too bossy, opinionated, and *always* had to be right." I grinned. "Nothing's changed really."

Brooke's answering laughter was worth admitting one of the biggest failures of my childhood. Who gets asked to leave Girl Scouts? I turned off the flame under the tomatoes and olives, deftly swapped utensils and scooped a few pieces of penne pasta from the pot of boiling water. Squeezing one between my fingers, I declared, "Almost done I think." Then I popped it in my mouth.

"Let me test." Brooke made a *gimme* motion.

Inexplicably, instead of just passing the spoon over, I held up the second piece of penne. But she didn't take it from me. The edge of Brooke's mouth twitched before she carefully placed her hand over mine to steady it and ducked under my fingers. As she took the pasta in her mouth, her lips brushed my fingertips in a touch so soft it could have been my imagination. But I knew it wasn't. My heart hammered double time and the unmistakable twist of excitement in my stomach meant only one thing. One confusing thing, because this was real life not a dream.

I wanted to kiss her.

That dream came back in full color, Dolby-surround audio. Oh fuck. I cleared my throat, hoping desperately that my expression didn't match my thoughts. Get a grip, Jana. "Brooke. I, uh…" Yes, *Brooke*, who'd come to see me because she was upset. Brooke who didn't need my weirdness on top of that. Brooke who could go out and find any girl and didn't need a straight girl who was suddenly having lesbi-thoughts.

But she skipped right past my awkwardness with a calm, "Yeah, needs another minute I think." Then she smiled, as if she knew what I'd been thinking. But underneath the serene expression I thought I could see something else—her own confusion and what seemed like desire?

"Okay," I managed to get out before turning away from her and setting the slotted spoon beside the stove. Too cowardly to face her, or rather face up to that expression, I busied myself pulling plates down from the cupboard. "Could you please grab some cutlery, the drawer just to your right."

She collected knives and forks, then peered around. "Do you have placemats?"

"No, I never use them. Don't tell my mom, it'll give her a heart attack. Not married, except to my job, I don't have kids yet *and* I don't use placemats."

"Promise I won't. I don't want to tip her over the edge," she said dryly.

"Bless you. I don't think I could stand a lecture on table etiquette right now."

Brooke helped me set the table, then stood awkwardly while I finished putting dinner together and placed the large bowl of pasta on the table. We sat opposite one another and I pushed the bowl closer. "Help yourself."

She stared at the meal, eyebrows drawn as though she couldn't quite work out what to do or say. Cooking for new people was almost like exposing myself for the first time to a lover, the edge of fear and excitement and that hope the other person would approve.

Brooke ate carefully. Nothing like the tipsy woman from the other night who'd used cheese sticks and fries to gesture while she made her case for why every cereal ever made is better than Grape-Nuts.

One thing remained the same—the little murmur of enjoyment, which was a borderline moan. "This is fabulous, Jana. So good."

"Thanks, and ugh, this sounds like such a cliché but it's really nothing, just something thrown together."

Brooke paused, fork hovering above her plate. She raised her eyes to mine, and the gratitude in them floored me. She had the most expressive eyes, telegraphing every emotion, and I wondered if she knew how easy she was to read. "This is one time you're wrong. It's everything, and not just the meal. Thank you." Then she dropped her gaze back to her plate like she couldn't bear to see my reaction.

"You're welcome." It sounded soft, tender, and I waited until she'd eaten another mouthful before asking, "Do you need to talk about today?"

"Hmm. Need? Yes, probably. But honestly, I don't *want* to." Brooke's smile was tremulous. "Kinda drags the mood down."

"I don't mind, but I get it." I pushed pasta around my plate, struck by the sudden urge to *help* her. "I'm always around if you need to talk, any time of day or night. Unless, you know, I'm caught up with a client or yelling at dickhead attorneys. But other than that, totally available."

She carefully speared pieces of pasta and tomato. "I know, thanks. I just don't want to burden you with all of my shit. Especially not just yet, in case you run screaming. But maybe in a few months, I'll dump it all on you." She leaned back in the chair, her grin a touch on the cheeky side. "That is, once I've wowed you with all my charm and you find me too irresistible to get rid of."

"I look forward to it." And I did.

The grin turned to a pleased smile before she dipped her head and dove back into her dinner. She had seconds, insisted on helping me clean up and accepted a container of leftovers, laughing in agreement when I admitted ruefully that I had a tendency to cook for an army.

"I'll drive you home, just let me grab some shoes." There was no way I was letting her walk six blocks for a bus and then go home by herself, even if she did it all the time.

"Ah, no I can't ask you to do that."

"You didn't ask. I told you that was what I was doing. Bossy, remember?"

"Seriously, it's fine. I'll call for a cab, it'll be here in no time." She smiled, arranging her handbag and coat and the container of pasta into one well-balanced handful. "You've already done so much tonight, I'd feel better not asking for any more."

I could have pushed but sensed it would only make her feel worse. "Okay, sure thing. Text me when you get home though?"

"Absolutely." She placed a hand against the wall to steady herself as she slipped back into her shoes, then she straightened, staring at me with an expression of uncertainty. "Uh, well, I guess I'll be off."

I'd already hugged her once today. Fuck it. I opened my arms and she instantly stepped forward into them as though she'd just been waiting for me to initiate it. The embrace was less needy than our hug in my office, but still warm and comforting. I relaxed into her. "See you for coffee in the morning?"

I could feel her nod against my ear and she exhaled as though expelling all her upset on a breath. "Thank you," she murmured. "Tonight was exactly what I needed."

"Any time."

She squeezed me tight then backed up while I opened the door. I stood in my doorway, watching her walk away, waving as she stepped into the elevator. Then she was gone. And I went back into my empty apartment with a strange sense of having just lost something.

Brooke ticked things off a small grocery list resting on the handle of the shopping cart. "Pasta, tortillas, tomatoes, milk, tea, um... tampons, barbeque sauce. Oh, can you duck over to the other aisle and grab some lube?"

"What for?"

"Never know when you might need lube." She made a slow up and down inspection of my body, mouth twisting into a wicked grin. "Probably not for you any time soon, though."

"Probably not," I agreed, leaning against the shelving. "I'm hungry, are you hungry?"

"I am." She handed me a box of Grape-Nuts. "Here, munch on these."

"And what are you going to eat?" I asked, opening the box and pulling out a single piece of cereal.

"I think you know," she said, voice husky with promise. Brooke pushed the cart away then knelt in front of me. She slid her hands under my dress and dragged my panties down my legs before slipping them off. With the lightest caress the tips of her fingers danced against my skin. Then she licked her way up my inner thigh and buried her face between my legs. Unexpected. Not unwanted.

I wedged the box on the shelf beside me so I could pluck cereal from it while Brooke attentively worked her magic. My other hand dropped to her head, gently pushing her hair back and holding it in a loose fist. She made the sexiest sound, something like the love child of a growl and a groan. "I don't think this is going to satisfy me for very long. I'm going to be hungry again very soon," she murmured before getting back to her intense attention to my clit.

I worked at trying to break a Grape-Nut between my molars. Most unsexy cereal ever. "Maybe I'll try it sometime."

"I think you should. I volunteer as your test subject..."

"I'm not sure I can wait long, I want to taste you. Fuck that feels so good." I gasped as she hit a particularly sensitive spot.

Her tongue made another slow sweep, lingering warm and wet against my flesh before she closed her mouth and drew my clit between her lips.

"Oh shit, fuck…yes, do it just like that and I'll co—"

I came awake on the brink of climaxing, heart hammering and my breath catching in my chest. Clutching the sheets in tight fists, I squeezed my thighs together to stave off the imminent orgasm. But my automatic response to waking up hyper-aroused had the opposite effect and the pressure against my clit sent me spiraling into release. Back arching against the climax, I could do nothing but helplessly ride out the exquisite sensations.

When I could finally think again, I realized what'd happened. I'd had a wet dream like a damned teenager. What the actual fuck? I hadn't even *touched* myself. Not to mention the fact I'd spent most of the evening comforting her, and here I was treating her like some warped erotic object. This was getting beyond ridiculous. I rolled over and buried my face in my pillow, trying to ignore the remnants of pleasure coursing through my body.

But…I had to admit to myself that despite my confusion, I'd liked what'd just happened.

Scratch that.

Really, *really* liked it.

CHAPTER TWELVE

The next morning when we met up for coffee, Brooke seemed to avoid talking about her meltdown the night before. As for me, I managed to keep myself together and mostly not think about those dreams. Mostly. While we talked, my mind wandered until I had to yank it back like a toddler on a safety leash. And then off it went again.

The mind wandering was not helped by small things like the way she kept fiddling with her takeout coffee cup, which of course had me staring at her hands while she tapped and turned. Slender fingers, nails painted a deep purple, that silver ring she always wore on her right middle finger.

And with every realization and new observation came an answering jolt in my stomach. Excitement? Guilt? No, not guilt but definitely confusion. Clearly these random thoughts plus the two dreams about Brooke were a sign I needed to get laid. Or start allocating more me time during the week to quiet down those urges. It wasn't like batteries were expensive and the way I was going, I wouldn't need much time to get the job done.

Maybe I'll volunteer…

Oh shit. The remembrance of last night's dream sent an unconscious shudder down my spine. Right, that's it. Brooke is not an object to be lusted over, she's a friend. A woman friend at that. The moment I got home, I was sorting this out.

The object of my lust, er...confusion glanced at her watch, grumbling, "I have to get going. Work awaits."

"Don't remind me." I pushed my chair back. "Plans tonight? Hot date?" Casual question asked friend to friend, no big deal.

"Not in the slightest, unless you count TV, your leftovers, and wine as a date."

"Actually, I think I might."

Brooke grinned and stood, moving quickly into my space to give me a quick, one-armed hug. She disengaged before I could do anything but pat her back. Her voice was low, almost intimate. "If I don't see you later, then have a great weekend. Try not to work too hard, or actually—try not to work at all."

"I'll try. You too."

"Oh I don't intend on doing anything but play this weekend." She squeezed my shoulder, and with a quick *bye*, slipped out of the café.

And I watched her go, wondering why I'd never noticed before what an enviably great ass she had. Enviable, yes...that's it.

Overwhelmed by hunger on my drive home, I caved and detoured for pizza. I ate a slice as I drove and another slice as I stripped out of my court clothes and into sweats and a tee. Stomach temporarily satisfied, I planted myself on the couch to eat pizza straight from the box, with a bottle of cheap champagne to wash it down. Classy.

After another slice of supreme, I felt human enough to work on my other problem. My wayward libido. Holding the pizza box aloft, I stretched to grab my phone from the coffee table and once I finally got a grip on it, navigated straight to one of my dating sites and began my quest.

The quest was unsuccessful. Too young, too scruffy, too illiterate. Boring, boring, cute but still boring. Every profile was beyond uninspiring, and the more I tried to find a guy who I'd be willing to get to know before sleeping with him, the less I felt like doing exactly that. Of course I *could* have slipped out and gone to a local bar to pick up a random, but despite the fact I'd decided getting laid was the perfect answer to my issues, I couldn't set aside my standards to just go out and hook up with a stranger.

A text saved me from slow death by unsuitable partners. Brooke. I realized I was grinning. Hugely. Like a fool.

Sorry to bug you but your dinner is even better reheated.

You're not bugging me ☺ *I'll take your word for it. I went with old faithful. Pizza.*

Oh good call, but I still think I got the better deal.

Trying to juggle pizza box, glass, and phone was proving troublesome after a couple of glasses of champagne. So I called her, put my phone on speaker and set it on the couch arm. She answered with an exuberant, "Jana! Ahoy!"

"Ahoy. Wait, am I supposed to follow up with some more pirate stuff? Because I pretty much used up my entire repertoire just then."

"Ha! No, just ignore me. I'm a weirdo, and also two and a half glasses of red down. To what do I owe the pleasure of this call?"

"My clumsiness. I only have two hands and they're currently occupied with food and drink."

"Ah. Well in that case, I'm glad you have busy hands."

Oh, you have no idea. Though apparently not as busy as hers if my subconscious was to be believed. With my brain stuck on how talented Subconscious Brooke was, I could do little more than offer a lame, "Mhmmm."

There was a brief pause, then her quick, "A quiet Friday night then?"

"You know it. I mean I have work to do but I'm trying to be a normal human so I'm ignoring it."

"Sounds like a good strategy. Hey, on that note, do you have plans tomorrow?"

Trying not to think about the fact I keep having erotic dreams about you. You know, the usual. I cleared my throat before answering, "Yoga in the morning, then some work so I can have a gloriously free Sunday. Why?"

"I have an Ultimate match in the afternoon and I could use a cheerleader. Do you want to come and help a gal out?"

"And what makes you think I'm qualified to cheer for you?" I'd known right away when she asked that I'd agree but for some reason wanted to make her work for it.

Brooke laughed. "Well, you seem pretty upbeat and I get the feeling you're good at screaming when you want to be." Hmm, yeah there was a definite undertone.

Or maybe I was just reading into it. See aforementioned erotic dreams. I decided to test the water a little, see if I could get a better read on the situation. "Oh, I am…with the right motivation."

There was a long pause, a clearing of her throat. "Mmm, I bet you are. So can I count you in?"

Oh yeah. She was flustered. The thought was pleasing, and also made me feel slightly better about my runaway thoughts. "You can. Where will I meet you?"

"We play at the community park a few blocks from my house, so if you want to come by I can take you."

"Perfect."

"I'll have to leave around two fifteen so why don't you drop by any time before then and maybe we can have lunch? Though I doubt it'll be anything near as tasty as this pasta I'm currently inhaling."

"Ms. Donnelly, if I didn't know better I'd think you were trying to flatter me into cooking for you again."

"Shit, am I that obvious?"

"Totally."

"Mmm, I'll have to work on my subtlety."

"Oh no, please don't. I spend my whole life trying to tease the truth out of people and even then I'm pretty sure most of what I'm told is twisted. I adore your no bullshit, good communication approach."

"Oh…well that's good to know," she said softly and I could hear the relief.

"Why don't you text me your address and I'll call before I leave."

"If you want, but no need to call, really. If I don't answer the door, I'm probably working out the back. The side gate will be unlocked, so come on through to the yard and find me." There was a pause and I could hear her shuffling something around. "Some of us go for a beer afterward to celebrate or drown our sorrows. You're more than welcome to come along."

"You sure? I don't want to push in on your team thing."

"You won't. Plenty of the others bring their girlfriends." She spluttered, made an almost choking sound and before I could say anything, words rushed out of her in a jumble. "Fuck, I didn't mean that you and me, or anything like that, uh…just that…um…the others bring people along and it's totally not a big deal at all so don't worry about being a non-player because nobody else will care. That's all. Jana? Are you there?"

"Of course I am." While she'd been rambling, I'd been primed to tease her about her slip of the tongue. But the rising panic in her voice had reined in my reply, and I decided that rather than draw attention to it, I'd just steamroll past like she'd never said it. "If you're sure then that's good enough for me."

She let out a long exhalation. "Mhmm, totally. Excellent. I, uh, guess I'll let you get back to your pizza and I'll see you some time tomorrow?" Her voice rose hopefully at the end.

"That you will. I look forward to it."

"Me too. Oh, wear something purple." With a quick goodbye, she hung up.

I slid my phone back onto the coffee table, my urge to find a guy to sate my libido well and truly evaporated.

CHAPTER THIRTEEN

Brooke's house was a cute double-story, smoky-blue and white house in Clarendon, a little over twenty minutes' drive across the Potomac from my place in Logan Circle. Nestled in the pointed roof was a small dormer that reminded me of my childhood bedroom. Her front lawn was recently mown, a large tree shading the patterned brick driveway.

I checked my watch, slightly anxious about the fact it was only twelve thirty. I'd finished my yoga class plus all my work, and hanging around the house was only boring me. She'd said come around whenever, and this was whenever. Stop worrying. There was no answer when I rang her doorbell and after waiting a minute to make sure she wasn't about to open the door, I backtracked down the brick stairs and around the side to the low paling gate.

Her backyard was as neat as the front, or rather what wasn't taken up by a huge metal shed painted to match the house. The roller door was all the way up and a coveralls-clad Brooke was bent over a pile of metal, her back to me as she welded. Not wanting to startle her into an accident, I waited and watched her working.

When she'd said she did art as a hobby, it had made me think of something casual and second-rate. She was selling herself way short and despite having seen that painting in her office, I had mistakenly underestimated her talent. I shifted slightly to get a better look at the angles of her piece. It was incredible, mesmerizing.

It was a metal frame upon which she'd welded closely-packed wire and pieces of metal to give the sculpture depth. The life-sized person—a woman I realized upon closer inspection—was curvy and full-breasted. Though the figure wasn't anywhere near complete, it immediately conjured an image of an Amazon. Proud, chin up and a hand on her hip as she gazed into the distance as though readying for battle.

Brooke moved around to the back of the sculpture until she was facing me. She straightened and held up a hand, fingers splayed wide. Apparently satisfied I'd stay put, she fiddled with a boxy device that showed digital numbers, turned valves on the tall gas cylinders, did something with the thing in her hand and set it down. She checked everything again, flipped some switches, then finally turned to me. Complicated.

The welding mask came off first, then the faded backward baseball cap and finally her thick leather gloves, all of which she set down on a nearby bench. After wiping her face with a forearm, she grinned. "Hey, you're early."

"I am," I answered, holding up a six-pack of beer. "And I brought gifts for now or after the game."

Her mouth fell open, shoulders dropping in relief. "You're a lifesaver, and a mind reader. I was just thinking I'd kill for a cold beer. It's hot as hell in here. Come on through but there's not much free space so watch out for things that might snag you."

I picked my way around benches and neat stacks of wire and scrap metal. The overwhelming smell of steel and something akin to fireworks was pleasant and earthy, and I breathed in deeply, savoring it. Now I was closer, I could see the sculpture remained upright with rods that were actually her calves affixed to a large metal plate. Gesturing to the mass of metal, I said, "This is absolutely fabulous, seriously mind boggling. How long does something like this take from start to finish?"

Her cheeks pinked. "Ah, thank you." Brooke glanced at the sculpture, rubbed the back of her neck. "I haven't been able to stop thinking about her, so instead of working on a few things I've been focused only on this one. Usually it'd take three months or so but I think I could have her done in another few weeks."

"How do you make the face like that?" Though rough and almost mask-like, the features were clearly visible. I tried to figure out how to get something so three-dimensional from all the one-dimensional pieces around me.

"Oh, uh, I cut up a bunch of metal into small geometric shapes, lay them out like a face and then weld them together. I build the features up with weld too, then grind it back to shape it. It's basically endless welding, grinding, welding, grinding. It'll be way neater than this once it's finished, ground smooth and polished," she added quickly.

Everything she was saying was like a foreign language, but I still knew one thing. "It's fucking incredible. Do you sell them?"

"Mostly, yes." Her face softened into reverence as she gazed at the sculpture. "But I think I might keep her. The image kind of just hit me and I can't get her out of my head."

"I can understand that." I passed her a beer before opening one myself.

Brooke took a deep swallow and raised the bottle to me in salute. "Seriously, you're a goddess. Thank you."

"No problem." I glanced around, and finding a bench that seemed safe, leaned against it. "Do you do commissions?"

"Sure, I've made some things for friends. And not just naked women. Animals, objects, I can do pretty much anything."

"Could I commission you? Paid of course."

Her voice pitched up an octave. "Absolutely, what are you thinking?"

"I still haven't bought Sabine and Bec a wedding gift. I think in this case, naked woman or women would be apt. Probably something small that could fit on their coffee table or in their bedroom?"

"I can do that. When's the wedding? In four weeks?"

"Mhmm."

Slowly she nodded. "That'll be fine. This one is just a vanity project so I can put her down and pick her up again. I'll get you some concept sketches in a few days and do up a quote. Do you have any idea of what materials you'd like?"

"Not a clue, I'm art-inept. All I know is *that* looks amazing and I'm sure whatever you come up with will be perfect. You can do up a quote if you want, but I'm sure whatever you're asking is more than fair." I dug in my handbag for my checkbook. "Do you need a deposit or something?"

"Nope." She grinned, lazily tipping the bottle toward her mouth. After a long swig of beer she said, "I've seen your car, I know you're good for it."

True, but I still would have paid Brooke whatever she wanted to create something for me to give to two of the most important people in my life. Because I wanted her to make art, to be fulfilled by it, to see that people were interested in what she had to offer. Because if I did that, then maybe she'd do it more and maybe that little sparkle in her eyes would stay longer.

"I'm starving. Have you had lunch yet?" Brooke set the beer on a nearby bench and shucked her torso out of the coveralls, absently tying the sleeves together at her waist. But it wasn't the way the faded red tank top clung to her body, or the glistening sweat on her bare skin that drew my attention and made my answer stick in my throat.

What caused my brain to stall were the rows and rows of neat scars encircling both biceps, ending a few inches above her elbows. Unable to help myself, I simply stared, also noticing lettering I couldn't quite make out tattooed in black on the inside of her left bicep. When I realized how long I'd been staring I raised my eyes to find her gentle ones.

Brooke lifted her arm. "It's Latin. *Dum spiro spero.* While I breathe, I hope."

"Oh. That's powerful. Profound. I like it."

Her smile was almost facetious. "Me too, that's why I had it permanently marked on my body."

Dumbly, I nodded, unable to think of anything else to say because what could I say? I knew about this sort of mental health issue, knew intellectually how she'd gotten the scars, but I couldn't quite reconcile the whole picture. Though I knew she suffered anxiety, this just didn't seem like *Brooke*, which was such a stupid thing to think.

"It's all right, Jana," she murmured. "You can ask."

So many questions sprung into my head. Did you do that to yourself? Why? When? But there was really only one question that mattered, and it came out shakily. "Are you okay?"

Her eyebrows rose fleetingly. "Mhmm, I am. Just emo teen stuff that I got over a long time ago. I had a pretty hard time coming out, if you could even call it that. Maybe coming to terms is the better way to phrase it."

"What do you mean?" I moved closer.

She blew out a breath. "My father is a homophobe. Actually…I'm not sure if that's totally true. I don't know if he's a homophobe or if it's just *me* who he can't stand being gay. He refuses to acknowledge that I'm a lesbian. I've never introduced him to my girlfriends, and so we pretty much just ignore the entire thing. My mom's incredibly religious and her reaction was much the same as my dad's, with some added disgusting sinful daughter and going to hell stuff thrown into the mix. Oh, and you know—her trying to keep my brother away from me. Just the usual unaccepting family stuff." She laughed humorlessly.

"Shit," I breathed. "Brooke, I'm *so* sorry. That must be awful." My family had been nothing but supportive of me and Sabs our entire lives. Sabine always knew she was same-sex attracted, and when she was ten told Mom that she was going to marry Wonder Woman. Mom had told her matter-of-factly that unfortunately Wonder Woman was a fictional character, so maybe Sabine should aim to marry the actress instead, when she was old enough. My older sister's sexuality had been a complete nonissue from the time she'd officially declared what we'd pretty much known for years.

No matter what we did, Mom and Dad had always been there to support us and love us. They'd practically adopted Sabine's best friend, Mitch, into the family when Sabs had brought him home at Thanksgiving their first year of med school. His family want nothing to do with him because he's gay. Mom nearly had a stroke, and I'm certain my father considered marching into Texas to give Mitch's family a piece of his mind. My whole family, close and extended on both sides, had also absorbed Bec—an orphan with no living relatives—into the fold from the get-go. My family just loved family.

"It's fine, really. Well it's not fine, it's kind of shitty but it's also just the way things have always been, so…" Brooke shrugged. "C'est la vie." She glanced at the large metal clock on the wall, one I suspected she'd made, and asked again, "So, did you eat lunch?"

"Not yet."

"Shall we take this beer inside and have something to eat before we have to go?"

"Sounds good."

Brooke pretended to crack her knuckles. "Right. Guess I'd better try to wow you with my expert food-ordering skills because I have fuck all to eat in my fridge."

The interior of Brooke's house had a homey, old-world kind of vibe and as she ushered me through the back door I felt immediately at ease. There wasn't a lot of furniture cluttering the living room, just a gray suede couch opposite a huge television on the wall and an amazing coffee table that looked like it was made from an old wooden door with glass laid over the top. The walls were full of bright paintings, poster-sized photographs of European architecture and an incredible black-and-white photo of a group of some sort of nomadic people with their horses, against a backdrop of snow-tipped mountains.

"Could you give me five minutes to shower off this sweat so I'm ready to get sweaty again at the game? Make yourself at home, help yourself to anything, not that there's much to eat. Would you mind putting those beers in the fridge?" She pointed. "Kitchen is just through there."

"Mhmm, sure," I murmured, absorbed in a baseball bat-sized metal artwork in the corner. A mermaid this time. "You made this?" Dumb question.

She walked backward as she talked. "I did. Just whipped her up quickly, one of my sanity-saving projects where I just *have* to make something."

Sanity-saving…

I watched her backing down the narrow hall and just before she disappeared I said, "Brooke?"

She stopped immediately. "Yeah?"

I ducked around the couch and rushed toward her, wanting to be near her rather than calling across her living room. The question felt so shallow but I had to ask. And I had to touch her, to give myself the small comfort of knowing she was there. I grasped her hand, knowing even as I did it, the gesture was entirely inadequate. "Are you sure you're all right?"

She squeezed my hand, her thumb sliding over my knuckles. "Yes. Right now, I'm perfect." With a smile, she let go, and left me to hang around while she got cleaned up.

I exhaled a few long breaths, hoping to settle the uncomfortable feeling in my body, then put the rest of the beers in the fridge, sneakily checking out her small neat kitchen and her fridge which was indeed bare. As I wandered around her house, I felt angsty and out of sorts, and knew exactly why. I was upset about what I'd recently learned about her.

I'd seen Sabs struggle with her PTSD, knew quite a few friends with other mental health issues, had even had a touch of anxiety myself on occasion. But the thought of teenaged Brooke hurting herself like that and not having family support made me want to barge into her bathroom, pull her into my arms and hug her for the rest of the day. Then ask Mom and Dad to pseudo-adopt her like they had done with Mitch.

She came back after five minutes, dressed in jeans and a faded tee with a screen-printed Eiffel Tower on the front. My eyes automatically went to her upper arms, now covered by fabric, and when I realized what I was doing I averted them again. My brain decided I needed to blurt something to try to cover up my very obvious staring, and decided on a very clever, "Um, are you hungry?"

"As established about ten minutes ago, I am." She grinned, pulling her hair back and securing it in a ponytail. "You seem kind of wigged out about the self-harm thing. Are you sure you're okay?"

Brooke, asking *me* if I was okay…

"Yeah, I am. I mean aside from being really upset that you had to deal with all that shit. I think it's just that you, uh, surprised me I guess because I've never seen you without a blouse or jacket or something on."

"You're right, you haven't," she said calmly. "It makes my dad weird, so I always wear sleeves at work."

"Oh. Makes sense." I cleared my throat and decided I needed to suck it up and get over it, because apparently she had done just that. "Thanks for, well, sharing with me."

Her eyes widened. "You're welcome," she said quickly, then came a softer, "I trust you with my cruddy childhood shit."

Long moments passed just looking at each other, not needing words to fill the space between us. A weird sensation for me who could talk underwater, but not at all unpleasant. When the air settled, Brooke broke the quiet with a smiling, "I'm really sorry but I wasn't actually expecting you to come around and I wasn't joking when I said I didn't have any food. Do you mind if I just order something?"

"Course not, that sounds great. I'm not fussy, and I don't want you to have to go to any trouble."

Already on her way to the kitchen, Brooke glanced over her shoulder, smile already in place. "You're not trouble, Jana." A pause, and a laugh. "Well I'm sure you are, but it's no trouble I should have said. There's great Thai and Japanese a few blocks away. Or I probably *could* scrape up enough crap to go totally college student and we can have ramen and tuna with potato chips."

"Any of those would be good."

"Ramen it is!" She chuckled, and amended, "Kidding. Thai?" She opened a drawer and pulled out a menu.

"Sounds great," I agreed, though I would have been fine with ramen. I would have been fine with anything as long as we were hanging out together. "But beer and Thai before you play sport? That's brave."

Brooke laughed and patted her belly. "I won't each much. Did you want a few things to share and then split leftovers for dinner? If you don't mind mild on the spice-side that is."

"Sharing sounds great, and I'm totally fine with not-spicy."

Her smile was sheepish and self-deprecating. "Thanks. I'm a total wimp when it comes to hot food. I just can't handle it. I like to be able to feel my tongue after a meal."

I smiled, that strange nervous excitement feeling in my chest making an appearance again. "No, mild is fine by me." It's perfect.

We arrived at the park a little after two thirty and she settled me on a folding chair at the edge of a marked-out rectangle, with instructions to guard her water bottle and the cooler with my life. Brooke flashed me an almost maniacal grin before jogging over to join a group of women milling about in the middle of the field. She'd changed into a pair of running shorts, sneakers and a purple tank top, all of which served to showcase the fact she had a very capable body.

It didn't take long to confirm my suspicion that Brooke's Ultimate Frisbee team was made up of sporty, charming and funny lesbians, and the team name *Disc Dykes* simply confirmed it. I had no real clue of the mechanics of the game except for the fact it involved a lot of running, throwing, catching, diving, and leaping. Watching Brooke do all of the above, I realized just how athletic she was. A brief stab of jealousy at said athleticism was replaced by admiration and then something I didn't want to admit could be akin to lust. Okay, it wasn't akin to lust. It *was* lust.

Time to stop pretending those dreams and thoughts don't mean anything. Time to stop pretending you're in the dark about what you're feeling, Jana. You're physically attracted to her. *Her*, a woman, for the first time ever. Maybe not romantically, but you like the way she looks, you enjoy spending time with her. Wait, isn't that kind of romantically?

Well great, knowing I felt that way was one thing. Knowing what to do about it or having the guts to do what I thought I wanted to do was a whole other thing. Mmmph. I stuffed my sexual identity crisis aside to concentrate on cheering.

The match went for about an hour and a quarter, with a few timeouts and a halftime break. Brooke had run over, winked at me and squirted water into her mouth before running off again. Mmm. Very athletic. I'd spent most of the game watching her, cheering every time she caught the Frisbee or made a good throw or caught the disc in the goal area to score, and had to remind myself to also cheer for the other women wearing purple.

The Disc Dykes gathered around each other for excited shouts and high fives. Weird game but fun. Sabs would definitely like it, and undoubtedly be excellent at it. Brooke came running over and paused ten feet away to do a cartwheel. Then she slowed to a walk and strolled over. I passed her the water bottle, received a smiling thanks in return.

Breathing heavily, Brooke lifted her tank to wipe her face, showing a flash of tight tanned stomach and a red-gemmed silver navel piercing. I stared, all too aware of something strange flitting through my chest and curling into my stomach. The *something* felt suspiciously like the feeling I got when I saw a cute guy at the gym. Or…the way I'd felt during the Grape-Nuts dream. And the first kissing dream. Yep, totally attracted to her. Stop staring, Jana.

Brooke dropped the water bottle into the cooler. "What did you think?"

I forced down the inappropriate feelings and responded with a bright, "Very energetic. You were great. Congratulations on the win."

"Thank you." Brooke extracted a container of orange segments from the cooler and offered it to me before taking a piece herself.

I popped the orange into my mouth, crushing it between my teeth, enjoying the sweet juiciness of the cold fruit. Brooke sucked the end of her thumb and forefinger before eating her own portion of orange. Sweat glistened on the dark golden tan of her arms and shoulders, and the ridges of scars. Seeing them now wasn't quite as upsetting as earlier.

She grabbed another segment, and when I shook my head, she took the last piece as well. "Are you sure I can't convince you to join the team?"

I spluttered a little before answering, "Hell no. Thought I told you, I'm the kid everyone laughed at in gym class. I can't catch or throw to save myself. But Sabine said she wanted to come check out a game and she might join the league."

"Oh, awesome. I'd like to meet her." She seemed genuinely pleased at the idea. "It's a pity I can't tempt you. Purple suits you." At my smiling head shake, she sighed. "Fine, I'll give up. Listen, I think everyone's pretty much done so we're ready to head off."

Once Brooke had called out to her teammates that she'd see them at the bar, we gathered our stuff. The walk back to her car was silent, the cooler carried between us, and she swung it lightly, forcing me to do the same. Silence had never been my strong point and once we'd stowed our gear, I felt the urge to say something and managed possibly the lamest thing. "Thanks for inviting me."

Brooke grinned. "Thanks for screaming out my name. Really helped my performance."

Jesus. Christ. I opened my mouth to respond, but nothing witty came to mind. I managed to push out a slightly wavering, "You're welcome." Even lamer than saying nothing at all.

Brooke's eyebrows raised fractionally. "Are you all right?" She reached around me to snag a gray linen hoodie from the backseat.

"Yep. Absolutely." I took a step back and bumped against the front passenger door.

As she shrugged into the hoodie, Brooke stared at me. Then a lightbulb-moment smile lit up her face. "You seem uncomfortable, Jana. Does my flirting bother you?"

"No, not at all." I wanted to add that I liked it, but I couldn't quite find the right combination of words, which was utterly stupid. I...like...it. There, easy to say. Only not so, especially for me who'd never thought of a woman as anything other than a friend until very *very* recently. Now, maybe-want-to-be-more-than-friends was pretty much eighty percent of my thoughts when near Brooke.

She nodded slowly, still holding my eyes with hers. "And does me being a lesbian bother you?"

"No!" I said quickly. "Not at all, I mean you know my sister's gay, so obviously I have zero issues with it. Ugh, God, I'm so sorry. I *hate* when people say that, you know like I'm not homophobic because I know a gay person. I'm not racist because I work with an African American. Shit, fuck! I'm *not* racist. I'm *not* homophobic or anything phobic except arachnophobic. And sometimes my sister's friends flirt with me, and it's seriously not a problem. Also sometimes women who aren't my sister's friends do it too and that's also not a problem. Aaand I'm going to stop rambling and shut up."

Brooke laughed, the sound echoing around the parking lot. "Your rambling is really cute. I'm sorry, the flirting is kind of an unconscious thing. I know you're not, uh, inclined that way."

"No, I'm not." Those three words sounded choked, like my throat wanted to close to stop them coming out. I *wasn't* inclined that way, was I? How could I be inclined toward women if I'd never thought of it before now? I'd never thought of a woman the way I thought of Brooke—as a good friend, someone I really enjoyed spending time with...but with something more, something romantic-ish teasing at the edges of our friendship.

"Great. I promise I'll try to tone it down. Girl Scout's honor."

"But I didn't think you were a Girl Scout."

"Busted." Grinning, she stepped closer, reached around me again and pulled the door open for me. "So, can we go get beer now?"

"Mhmm. Absolutely."

It was a short drive from the playing fields. A short, slightly awkward drive because every time I thought about something to say, it turned into innuendo. So I mostly said nothing. As we walked from the car, Brooke fumbled with the zipper of her hoodie, muttering expletives under her breath. Laughing, I dragged her to a stop just outside the bar. "Let me. Clearly walking and zippering are beyond your capabilities at the moment."

"Thanks. Seems I used up all my coordination on the field."

Head down, I zipped her up, careful to stop just below her breasts. "There, all done."

"Thanks." She cleared her throat, then tugged open the bar door and gestured that I should go inside.

As thanks for the motivation I'd provided, Brooke insisted on buying me a drink, and with a bottle of Bass in each hand, she led us to a table where a petite platinum blonde sat with a pint of beer. Brooke made quick introductions. "Jana, this is Beth. Beth…Jana."

Beth rose slightly from the chair so she could reach over to shake my hand. "Nice to meet you."

"You too. Congrats on the win. You caught the winning throw, right?" The almost-white hair sticking out the back of her ball cap was hard to mistake.

Beth's smile was immediate, and cocky. "That I did."

Brooke set our drinks down on the table then pulled a chair out for me. "And she'll never let us forget it. Where's everyone else?"

I stared at the chair for a moment before I sat down, trying to figure out why I felt suddenly emotional. It didn't take long to work it out. Brooke had pulled a chair out for me, and the way she'd done it had been so natural and unaffected. Just a polite gesture. The woman may as well have just issued an invitation for a date.

Beth pointed over her shoulder. "Immy's at the bar. Everyone else bailed after the game." She raised fingers as she listed, "Hangover, sick kid, first date that needs four hours of prep, a sick girlfriend."

"Ah, well I guess we'll have to make up for our missing comrades."

"Damned straight." Beth raised her beer and took a long gulp as another purple-shirted woman rushed up, armed with a wineglass.

Before the newcomer said anything to anyone else, she thrust a hand at me. "Hey! I'm Immy. Great to meet you."

"Jana." I shook firmly. "And you too."

"I heard you yelling from the sidelines, you've got a nice set of pipes."

I dipped my head. "Why thank you. If I'd known how competitive it was I would have practiced."

"She actually started practicing her yelling almost a month ago. At me," Brooke supplied.

I nudged her. "That was unintentional. And only one time."

"Yeah, but you have to admit it was a time to remember." The way she said it, low-voiced and almost sensual sent an unexpected thrill through my stomach.

"Mmm, it was," I said because it was the only thing I could think of to say around the unnerving but admittedly pleasant feeling she'd evoked. Such a wordsmith, Jana. Who the hell lets you get up in front of judges to speak on someone's behalf about life-changing things?

Brooke smiled, brushed her hand over my forearm then turned back to her beer and her teammates. The conversation flowed naturally, and it was easy to fit in with these long-time friends even though most of the talk revolved around the game, partners and kids before looping back to the finals match for which they'd just qualified.

"Will you come cheer for us again, Jana?" Immy asked, cheeks flushed with excitement and maybe wine, as she leaned on the table. "You seriously drowned out most of the other team's cheer squad."

I glanced at Brooke, whose pleased smile confirmed I'd be welcomed back. "Sure, if I can make it. I'd like that."

Beth nodded absently. "Cool." She'd been staring at me since we'd arrived, but not in an appraising or appreciative way. Rather it was curious yet tentative at the same time. Three-quarters through my beer, I decided I had to bring it up. "Do I have something on my face?" I asked, hoping she caught the teasing tone.

She straightened, dragging her sweating pint glass toward herself. "Huh? Uh, oh no…sorry, it's just you look really familiar and I can't quite place it. Are you sure we haven't met before today?"

I offered a smile. "I'm pretty sure we haven't."

She frowned, still looking thoughtful. "Have you done any sort of television or magazine modeling stuff?"

"Nope."

"Never been in porn or had a private sex video leaked online?"

Brooke half-rose out of her chair. "Hey, come on, where are your manners? There's *boundaries* for new people, Beth."

Grasping a handful of Brooke's hoodie, I tugged her back down. "It's okay," I murmured.

Beth's smile was charming. "Sorry, you know it's just a logical conclusion."

"No worries. And no, no porn. Must just be a doppelgänger then."
She bounced her eyebrows. "Hmm. Sounds hot."

Brooke grunted and took a long swallow of her beer.

"Thanks. I think." Suddenly it twigged as to why she thought I
looked familiar. It was a long shot, but entirely possible. "You might
have seen my sister, Sabine around the, uh…" I made air quotes.
"Scene. Before she got old and boring that is."

Beth stared some more, her eyes narrowed and forehead wrinkled.
I could almost see the cogs turning, and it took her another few
seconds before she exclaimed, "Ha! Holy fucking shit, you're right.
You're Sabine Fleischer's younger sister? The lawyer?"

"Mhmm, the one and only." Of course I felt compelled to add, as
I always had when someone did the "Oh, you're Sabine Fleischer's
younger sister, I hope you're as good a student-slash-athlete-slash-
human as she is" thing, "But you know, I'm my own person too, not
just her sister."

"Oh, well I'm a friend of Sabine's from the bad ol' days." She
snorted. "So, last I heard, she was getting married." At my nod, she
barreled on, "About fucking time. That woman's been marching
toward eternal commitment for as long as I could remember."

I turned the bottle in circles, leaving smears of condensation on the
wooden table. "Yeah, Rebecca's great. They're really happy."

"I should call her. I will call her." Beth leaned in. "So, uh what
are you doing hanging out with the Disc Dykes? I didn't think you
were gay, if what your sister's told me—and it's a lot because she never
fucking shuts up about her family—is true."

"No, I'm not." I glanced sideways at Brooke, who now wore an
oddly neutral expression. "I'm just a ring-in cheerleader who's also
crashing your pub time."

"I see…" Beth drew her answer out, musing as she looked between
Brooke and me. "Well, the more the merrier, I say." She raised her
glass. "So, is Sabine's number the same?"

We had another drink, and more easy conversation for almost
an hour before Beth declared she had to get her ass home to her
girlfriend, and Immy groaned that she had to pick up the kids from her
mom's place. We said our goodbyes, went through the usual *might see
you at another game* scenario, and Brooke led the way back to her car.
She stuffed her hands in her pockets as she walked, jangling her keys.
"Sorry about Beth. I forget that she can be a little full-on, especially
with new people."

"No, it's fine. That sort of thing doesn't bother me."

"You sure? You seemed kind of upset about her being your sister's friend."

She'd noticed my mood shift? I'd barely noticed it, and it'd been my mood that had shifted. "Oh, no, that's not it. It doesn't bother me whose friend she is." About to leave it at that, I decided I wanted to share my childish annoyance with her. Feeling like an idiot, I elaborated, "She just hit a raw nerve that's all. I feel like I've spent my whole life being *Sabine's younger sister*, you know? Like at school, or meeting the parents of her friends, or going to her horse competitions, her track competitions, her gymnastics competitions—it was always that thing of *Are you as good as Sabine?* It kinda grated on me, like this constant feeling that I wasn't as good as her. And I guess it's never quite gone away."

"That must be hard," Brooke said gently.

"Yeah, but it shouldn't be because there's never been any pressure from my family. My parents love us equally, I *know* that. I also know for sure my sister doesn't think of me as being a second-rate version of her. I adore her. She's smart and funny and athletic and kind and just…great, and she's overcome some pretty fucking shitty things." I shrugged. "I guess it's mostly pressure from myself, never feeling quite good enough. Kind of like I've always been standing behind her instead of beside her. She did the Army thing for my family and she saves the lives of heroes every day. It's hard to top that."

Brooke pulled me to a stop, then tugged my hand until I turned to face her. "Obviously I haven't met your sister and I'm sure she's wonderful, but you're wonderful too. All those things you just said about Sabine? You're all that and more, and you save lives too, just in a different way is all."

Her words were so earnest, so kind that I wanted to throw myself at her and hug her. I settled for a self-deprecating groan, which was nowhere near as satisfying. "Oh God, I'm sorry. This really wasn't a pity-party-fishing-for-compliments thing, I swear. And thanks, you're really sweet."

"You're welcome," she said, the two words husky and soft.

It was then I realized our bodies were barely inches away from touching. There wasn't enough air between us, like the atmosphere had sucked it all out somehow. And all I could think was this was a movie moment, the one where the leads are about to kiss, and they're standing there staring into each other's eyes and everyone knows it's about to happen and ever…so…slowly they lean in.

"I like guys," I blurted.

Brooke let out a short laugh. "So do I." She smiled, clearly amused.

"No, I mean I like them as in I date them."

The smile widened, eyebrows raised. "That's really great, Jana. Guys are fabulous, of course."

"Mhmm. I just, um wanted you to know."

"I did know but thank you for the reminder." Every word sounded like she was struggling to hold back more laughter.

"Okay then." I cleared my throat, aware of a strange lingering disappointment layered over my other emotions. Despite what I'd just panickingly affirmed about my sexuality, I'd *wanted* that movie moment to continue to its inevitable conclusion. There had been undeniable anticipation that it *could* happen, and I'd desired the testing and teasing that comes with new romantic entanglements. And in that moment, I'd wanted all of that stuff with Brooke. I swallowed, took a shuffling step back.

Brooke tilted her head, the amused expression turning to one of confusion. That made two of us. She tucked both hands back into her hoodie, shoulders hunching forward. "Ready to go home?"

"Mhmm. Sure." Ready to go home and figure out what the actual hell was going on.

CHAPTER FOURTEEN

Sabs met me after work at one of my favorite coffee shops, just a few blocks from work and nowhere near hers. She never insisted we meet somewhere closer to her and secretly I thought she did that so one day she could shove every magnanimous thing she'd ever done—like regularly drive forty minutes out of the way to meet me for coffee—to force me into doing something huge for her. She was sneaky that way, but I already had *Putting up with you planning a wedding* ready as a rebuttal.

She wound her way through the half-empty café, dumped her backpack on the chair next to me and caught me just as I was standing for a hug. "How was court today? Kick some ass?"

"Unfortunately not. Sick judge so we had to reschedule. Now next week is busy as hell, and I have all this winning energy and nowhere to put it. Sucks."

"Bummer. I lost a patient today. Almost lost him last week and managed to get him stabilized again, but…today just sucked."

Okay, she won. I held both of her shoulders. "Sorry, Sabbie."

"Yeah, but it happens." She smiled her *it'll be okay smile*, the one that always made me feel it really would be okay. Sabs rummaged in her backpack. "Ready for coffee?"

"Please. Surprise me."

While she went up to the counter I dealt with a work email and tried to ignore the low throbbing of a tension headache behind my eyes. Sabs returned after a few minutes, and before she sat, placed a warm hand on the back of my neck. "Have you taken something for your headache?" She massaged gently, then sat next to me.

"No. It's not that bad."

"Yeah right. You're making the my-head-is-going-to-explode face."

"Am not."

"You are too." Sabine's phone vibrated and chimed with a text alert, ending our childish back-and-forth. "Bec," she breathed. Sabs snatched up her phone like it was her last meal, texting furiously with both thumbs. She had that ridiculously goofy smile she always got whenever Bec was near or she spoke to her.

What a sap.

Come to think of it, I'd kind of had the same expression lately when I was near Brooke. Hmmm, oh shit oh shit. Or maybe not oh shit, maybe…so what? Brooke was a good friend who made me happy during both conscious and unconscious hours. I smothered a groan. Remember what you decided about being honest? At least to yourself. You were checking her out on the weekend, Jana, and found her *very* pleasing to the eye. And other parts of your body.

The moment Sabs set her phone back down, I blurted, "You ever thought about guys, you know, sexually? Like weird dreams or anything?"

Her smile of pleasure turned to a look of confusion. "Nope. Oh, wait. I did have a vague kinda sex dream about Robert Redford after we watched *The Horse Whisperer*, but midway through he turned into Kristin Scott Thomas. So I guess no."

"Ah, okay then." Well shit. I was on my own.

"Why? Something you want to tell me?"

Way to be subtle, Jana. Why not just pass her a note saying *I think I might suddenly and inexplicably be a bit gay, got any tips?* "Nuh-uh, nope, just curious that's all, seeing as you're about to hitch yourself to Bec's wagon for good."

She stared as though trying to work out exactly where I was coming from, then her face relaxed as though she'd figured it out. "I've checked out other women, if that's what you're asking, and so does Bec. I know for sure she ogles the mail lady, and with good reason. She is hot with a capital H." Sabs made an *okay* symbol with thumb and forefinger. "Appreciating nice-looking humans doesn't necessarily mean we want to drag them into our bed."

"No, that's not it." Nowhere near what I was getting at. "I was just curious, that's all. You've always been so straight down the line with your preferences."

She grinned. "Not so straight."

Oh I'd walked right into that one. I swatted at her. "Ha-ha."

"Look, Jannie, I'm less than a month away from marrying The One, and I am so supremely fucking content that sometimes I just have to sit down and wonder how the hell I ever managed to get this lucky. I cannot *wait* to hitch myself to Bec's wagon."

I glanced at my watch. "Holy shit. Nine minutes into a conversation and we've only *just* had our first mention of the wedding." I leaned close, widening my eyes. "Are you feeling all right?"

"Oh…" Sabs spluttered, hands working ineffectively as she searched for a suitable comeback. Eventually she just mumbled, "Screw you."

I placed a hand on my breast. "I'm wounded."

"Whatever." She fidgeted with the paper napkin, twisting it between her fingers. "Look, Bec kinda mentioned that maybe I was getting a little out of hand with all this ceremony shit, and now I'm trying to just let things happen as they happen and not be so, you know…"

"So completely and utterly fucking over the top and annoying about the whole thing?" I asked dryly.

She held up both hands. "She's right, you're right. You know I just want it to be perfect for us. But I talked to my shrink about it and he helped me unpack a few things, and we agreed to increase just my anxiety meds for a short while. I took a good look at everything, checked all my notes and our spreadsheets and shit and I realized that everything really is under control and I need to trust everyone else and stop stressing and micromanaging."

I squeezed her hand. "I love you, stress and micromanagement and all. And I promise everything is going to be perfect." I scoffed. "As if I'd let it be anything but. As if Bec and Mom and Dad and everyone else would let it be anything but."

"I know." She inhaled deeply, eyes fluttering briefly closed. "So, what else is news?"

"Not much. Working my ass off, trying to have some sort of a social life. I met a friend of yours on Saturday. Beth?"

Sabine's blink was comically slow. "Beth, shit. I haven't seen her in a few years. She was part of the crowd when Vic and I were dating yeeears ago." Sabs gave a mock shudder. "Thank fuck that's all over. But Beth's pretty great. How is she?"

"I'd say okay, given she's alive and seems to have all her body parts intact."

"Smartass. So how'd you meet her?" She peered up, smiling as the server came over with our coffee. "Thanks."

I murmured my thanks too and dragged the cup closer. "She plays Ultimate with Brooke, and we went out for beers after the game."

"Ah. I see." Sabs frowned, turning her coffee cup around before taking a sip. "So you and Brooke are doing a lot of shit together."

"I guess." I added a fake sugar to whatever coffee she'd picked for me. "It's just nice to have someone to hang out with when you guys are working or busy or whatever."

"Fair enough," she mused. "I'm glad you've got someone else to spend time with."

"Me too. Oh, and I told Brooke you were going to come watch one of her games. She seemed pretty excited." I sipped the coffee, which was actually some flavored latte concoction. Oh boy, way too sweet. Next time, test and then add sweetener, Jana.

"Excited to meet her friend's sister? I mean, I know I'm fucking awesome, but still. Seems a bit weird."

"I don't think so. She's just like that. Maybe she's curious about my family, I don't know."

"Hmm, okay then." Sabs drummed her fingers on the side of the coffee cup. "When's their next game?"

"Saturday, big final or something."

"You going?" At my nod, she added, "I'm not working so I'll tag along."

"Sounds great," I said quickly. For some reason, I wanted her to meet Brooke. Wanted her to like her, to…approve of her or something. Approve? Why? I'd never felt any need to have my sister vet my friends before.

It took us another half hour to catch up on what'd happened since we'd spoken on the phone a few days ago. Sabine declared she *had to jet* because she needed to get to work, and screw night shifts and her fucked-up circadian rhythms. And, according to her—I had to get my ass home, take something for my headache, most definitely not do any work, and go to bed. She walked me to the street, where we hugged tightly, said our usual byes and love-yous before splitting off to go our separate ways.

I let myself into my work building and headed straight for the elevator down to the parking garage. As I did every afternoon, I checked the silver paint of my car for green scratches. Nothing. Damn.

Just once I wanted that asshole to be taught a lesson. The moment I settled in the driver seat, I let out a long breath, leaned my head against the headrest and I tapped out a quick text to Bec. *Whatever you said to get her to calm down, THANK YOU. I'm not sure how much more I could have taken. Love you xx*

Trust me, it was for me too… ☺ Love you too x

* * *

A familiar edge of my vision blurring caught my attention—the weird, almost underwater light refraction in my peripheral was a telltale sign that I was about to be whacked over the head with a migraine. Oh fuck, please no. Argh. With one hand I fumbled in my purse for a nasal spray, hoping it wasn't too late, and with the other I quickly saved what I was working on, knowing that it probably *was* too late and I didn't have long before I'd be incapacitated.

Yep, I was too late. The background headache I'd been mostly ignoring since having coffee with Sabine the day before suddenly coalesced into a knife-boring-into-skull kind of pain, followed up with a surge of nausea so strong I only just managed to hold on to my stomach. Instinctively, I closed my eyes. Idiot, I should have known it wanted to turn into a migraine when the headache from yesterday hadn't gone away overnight, or been dulled by my strategic doses of Advil and Tylenol all day.

Everyone had left the office an hour ago. Fuck. I whispered a pathetic, "Help" in the hope the universe might grab the word and send it out to someone for me. Sabs and Bec were both on night shifts. Maybe I'd get lucky and catch one of them on a break. Great idea, Jana. What exactly are two busy surgeons going to do? Say, "Sorry, my sister has a migraine and your life-threatening thing has to wait while I go get her, just put your hands over that hole where your insides are coming outside and I'll be right back"?

Okay then, only one option left. Curl up on the floor of my office and die. I pushed my chair back and blindly fumbled my way to the floor, crawling until I reached the edge of my plastic chair mat where I lowered myself to lie in fetal position on my thick soft carpet. Though the movements were slow and cautious, I still felt each one as a delightful mix of scream-inducing pain in my head and puke-inducing grossness in my stomach.

I concentrated on deep, slow breaths. Just lie still. It'll pass. Eventually. Even with my eyes closed, the crystal rainbows still shimmered against a black backdrop in my vision. When everything had settled enough for me to move again, I thumbed my phone to silent and held it clutched to my chest. Fuck this shit. Stupid head. Stupid work and stupid fucking Weisman and his asshole-client stress.

An eternity of migraine horror later, my phone vibrated. Then again and again. A call. I tapped at the screen, hoping muscle memory would get my finger in roughly the right spot to answer. Please be Sabs or Bec somehow sensing my misery and calling to help. Please please please.

"'Lo?" I whisper-croaked.

"Jana, it's Brooke. Hey, sorry to bother you but one of my friends just pulled out of going to the movies tomorrow night and I already arranged tickets. Are you free?"

"Mhmm," I managed to get out.

A long pause. "Are you all right? Is this a bad time?"

My voice was a hoarse mumble. "I'm being held hostage."

Her voice dropped but the urgency was unmistakable. "What's going on? Who's there? Where *are* you?"

"Office. Migraine."

Brooke's voice remained quiet, but now it lacked inflection as though she was trying to be as flat and soft as she could. "Crap. Do you need help?"

"Very much."

"What do you need me to do?"

"Just…help please. If I open my eyes I'm going to puke or die." That was as far as I could think, and I hoped she could take what little information I'd provided and figure out what might help.

"Okay, I'm leaving home now, be there in twenty minutes. Is your office accessible or do I need to grab security?"

"It's open." Because I was still working, nobody had locked the front door as they'd left and the cleaners hadn't been in yet. Not that it would have bothered them—I'd been struck down by migraines in my office before and they'd quietly emptied my trash, skipped the vacuuming and left. "You can come through," I whispered.

"Sit tight. I'm on my way."

Sitting, or rather lying, tight was a good plan and pretty much all I was capable of. I curled up, clutched the phone to my chest and waited for my savior to arrive. Good job, universe. You really delivered. I owe you big-time.

An indeterminate time later, the front office door opened, closed and then I heard a raised whisper of, "Jana?"

Without moving, I said as loudly as I could, which was pathetically soft, "I'm here."

"Oh, sweetheart. Let me turn off the light." The light in front of my closed eyelids suddenly disappeared, replaced by a red haze.

"What's the red? Are my eyes bleeding?"

"Red-light headlamp. It's great for nighttime when I'm hiking and hopefully won't affect you as much as white light."

"Clever," I mumbled.

A warm, dry hand pressed lightly against the back of my neck. "Can you sit up?"

"Haven't tried yet. Too scared."

Fingers stroked the skin of my neck. "Is there any medication I can get for you?" She kept stroking lightly.

"Time is it?"

"Almost eight thirty."

"Mm, in my bag or my drawer, a nasal spray please."

I could feel her moving around me, hear the quiet sound as she tried to find what I needed. She curled my fingers around the bottle. "Can you manage that on your own?"

I was a pro at closed-eye administration and given this was only a six out of ten migraine I was still functional on a basic level. "Yes." I fumbled, getting my bearings on the single-use spray before quickly stuffing it up my nose.

When I was done, she took it from me, hands closing around mine. "Let me know when you want to move."

"Never, I never want to move…but let's try now." I was fairly certain that I wasn't going to become capable of anything but doing nothing for quite some time, and there was no point in waiting. I wanted to go home to my bed so I could at least die in comfort.

With Brooke's supportive hands on my shoulders, I managed to get upright and stay that way because she pressed into me so I could lean. I could only imagine how graceful I looked, slumped on the floor of my office like a drunk. My disorientation was exacerbated by being voluntarily blind. But it was better than the alternative.

Soft satin was pressed into my hands. "Here's an eye mask. It'll keep the light out when we leave."

"Thought of everything." I fumbled. "But I can't work it out."

"Here, let me." Fingers slid over mine then the mask was carefully slipped over my eyes. Something brushed my cheekbones.

I reached up to make sure the mask was in place and cautiously cracked open my eyes. Not a bit of light came through. "Thank you," I breathed. "Sorry to take your sleeping mask."

A low chuckle. "Actually, it's my kinky sex game mask, but... whatever."

If I hadn't felt so fucking awful I'd probably have laughed and made some comeback. But all I managed was a weak, "Even sorrier then."

"No problem. My mom had migraines, or still has them I suppose. I always remember being in the car with streetlights flashing by used to really get to her." Brooke cleared her throat. "And I have a bucket, just in case. Hold out your hands."

I did as asked and she carefully folded my fingers around the edges. Brooke pulled my heels off, replaced them with something soft. Slippers? The woman was a genuine saint.

"Bless you. Thanks, sorry for being so pathetic."

"You're anything but. Come on, let's get you home and to bed."

"Could you please get my laptop and handbag?"

"Sure."

As I sat with a hand braced on the floor, the other gripping the bucket, and legs curled underneath myself, there was the sound of her quietly packing up. She carefully helped me to my feet, made sure I was steady and then led me through the office with her right arm around my waist and her left holding my arm to guide me. She turned out the lights and locked the door, the click of the switches and locks stabbing so fiercely through my head that I had to stop moving to ride out the waves of pain and nausea.

Brooke's hand swept up and down between my shoulder blades as she waited for my brain and stomach to settle. She didn't say anything, didn't push, just held me close and kept up the gentle strokes. I breathed slowly. "Okay, I think I can move. If you help me."

"I will," she murmured. "Don't worry, I'm here."

Brooke drove home carefully, taking every turn wide and slow and at every one of my surprised or pained grunts, murmured her apologies and assured me everything was okay, we were nearly home. Somehow she managed to figure out my garage access card and then keys and whatnot for my front door.

"Alarm code is seven, two, eight, three, then press one." I braced myself for the sound.

"Got it." Quiet sound of the door closing, then beeps as she disarmed my security system. Blargh. Brooke kept her arm around me. "If you don't mind, I'll stay on your couch. I don't want you to be alone."

"Don't need to, is fine."

"I want to. Please." That single *please* was almost desperate.

I was too sick to argue, so waved my assent. "Guest room, first door on right. Bathroom next door. You'll figure it out. Thanks. Eat and drink and do what you want. Can you get me to the hallway please?"

Brooke helped me get to my room, my fingers trailing along the wall the whole way, and guided me to my bed where I cautiously sat down. "This feels like a weird blindfolded party game," I mumbled.

"Should I put up a poster of a donkey for you to pin the tail on?"

I huffed out a laugh, wincing at the immediate lance of pain in my head which was followed by a slow roll of nausea. I barely managed to swallow my groan.

"Sorry," she whispered. "Do you want me to call someone for you? Sabine or a, uh…guy friend?"

Eyes still protected by the mask, I held my phone in what I thought was Brooke's general direction. "Sabs and Bec are working. Could you please text Sabs that I've been attacked, but you're here and I'm okay? Need to keep phone on silent and sleep."

She paused, exhaled audibly. "Of course." Her fingers brushed mine as she took my phone from me. "There's a bucket on the floor, and I'll leave the doors open a little in case you need me."

"Mhmm, thanks." I kicked out of my borrowed slippers and tried to work my arms from my suit jacket, but with the general disorientation and uselessness only ended up getting tangled.

"Here, let me." Brooke carefully helped me out of the garment. Hyperaware of every sensation, the brush of fingers through my jacket and then the bare skin of my arms made me shudder. "Can you manage the rest of your clothes?" she murmured.

"Yeah."

"Okay then. Make a sound if you need me."

"I'll try. Thanks." God I sounded pathetic.

Her hand gently touched my forehead and then was gone. When I heard her footsteps and my bedroom door creak, I clumsily undressed except for bra and underwear, dropped everything on the floor and climbed between the sheets. Sorry, face but you'll have to cope with makeup staying on overnight. I rolled onto my side, slowly curled into a ball and begged myself to fall unconscious.

CHAPTER FIFTEEN

I shoved the eye mask up to my forehead, pushed the covers off my body and reached over for my phone. I fumbled and pushed it off the bedside table. Clever. The clunk of it hitting the floor sent a minor shockwave through my brain, but mercifully I was clear-headed enough to discover that it was nothing more than my typical post-migraine hangover. A little weak and out-of-my-body feeling, but pretty much lucid and pain free.

Brooke barged into my room. "You okay?" She slammed on the brakes, a cartoonish stop that would have made me laugh if I'd been more awake. Her spin around was equally cartoonish. "Shiiiitt, sorry. Didn't expect the naked."

"Not naked. I'm wearing underwear. It's like wearing a bikini." It would have been the perfect time to test the waters of my possible attraction, and of course I felt too fuzzy to make any sort of suggestive comment.

"Mm, yes, but close enough to naked." She cleared her throat. "How're you feeling?"

"Groggy, but better." My voice was rough and raspy with leftover migraine fatigue. "How'd you sleep?"

"Really well, your spare bed is super comfy. I hope I didn't wake you just now."

I swung from the bed, testing my legs before I stood properly. Wobbly, but capable. "You didn't. I dropped my phone. Would you mind picking it up please? I think bending over would test my limits."

She turned around, very carefully keeping her eyes averted as she bent down. Sweet of her, but some distant, insistent part of my brain wondered if she wasn't looking because she found me repulsive sans clothing.

"Thanks." I checked my phone, grateful that my vision had lost the weird rainbow crystal effect. There was only a message from Sabs. It was a simple response to the message Brooke had sent—a thank-you and that she'd call when she had a moment. I scrolled up to read what Brooke had written.

Hi Sabine – it's Brooke Donnelly, a friend of Jana's. I'm with Jana at her place, she's been attacked by a migraine (her words). She's turned her phone to silent, but I'm going to stay here tonight to make sure she's okay. You can contact me at any time if you need to.

She'd listed her phone number and the thoughtfulness made my eyes sting. I pulled on sweats, a threadbare Penn tee and my grandma cardigan. Comfort wins over fashion. "Did Sabine call you?"

"Mhmm, around ten thirty I think. I told her you were sleeping and seemed okay. She wanted me to go in and take a photo of you, but she seemed to calm down after I assured her a few times that I'd just checked and you were asleep and yes, still breathing."

"Fuuuuck, she's an over-the-top pain in the ass. Still breathing? Really? And doesn't she get that any time doesn't really mean *any time*?" My brain stalled then reversed back to Brooke apparently checking on me. The woman really was the sweetest thing.

"Sure it does. I said any time because I meant it and I thought she'd be worried about you. It wasn't that late and I was awake anyway. She said she's going to come by on her way home from work to check on you and you'd better be here and not at the office."

"She's so damned bossy." Of course I had no intention of going in, and as we wandered to the kitchen I took a moment to send Kelly a text to let her know I'd be out for the day, to please reschedule my two meetings and deal with anything else that needed taken care of. There was nothing urgent requiring my attention and a day at home was definitely on the agenda. I nabbed the closest chair, sat down and pulled my leg up to rest my heel on the chair with my chin resting on top of my knee. "Thanks for staying."

"You're welcome, but it was selfishly for me too. I would have worried about you all night, being here on your own." Her voice was quietly intense, almost protective. Brooke settled at the table, to the right of my usual spot, where a mug of coffee sat waiting on a saucer next to a used plate with knife and fork lined up neatly atop it.

I fiddled with the ankle of my sweats. "You're a really good friend, and I know it's weird because I've only known you for ten minutes." Friend. The word still felt odd. I didn't have many friends. Sabs and Bec filled all my important friendship requirements. Then there was that circle of acquaintances—people I caught up with on an irregular basis for drinks or whatever, but always kept superficial. And guys... guys were for dating. Aside from Mitch and his boyfriend, Mike, who were obviously off the menu, I'd never just had a male friend. Every guy was a potential partner and if they weren't good for that, then they weren't good for friendship either.

So all of my friendship notions left my relationship with Brooke in some weird, confusing gray area. She was a *friend* friend, but I was also attracted to her, but I didn't usually do friendship with people to whom I was attracted. The whole thing was one great circle of confusion. I cleared my throat. "I mean, I'm glad you were here."

"Me too." There was the briefest moment when I thought she was going to say something else, something important. Instead, she flashed a smile and nabbed her mug. "There's plenty of coffee, I wasn't sure if you'd feel up to eating anything."

"I think I will be, but not quite yet."

"Do you want some water?"

I checked in with my stomach, and after mutual agreement that it wasn't going to throw a tantrum, nodded. When I shifted to get up, Brooke held out a hand to stop me, and jumped out of the chair. "I've got it."

She moved around my apartment like she'd been here hundreds of times, and watching her open cupboards and pour cold water from the fridge I decided that I liked her being there. She fit in my space and for the first time I could recall, having someone in my kitchen who wasn't family didn't make me feel uncomfortable, like they were going to put something in the wrong spot, or mess up my recycling system.

As she leaned over to place the glass in front of me, Brooke held my chair, her fingers brushing my back.

"Thanks." After a cautious sip I nodded at her plate. "So you already had breakfast?" Egg and toast by the look of the plate. A quick check of the kitchen confirmed she'd already cleaned up whatever she'd cooked with.

"Yeah." Brooke hastily gathered the plate and cutlery, the movement fluttery like a bird. Her gaze was fixed on the plate and like clockwork, her ear blush appeared. "Sorry, you said to make myself at home and eat whatever. I hadn't had dinner when I called you last night, so…"

"I did say that. And I meant it." I reached over to grab her hand, sliding my thumb over her fingers to make her look at me.

Finally she turned her attention to me. "I know. I just realized I kind of invaded your fridge and pantry like a kid come home from college." She pressed her forefinger to the table a couple of times to snag crumbs, which she brushed onto the plate. "I should probably go home and get to work. Are you sure you'll be okay here by yourself?" She added the mug and saucer to her pile then carefully pushed the chair back under the table. She reminded me of ten-year-old me at friend's houses, overly aware of my manners.

"I will, yeah. Just going to bum around and probably sleep most of the day."

"Good." Brooke backed toward the kitchen. "Call me if you need anything at all. I don't have anything on today so I can come back at any time. What will you do about your car?"

My car was still at work, parked crookedly as usual. Racing Green would have a heck of a time getting into his space this morning. Excellent. "I'll catch a cab or something in tomorrow."

"Oh, sure, okay then." She opened the dishwasher.

"You don't need to do that, just leave your stuff in the sink and I'll sort it out."

Cutlery and crockery clinked, and over the top of that came a muffled, "Too late, it's done. If you decide you need a ride in the morning, give me a call."

"You'd break your bus ritual for me?"

"Of course I would." Brooke wiped her hands on a dishtowel then slipped out of the kitchen. It took less than a minute for her to gather her keys and handbag and push feet into her sneakers, by which time I'd managed to get up and meet her near the door.

There was no thought, no hesitation, I just stepped in and hugged her. She held me close, fingers massaging the back of my neck. "Rest up, and *please* call me if you need anything."

I relaxed into her embrace, aware of the little sigh that escaped me when I rested my cheek against her shoulder. "I will. Thanks for everything, drive carefully."

Brooke squeezed me gently, and then with what felt a whole lot like reluctance, slowly let me go. She softly thumbed my cheek, gave me a shy smile and slipped out the front door. And I stood rooted to the spot, my hand against the cheek she'd caressed, like a teen who'd just been kissed for the first time.

Sabine's arrival just after ten a.m. interrupted my nap on the couch. She turned off my white noise machine and came to crouch in front of me. "How're you doing, Jannie?" She kissed my forehead, smoothing hair back and tucking it behind my ears.

"Okay, just tired."

"Any dizziness or nausea now?" Sabs took my hand, drew it toward her with her fingers resting on my wrist. Though she tried to pretend she wasn't, I knew she was checking my pulse. Just as I knew that her forehead kiss had doubled as a fever check.

"Nope." I rolled into a sitting position, grateful my body didn't make a liar out of me.

"How's the actual headache?" She cupped my face in both hands, thumbs gently massaging my cheekbones and her fingers doing the same just behind my ears.

"Very vaguely there in the background, the way it usually is after an episode. It's fine." I swatted her away. "And stop disguising a clinical exam in gestures of affection." She always did that—she couldn't help herself and just had to reassure herself the person was okay. And once she was reassured, she turned into Doctor Annoying.

She mmph'ed at me and pulled a small light from her backpack. "Look at me." She clicked the light on and beamed it right into my eyes.

I scrunched my eyes closed, turning my head away for good measure. "Fuck, can you *not* do that?"

"Does it cause a reaction?" my sister asked, voice tight with urgency.

"No, it's just fucking bright and not really what I want in my eyeballs the morning after a migraine, Sabs."

"I know, sorry, but I need to check your response."

"My response is not something you want to hear right now." Cautiously I opened my eyes and pushed her hand out of the way.

But she was on a roll. "Maybe you should go for a CT."

"As if."

"When was the last time you had your eyes checked?"

"My eyesight is fine, I don't need glasses. It was a migraine, Sabbie. You know, those things I've been having every few months for the past fifteen-odd years? Not a tumor, not a hemorrhage and not brain-eating bacteria. Just the usual things—stress, not enough sleep and too much time in front of a screen. Now put that medical degree away and make me a cup of herbal tea please. Then go home and go to sleep. You look like shit and you're back on day shifts tomorrow. You know how grumpy you get if you don't sleep transition properly."

She mumbled something under her breath that sounded a lot like calling me a mean name. "You had a headache the day before yesterday when we had coffee. You need to reassess your treatment. When did you last see your physician and specialist?"

"Sabs, I love you and I know you're worried and trying to help but I'm not capable of taking in anything right now and I'm going to get snarky."

"You're such a brat." She kissed my forehead again, then stood and made her way to the kitchen. "So Brooke stayed here all night? Sorry I couldn't leave work to come help."

I leaned my head against the back of the couch and flung my forearm over my eyes. "Yep, she did. And it's okay. Our nation's wounded heroes are far more important than my neurological issues."

Sabs made a noise that made me think she thought her family was more important. "That was really great of her. I'm glad you didn't have to be here alone."

"Mhmm, yeah."

"You hungry? Want me to make you something?"

I was set to decline and insist again that she go home and to sleep but my stomach chose that time to let out a loud grumble at the fact I hadn't fed it since lunch the previous day. "Egg and toast would be great. Thank you, best sister."

I curled back down onto the couch while she did her thing in the kitchen. The smell of her frying me an egg caused no nausea and I sent silent thank-yous to the migraine gods. My last one had incapacitated me for days and by the time it'd gone I'd felt like a hollowed out eggshell. It didn't take long until Sabs asked, "Can you get up or do you want to eat on the couch?"

I raised my head to stare at her over the couch armrest. "I can get up. I haven't had a stroke."

Her stare would have frozen water.

I'd managed three mouthfuls of food before Sabine blurted, "So you called Brooke for help then?"

I blew on my tea. "Actually she called me about something else. It just happened to be at the right time to help me."

Sabs bit off a huge mouthful of peanut butter toast, offering nothing more than a thoughtful, "Mmmm." Once she'd swallowed, she asked, "Does Brooke have a girlfriend?"

"Not at the moment. Why? Are you thinking of setting her up with one of your friends?"

Her left eyebrow shot up. "Yeah, something like that," she mumbled before stuffing the last of her toast triangle in her mouth and getting up to take her mug and plate into the kitchen.

A setup. Though I knew Sabs's friends were good people, the idea of Brooke dating one of them niggled at me. More than niggled. I managed what I thought was a very neutral, "Oh, okay."

"You don't like the idea?" Sabine leaned back against the counter near the sink, arms folded.

"It's not for me to say." I was surprised how sharp the words sounded.

"I see," Sabs said carefully. "Sounds to me like you care whether or not she's dating."

"Well...yeah I guess I do. If she starts dating someone then she's going to have less time for our friendship." The excuse sounded even weaker once I'd actually said it. "And I like doing shit with her." More than liked.

"Ah. Sure. That makes sense." Sabs pushed off the counter. "On that note, I'm out. Get some rest, stay away from screens, call your specialist about getting some scans."

"You're not my doctor and you're not the boss of me."

She let out a long, exasperated sigh. "You know, when you were three I asked Mom to help me put you up for adoption in the paper. If only she'd let me do it." Sabs hugged me and kissed the top of my head. "Love you. Call if you want anything."

"Love you too, but you'll be asleep and Brooke already offered to be my on call standby person."

"Did she now?" Sabine grinned, then clamped her mouth closed. She nodded vigorously, the grin still teasing at the edges of her lips. "Isn't that nice of her."

CHAPTER SIXTEEN

After my migraine-recovery day, where I did nothing except nap and engage in a brief text exchange with a guy, I was back at work the next day. Brooke was nowhere to be seen when I arrived at the café for our morning coffee, so I slipped into line to wait for her and read the news on my phone. I'd made two feet of progress in line, and an article and a half worth of progress on current events when someone touched my shoulder. I turned, and Brooke slipped around to the other side, laughing like a kid caught in a peek-a-boo game.

Her hand lingered on my shoulder for another few seconds. "Morning, how're you feeling?"

Great now you're here. "Human."

"You look much better." Though she didn't move her head, her eyes wandered. Mostly downward from my face. "Actually, Jesus, you look amazing. New dress? Do you have court today?"

"Thanks. And no, just a drinks-date tonight with the workmate of a friend of a friend of a...well, you get the idea." I ran my hands over my stomach to smooth down the dress. "Last-minute thing. Trying to line up schedules has been a nightmare, so we're doing the 'we both work in the city, let's just meet up after work' thing. It's a pain in the ass because I had to leave my car here for the migraine thing, so I have to drive home and I can't drink much."

An odd look flashed over her face and if I didn't know better I'd have thought it was jealousy, tinged with a touch of regret. *You're flattering yourself, Jana.* Brooke's easy smile quickly covered her expression. "Ah, damn. I was going to see if you wanted to join me for a TV binge session and some baby-spicy Mexican tonight."

As she laid out her plans, I knew that was all I wanted to do and briefly wondered if I should just call this guy and cancel. Only the fact that he was associated with someone I knew and canceling would make me look bad stopped me. "Shit, I so would have. Sorry. They've been trying to throw us at each other for months now so I kind of have to go. Total rain check though, first chance we're both free?"

Her smile was bright, but her eyes remained wary. "Sounds great. I hope you have a blast."

"Honestly, I think I'd just settle for some interesting conversation."

The smile dimmed and her expression intensified. "You're too special to *settle* for anything, Jana." She straightened, cleared her throat. "Shit, sorry, that was really rude of me. It is so not my place to tell you what you should and shouldn't do. Especially not with guys. I, um, sorry, I'll keep my opinions to myself." She appeared mortified and with flustered movements, opened her purse.

Gently, I grabbed her forearm. "Hey, you don't have to do that. I like your opinions." More than that, I wanted her to care enough to have opinions about me and feel comfortable enough to express them. "Hanging out with you tonight sounds *so* good, but I just can't. Sorry."

"Oh no, I get it. Sorry, bit of an overreaction there." She looked up, her not-real smile still in place. "Already in the *work sucks* headspace I guess."

"Can I try to drag you out of it by buying you coffee? I owe you for the migraine thing. I mean, coffee's pretty inadequate but it's all I've got right now."

"You don't owe me anything, Jana." She drew in a long breath. "But coffee sounds great."

* * *

My date with Todd the financial analyst was not going well. *Not going well* was possibly one of the bigger understatements of my life. General boredom and complete lack of attraction aside, he was also completely unapologetic about his political views. As in—he had none. On its own, that would have been a teeth-grinding moment but when

I added it to the fact pretty much everything else about him was wishy-washy too, and every conversation I'd tried to start had been dead-ended by his "Hmm not sure" or "I really don't know," he'd quickly moved to the Nope list and then to the Hell Nope list.

Mentally, I headdesked. Then immediately smiled when I thought of how Brooke would actually say *headdesk* in the middle of a conversation to indicate her frustration when she couldn't find the actual words. She'd also thrown out a spoken *LOL* or two, and listening to her say it as a word instead of acronym always made me laugh.

Thinking of how animated Brooke was when discussing pretty much everything made me suddenly desperate to not be where I was. I wanted to be with her, talking about how good the margaritas were at the bar down the street from our work building, and the chemical composition of volcanic ash, and everything in between while we inhaled our not-spicy Mexican food and picked apart whatever we'd decided to binge watch. But I was stuck with Tedious Todd.

For now at least.

There was a football replay showing in the far corner of the bar, and desperate for conversation topics, I tried to prompt Todd into giving me his feelings about the NFL.

"It's all right I guess. Sometimes I like sports." He smiled cheerfully as he pushed his chair back. "I'm just going to visit the little boys' room."

Little. Boys'. Room. Wow. Just, fucking...wow. If everything else hadn't already convinced me he was a dud, that gem certainly did. I watched him wind his way through the bar and when I was certain he was out of sight, fumbled my phone from my purse and sent Sabine a text I knew she'd understand.

CALL 10!!!!

As I pressed send, I simultaneously hoped that she was awake and near her phone, and wondered what bizarre and disjointed conversation was in store for me when my sister would hopefully call in ten minutes. I checked my phone sound was on loudly. Then I thought up a plausible story to tell him on my way out the door, yet another skill I'd perfected over years of date abandonment.

Todd walked through the bar, checking his zipper with one hand and his hair with the other. His gaze was directly on me, and his laser focus gave me a brief stab of guilt. Statistically, most guys on their way back from the bathroom checked out other women around the room. Stay strong, Jana. He's probably going to tell you he had a successful peepee.

He climbed back onto his barstool, peered at my glass of red, which was still half full, then his empty beer glass and signaled the barman over. While we waited, I made a few more valiant attempts at conversation. Did he like to hike or camp? No, afraid of wildlife. What about indoor stuff like video games? They made him motion sick.

The first text alert sounded from my purse a few minutes after he'd received a fresh beer. Five minutes since I'd texted Sabs, good timing, not too suspicious. I laughed lightly. "Sorry. Probably a client."

"At eight thirty at night? Do you always work after hours like this?"

"Mhmm, that's me. Always available." Lowering my voice to the perfect pitch of earnestness I added, "I think it's really important for people to know they have someone they trust and who will be there for them during such a difficult time." In truth, being always available was a mistake. I'd learned early on, with some help from Will and Ollie, that if you wanted to maintain some work-life balance one of the worst things you could do as an attorney was to be overly available for your clients.

Todd mused noncommittally and sipped his beer. I asked him about the financial market and received a vague answer in response. I asked if he liked to travel and was told only for work. Come on, Sabs, I'm dying here. Mercifully, my sister came through and two more text message alerts landed within thirty seconds of each other. I studiously ignored each one, making a face that was the perfect mix of apologetic and *how annoying*. The texts were just for effect, to strengthen the punch of Sabine's big finale.

Exactly five minutes after the first text—leave it to Sabine to be ridiculously punctual even at a time like this—my phone rang. "Sorry, Todd, I should probably take this." The apology was a mix of contrite and no-nonsense, a tone I'd perfected over the years for this exact situation. When I fished my phone from my handbag, I saw three texts on the display.

The skin cells in your mouth are the same as the skin cells in your vagina.
I spat in your Pepsi after you ruined my R.E.M. concert tee with paint.
Koalas have unique fingerprints just like humans.

I had to clench my molars to keep from laughing and with great effort, forced a frown and said, "Oh, it's my sister." I tapped the phone screen to answer, "Sabs, what's up? You keep texting me."

"Rubber Ducky Sixty-Niner, this is Root Beer Float Eighty-Eight. Do you copy? Also, I'm not kidding, I really did spit in your drink because I was *super* fucking pissed at you. Over."

Eww, gross. "Oh my God. Jesus, oh no, seriously? Is she okay? How bad is it?"

"Pretty bad. I may have added some hocked-up throat stuff too. I don't regret it though, it was my best and favorite shirt from my first ever concert. Over."

"Oh…my God. Shit. Oh shit." Bitch bitch bitch. And double ewww.

"Jannie, come on. We need to work on your radio comm skills. How will I know you're done talking if you don't say over? Over."

I cleared my throat, fighting the giggle that was trying to work its way out. "What did the doctors say?"

"The doctor said Titus is still in the tree out the front and won't come down for dinner. Should I call for a hot firefighting woman to get him? Actually, Bec's good at tree-climbing. Maybe I'll make her put on a firefighter uniform…without a few bits of course. Gotta make it sexxxy. Overrrrr."

"Oh God that's not good. Okay, look I'm across town but it shouldn't take me long to get there." I reached for my purse, pulling out some cash to cover my one and a half drinks. No way was I going to let Todd pay for me and get any ideas about there being a next time.

"Ten-four, copy that, sis. On second thought, maybe I should get an industrial vacuum cleaner and suction him to the end of the hose, so I can pull him down like that? Over."

"I'll be there as soon as I can." I hung up before she could say anything else that might break my fraying self-control.

Sad things, think of sad things. I was quite pleased when, thanks to my attempt at holding laughter back, my voice came out with just the right amount of tightness. "Todd, I'm so sorry, but my sister's had a bad car accident and she's in an induced coma and I have to go." Perfect. The trick with this kind of situation was to lie while skirting the edges of truth. My sister had indeed been in a bad accident, albeit a few years ago now, and had been pretty fucked up at the time. If anyone decided to check in with me after hearing about my *sister's mishap* from Todd, it'd be easy to carry on the lie. I should really teach a class or something.

Todd jumped to his feet, his face a mask of such genuine distress that I almost felt bad. Until I remembered the *little boys' room*. "Oh no. Jana, that's terrible." A light hand touched my shoulder. "Will you be all right getting to the hospital? Do you need a ride?"

I sniffed, set the money on the bar and took a step back, ready to make my exit. "I'll be fine, thank you. I'll just run out and grab a cab." Back to work to get my car, which was only five blocks away. But he didn't need to know that.

He bent to kiss me and I deflected with a head turn so it landed squarely on my cheek. Barely two hours of boring-as-fuck first-date drinks does not entitle you to a kiss, mister. "I'll check my schedule and call you." Like hell.

"Okay. Um, well…good luck."

"Thank you. Take care." I squeezed his hand, then backed away.

Safely outside, I flagged down a cab and dialed Sabine. She answered almost right away and I jumped in with, "I hate you."

I could hear the smile in her voice. "No you don't. You love me. So, who's in dire straits this time?"

"Our nonexistent other sister had a super serious car accident and is in a coma. It's dicey. She might not make it."

Sabs chuckled. "It's okay, me and Bec'll save her."

I snorted. "I'm sure you two are excellent at your jobs, but I don't think even your skills can save this poor imaginary woman."

"You underestimate us. Also, you are so going to hell for all the lying you've done to these poor defenseless guys. I bet they don't even know what hit them when you rush out of there in a whirlwind like the Tasmanian Devil."

"I know, I knowww, sometimes I'm awful. But, Sabs, he used the phrase 'little boys' room' when he went to the bathroom."

All the teasing left her voice. "Oh. Fuck. Really? Well why didn't you ask for a bail out sooner?"

"I messaged you the moment he was gone!"

"Good. That's even worse than the one who ordered your dinner for you. What else was wrong with this guy?"

"Ugh, just…no. I can't even explain it but he was just wrong. A bar of soap would have been a better conversationalist."

"I see." She sighed and I could hear her genuine concern when she said, "Jannie, I really hope one day you find the right person."

"Mmm. I'm not even sure the right person for me even exists." I stared out the cab window. "Oh, are you still going to come watch Brooke's Ultimate Frisbee game with me on Saturday?"

There was a long pause. "Yes. As confirmed twice already."

Her odd tone made me wonder what exactly the issue was. "What?"

"Nothing."

I waited silently, knowing she wouldn't be able to resist telling me exactly what she was thinking. Sabine didn't disappoint. After five seconds she amended, "Nothing except within moments of saying *the right person*, you mentioned Brooke's name. Herr Freud would be having a field day with this one."

"Seriously? I was just thinking about my schedule for the week, that's all."

"Mhmm. And all the other times you've casually mentioned Brooke out of the blue? You must think about your weekly schedule a whole lot."

"You're insufferable." And maybe not that far off the mark…

"I know. I'm also usually right. So did I teach you some new fun facts tonight?"

"Aside from the disgustingness of you spitting in my drink, you bitch, you did. I knew the koala fingerprint thing but didn't know about the skin cell thing. Interesting, and a little off-putting."

She laughed. "Not for me it isn't." With a kiss down the phone and an, "I love you. See you Saturday for the big game." Sabine hung up.

"Shithead," I mumbled.

I opened my texts and scrolled up to find the back-and-forth between Brooke and me about the Ultimate game.

Hey! No pressure but just wanted to check if you're still in for ultimate finals cheering on Saturday and if you need a ride. Let me know? Drinks afterward regardless? x

I'll be there! Sabs too, so she'll drive me. Should I have pom-poms this time?

Great! Looking forward to meeting Sabine. And I wouldn't dissuade you from whatever cheerleading outfit you decide to wear.

Shit. Time to go to a costume store—I think it's a proven fact people cheer louder when they have pom-poms. Might even go full outfit, short skirt and all.

They'll eat you alive.

I don't think I'd mind.

I might… Wear whatever you want ☺ As long as you cheer loudest for me.

Of course! You're my star player xx

I read the thread again, aware of a strange sensation worming its way through my body. Sure it was a friendly exchange but it was also something more. I pinched the bridge of my nose. Stop skirting around it, Jana—if it was a guy then you would definitely class it as flirting. *Reciprocated* flirting. I was flirting with a woman, and it'd moved from harmless playful I'm bored kind of flirting to I kinda really mean it kind of flirting.

Oh, shit.

I took a moment to sift through the assorted feelings of confusion, excitement, and anticipation. Okay. Openly flirting with Brooke and enjoying it. Right. Add that to the newly discovered feelings you have for her. Once I'd acknowledged what was happening and confirmed that not only did I not care but that I liked it, there was only one thing to do.

I sent her a pointless text. *You up?*

Her response landed less than a minute later. *Yup! I got caught up in an America's Next Top Model replay marathon straight from work. Have not left couch in 4 hours. Numb butt. How was the date?*

I tried to ignore the reference to her butt to focus on her question. *On a scale of 1 to 10, he was -3.*

Ouch. Sorry. Good food at least?

Just drinks. What season of ANTM?

Cycle 7, they just did that weird ass circus shoot. Megg's bearded lady and CariDee's elephant lady WTF?

CariDee won the whole thing, didn't she? Did you know the real Elephant Man died of a dislocated neck in his sleep because his head was so heavy?

I did not know that.

I was so absorbed in my back-and-forth with Brooke that I hadn't noticed the cab had stopped in front of my work building. A pointed throat clearing tore my attention from my screen. "Sorry." I glanced at the meter, handing him more than enough to cover the fare and slipped out of the cab with a hasty, "Thanks!"

I drove home at my usual breakneck speed, then beelined for the mail room and collected a stack of mail which I tucked under my arm so I could keep texting Brooke.

Just got home. Time to undo all my hard work. Can't believe I redid my makeup after work for such a dud guy. Ugh.

Mm. You looked amazing. Stupid boring guy is an idiot.

He is. Such a waste of time. Kinda wish I'd taken you up on tacos and TV. I missed your company tonight.

There was no answer, and my worry escalated. Maybe I'd overstepped that friendly flirting line that we seemed to have drawn. Maybe I should stop sending mixed messages—the confused straight girl maybe testing the waters wasn't fair to Brooke. To be honest, it was starting to feel a little unfair to me too.

It was starting to feel like it wasn't quite enough.

My phone pinged as I was setting my keys in the clay bowl Sabine had made for me during her recovery. Boredom makes people do weird things, like a brief bout of dabbling with pottery.

Mouth dry, I raised my phone to read Brooke's message.

Me too, a whole lot.

CHAPTER SEVENTEEN

Sabs leaned close, a hand cupped beside her mouth. "I think Brooke's about to make a sneak play for a goal. This game is awesome."

"Why are you covering your mouth?"

"So the other team can't read my lips."

"Are you serious? It's not the fucking Frisbee Super Bowl. And they're all far enough away that I'm pretty sure they can't figure out what you're saying." I glanced at Brooke, who stood bent at the waist with her hands on her thighs, and tried to figure out what gave her motive away to Sabine. I could find no answer, probably because I wasn't really a sports person. As if she'd heard us talking about her, Brooke turned her head and stared right at me and even at this distance I could see her grin.

Sabs leaned forward, resting her elbows on her knees. After a few moments, she hmm'd and mmm'd, twisting around to look at me. "Brooke's cute. Really good at this game. Very, uh…lithe."

I only just suppressed the snarl rising up my throat, settling for a choked sort of growl. "Don't."

"What? You don't think she's cute?"

"Yes I do, I mean no, I mean…that's not it. She's my friend, Sabs."

"So? You've never cared if I've thought your friends were cute before."

"This is different." Different how? Different because I wanted Brooke for myself? Different because my out-and-proud-her-whole-life sister was free to express herself as she pleased while I fumbled about in what I was now beginning to realize might be a closet.

"Mmm, right."

I could tell she was being deliberately antagonistic and I chose to ignore her annoying digs and focus on the task at hand—enjoying watching Brooke and its associated pleasure. So with knowledge of that pleasure, what was stopping me from marching up to her once this game was done and declaring, "I think you're cute and you have a great ass and a fabulous smile and you're funny and just great and also I really love your ears"?

Actually, that was a good point. What *was* stopping me?

Fear? Maybe a little, though about what specifically I wasn't sure. Fear of the unknown? That it was one-sided?

Uncertainty? Maybe I was confusing the sudden rush of a quickly formed friendship for something more. Maybe I was just trying out another thing Sabs did, the way I had my whole life. No, being gay wasn't something Sabs *did*. It was who she was, as much a part of her as her intellect, her weird but hilarious sense of humor and her intense compassion.

Maybe the thing holding me back was the niggling doubt that this whole Brooke thing was just a casual dip of my toe into the lesbian waters and it wasn't really real.

Brooke's sprint and leap to catch the Frisbee immediately nixed the idea of my attraction being a casual thing. The movement, at once strong and graceful made my stomach flutter not unlike the feeling I'd had upon waking up after the Grape-Nuts dream. As sneakily as I could, I tilted my head to get a better look. Oh. Yes. Mhmm, yeah, it's really real.

Brooke flung the Frisbee to the end zone, then threw both hands up in the air when it sailed right over the line and into the hands of a teammate. I jumped to my feet, cupped both hands around my mouth and yelled, "Way to go, Brooke!" followed by a loud cheer and clapping.

"I don't remember you ever cheering that loudly for me," Sabs commented dryly, clapping as well, though with a little less enthusiasm than mine.

"That's because you never scored game-winning goals."

My sister laughed freely. "I never played anything as a kid that needed goal scoring." After a nudge, she reminded me, "She really is a great athlete."

"I know," I murmured. "She's great at a lot of things."

Sabs mumbled something under her breath, but I was too busy watching Brooke to catch what she'd said.

Brooke's team surged to a thrilling victory, helped by her five goals—each one to enthusiastic cheering from me, and appreciative cheering from Sabs. Once she'd celebrated onfield with her teammates, Brooke jogged over to us with a huge grin splitting her face. She looked so pleased with herself that I couldn't help but open my arms to her and she stepped into my embrace immediately.

The hug was natural, no hesitation from either of us, and the moment her grip tightened around my waist I relaxed into her and squeezed back. As sneakily as I could, I inhaled her scent. The mix of soap, shampoo, and sweat was some seriously incredible pheromone or something. Then I remembered I was supposed to be supporting her, not sniffing her and dialed myself back a few degrees. "Congratulations! That was awesome."

"Thanks," Brooke mumbled against my ear. She held the hug for a few more seconds, then slowly released me.

When we'd separated, Sabs stepped forward. "Great game," she agreed. "You looked very capable. And fabulous winning throw. You guys looking for any new players?"

Brooke laughed. "Thanks. And we're always keen for fresh blood." She offered her hand to Sabine. "I'm Brooke Donnelly."

"The dress guru and migraine rescuer. Great to finally meet you. I'm Sabine, Jana's sister, as you'd know if she had any manners and introduced us."

I kicked her ankle, gratified by the grunt huffed out in response. After a smiling, eyebrow-raised look at me and my sister, Brooke turned her attention back to Sabs. "I can see that. A pleasure to meet you too, and congratulations on your upcoming nuptials."

"Oh, thank you." Sabs shot me a sideways look, but instead of saying something snide or teasing, she sobered. "And seriously, thanks for taking care of this one while I was stuck at work, and for making sure she didn't bring home her dress with some gaping hole in it or something."

Time to pipe up. "Hey, right here and also not five years old."

Sabs absently patted my shoulder. "Yes, yes, of course. You're an adult and capable and clever and all that." She dodged my second ankle kick. I really needed to learn to go for a different body part the second time around.

Brooke chuckled. "Can't argue with that." She shot me a questioning look. "Are you still coming out for drinks with us, Jana?"

"Absolutely. Whenever you're ready."

Brooke turned her attention to Sabine. "You're welcome to come along of course, Sabine."

"Thanks, but I might pass. Long work week and I'm looking forward to some book and couch time."

Brooke's response was lightning fast. "No worries. I can take Jana home."

I nodded, and Sabs offered her thanks as something caught her attention and her face split into a wide grin. "Excuse me, sorry, I've just spotted a friend."

"Sure," Brooke and I agreed together as Sabs backed away.

My sister loped over to Beth, who was already squealing and opening her arms to receive Sabs for a hug. The two of them embraced wildly, and from where we stood fifty feet away, I could hear their excited chattering. Beth pinched Sabine's cheeks, and they laughed and hugged again. I shook my head. "I didn't know they were such good friends. She said they were part of the same crowd years ago, but this looks like some serious long-lost friend shit."

"It does. I guess that'll make it easier if she ends up playing Ultimate with us."

"Mmm." I turned away from my sister's reunion to grab Brooke's hand for another congratulatory squeeze. "Speaking of, you played so well! Seriously awesome. They should give you the woman of the match award."

"It's your cheering that makes me play better." Her grin was smug, almost cocky. "I especially liked the way you yelled that rhyme. Something about Brooke and cook wasn't it?"

"Ah yeah." I had to fight the urge to scuff my foot in embarrassment. "Sorry. Sabs was egging me on and I *really* didn't put much thought into it."

"Not at all, it was hilarious, we were all laughing. Sabine seems really great. Are you guys always like that?"

"Pretty much. Usually worse. We try to behave when we're in public but aren't always successful."

"It's super cute. I can't imagine playing around with Marshall like that." Her eyebrows scrunched. "My family is pretty serious."

"And mine's pretty wacky."

"Wacky is fun." She peered around at the other women all chattering and laughing as they packed up their gear. "I think we're done. Ready to head to the bar to celebrate?"

Ready to do pretty much anything with you, yep, whatever you want. Dial it down again, Jana. Keep it simple. "I am." Okay, maybe that was too simple.

We headed to a different spot this time, Lola's, which I quickly realized was a lesbian bar. And apparently a place The Disc Dykes and Co. frequented regularly. The staff greeted a couple of them, including Brooke, by name and helped us drag a few tables together to claim a corner in the back near the empty stage and a life-size painting of Marlene Dietrich. The space quickly turned raucous but fun.

Brooke had a single beer then swapped to soda, while I worked on a few glasses of wine. Same as the other post-game gathering with Brooke's friends, I was enfolded into the group immediately. Most importantly, as the afternoon wore on, I was ever conscious of Brooke's knee resting against mine, with neither of us seeming to feel the need to move. My instinct to press against her and slide my hand onto her knee and up her thigh was so overwhelming that only constant censure kept my hands above the table.

The group began to thin after a couple of hours, citing various reasons for having to bail—mostly because of a partner or kids. Brooke lightly touched my arm and leaned over to murmur in my ear, "Whenever you want to go, just say the word."

I turned my head, and was immediately aware of her proximity, barely two inches away. The tight hold I had on myself slipped a fraction and for a moment I leaned closer until I caught myself and moved back again. "Your call. Happy to stay or leave at any time."

She bit her lower lip and when she spoke her voice was still quiet. "In about ten minutes, it's going to devolve into tabletop dancing and knowing this group, likely with a fair bit of skin bared."

Immediately, an image of Brooke doing just that jumped into my head. The wine loosened my tongue. "Oh. Will you be joining in?"

"That depends."

"On…what exactly?"

Her voiced dropped even lower, husky almost. "On whether anyone asks me to, and then cheers me on."

"I—" That single syllable stuck in my throat. I swallowed, and the rest of my words came out a hoarse whisper. "Might just do that."

Heat flared in Brooke's eyes. "Mmm. On second thought, maybe we really should go before things get dangerous."

Things already felt dangerous. The only safe thing to do was to nod my agreement that yes, we should go.

The drive back to my place was quiet. Being quiet let me think. And think I did. At a million miles a minute. The moment in the bar was just one of many *moments* that were all coalescing to point to one thing. Brooke parked, and left the car running while I collected my things. "Did you want to come up for an early dinner? You must be starving."

She hesitated for just a moment. "Sounds good."

Riding the elevator, I was all too aware of how close she was again and the sensation made me both nervous and excited. "So what's next? Will you play another sport until Ultimate season starts up again?"

Brooke turned slightly to face me. "Mhmm. We'll have to go indoors for winter, so probably volleyball or something like that. Why? You looking for a full-time cheerleading gig?"

I started laughing. "You want more of my *Brooke, Brooke! She's so great your goose is cooked!* rhyme? Actually, it doesn't even rhyme."

I barely heard her quick, quiet admission over the ding of the elevator. "God, you have the best laugh." But I couldn't say anything in response, because not only was I too stunned, but because she followed up with, "Yeah, I do. And all of your other rhymes."

I didn't know how to react, too stuck on what I thought I'd heard her say about my laugh and wondering if I should make a move. Nice ego, Jana. Just because she seems to enjoy your company and is a lesbian doesn't mean she wants anything more than friendship. Just because you're suddenly deciding that you're not entirely at the straight end of the spectrum doesn't mean you should be jumping on her. "Well all right then. You've got yourself a staff cheerleader. Come on in and let's figure out what we want to eat."

Brooke leaned against the counter while I fussed around the kitchen. Leaning into my walk-in pantry, I offered, "I could probably rustle up something or do you want to just order in?" As I stepped back, I found her right in my personal space.

"I'd do pretty much anything for your pasta right now." Brooke studied me, her eyebrows drawn slightly together. "Here, you've got a little bit of…" Slowly, carefully, she pulled something from the edge of my mouth, then held it up between her thumb and forefinger so I could examine it. "Just a piece of fluff."

"Thanks," I whispered.

She opened her fingers, letting the lint flutter to the ground. Her eyes lingered on my lips before her gaze slowly came back to meet mine. "You're welcome."

I took a half step backward, away from her enticing heat, the soft caress of her fingers and the inviting part of her lips. My only options were step away, or kiss her, and though I knew I wanted the second option more I still didn't think springing it on her was a good move.

She didn't chase. "You okay?"

"Mhmm, perfectly." I stepped sideways this time, all too aware of *her* and how much I wanted to step forward and press against her, instead of back away. "Just uh, you know…um, this." I gestured awkwardly between us, hoping that would encompass what I wasn't sure how to say.

"Ohh." Brooke's expression changed to one of pondering, then to one of mild panic. She let out a long breath, mumbled something I didn't quite catch but sounded like self-admonishment. All her words came out in a panicked rush. "Sorry. Jana, look, I really enjoy this friendship or whatever it is that we've got. I don't want to jeopardize that just because I'm an idiot who's apparently forgotten her manners. I'm really sorry, I promise I'll tone it down. It's just…" She shrugged helplessly. "You're so easy to be around."

The mini-Jana in my head was grabbing her, shaking her and telling her that I didn't want her to tone it down, that I was interested in it, that I *liked* it. I wanted to tell her that whatever was happening between us, even if it was more my thing than hers, made me excited, but so afraid of all the possibilities. This was my chance to throw it all on the table, and I blew it. The only thing that came out of my mouth was a soft, "Brooke, it's okay, really. I'm—"

Smiling, she shook her head, cutting me off. "Look, uh, I might head home and just grab something there. I really should eat a salad or something. Thanks for coming along today, it was really great having you there." All the words blended together in a nervous rush as she backed slowly away.

"I…uh, sure. If that's what you want. And it was my pleasure," I said dumbly. Jana, you idiot! You're shoving opportunity out the door. But no matter how hard I tried, I couldn't make myself be brave enough to stop her. To tell her some of what I felt. As I walked her to my front door, I felt uneasy, my want warring with my confusion.

Brooke shrugged into her linen hoodie. "I'll talk to you soon."

"Mhmm. Drive carefully."

She favored me with her easy smile. "Always more carefully than you."

"Ha-ha. Very funny."

She leaned in, seemed to think the better of it, then raised her hand in a tentative wave. Then she was gone. I turned and leaned my back against the closed door. That went well. Good job. She practically handed you an opportunity on a platter and you were too afraid to take it.

From the moment I first discovered my hormones, I'd never had any sort of real romantic or lusty thoughts about a woman. Until Brooke. Until the kissing dream. Actually, maybe even a little before that if I was being completely honest. Of course I admired attractive women, enjoyed looking at them the way someone appreciates beautiful things, but I had never *ever* felt this stomach-tingling arousal before.

Why now? And why had it hit me so suddenly? Like spending some time with her during the week plus some erotic dreams suddenly equals intense attraction? It was literally like someone had flipped a switch from "Dates guys" to "You think Brooke Donnelly is cute now."

Hormone weirdness?

Early midlife crisis?

Taken over by a Body Snatcher?

I grabbed my personal laptop and hopped onto the couch with my legs crossed and it resting on my knees. I did searches for *naked women*, *athletic women* and on a whim *naked breasts*. After discarding gross and unsavory sites, I settled on a few tasteful images and steeled myself for the rush of arousal. But there was nothing. I could appreciate the aesthetics of the women, but aside from that, zip zero zilch.

So, random images did nothing. Watching Brooke's teammates had produced absolutely no response. Attractive women were attractive but that was it. So, the only time I got *that* feeling was looking at Brooke. Thinking of her. Scrunching my eyes closed, I tried to eliminate the memory of her sweaty, panting body. The curl and release of muscle as she sprinted across the field. The arc of her body as she leapt.

It didn't work.

Instead, I got a bonus vision of Brooke working in her shed, the welding, her pleased grin whenever she saw me, the way she always lifted her shirt to wipe sweat from her face and how it exposed her belly. A low hum of arousal set up shop, refused to go away and only got worse the more I thought about Brooke...sweaty...panting. Oh

God. Then my brain jumped to the thing I'd been trying *not* to think about. The Grape-Nuts dream. Help.

My whole life, I'd liked men. Tall men. Brooke was obviously a woman, an incredibly pretty woman full of lovely muscular curves and barely an inch taller than me. I should not be feeling like this. No scratch that, not *should not* because there was nothing wrong with it, but *why* the sudden turnaround? Despite my feeble attempts at rationalization and explanation, no matter how hard I tried to shove her aside, she slid back to front and center.

I closed down the browser and opened a blank document. My fingers took off, words filling the space.

Why do I suddenly want to kiss (and more) Brooke Donnelly?

-I like spending time with her—don't like being away from her but not in a weird creepy way. More like being excited to see her, and when we do the goodbye thing it's kind of hard because our things are always so short.

-She's so funny and gets my humor too.

-Adorable with her kinda social anxieties and blushing and stuff.

-Sometimes she looks at me and I feel like she's having dirty thoughts and I like it.

-She's ~~cute~~ hot, pretty/beautiful, great body, oh her ass and legs. Ears…

-She makes me feel comfortable and I hope vice versa.

-I want to know more about her, but the things that are more than just what friends know.

-Her lips look so soft.

-Is it just because of those dreams? Don't think so.

-I care about her, care about her feelings and her hopes and dreams and that sounds SO lame but it's true.

-She gets how important family is to me.

-I think about her a lot when we're apart. Why? See above.

-Sabs likes her. Not a reason, but helps if something happens between me and Brooke.

-If (huge if) something happens (!!!) she's someone I want my family to meet and vice versa.

Brilliant list, Jana. That helps exactly…zero. All these things and I still couldn't figure out the root cause of my sudden intense attraction. Basically all I had was I like her because I like her. Only one thing left to do. Shower and orgasm to clear my head. I stalked through my apartment, stripping off my clothes.

My go-to fantasy for a fast climax was being lifted onto a table and fucked senseless. Leaning against the shower wall, with blissfully hot water cascading over my head, I closed my eyes and let my brain take over. A hand played over my breasts, lightly pinching my nipples before sliding down my stomach and slipping between my legs. Squeezing my clit lightly between thumb and forefinger, I jerked as a wave of fresh arousal overcame me.

Unannounced, the fantasy took an abrupt turn. Hopping up onto the table, I opened my legs to Brooke and pulled her in. Her tongue made a wet path over my neck, licking and sucking and lightly biting, sending tingles of pleasure through my nipples. She yanked off my panties and thrust her hand between my thighs, stroking me firmly. Oh my fucking God. I opened my eyes again. My clit throbbed almost painfully, and I was so wet, I could feel it thick and hot against my fingers.

In that instant, I decided to drop all pretenses, run with whatever my brain wanted and let the rest of the fantasy play out. There was no teasing myself, trying to draw my orgasm out. I wanted desperately to come, and I wanted to come hard. In my head, Brooke finger fucked me, curling forward to find that perfect spot before pounding me hard until I began to cry out. Then she withdrew, spread my legs and bent down to lick me, tongue stroking my clit and knowing fingers tweaking my nipples.

My climax rose swift and hard, lingering with delicious heat until my knees almost gave way and I was left panting against the wall of my shower. And the whole thing was brought about by the image of Brooke's head between my thighs. Fuck. As quickly as I could, I composed myself, finished my shower and dressed.

I needed something to drink, smokes, and a sister.

CHAPTER EIGHTEEN

Hoping Sabine had meant it when she'd implied that she'd be home all night, I let myself in and quickly closed the door as Titus, their ginger and white cat, came sprinting toward me with his tail in the air. I picked him up, slung him over my shoulder and walked through the house. "Sabs?" I called in case she was in a compromising position.

My sister's response came from the den. "In here."

I bent down to drop her cat and my overnight bag on the floor at the entrance to the room. "Bec still at work?"

"Yep, back in the morning." Sabine rolled over on the couch and bookmarked her page. She was reading Kafka in original German, probably for the eleventh billion time, the fucking nerd. "I didn't expect to see you so soon." She glanced at the bottle of whiskey in my hand, a grin lighting her face. "I'll get some glasses."

While she fiddled in the kitchen, I dropped onto the couch, rested my feet on their heavy wooden coffee table and opened the bottle of Redbreast I'd picked up on the way over. The name seemed appropriate. For a brief moment I considered just swigging from the bottle before I remembered that firstly I wasn't at a college party and secondly my problem wasn't actually that bad.

From the kitchen, Sabs called, "Did you guys eat at the pub? Are you hungry?"

"No, and yes." Didn't eat, been kind of preoccupied fantasizing about a woman, you know how it is.

She returned with glasses, and a hastily assembled plate of cheese, salami, crackers, and dip. Best sister. I shoved a cracker and cheese in my mouth and lined up the glasses. My pour was long and I gulped down an eye-watering mouthful, sucking in a few breaths to quell the burning in my chest.

"Like that is it?" Sabine stared first at me, then the single finger of whiskey I'd pushed over to her. She took a measured sip and made a sound of enjoyment. "What's going on? You don't seem like you're about to drop a health bombshell on me, I talked to Mom an hour ago, and I know you're kicking ass at work. So I have to assume this is about a guy."

"Not exactly." After a much smaller swallow I mumbled, "A girl."

Sabine's eyes went wide before she uttered a quiet, "Oh. Shit."

"Mhmm. Pretty much."

"Care to elaborate?" Her overly expressive hands were the stillest I'd ever seen them. Oh dear. I'd totally shell-shocked my sister.

I shrugged. "I'm having lusty thoughts about Brooke. Actually, I think it might be more than just lust. I think there's *feelings* in there too, like on top of the great friendship feelings I think maaaybe it could be a bit of plain old romance as well."

"Shit," she said again, this time drawn out and a touch incredulous. Sabine chewed the inside of her cheek, apparently trying to figure out how to best approach my revelation.

I said nothing more, happy to drink and wait for her to tell me what to do. When I'd lowered the level in my glass by another wonderful burning spicy mouthful she said, "I was just teasing you about her but we've never really talked about this sort of stuff for you, have we? I mean I just assumed because you've always dated guys so…" Her eyes widened further. "Oh no, that conversation when we had coffee the other day. I totally missed the point, didn't I? Fuck, sorry."

"'S'okay, I wasn't exactly forthright. And yeah, I think the assumption about my sexuality thus far goes for you, me, and everyone else too."

"Mmm, yeah. I mean, it's a surprise but honestly, not that it's Brooke. I've never known you to spend this much time with anyone, or casually mention someone as often as you do with her. And watching you with her…" She made a *you know* gesture, not needing to say what I was well aware of.

"You're telling me. So what am I supposed to do about it?"

She lifted her feet onto the couch, knees bent and an arm wrapped loosely around her shins. "First of all, are you bothered by it? By feeling this way?"

"Bothered, no. Confused, yes. Very." My ears heated as I confessed, "I've had dreams about her, like the other night it was one where she was going down on me in an aisle at the supermarket and I was eating Grape-Nuts the whole time. And you know I hate Grape-Nuts."

Sabs let out a low whistle. "Sexy."

Obviously it had been, if the benchmark for *sexy* was measured against the fact I'd woken up and climaxed almost immediately. I sliced off some more cheese, and carefully assembled a sandwich with crackers and salami. "I've honestly *never* really considered a woman romantically, Sabs. Like my whole life has been mapped out—find a guy I can actually stand being around for long periods of time, marry him, pop out a couple of kids, give them funny German names like Hubertus and Brigita and make them keep my last name to carry on the Fleischer line. Then give them to Aunt Sabine and Aunt Bec to babysit because you both love kids *so much.*"

She flipped me the bird.

I answered with one of my own. "I think my brain has always seen a guy as the path of least resistance to my end game. This…attraction to a woman was not part of my plan."

"So it's physical as well then, not just like a personality or friend crush?"

I thought about my orgasm in the shower, and my reply squeaked out. "Yeah, I'm pretty sure it's physical too."

"It's no wonder you're confused," she said sweetly. It would have been so easy for her to be smug and superior, but she was gentle and methodical. Typical Sabine. There'd undoubtedly be teasing later, but for now she was in fix-it mode.

"I'm just…how does…why? And it's so fast, I've only known her for a month."

"True, but you've been doing a lot of activities with her, right? Your morning coffee, the Ultimate games, drinks and stuff. Kind of like going on dates with guys to test the waters. You either get a feeling or you don't."

"Mmm, you're right. I need a smoke." I wanted more burning, more feeling, more…something. I wanted to be drunk and to wake up hungover and with all the answers magically in my head.

Sabs grimaced, shuffling backward as if I'd lit up then and there in her house. "Really?"

"Don't be such a nag." I very rarely smoked and only ever when I was drinking. I suspected Sabine's hatred of smoking was partly because of the health thing and partly because she was jealous when our father and I snuck off for cognac and cigarillos. She shared the military with him. I shared a health vice or two.

We sat together on her front step with glasses in hand while I sucked hungrily on my cigarette. Sabine made a show of leaning away or waving her hand whenever the smoke curled anywhere near her, until I twisted away, exasperated. "Your ex smoked, remember?"

"Yes and I didn't like it. It's even worse when you do it. You know I hate you killing yourself with those things."

So dramatic. "They're ultra lows and I haven't smoked in months and then months before that." After another deep inhalation, I quietly confessed, "Sabs, I'm terrified."

"Of what?" she asked.

"Pretty much everything. I mean, what if I'm wrong about what I'm feeling? What if it's just hormones, or an early midlife crisis or something? I'm *so* bad at relationships, what if I end up bailing on her and hurting her? What if I'm crap at sex with a woman? What if I don't even like it? I've only kissed a woman once in college when we were both kinda wasted, and from what I remember, it was…not good."

The glass on its way to my sister's mouth stopped immediately. "Whaaat? Fuck, I had no idea you'd even done that." Both eyebrows lifted, she seemed to consider this as she sipped her drink. "Does it feel wrong thinking about Brooke as a potential partner or even…lover?"

"Not at all. You *know* it's not that I've got issues with it, but the opportunity never arose again after that one time and I never felt compelled to go chasing after it. I've never enjoyed spending time with, or been physically attracted enough to, any woman to want to deviate from my plan." Somewhat embarrassed, I added, "I don't even know what to expect."

"We aren't mystical creatures, Jannie. You know we live just like other couples with jobs and bills and pets and arguments and vacations et cetera."

I attempted smoke rings. None of them worked. "I know that, obviously. It's not that, it's just that I can't get past how did I get from never even considering it to this?" Frowning, I amended, "Or maybe I've always had those sorts of feelings but deep down, and I mistook them for just admiration or whatever because no woman has ever made me feel like Brooke does. Nobody's ever uh, sparked me before.

Only Brooke. *One* woman, Sabs. And I checked, like I went online and...looked at things. No reaction. At all."

Sabs looked like she was considering asking what *things* exactly I'd looked at, then changed her mind. "It wouldn't be the first time. You know my friend Megan from med school? She only dated men before she met her partner at yoga. Same thing. She'd literally never thought of it until it was right there in front of her, a great ass in yoga pants. True love. And they've been together twelve years and she always says she doesn't look at other women sexually. You don't have to find every woman attractive to be admitted to the club, you *can* just be gay for one person. And you can change your mind later and date guys again. Or date another woman. The only rule in the Lady Love Club is don't be an asshole."

I was pretty sure I could manage not to be an asshole. "Brooke has a great ass," I admitted. I'd looked. A few times. Along with a few other parts of her. That now-familiar curl of heat flared again.

Sabs clapped enthusiastically. "Jannie! Look at you, already checking out her assets!" She wiped fake tears. "I'm so proud of you."

"Thanks," I mumbled. "I just don't know how to approach it. How to approach her. Oh hi, I think I previously classified myself as pretty much straight but now I think I might be a little bit gay for you but I'm not sure and would you be willing to let me experiment a bit just in case? That hardly seems fair."

Sabine grinned. "I think something along those lines would be a start. Or you could do the classic scared gay crush thing."

"Which is?"

"Get drunk with her, say some suggestive shit until it leads to making out. If it doesn't go well then blame it on booze and feel like crap and mope for ages. If she's into you then she'll go for it regardless of how you put it to her, and if she's not then problem solved anyway."

A new panic overtook my original panic. "Oh shit. I hadn't even considered that the flirting and stuff wasn't genuine. Fuck, what if she's just playing around? I mean if she was into me, shouldn't she have made a move by now?"

"Ehhyeah, I don't think she is playing," Sabs said carefully.

"How do you know?"

"Because I've seen the way she looks at you. Part lust, part admiration, part awe, and part like she wants to hoist you over her shoulder and drag you back to her cave to have her way with you."

I relaxed by a micro-fraction, then imagined Sabs's metaphorical cave scenario and tensed again. But it was a good kind of tension.

Sabs bumped my knee with hers. "Trust me on this one. So when she says okay, and I'm ninety-nine point nine to the power of infinity percent sure she *will* say she wants to ravish you, where do you go from there? What do you want from it?"

Ah, there was the problem. I really didn't know. Usually I went on dates with men then said no thanks after a few. Sometimes they lasted more than five dates and sometimes there was some sex thrown in. Sometimes the sex was even passable. I'd had a couple of months-long relationships but I hadn't had a long-term relationship since my second year of college and even then it'd only lasted eight months.

But with Brooke, we were already good friends and enjoying each other's company quite a bit throughout the week and on weekends. None of her quirks annoyed me, which was a goddamned miracle itself. Would we perhaps go on a few dates, add sex to it a couple of times and then I'd be done like I was with everyone else? What if she decided I was no good at sex with a woman? Fuck, what if I *was* bad at sex with a woman? Would that be the end of our friendship too because I'd ruined it by wanting to see if the reality of being with her matched up to my ever-increasing fantasies?

I groaned, stubbed out my butt and drained the last mouthful of Redbreast.

"What's wrong?" Sabine stood and offered me her hand, hauling me to my feet. Those feet grew uncooperative as we walked back inside, with me repeating my inner ramblings for my sister.

"Valid points, but I think you're getting ahead of yourself." Sabine shot a pointed look at my hand. To keep her happy and appease her ridiculous paranoia about cigarettes spontaneously reigniting, I rinsed the butt under the running faucet then put it in the trash.

We settled back onto the couch, me a little sloppier than her, and I refreshed my glass. The bottle was down almost two inches—one and three quarters of which were mine while Sabs was still working on her first drink. I was starting to feel mercifully intoxicated. Goodbye, problems. At least temporarily.

"Don't lesbians dislike women who aren't full lesbians?" I asked around a mouthful of cracker and dip.

"Maybe some do. But I also think women who love women love women who love women." Sabs burst into laughter. "Sorry, that was dumb."

"Heh. No it wasn't. But I'm pretty sure I'm not quite at the love stage. Not sure what stage I'm at except maybe the how the hell do I do this stage."

"Why are you so hung up on the whats and hows? I say just dive in. Literally and figuratively. 'Cause you know, muff diving." She snorted, clearly pleased with herself.

"Thanks."

Sabine set her glass on the coffee table and squeezed my leg. "Jannie, listen. The only way you're going to know is if you talk to her about it."

"I hate it when you're logical," I mumbled. Aware of my drunken mumbling, I did the only thing I could. I swallowed another mouthful.

"I know. It's a flaw," she said nonchalantly. "Look, she'll either decline or accept, but I'm pretty sure it'll be the latter. Or you can try and pretend this isn't happening and be miserable with your what-ifs for the rest of your life."

I was well beyond pretending it wasn't happening. I threw my head back and covered my face with my hands. "Ugh!"

"Are you worried about the actual sex part?" The question was part amused and part concerned.

Letting my hands drop, I admitted, "Yes. Very."

"Nothing to it." Sabine smiled, almost to herself. "Just think about what you like and try that to start with."

That wasn't really helping. I knew how to fuck, clearly not another woman, but I certainly wasn't a novice at the ins and outs of sex, and I knew what I enjoyed. But I felt like I needed some explicit instructions about what I was supposed to do, assuming Brooke and I ever got to that point. I was getting way ahead of myself. The shower fantasy came back in glorious detail. Oh boy, did I want to get ahead of myself. "Can't you just tell me what to do?"

"You're my sister. I'm sorry but I can't help you. Waaay too weird. Hang on." Sabine hopped up and went straight to one of their bookshelves. Moving her finger over the spines of books, she extracted a worn and torn book and brought it back.

I turned the book over. "*The Joy of Lesbian Sex*..."

"Oh it's very joyful." Sabine's grin grew wider until she couldn't contain it anymore and she burst into peals of laughter. Her glee leached into her words. "Okay, so this book is more for laughs than anything but you *have* to read it."

"How old is this thing?"

"Came out in the seventies? You'll learn more if you just look on the Internet, Jannie, but this book is practically a rite of passage. *Promise me* you'll read it."

I dropped the book onto the coffee table. "You're so cruel. Don't you have anything that came out more recently than the decade we were born? Or better yet, a step-by-step how-to guide?"

"As I said, Google is your friend, or watch some porn if you must. But good lesbian porn, not stuff made for straight men." I opened my mouth to ask, but Sabine cut me off with a firm, "No. You can't borrow ours. How many times do I have to say it's too weird."

By the time we, or rather me mostly, had drunk almost a third of the bottle, we'd moved on to topics other than my possible one-woman lesbianism. Unsurprisingly, The Ceremony featured heavily.

"I'm about to be married, and maaaybe you're about to be married," Sabs drawled.

I choked on a mouthful of my cheese and dip combo. "Dial it back a bit. For now I think I just want comfortable companionship."

"Companionship is good. I like it very much."

"Yeah…I think it will be. I like her a lot." Now that I was really digging into my attraction to Brooke, so many things had become clearer. "Maybe I've been holding out because I've always done everything you did, Sabs. The horses and your sports and then moving to D.C. because I couldn't stand being away from you. Do you think maybe I was ignoring liking women thinking it was admiring them or whatever it was, because I assumed it was just me wanting to be like you again? I dunno."

"It's not about that, Jannie. Do you really think it matters if we both like the same things? Even women?"

"Naw, I guess not."

"Even with all we've done together, all the stuff you've followed me with, you've always marched to your own beat."

"Mmph. Think I need to march upstairs." I rolled over and slid off the couch, managing to land on my knees instead of puddling to the floor. Seven out of ten drunk. Oh I was going to regret this. "Come on, the sooner we go to sleep the sooner I can wake up with a hangover. When's Bec home?"

"Probably around nine, assuming nothing comes in at the end of her shift."

"Will you sleep in my bed with me?" I mumbled, the epitome of pathetic. When we were younger we'd often cuddle in bed when we were upset. When she was recovering and Bec was still in Afghanistan, Sabs would wake up screaming and I'd hold her and soothe her until she'd fall into uneasy sleep again. Then I'd lie there, making sure she was okay for the rest of the night, imagining I was protecting her from whatever was in her head trying to harm her. Now, all I wanted was sisterly comfort.

"Course."

Sabine forced me to drink two glasses of water and swallow some ibuprofen before we giggled and I wobbled my way upstairs. She left another large glass of water on the bedside table and a bucket on the floor.

"Puh-leeease. I'm so not near puking stage." The water and bucket made me think of Brooke's sweet migraine care and a sudden rush of longing made me desperate to see her. Bad idea. It's late, you're drunk, you'll say and do stupid shit. I swapped my top for a tee then stripped down to my underwear, pulling my bra off under the shirt and whisking it through one of the armholes. "Ta-dah!"

"Oh you're going to be so sorry in the morning," was the only response I got to my magic act. She made me brush my teeth and drink yet another glass of water before letting me go to bed.

Sabs had pulled on one of Bec's tees to sleep in and it smelled like her. I poked her arm. "I love Bec and she always smells nice and is very attractive, but I don't want to kiss her."

My sister rolled over to face me. "I'm glad. Because she's my fiancée."

"I also think Jennifer Lopez is pretty hot, but I've never thought about kissing her either. That painting of the nude woman downstairs? It does nothing for me. I mean it's a nice piece of art, but it doesn't make me hot. Women in porn, nada. I look at women and I think they have a great haircut, or dress stylishly or have enviable legs or tight abs at the gym but I don't want to kiss them. It's just Brooke."

"Mhmm, so you've told me. Multiple times tonight."

Stupid whiskey repeats. "Because it's true! I just want to kiss Brooke!"

"Just Brooke, and just kissing?" Sabs asked, all sly innocence.

"Well, I uh…um…" Again, I thought of my orgasm in the shower and how I'd climaxed with the image of Brooke between my legs, her hot tongue making laps around my clit. Her fingers pumping inside me. I ran a little further with it and pictured her nipples in my mouth and my hands on her skin. A flash of arousal made my cheeks heat and my stomach clench tightly.

Sabine laughed quietly. "Judging by that response and the look on your face, I'd say you've thought about a lot more than kissing, Jannie."

"Yeah." I pulled the pillow over my face and groaned into it.

"Chill out. You're attracted to her, big deal. Like I said, sometimes that's the way it goes, you *can* just be gay for one person. It happens."

Yanking the pillow off my face I sat up again. My head spun. "Are you *really* sure it's okay? You're not just saying it to make me feel better?"

"Sure it's okay." Sabine patted my shoulder. "I think you should worry less about labeling it, and just go with what you feel." She rolled over and turned off the bedside light.

"But I like labels." Though less uptight than Sabine, I still like a little bit of organization and order.

Sabine kicked and fussed into a comfortable position. "Fine, if you want a label, then maybe you're bisexual."

"Maybe...but for the millionth time, I don't feel like this with anyone else."

"Then maybe you're Brooke-sexual." She sniggered and I could tell she was pleased with herself.

"I think I am." I snuggled into her, desperate for comfort. "What if I'm no good at it? What if I don't like it?"

She slung an arm around my shoulders. "You like orgasms right?" Sabs asked, her voice dropping into the low, almost-slurred drawl I knew meant I had about three minutes until she was asleep.

"Well, yeah. Of course I do."

"Then I'm sure you'll be fine, but if you don't like it then it's no big deal." A long pause and a muffled chuckle. "In either case, I'm sure Brooke will be willing to help you figure it out. Over and over and over again."

CHAPTER NINETEEN

Sabine and Rebecca's quiet talking dragged me from a crappy, uneasy sleep. Why oh why had I not learned yet that I was too old to do excessive booze?

Bec sounded utterly beat as she spouted a bunch of acronyms. "Multiple MVAs with two DOAs, a motorcyclist with a BKA, and I lost one to GSW. Got really busy after midnight, I haven't slept."

"Oh, I'm sorry, honey. Are you all right?" The sound of a kiss, then more quiet murmurs I couldn't make out.

"What's this about? Everyone okay?"

"Yeah it's fine, she's just kinda confused about Brooke. Romantically."

A long pause. "Really? Oh wow."

"Mhmm. I'll fill you in…"

When I fully opened my eyes something stabbed my eyeballs right through into my brain. Ah, crap. Squinting, I took in the scene. Rebecca sat on the side of the bed, still murmuring to Sabine as she stroked her cheek with a thumb. Sabs held Bec's free hand, their fingers entwined.

Bec looked up, her sweet smile coming easily. "This was a pleasant surprise, coming home to two beautiful women in my house this morning." Her thumb moved up to brush over Sabine's eyebrow. "Two beautiful *hungover* women by the look of you both, and the bottle downstairs."

Sabs protested quietly that Bec was wrong and she wasn't hungover, just tired. Bec wasn't wrong about me though. A persistent throbbing had taken up inside my skull but my stomach seemed okay. I stretched, kneeing Sabine in the back. "Morning, Bec. Bad night at work?"

"I've had better." Bec ran her hand through Sabine's hair. "I'm going to take a shower then we can have breakfast? I assume it'll be something fried and greasy for you, Jana?" Bec grinned, then slipped out of the room.

Sabine sat up and swung her legs over the side of the bed, glancing over her shoulder at me. "Jannie, get out of bed and put coffee on. I'm going to join my fiancée."

"Sure. So, and I'm only asking for research purposes, how long roughly should lesbian shower sex go for?"

Sabine tossed a pillow at me. "We'll be downstairs in twenty minutes."

Hmm, not bad...

I rolled clumsily out of bed. Oh, wait. On second thought, stomach is not all that okay. Not in *puking is imminent* mode, but definitely on the queasy end of the scale. I made my way carefully downstairs, ignored Titus who was trying to convince me a half-full bowl of kibble was a cat catastrophe, and started the coffee machine.

I was nursing an untouched cup when they came down after only fifteen minutes, arms wrapped around each other's waists. Sabs snorted. "You look like absolute shit on a stick, Jana."

"Go away," I mumbled. "Can you get me something for this god-awful headache please? And something for my nausea would be really awesome."

"Ibuprofen, yes. Pepto, no. You feel sick for a reason, and if it wants to come out, it should so it's not poisoning your system."

I bent forward to rest my cheek on my folded arms so I could look at her. "Shut up, Doctor Fleischer. I don't want a medical lecture. I want sympathy and something to make it better. And it was whiskey, not poison."

"An abundance of whiskey, so yeah...kinda like poison." She looked exceedingly smug and if I hadn't felt so crappy, I'd have been able to come up with a retort. As it was, I barely managed a grunt.

Bec laughed softly. "Don't be cruel, darling." She dropped a single slice of bread into the toaster then caressed Sabine's cheek, following up with a light kiss. "Go get your sister something to help her feel better."

Sabine did as Bec had said, but I could hear her grumbling and *tried to tell her* all the way up the stairs. I straightened up, staring into my coffee until Sabs came back with some Pepto chewables and a bottle of ibuprofen, which, along with a glass of ice water, she set on the table within my reach.

"Thank you, mean bitch."

"You're welcome, idiot who thinks she knows better than to listen to her big sister." She kissed the top of my head, gently massaged my shoulders and moved into the kitchen.

As quickly as I could with slightly shaky hands, I palmed the pills into my mouth, swallowing with the water Sabs had so thoughtfully provided.

Bec placed a plate with a single slice of dry toast in front of me. "Here, sweetie. Try chewing slowly on that."

"Thank you."

Bec lingered. "So. Crush on a woman."

"Mmm."

She slung an arm around my shoulders, pulling me against her. "Welcome to the club." Her fingers combed soothingly through my hair.

I relaxed into her. "When do I get my membership card?"

"Filled in your forms? Nominated your sponsors? Listed at least three k.d. lang songs?"

Despite the general malaise I felt—fuck you, booze—I couldn't help laughing. "I adore you."

"Well that's good because I adore you too." Bec kissed my forehead then sat down opposite.

"So you've made up your mind, Jannie?" Sabs asked from her position at the counter.

"Mhmm, I've decided fuck it, I'm going to go for it and tell her. Why not, right?"

"Don't you mean, fuck her?" she quipped.

"Ha-ha. What I mean is, *clearly* I'm feeling something for her that goes beyond friendship and teeters right into lust or desire or whatever the hell you want to call it. Why fight against that? I mean, yeah I'm a little nervous but it's not like it's repugnant or anything."

"Gee, thanks," Sabs said dryly.

There was nothing to throw except a magazine resting on the kitchen table, and in my pathetic state it barely made it two feet. "You know what I mean, you ass."

Bec interrupted our bickering with, "How's that toast going down, Jana?"

I made a *so-so* gesture.

"Good. Now what can I make you two to eat?" Bec started to rise, the movement slow and halting in the way of the truly exhausted.

Sabine sidestepped quickly around the counter as if to block her. "Babe, no, you don't have to cook breakfast for us, especially not for Whiny Whineface over there. You've been at work all night. We'll do it." She glanced back at me, hunched over my untouched mug of coffee and still working on my now-cold dry toast. "On second thought…I'll do it myself."

They engaged in some back-and-forth about who should prepare breakfast, indulged in some kissing and giggling, and I tuned them out to keep staring into my mug. Right, so…choice made, time to put the Brooke plan into action. I couldn't deny the twinge of anxiety but more than anything, I felt excited. It was either going to be the start of something amazing, or possibly the end of a great friendship.

No pressure at all.

CHAPTER TWENTY

Mercifully, after some strategic moping on my couch, my hangover dissipated around two in the afternoon. After a gentle late lunch and a shower I felt human enough to tackle the issue at hand. Brooke.

I sent her a quick message asking if she was free and if so, could I come around. Brooke responded to my text within minutes, letting me know she was indeed home and to come on over whenever. Emoji, emoji xx. Oh help.

I showered, brushed my teeth twice and trawled through my closet for something that said, "I've just realized that I like you and do you find me hot?" Eventually I just pulled on linen shorts, a sleeveless blouse, and casual sandals. Good enough. Chill, Jana, it's Brooke. Brooke who has seen you in court clothes, work clothes, old sweats, and pretty much every fashion combo in between. Including only underwear.

The whole twenty-minute drive, I rehearsed what I wanted to say, discarding what I'd decided upon, and then starting again. Brooke must have heard me, because I'd barely made it up the front steps when she pulled the door open. After our usual hellos and a quick—too quick—hug she ushered me inside and to the couch. There was no trace of the weirdness from the conversation we'd had in my kitchen the previous afternoon when she said, "I would have thought you'd be sick of me after yesterday."

"Not at all." And judging by the way things were going, not any time soon either. "How're you feeling after the big win?"

"On top of the world, thinking I need to start looking for sponsors, building up my athlete image and all that." Grinning, Brooke rummaged in the fridge and pulled out two bottles of Sierra Nevada. "Beer?"

"Ugggh, no thanks." Just the thought of alcohol made my throat work convulsively and I had to draw in a few slow breaths to get myself under control again. "Long soul-searching night with whiskey. I'm still feeling a little delicate and a booze-free week is definitely in the cards. Maybe even a booze-free month."

"Oh, is everything all right?" She put both beers back and extracted a jug of cold water. As she poured two glasses, Brooke teased, "What happened to *getting too old to drink a lot?*"

"Yeah…that dissipated with a healthy bout of uncertainty that seemed like it could only be cured with cigarettes and drinking to excess."

She handed me a glass of water. "I see. And did it work? Was the misery worth it?"

"Thanks. And, I think so." Assuming the conversation I was about to dive into went as I wanted, then yeah it was worth it. I recalled what I'd talked about with Sabs. Brooke, I really like you, like *like* you, like you. Brooke, I can't stop thinking about kissing you. About your hands on my…ahem. Instead, all that came out of my mouth was the most idiotic of openers, "Can we talk?"

"Oh dear. I've found nothing good usually comes of that question." Her smile, guarded as it was, softened the words. She dropped down onto the couch beside me.

Stupidly enough, I knew that too and hastily tried to cover my ass. "Perhaps not but maybe I'll change that. I don't think it's bad. Well I know it's not bad for me, but I'm not sure for you. Actually no, I really don't think it's bad at all for anyone." For fuck's sake, spit it out, Jana.

She set her water on the glass-topped coffee table and made a *gimme* gesture. "Okay then, hit me."

Deep breath, just say it. "Brooke…I really like you."

"I really like you too. Yay, friendship!"

"Yeah, yay friendship. Umm, also I'm straight." Okay, back up. That was maybe not the best place to go from there.

"Yes, I know and good for you." She grinned and held up a fist. "More power to the heteros and all that." The grin faded slightly and her hand dropped to her lap. "Wait. Is this about me? About that weirdness yesterday?"

I nodded. "Partly, yes."

"Oh." Her eyebrows knitted together, and she was so utterly still that for a moment I was worried. Then she let out a breath and shuffled backward a few inches.

I shuffled forward. "I'm just…it's…I feel like there's this flirting and we keep having all these *moments*, you know? Like where there's that intense connection that's not just us being great friends, which I think we are. And if you were a guy, I'd just kiss you and be done with it. But, you know…"

Frowning, she nodded as though working through what I was trying, badly, to say. "Right, okay. Sure. Shit, I'm such a dumbass." She grew wide-eyed, almost panicked. "Jana…fuck, I mean…I'm sorry if I'm making you uncomfortable somehow, it's not intentional and I think I just forget that you're not into women. I really don't want that to cause an issue between us."

I grabbed her hand to reassure her. "No, Brooke, it's not that. That's not exactly what I'm talking about." Holding her hand felt so natural, so right, that I kept doing it. "You haven't done anything *wrong*. I've realized these past few weeks that I'm not being entirely truthful with you, or with myself really. My mouth is constantly saying one thing and I think my brain is making my body say another, and I'm sure that would be causing some of that weird uncertainty."

Brooke's gaze flicked down to our joined hands then came slowly back to my eyes. "What do you mean, Jana?"

Hold your breath, jump into the deep end. "What I'm trying to say is that I've always assumed I was straight, but with you…I kind of feel like I'm not."

Her eyebrows rose so slowly it was almost amusing. "Oh. Ah. Gotcha."

"Yeah. So that's it."

She squeezed my hand. "Top tip for next time? Start with that. I think my heart's still quadruple-timing."

"Got it. Sorry…I guess I'm nervous."

"Why? It's just me, the same Brooke as always." Her thumb slid slowly back and forth over the back of my hand.

"I know but I've just dropped something pretty big on you."

"True," she mused. "I bet it's pretty confusing." She was still caressing my skin with soft rhythmic strokes, the movement gentle and soothing.

"Mhmm, that's the understatement of the month." Year, lifetime.

Brooke let out a long breath, and I could almost see her tension exiting along with the air. "I'd thought you seemed kind of interested but honestly was just dismissing it as my wishful thinking." She laughed softly. "So, what does it mean to you? Are you saying you'd like to try dating women?"

"No. Not women." I closed my eyes and summoned another burst of courage. "You. It's literally *only* you."

When I opened my eyes again, her expression had changed. It was still kind and encouraging but now a hint of cockiness simmered under the surface. "I see."

"It's true," I insisted. "I tested the theory. Nobody makes me feel this way except you, and I don't know how to describe it. I've only dated men, only slept with men. I've honestly never really even considered dating women." Frowning, I amended, "Well I think I've thought about it but not really? Like I just dismissed it as normal human admiration instead of possibly something more. I've kissed a woman exactly once, in college and it was beyond mediocre."

"And now?"

I raised my eyes to hers and, not that I'd expected anything else, still found kindness and encouragement. "And now it's pretty much all I think about when I'm near you. Also when I'm not near you. Brooke, I think about you constantly during the day, even after I've seen you in the morning for our coffee, uh…date. It's just random shit like what did you have for lunch or I hope your meeting went well and you got that engineer off your case, or finished your designs and drawings and can relax for half an hour, and that your dad isn't hassling you about stuff, or how much I'm looking forward to whatever activity you might suggest. You know, all our hanging out? Except for Sabs and Bec, I don't even do that with people I've known for years. I might see them every few months if that. But I'm in this space now where I want all my free time to be taken up by being with you."

The cockiness exploded into a smile, confident and encouraging. "I see," she said again.

"I don't *do* that, think about people like that or want to spend time with people the way I do with you. I just…I can't stop thinking about you but I'm not quite sure how to categorize how I feel." I let out a long breath. "But I'm so tired of trying to pretend it's not the truth. I'm sick of second-guessing why this is happening, and what it means. I'm sick of pretending this, *you* isn't what I want because it's exhausting and frankly, pointless. So I've decided to stop pretending, and now I'm terrified." Finally I ran out of steam. "So, yeah. That's it."

She slid closer, took both of my hands in hers and when I curled my fingers around hers she exhaled softly. "What're you worried about? Truthfully."

I didn't even need to think before words spilled out. "Changing our friendship and I don't want to because that's really important to me, Brooke, and I don't want to lose it. And maybe that I'm not going to be any good at it. I'm a little scared that you don't really feel the same, and are just playing around for the fun of it. I'm worried that I'm not cut out for a relationship or wherever we might end up. And so much more that I haven't even begun to unpack yet."

"Sounds like fairly standard fears for any sort of new experience." Her tone turned intensely serious. "Let me put one of those fears to rest. I'm not playing with you, Jana."

"Okay, good," I breathed.

Brooke turned our hands over, twined our fingers more tightly together. "So, you didn't like your previous attempt at kissing a woman?"

I shook my head, feeling suddenly very shy. "Nope. Zero fireworks, just tequila-flavored sloppiness."

Her smile started slow, blooming into my favorite playful one. "I'm more than happy to try and change your mind about kissing a woman. Just hang on a moment." She extracted her fingers to fluff her hair, ran her tongue over her teeth, then cupped both hands under her breasts, shifting them around. "Okay, I'm ready."

I couldn't help laughing, and she joined in with my mirth. I was so grateful to her for keeping what could have easily turned into a full-blown anxiety moment light and sweet. Despite the playfulness, my heart hammered with the anticipation of what was close. Once I'd regained control, I confirmed, "You sure are ready. And maybe I'll take you up on that."

She came back with a quick, "Maybe I'll let you."

The tenuous grip I had on my control slipped a fraction. I swallowed, tried to wrangle it again. "Are you sure you're not weirded out by my sexuality backflip?"

"Not at all." She grinned. "Sorry to break it to you, but you're not the first person in the world who's decided they weren't what they thought. Feelings, ideas, whatever you want to call it, adapt and evolve." She took my hand again, brought it to her lips and brushed the lightest kiss over my palm. "And honestly, Jana, I've wanted to kiss you since the moment you opened that gorgeous mouth to yell at me."

"Oh. Phew," I said dumbly.

Brooke rolled her eyes, her words tinged with reluctant

embarrassment. "Yeah, I've been that clichéd lesbian lusting after their straight friend. It's been kind of pathetic."

"Lusting?" I squeaked.

"Mmm. Like you wouldn't believe."

We'd moved together, almost unconsciously, and her lips were so close I could feel their heat. But she didn't move further, except for her eyes which shifted from mine to my lips and then back again. The decision was left to me. Emotionally I was there and had been for quite some time. It was more than caring, more than liking, more than a crush. All that was left was to see if the physical matched the mental.

I brushed my thumb over her lower lip, my decision made in a split second. "Can I?" The two words came out so quietly I wasn't sure she'd heard me, but she nodded and made a small sound of agreement. I pressed my mouth to hers and the moment our lips brushed, all my uncertainty fled. Why had I waited so long?

Everything about the kiss was different—the smoothness of the skin along her jaw when I drew my fingertips along it, the feel and taste of her mango lip balm, the gentle press of breasts against mine and the curl of long hair through my fingers. Despite all that was new, I was filled with a sense of utter rightness.

The kiss was soft, almost chaste and Brooke didn't push for anything more. Her hands tightened on my waist and when I opened my mouth a little to deepen the kiss, she let out a soft sigh, but still didn't go further. But when my tongue sought hers, she broke and gave everything back to me. With interest. The butterflies that'd been quietly flitting around in my stomach went into full-on swarm mode.

I pressed against her like she was the only thing keeping me upright, and she pressed right back. The kiss was unhurried, sensuous, a gentle give-and-take without any push for dominance. She ran her hands up my sides, over my arms and shoulders, along my neck until she was cupping my face. Her hands were steady and warm, thumbs gently stroking my cheeks. It was a kiss purely for the sake of kissing, rather than a prelude to something more. But the possibility of something more was evident from the soft stroke of her tongue on mine, the quick pull on my lower lip.

It was a possibility for later. Or maybe now. Yes, now. Ideas came rushing into my head, and the low, pleasant hum in my belly turned sharply erotic. With a reluctant groan, I broke the kiss but not my contact with her. I needed a moment to think and process exactly what was happening.

Brooke rested her forehead against mine, kissed the tip of my nose.

"You okay?" she asked, pulling back slightly but not letting go of my face.

"Mhmm. Better than. That was…good." I'd expected to enjoy it, for it to be a far better experience than my first and only other woman kiss. What I hadn't expected was to be so thoroughly turned on that I felt like stripping naked and begging her to make me climax.

"Just good?" Her nose brushed through the hair above my ear. I heard her inhalation, the sound sending a shiver down my spine and raising the hairs on my arms.

"It was really good, amazing," I amended. "So much better than the dream kiss."

"Dream kiss?"

"Oh, uh, two dreams really. About you. Never mind."

She arched an eyebrow. "Well I'm glad real me is better than dream me." Brooke pressed her lips to my hairline, lingering for a few seconds.

"Way, way better," I murmured, tightening my grip on her. Kissing her had ignited a fire in my belly, and touching her, I had the sudden realization that in all my thoughts and fantasies it'd been *her* making *me* come. Selfish, and also silly of me. The more I explored, the more I realized I *wanted* more. More of her. More kisses. More of her body against mine. More skin and heat.

She muttered a helpless sound, grasped my shoulders and pulled me back to her.

We ended up indulging in a very hot make-out session that seemed to be leading straight to sex until Brooke muttered something indistinct, lifted herself off me and shuffled back a few inches on the couch. I groaned. I was moments away from yanking her shirt over her head and opening her bra. From my careful explorations I knew that her breasts fit nicely in my hands and that when I stroked her nipples through the fabric, she made a sound that sent a shudder straight to my clit.

And I liked both of those facts.

My pulse pounded between my thighs, and I could feel how thoroughly aroused I was. It'd been at least a decade since I'd done anything like this, make out on a couch, and I felt like a horny teenager. And I liked that too.

She swallowed hard, eyes slightly glazed. "I don't want to stop, Jana, but I don't want to rush you."

I dropped my head to rest on the arm of the couch. "I know. I know. You're not rushing me, I swear. I'm just, fuck, I *want*."

"I know. I want this too. I want you. I want to strip you naked and make you come over and over again. But not yet." She sucked in a deep breath and pulled her shirt down over her stomach. "I want you to be comfortable with this."

"I am," I countered instantly. "Totally comfortable."

She grinned. "Oh I can see that. What I meant was comfortable with the concept of us and what it means if we go *there*. I want you to really think about it. And…I need to think about it." Brooke took my face in her hands. "There's no rush."

"Tell that to my nether regions right now," I mumbled.

She snorted out her laugh, which was my favorite of her laughs. "Nether regions?"

"Well…yes? What do you call it?" It didn't seem appropriate to say my clit was pounding so hard I thought I might come apart if she didn't touch me.

"You can call it anything you want to, Jana. I prefer clit myself. We're adults."

"Good, clit works for me. And honestly, I am so fucking horny I'm about to explode."

"Really?" Brooke's eyebrows shot up.

"Ohhh yeah."

A lazy grin formed on those beautiful lips. "I'm glad. And feel exactly same way. You make me insanely hot. Remember that."

I swallowed hard at the implication of her words. "Do you think we could maybe…see if I really am comfortable with all this kissing?" It came out a little coyer than I'd intended, but she seemed to like it.

Ever so slowly she lowered herself back down. "I think we could manage." She drew in another long, audible breath. "God you smell good." She kissed my neck, my collarbone, sucked gently. Her words were muffled against my neck. "You know, this was not where I thought this day would lead, especially not after you did the whole we-need-to-talk routine."

"What exactly did you think was going to happen?"

Brooke backed away from her worship of my skin. "Honestly, I was sure you'd tell me I was being too forward and making you uncomfortable, then leave and I'd be minus one friend. But now it feels like I'm going to keep one friend and possibly add a friend with benefits?"

"So what does friends plus friends with benefits equal?"

Both of her eyebrows shot up. "Uh, well to me, I guess it eventually equals girlfriend?" She sounded adorably uncertain.

"Sexy math."

She laughed, kissing me again. Yes, I was definitely comfortable with kissing. I pulled her back down on top of me and indulged in my comfort until I lost all sense of time. I lost myself in kissing her, in the wonderful heat and softness of her mouth until inevitably, the need for more than a few hastily grabbed lungfuls of oxygen overtook us. We both drew back at the same time, though Brooke remained close.

She softly kissed my cheeks, my chin, that spot on the underside of my jaw that made me shiver. Shifting just a little, she propped herself up on her elbows, and I almost groaned at the loss of contact, wanting nothing more than to keep feeling the weight of her on top of me.

Light fingers traced my lips. "Could we backtrack just a step?"

"Sure. But you're going to have to stop doing that."

"Sorry." She dropped her hand. Her eyebrows scrunched, mouth twitched as though it couldn't decide what words to push out. After a few seconds she quietly asked, "What do you want from this, Jana? Like what's the next step for you?" Quickly she added, "Sorry, I don't want to push but I'd just like to know what your thoughts are."

"Thank you. I do love how you communicate, and not just with words." I gave in, stretching up for a kiss I kept intentionally brief lest I get drawn back in to the sweetness of her mouth.

"Yes well, communication is important, in *all* aspects of a relationship." The emphasis she placed on that word wasn't lost on me, and I felt the anticipation as a quick surge of adrenaline.

"Mmm. I'd kind of only got to 'tell Brooke how I feel and cross my fingers she doesn't freak out.' From here on out, I'm winging it." What *did* I want from this? It didn't take long to find my answer. "I think I want what you said before, what we already have, the friendship and activities and fun and all that. But with something extra on top and we can see where that leads?"

Her shoulders dropped fractionally, relief evident in the slow grin that spread across her mouth. Her mouth. Focus, Jana. Plenty of time for kissing and *more* later. She nodded. "That sounds like a very good starting point. Maybe we can reassess goalposts and the speed of our progress as necessary?"

"That sounds like a solid plan."

"Good." Another kiss, and this time she lingered to suck my lower lip. "So, just to confirm. What are we calling this exactly?"

I pondered for only a few seconds until I realized exactly what I wanted to call it. Something I hadn't wanted in more years than I could recall. My response came out with a little bit of uncertain squeakiness. "Dating?"

CHAPTER TWENTY-ONE

By the time Brooke walked me down to my car, I was so keyed up from hormones and adrenaline that I was about ready to burst out of my skin. Her goodbye kiss, delivered as she leaned through my open car door, seemed intentionally chaste and I was both grateful and frustrated. Grateful because if she went further then I'd never leave, and frustrated for the same reason. I gathered some of my wits to ask, "Do you want to come around tomorrow? Dinner and TV?" And making out.

"Sounds great." She gently took my face in both hands and kissed me once more, tender and sweet before murmuring her goodbye. You're really not helping the hormones, Brooke. Though of course she couldn't know yet that someone holding my face while they kissed me was an instant aphrodisiac.

"Okay, great," I mumbled.

She closed my car door, her expression making it clear she was suffering the same issues as me. With a reluctant wave, I drove away from the woman I was now apparently dating.

Dating.

I drove for a few blocks with that word bouncing around in my head, then crossed two lanes—to the pissed-off honking of at least two cars who were apparently blind to my indicator—to pull over with my hazards on. It only took ten seconds to tap out a text to Sabs.

I think I might have an almost girlfriend.

Then I turned my phone to silent, tossed it facedown onto the passenger seat and the whole way home listened to the vibration of a zillion texts and calls from my undoubtedly frantic sister. Heh. Consider this payback, Sabine, for being such an evasive shithead when I first asked you about Bec.

When I checked my phone once home I had five missed calls and seventeen text messages, each one escalating in "Answer me, you annoying bitch" factor. I knew she'd think I'd had an accident or something, so I responded to her with a simple *Amazing, right?*

I spent a while in the shower releasing some pent-up energy, which was made all the sweeter by the newfound knowledge of exactly how Brooke's hands and mouth felt. Then I made dinner, enough for at least seven, and bundled up the leftovers into the freezer to take over for Sabs and Bec. And only then, an hour and a half after I'd sent my last text to Sabs, did I call her.

She answered with a grumbled, "Fuck you and your dramatic pauses. I've been dying here waiting for details."

In the background I heard Bec call, "She's right! Driving me insane!"

I smothered a laugh and laced my response with innocence. "What? I've been busy. Cooking for you and Bec actually."

"Mmph. Enough bullshit. Come on, spill!"

I toed the dishwasher closed. "As much as I hate to admit it, you were right. Short version is I told her how I felt, and she said okay let's do this and see what happens. And then we, um…tested if I was comfortable with the idea."

"Ha! I told you! Didn't I fucking tell you? When are you seeing her next?"

"Tomorrow night, here, for dinner and stuff."

"Stuff? You are so going to sleep with her!"

"Jesus, Sabs. At least *pretend* to be discreet."

My sister's laughter was loud and mirthful. "Jannie, not that we had much to begin with, but we lost all discretion and modesty when you had to help me shower and use the toilet after The Incident."

"Good point." I leaned against the counter. "And I don't know what's going to happen tomorrow. We'll just have to wait and see what happens." But I hoped for more of the same of what'd happened at Brooke's place that afternoon. A lot more of the same.

The next day was a rainy late summer's day, perfect for being inside with your brand-new girlfriend. Brooke arrived in the early evening, now casually dressed in shorts and a polo instead of work clothes, and carrying a bottle of white. Her smile was tentative, until I pulled her close to share an unhurried kiss in my doorway. I had her pressed against the doorframe, my hand sliding under her shirt to clutch her hip before my brain realized that we could be sharing unhurried kisses inside and where my only floor neighbor wouldn't see.

Once the door had closed, Brooke offered me the bottle. "For you. Or us really. Sorry, I'm weirdly nervous all of a sudden."

"Thank you. And honestly, I'm a little nervous too." I snuggled an arm around her waist, pulled her close and maneuvered us to the kitchen. "But, it's just like any other time we've spent together, right?"

"Right, it is." She let out a long breath as though forcing herself to relax. "So are we staying in, or do you want to go out?"

I set the wine on the counter. "Stay in. Every moment we're outside these walls is a moment I don't get to cuddle on the couch with you. Do you mind if we order something? I cooked up a storm for Sabs and Bec last night, and I so don't feel like staring at the stove right now. Aaaand…see aforementioned comment about wanting to cuddle with you every moment I can."

"Jana Fleischer, you really are the most adorable softy." She brushed my hair back and kissed me again.

I could almost feel the nervousness draining from her, and the more she kissed me, the more at ease I felt too. I didn't think I'd ever get used to kissing her, the gentle thrill that coursed through my body from even the most innocent brush of lips. "Don't tell anyone. Big bad bitch image and all that." I backed into the kitchen. "Just so we're clear, when I said *cuddle*, I actually meant making out."

"Even better," she drawled. "But before that, I need to fortify myself with food. Stamina, you know. I'm craving something like Vietnamese."

"Sounds great. Why don't you check out some places while I pour us a glass?"

"Sure, but um could I use your phone or laptop? I forgot my phone." She grinned sheepishly. "I was so excited to see you that I left in a rush and forgot it."

"Now who's the adorable softy? Laptop's on the coffee table."

"Thanks."

When I came back less than a minute later with a wineglass in each hand, I noted right away that she wasn't Googling places to get dinner. She was reading the why I want to kiss her list. Oh holy shitballs. I'd totally forgotten that I'd just closed the laptop on it in my frantic *what the hell is going on?* from a few days before. My mild embarrassment turned to profound embarrassment. I rushed through a bunch of explanations, but all I managed to articulate was, "Oh. Fuck."

Brooke twisted around on the couch, then stood, her expression one of careful neutrality. "Do you mean this?"

I set the glasses down on the coffee table, acutely aware that my ears were hot and undoubtedly turning red. "Yeah, I did but it's stupid. I was just so confused and I thought if I could get some words out then maybe it'd help me understand why—"

A firm kiss shut me right up and the softening press of her lips on mine kept me that way. She lingered, her tongue stroking lightly over my lip. "It's fucking incredible, and so sweet." She kissed me again, just the edge of my mouth. "You like my ears?"

"Yes."

"You think I'm beautiful, with nice body parts?"

"Mhmm. Very much so, on both counts."

"And…you care about me?"

"Yes, I do. A lot."

Brooke pulled me close, nuzzling the spot under my ear. "Likewise, FYI, for all of the above. Seriously, where have you been all these years?"

"Oh you know, just hanging around waiting for someone to literally sweep me off my feet."

She pulled back, eyes narrowed but still creased with a smile at their corners. "You're never going to let me live that down, are you?"

I grinned. "Nope."

"I suppose I'll just have to replace that clumsy move with a slicker one." In a maneuver that surprised the hell out of me, both for its speed and strength, Brooke hooked her hands under my ass, lifted me up and onto the couch, then settled on top of me. I squeaked. She silenced the squeak with a long, toe-curling kiss. I made an indistinct groan-slash-moan-slash-oh-my-goodness sound. She silenced that one too. And every other sound I made for the next fifteen minutes or so.

We finally managed to pry ourselves apart to order fantastic Vietnamese, which we ate sitting on the couch watching a *Survivor* rerun. As it turned out, Brooke was a huge fan and she picked apart strategy and gave me running updates in between mouthfuls of pho.

Midway through a council thing I set my coconut shrimp on the coffee table and snatched up my vibrating phone to silence a notification. A dating site connection request. Snorting, I followed the link to my profile to decline, and by the time I'd opened the page my snort had turned to chuckles. "Oh, not a chance," I muttered.

Brooke swallowed her mouthful. "Pardon?"

"Just some guy on one of my dating apps." In the whirlwind that had been Brooke and me, I'd completely forgotten to deactivate my dating profiles.

"Oh." She shifted slightly, set down her dinner and wiped her fingers on a paper napkin. Her movements were slow, almost overly cautious.

"What?"

"I just realized we haven't really talked fully about this, about what *this* means." Brooke gestured between us. "How serious it is, or might get. If it's just some casual enjoyment or a potential long-term relationship or whatever else."

I muted the television. A sudden fear made my chest tight, and I was stunned by its intensity. "Do you think I'm not really into it?"

"I'll be honest, when you first told me yesterday, I *was* worried that maybe it was just a fleeting exploration thing. God I hate this term, but, a..." She made air quotes. "Phase. Then after you left I spent some time thinking about it, and I realized I didn't care about that. There are plenty of reasons why things might not work out and missing an opportunity because of my fear or whatever seemed silly."

"What about, you know...my past," I whispered dramatically.

"Oh, the guy thing? Doesn't bother me at all. Everyone has people they dated before." She pushed hair away from her face. "If you're going to cheat, or leave me to have another relationship then why does the gender of the other person matter?" Brooke's eyes widened. "Are you the cheating type? Fuck, sorry that's kind of weird and accusatory, but I think we should probably talk about that sort of thing before we, uh, really start anything beyond just making out on the couch."

"No, I'm *definitely* not the cheating type. Honestly there's been very few 'let's be exclusive' scenarios in my life. But I'm the-once-I-commit-then-I'm-committed type." I had to clamp down on the words that were about to follow. The words that were about to admit that I thought I wanted to commit to her long term.

Brooke's relief was palpable, but she still held an edge of disquiet. Her fingers went to a thread on the knee of her shorts and tugged until it broke. "As a kid I was really bad at sharing my toys, and I'm afraid adulthood hasn't improved me much."

"Toys? That's what I am? A…plaything?" I let the word roll off my tongue.

"Well you're certainly fun to play with," she said, her voice the low sultry whisper that promised delicious things later. Then she sobered. "Jana, my ex really wasn't the *let's be exclusive* type. I thought she was, but once we'd moved in together I discovered she was more the *let's have an open relationship* type. She dropped a bunch of very unsubtle hints about it and then laughed it off as a joke when I freaked out because that's not me, I'm not…like that. I kind of want you to myself if we're going to take this further."

"And that you shall have. It was an honest oversight. You and me literally just happened and I hadn't even thought about those profiles. Here, look." I turned my phone around, and despite her protests that it was okay and she didn't need to see and she trusted me to be honest, with a few swift finger strokes and taps I set all my accounts to inactive. "Done."

"Thank you," she said quietly. "Sorry, my dating history isn't really something that's ever come up, is it?"

"Not really. Do you want to talk about it? I mean we're already discussing such things as where this might go and what we're expecting from each other."

"Well…" She let out a long breath. "Like I said before my last ex wasn't the monogamous type so that didn't work out. The ex before that wasn't the sympathetic type, especially not with my um, anxiety and all that stuff so that really didn't work out. That stuff plus the weirdness with my family has made me a bit wary about things beyond casual, easy fling-type things."

"Oh, Brooke." I slid closer to her. "I'm sorry." Previously, it'd been utterly mind-boggling to me that someone like Brooke—sweet, kind, funny, thoughtful—didn't have women falling all over her. Now I realized that maybe she did but she was just as afraid as I was of commitment, but for different reasons. The simplest reason of all. She'd been hurt.

"I just want you to know that I'm into this, but I need some time to be comfortable with the concept of moving beyond just…spending time together getting to know each other more and um, physical enjoyment."

"Okay, sure. No pressure, just taking it as it comes."

She bit her lower lip. "I really do like the physical enjoyment stuff though."

"Me too…"

We spent a good portion of our supposed television evening not actually watching the TV but indulging in micro make-out sessions. All clothing remained on, though not in place. Brooke's careful exploration probably gave her a fairly good idea of exactly where and how much I love lips on my neck. And I discovered her ticklish spots. And also some not so ticklish spots that still made her utter a choked sort of groan that in turn made my stomach clench.

When ten p.m. rolled around, Brooke gently sat up, dislodging me who was on top and pressed full length against her, and mumbled, "I should get home."

"Mmmph. Bad idea." But I still pushed myself up and rolled off the couch.

Reluctance poured off her in waves as she gathered her things, and it was on the tip of my tongue to ask her to stay. To take me to bed and show me everything I'd been imagining. I was sure if I asked, she would without hesitation. Every time she touched me, kissed me or murmured sensual things in my ear she showed me she wanted this. But underneath it all was this almost gentlewomanly quality, a respectfulness that made me even more convinced that waiting a little while was the right thing. She seemed to know I was afraid—not only of the actual act of sex, or if I'd be any good or if I'd enjoy it—but afraid of what it would mean for us to take that next step.

"So I'll see you for coffee in the morning?" And try to restrain myself from kissing her the moment I saw her. Surprisingly, we'd managed some actual conversation in between the physical getting to know you. She was worried about her dad and we'd agreed that PDAs in the vicinity of our workplaces were probably not particularly professional.

"Wouldn't miss it."

"Great. So, listen. If it's not too much too soon, Sabine and Bec have a dinner thing at their place on Wednesday if you're free?"

"I'm free."

"And if you'd like to come."

She raised both eyebrows, a deliciously naughty grin forming on those kissable lips. "I'd very much like to come." After a wink, she amended her response. "And I'd like to join you guys for dinner."

Her teasing response had tightened my nipples, sent a thrill through my core and it was all I could do to not throw myself at her. "Just so you're not surprised, Mitch and Mike will be there too. Dinner, well dessert, is doubling as the final cupcake selection test for the wedding. But it's just them, so six of us in total. I think it'll just be a barbeque or something like that, nothing fancy."

"Sure thing, sounds great. Mitch is Sabine's best friend, right?"

"Mhmm. Best friends since college, just one of those weird friendships that you don't think would work but does. And he and his boyfriend Mike met in the Army."

"Is the military secretly doubling as some sort of LGBT matchmaking service?"

"Seems like it, doesn't it?" I passed Brooke her umbrella. "Both guys are really sweet, but if you're uncomfortable at all, at any time, we can leave."

"It'll be fine, sweetheart."

Sweetheart. Heh.

* * *

The next few days were wonderfully uneventful, except for the added Brooke time. I met her for morning coffee *dates* and then spent Tuesday at her place for more of the dinner/television/making out on the couch like horny teenagers. By Wednesday night, I was at an eleven on the ten-scale of "Want to have sex with Brooke" and climbing higher each hour in her company.

We stopped in at my place to change after work on our way to dinner at Sabs and Bec's and I could tell she was uneasy, though she did a good job of hiding it. By now I was tuned to the fine tension in her body, how she clipped the words at the end of sentences, and how she filled her anxious space with words. I let her be, except for reaching over to entwine my fingers with hers while I drove one-handed.

Brooke hung back a little when I rang the doorbell, having decided for once that using my key and letting myself in as I usually did was perhaps a little weird when I was bringing a guest for the first time ever. My plan to ease her into the group fell apart the moment Sabs answered the door, bouncing around like an excited puppy. Bec stood behind Sabine like a person who'd given up trying to control that excited puppy. I re-introduced Brooke to Sabs, then introduced her to Bec, who was a master at putting people at ease. They did their usual *fold a person into the family* gig, acting like they'd known Brooke for years, which for Bec involved being her usual sweet self and for Sabs being her bossy self and asking Brooke if she'd mind giving her a hand with some task.

I leaned close to Brooke. "Tell her to fuck off if you don't want to help. I do."

"Regularly," Sabs confirmed cheerfully.

Brooke laughed, kissed me lightly on the cheek and followed my sister into the kitchen.

Brooke and Sabs stayed inside working on salad and burger patties while Bec and I milled around on their back deck—her cleaning the grill and me setting their outdoor table. The lingering heat and humidity had driven us to eat outside in the hope of a breeze, yet to arrive. Satisfied I was done, I went to Bec. "Need a hand?"

Bec glanced up from the grill, her smile already in place. "Almost done. Stay and talk to me while I finish up. We haven't had much of a chance to chat lately. How're things with Brooke?"

I snuck a peek at the kitchen window, through which I could hear Brooke and Sabine's quiet easy chatter. "Everything's great."

"Wonderful. I'm so pleased for you, Jana. Really."

"Me too."

Bec wiped the grill plate a final time then closed the lid. She folded her arms over her breasts, a knowing smile teasing at her mouth. "You've been staring at the kitchen the whole time you've been out here. Are you worried your sister is going to tell some embarrassing childhood story?"

I laughed. "Oh I know she will. I guess I'm more worried about Brooke being comfortable even though I know Sabs isn't particularly scary."

Rebecca flashed her dimples. "No, scary is one thing she's not. She's been nervous all week about having Brooke here, about making sure she feels like part of the family."

"Really? Already? We haven't even been dating for a week."

"Yes already." Bec slid an arm around my waist and squeezed me gently. "Sabine saw it right away. And I've only seen you two together for a short time and I can already tell how you feel."

"How's that?"

Bec winked, squeezed me again then slipped back into the house, leaving me alone to ponder exactly what she meant. Exactly what she'd seen between Brooke and me. My pondering was cut short by the doorbell and Sabine's call through the kitchen window, "Can you grab that please, Jannie? Bec's gone upstairs and I'm up to my elbows in hamburger."

I swung the front door open but before I could say hi, Mitch exclaimed, "The M 'n' Ms are here!" He grinned. "Hello, my sugar pie." Six-foot-three inches of burly-bear Mitch stepped inside, picked me up and swung me around—his usual greeting.

I'd been nineteen when we'd first met and of course had had a massive crush on him. The man really was ridiculously handsome in a chiseled, all-American kind of way, and when you added that Texan drawl... Then I found out I had less than a snowball's chance in hell and moved him into the brother category. It hadn't taken long for him to feel like a blood relative. The guy was an utter sweetheart.

On my second circuit in Mitch's arms, I spotted Mike standing in the doorway, waiting for his overly-demonstrative boyfriend to finish twirling me. Smiling, he shuffled the two plastic cake containers in the crook of his arm so he could wave. Mike was a sweet, soft-spoken man with a wicked sense of humor and a love of baking—a good thing, given he'd opened his own specialty cake store after leaving the Army six months ago. Oh, and also an utter sweetheart.

"I thought I was your sugar pie," Sabine said dryly. She slipped past to kiss Mike's smooth cheek. "Hello, hon. Can I take any of that?"

"Nope, I've got it, thanks."

Mitch set me down and promptly scooped up Sabs, leaving me to hug Mike. As always, he smelled of aftershave and pastries. I kissed his cheek then moved aside so Bec could greet him. I hadn't realized until then what a round-robin greetings were when there were multiple couples involved. Speaking of...

I backed up, held out my hand to Brooke who took it and stepped close beside me. I squeezed her hand, hoping to reassure her. "Mitch, Mike." I indicated the guys in turn. "This is Brooke, my, uh maybe sort of girlfriend?" Shrugging, I turned my question to her.

"Maybe sort of girlfriend works for me." Brooke stepped forward to greet the boys' proffered handshakes. "Great to meet you. So...M 'n' Ms. Which of you is peanut and which is plain?"

Mike chuckled. "Good one."

Mitch burst into his deep belly laugh. "You know, nobody has ever made that joke before. Brooke, darlin', I like you." He leaned down. "And I think I'd have to claim myself as peanut."

She spread her hands wide as if surrendering. "I'm not sure if I should bite on that one."

Mitch's grin was broad. "Please do," he invited.

She grinned back, just the faintest flush coloring her cheeks. I readied myself to step in and help her out but I didn't need to. Brooke lowered her voice. "Truth be told, I'm not really big on plain or peanut..."

In his typical display of *personal space, what personal space?* Mitch slung an arm around Brooke's shoulders and directed her to the deck.

Laughing, he told her, "You 'n' me are gonna get along just fine. Now, let me tell you about the time Jana…"

Dinner was accompanied by our usual raucous, ridiculous conversation. Brooke settled into the madness easily, joining the laughter, sarcasm, and teasing that was inevitable when Sabine and Mitch were together. While we cleaned up, Mike prepared halved cupcakes for us to try. Everyone gathered reverently around the table like a nativity scene, waiting for Mike to elucidate. He pointed to each one as he explained, "Okay, so we have chocolate mud cupcake with peanut-butter buttercream, mocha buttercream, and my personal favorite—the Turkish-delight frosting. Then vanilla cupcakes with plain buttercream, a really subtle mint buttercream, and chocolate cream-cheese frosting." He exhaled. "Phew. I think that's it, but if need be there's still time to tweak."

"Marry me, Cupcake King," Brooke said the instant he was done talking.

"Git your own," Mitch shot back playfully. "This one and his bakin' are all mine."

She turned to me, clutched my hand and her question was almost hysterically desperate. "You'll bake for me, won't you?"

"Sure. Anything and any time you want."

Mike offered around plates and napkins. "I've already started shipping your mom boxes of supplies, and I'm going to run test batches in her oven a few days before the wedding, which will of course need to be eaten, but I think I'm all set."

Mitch piped up. "And I'm all set to take care of the test batches."

Bec squeezed Mike's bicep, stretching up on tiptoes to kiss his cheek. "Thank you, Mike. These look incredible. We're so grateful."

Sabs looked like she might cry. "You're an absolute baking rock star. Thank you so much."

Mike hugged her, lifting her a few inches from the ground as he kissed her temple. "You're welcome. Anything for my best girls. Now, time for cake!"

I started with a chocolate and peanut butter, falling into a paroxysm of ecstasy at the first mouthful. We worked our way through the samples, and everyone was in mutual agreement that Mike had outdone himself. The only comment that deviated from variations of *amazing* was from Sabine who thought the mint-frosted one was like eating cake after brushing her teeth.

Working on a vanilla with chocolate cream-cheese frosting, Brooke turned her attention to Mike. "These are all fabulous. You should do this for a living."

His smile was bashful. "I do. My bakery, Let Them Eat Cake, just celebrated its six-month anniversary and it's going great. We've had to put in a third oven, and I'm hoping to expand to another location in a few years."

She raised her hand a few inches. "I volunteer as taste tester any time you want."

"You'll have to arm wrestle Mitch for that job."

Mitch, with his mouth full, just nodded.

"I think I could take you on, if this is the prize." She nabbed another cupcake.

Everyone went back to quietly eating but my focus was solely on Brooke, whose eyes were half closed, her face holding an expression of what I could only describe as complete food lust.

"Oh my God." She swiped her thumb through the pink Turkish-delight frosting. "Have a taste," she murmured to me.

I grabbed her wrist gently to take her frosting-covered thumb in my mouth. Brooke drew in a quick breath, and I purposely took a little longer than necessary to suck the frosting from her thumb, sliding my tongue over her skin to make sure I had every last morsel. "Yummy."

Brooke's mouth fell open, her eyes widening. She swallowed and made a sound that was nothing more than few indistinct syllables.

Mitch nudged me in the back. "Hey! Stop bein' so sexy with your sister's weddin' cakes." He guffawed, and everyone laughed with him, even Brooke. I made myself join in, but I couldn't drag my eyes away from Brooke and the look in her eyes.

She looked *hungry*. But not for cupcakes.

CHAPTER TWENTY-TWO

We were two weeks out from the ceremony and Bec had gone to collect some specially ordered gift bags because Sabine insisted that everyone get a goody bag as a thank-you for coming, like we were having a kid's party instead of a not-wedding. Sabs and I were spending our Saturday creating the name cards to tie on to said gift bags. Or rather, I was using my high-school calligraphy skills while Sabine read out names, spelled them out repeatedly and then nitpicked over my shoulder. "Is that right? That should be capital T not F."

"It is a T. See how there's no line through it?" I kept writing, magnanimously resisting a dig that she should maybe get her eyes tested.

"You sure?"

"Could not be surer. It's cursive calligraphy, Sabs. That's how it looks, and you knew this when you asked me to do the cards in cursive calligraphy. I even wrote you and Bec a sample."

"Hungh. Okay then. And I know, I mean it looks great, just…"

"Like calligraphy?" I finished up the card and pushed it aside to dry. The careful penmanship, something I rarely did, was giving me a wrist cramp. After wiping my fountain pen and setting it carefully down, I rolled my wrist to ease the tightness.

My sister pounced. "Why's your hand so sore?" She grinned. "You *sure* all you and Brooke have been doing is just kissing?"

The things in reach were not things I wanted to throw, especially not in my apartment. "I'm not going to tell you anything ever again."

"You don't need to tell me, Jannie. I've seen you two together."

"We haven't had sex!" I insisted. Yet.

"But you want to, right?" Her eyebrows were sky high. Sabs seemed unusually troubled, as though she had some stake in my enjoyment of my foray into being with a woman.

"Yes, very much. But we're just taking it as it co—happens. It's only been a week, Sabs."

A wonderful week where we'd been inching closer and closer to the inevitable. A week where I'd learned even more about her, noticed things I hadn't before. Things I liked. While we'd been getting to know each other as friends, I hadn't been scrutinizing her as a potential partner, I'd just been enjoying the moments, enjoying being with her without tallying up the pros and cons and consequences of a partnership with her the way I normally would. Now in post *let's date* time, I realized that I'd missed all the things that would usually bug me or strike someone off the romance list. And now that I knew about Brooke's things, I didn't care.

"So, I'll add her to the ceremony list as a last minute plus one?"

I almost choked. "Fuck, no. I mean, yes but no. I don't know. I think that's a little presumptive, don't you?"

"Presumptive how? You have a girlfriend so why wouldn't you bring her as your date?"

"Because I only *just* have a girlfriend and asking her to come to a family event is a huge deal. Especially our family." Our wonderful, but loud, oddly-humored, and slightly weird family.

"Do you want her to attend?"

"Yes I do, very much, but see reasons above. And I just don't know how to ask her." I turned a pleading expression on her. "Please drop it, Sabs. I don't want to screw this up so soon by pushing her." Especially when I knew how cautious she was about relationships.

"Okay okay, it was just a thought. I only want you to be happy."

"I am. Now get me something to drink please so I can power through this batch."

We worked in diligent, mildly bickering productivity for another twenty minutes until the doorbell rang. Given I was working on forming a perfect *k* Sabs rose from the table. "I'll get it. Probably Bec."

"Thanks," I said absently.

"Not Bec," Sabs said, with what sounded like excessive enthusiasm. I looked up and found Brooke with bags of food hooked in her fingers. Bless her. She shifted her gaze from me to my sister. "I thought you guys might be hungry after all your writing."

I set my pen down, launched myself out of my chair and threw myself into Brooke's arms. Her surprised gasp when I kissed her turned to a little rumble of pleasure. "Hey."

"Hey," I repeated goofily. "Thank you."

Sabine was already on her way to the kitchen. "I'll grab some plates," she said without turning around.

We settled to eat on my balcony, and pretty much as soon as we were done with the deli sandwiches, Sabs unsubtly glanced at her watch. "Shit, it's later than I thought. I promised Bec I'd...be home to...look at the, uh, gift bags." Smooth.

After a cheery goodbye to Brooke, Sabine wandered to the door with me in tow. She lowered her voice, though her mirth was evident. "Have a good night. I'll come by to pick up the name cards tomorrow." She hugged me long and tight and as she pulled back, looked over my shoulder at Brooke. "Have a good niiiiight!" Grinning, Sabs made an *I'm watching you* gesture.

I turned around just in time to catch Brooke's smiling salute in response. Practically shoving my sister out the door, I called, "Love you, drive safe. Hi to Bec." I turned around, pressed back against the closed door. "Sorry, she's a shithead."

"No she's not. I like her a whole lot." Brooke pushed her hands into her jeans pockets. "How many more of these card things do you have to do?"

"Not sure. Maybe ten?"

"Anything I can do to help?"

"Actually, if you wouldn't mind reading and spelling out names then I could finish them all and get Sabs out of my hair tomorrow."

"Done."

We settled easily into a routine with Brooke beside me pushing cards along the table and spelling the names like she was in a spelling bee. And she didn't nitpick my writing, which was an added bonus.

"Uh, Jana?" Brooke held the paper under my nose and right away I realized Sabine had penned another name at the bottom of the printed list.

Brooke Donnelly (??)

Oh for crying out loud. "I didn't do that, it was her," I blurted. "I mean, clearly you're invited but it's in Ohio and it's my whole family as well as some friends of Sabs and Bec's, but I'd really like you to come. But I'll also have to do the maid-of-honor thing for a bit, but Mike will be there to keep you company. And I totally understand if you think it's too soon or you just don't want to then that's totally and utterly fine. I'd really like you to meet my family though."

She'd gone silent during my explanation and I hurried to add, "I mean, I don't want to presume or whatever about you meeting my family, but you've met Sabs and Bec and spent time with them and I guess—"

As she was prone to doing, Brooke effectively silenced me with a kiss. She lingered until I was breathless, then pulled back, kissing my forehead softly. "I like that you've presumed." She pushed another blank card over to me. "Brooke Donnelly. B-r-o-o-k-e."

I stared at her. "Are you sure?"

"Yes." She caressed my face, swept her thumb over my cheek. "Are you going to write?"

"Yes. Yes I am." I penned her name on the card and added a little heart in the bottom right corner, then carefully set it aside to dry. I couldn't stop staring at this simple gift card, the simple gift card that symbolized so much more than just a wedding invite.

"Looks great," Brooke murmured.

"It does." I glanced at her, suddenly feeling overwhelmingly shy. "Will you stay tonight?" Everything I felt was in that question. If she stayed then we would go to bed and everything would change. No turning back.

"Yes. I'd like to." Brooke drew my left hand to her mouth, softly kissed my knuckles. "Just to clarify, are you asking me to *stay* stay?"

"I am."

"Okay, good. Just wanted to make sure we're on the same page." She smiled. "You look nervous."

Excellent poker face, Jana. "I am a little. Mostly I'm just not sure exactly what to expect."

The gentle smile turned to a grin. "Expect the unexpected." Then the grin faded a little, her expression grew serious, earnest. "There's no rules, Jana, except mutual enjoyment. Sometimes it's quick and dirty on the couch or against a wall, and sometimes it's hours in bed, soft and sweet and slow. It's any way in any position you want it, until we've both had enough."

Oh help.

She leaned over and kissed me lightly. Kissed my jaw and down my neck, her lips lingering for a few seconds before a less-than-sensuous gurgling sound came from her mouth. She pulled back. "Um, I think I just tasted ink." Brooke's tongue ran back and forth over her front teeth a few times, the grimace unmistakable. She leaned around, studying my neck. "Yeah, I think you touched your skin with inky fingers."

I couldn't help but laugh at her expression. "Give me a minute to go get rid of ink that's in places ink should not be. Or…you could help me."

Her answer was to pull me to my feet. We kissed our way down the hallway, pausing to press each other against the walls and my bathroom doorway. I pushed her against the sink and slid my hands underneath her tee, noticing the slight tremble in my fingers as I stroked her skin.

When I swiped my tongue along her lower lip, she groaned and turned her head to the side. "Okay, stop, time out. I'm going to get rid of this ink, because if I don't do it now, I'm not going to." Her breath sounded shaky as she grabbed the washcloth. "Turn around."

I turned side on, hands braced against the sink as she lathered soap and began to scrub at a spot under my ear. Her thumb brushed against my neck, a soft counterpoint to the rough washcloth raising gooseflesh. She ran cool water to wash the soap away, succeeding in spreading the gooseflesh. I gripped the sink hard, tried to focus on staying upright while I imagined the sensations she might evoke if she were actually trying, instead of just cleaning ink off me.

"All done." Brooke set the cloth down, grasped my hips and spun me to face her. Her smile was knowing, and instead of words, she simply pulled me close, both arms wrapped around my waist. A few long moments passed before she asked, "You *sure* you're okay with this?"

"I'm very okay with it. Okay, but still nervous."

"What are you nervous about, exactly?"

I blew out a breath, trying not to sound as hyperactive as I felt. "Messing up, not knowing what to do or how to please you."

Brooke grinned. "Well I thought we'd start with me pleasuring you and take it from there. Jana, if you're not ready, or you're not comfortable then we don't have to do anything. But, honey, if you are then I want to help you to enjoy yourself. I want to enjoy myself with you…"

Instead of something sexy or clever, all I managed was a breathless, "Me too." The fluttering in my stomach was spreading through my limbs and low down in my core, excitement beginning to smother the nervousness.

Her kiss was light. "You can say no to anything at any time and there'll be no bad feelings or annoyance."

"Mhmm. And you too, obviously, I mean if you're not enjoying yourself or you don't like whatever I'm trying to do, or…you know."

She laughed. "I'm pretty sure I'm not going to want to stop but thank you for clarifying. Communication is sexy."

"Great, and yes it is. So um, I feel so clinical all of a sudden, like I don't know if we're supposed to talk about if we undress each other, or just get ourselves naked or what to do."

"What do you want to do?" she asked, voice low and encouraging.

My words came out a rush. "I think I'd like to undress you."

"I think I'd like that very much."

"Good, that's great." Yep, acting so suave and sexy and sensual right now. My tentative hands went first to her tee, then the waistband of her cargos and then back to her tee. Right. Though I wanted to tear the fabric from her, expose everything I'd been thinking about for weeks, I forced myself to slowly pull it upward and off, laughing when she raised her arms to help and instead became tangled.

It only took a moment to free her, and I tossed the tee onto my clothes hamper. Undressing. I could do this. I unhooked her bra, letting the cups fall away. Before I moved on, I indulged myself, lightly brushing thumbs over the silky undersurface of her breasts. Her skin was soft and smooth, and when I made another sweep up and over her nipples, she drew in a quick breath.

My hands paused. "Too much?"

"Not at all." She bent her head, watching my hands. "It feels good, that's all."

Her quiet assurance gave me the confidence to continue. Brooke helped where needed, stepping out of her shorts and underwear but mostly she stood still, letting me choose what to remove and how quickly or slowly to do it. Then she was naked, her posture relaxed and confident, almost arrogantly so and she had every reason to be. "You're frowning," she teased.

"No, this is my concentration face." I looked up to find her gaze fixated on me, making my stomach do a slow roll. Even though I was fully clothed and she was naked, she looked at me like I was something to be devoured.

I tried to take in the whole of her, but the whole was so incredible and overwhelming that I gave up to focus on the singular. The lift of her breasts and her small dark nipples. The long curve of her thighs leading up to the swell of hip. Tan lines. That bellybutton piercing catching the light of my bathroom. The patch of dark hair at the junction of her legs.

My pulse quickened. "Brooke...you're amazing. I'm just, like I... just don't know where to look, what to touch first."

"Then take your time, sweetheart. We're not on a schedule here."

"Right." I let out a breath, trying to ease some of my nervous excitement. I drew my fingers up her arms, pausing at her elbows before slowly tracing upward and over the minefield of her scars. She didn't move, just kept her head bent, watching as I took my time feeling the raised edges. I didn't know what to say, or if I should even say anything. In the end, it felt too uncomfortable not to acknowledge something that'd shaped her, something that'd brought her to this point where she stood naked and trusting in front of me. "I'm so sorry you went through this."

"Thank you," Brooke whispered, reaching for me and settling her hands on my waist. "I think you're the first person who hasn't tried to pretend they're not there." She kissed me, her hands slipping under my shirt, raising it ever so slightly. She paused and drew back, keeping eye contact with me until I nodded my assent. She lifted the tank, fingertips brushing the skin along my ribs and I raised my arms so she could pull it off. Instead of tossing the clothing to the floor like most of my previous lovers, Brooke carefully folded the garment and draped it over one of the towel racks. I stared. Her mouth quirked as she followed my gaze. "What?"

"Just the...folding. I've never had anyone do that before." The seemingly small gesture added another level to my already spiraling emotion and I knew right then that it was going to be very hard to stop myself from falling for her.

"Oh. Well, unless we're doing the frantic to get naked thing, it only takes a moment. I've always liked to take my time unwrapping my gifts." She grinned. "The first time that is." Brooke's hands gently stroked my breasts before her fingers brushed over the front clasp of my bra. "May I?"

"Please," I whispered.

She removed the material slowly, keeping eye contact with me the whole time. My bra joined my tank on the towel rack, and then her focus was back on me. Standing topless in front of her, I was hit with a sudden and unexpected wave of shyness. But she made it easy to be brave, to feel wanted with her undisguised desire and the way she softly drew her fingertips up my ribs before cupping my breasts. Her thumbs played over my nipples, the touch featherlight.

Her eyes fluttered closed for a few seconds and when she opened them again their raw need had all my blood pooling south. "God, you're so beautiful." She smiled, slow and seductive. "Come to bed with me."

Laughing, I reminded her, "It's my bed..."

The low huskiness of her response stole my laughter and turned it to a whirr of excitement. "Then ask me to your bed."

CHAPTER TWENTY-THREE

Brooke paused beside my bed. "Oh, I forgot about that," she said quietly.

"Forgot about what?"

"That very big mirror…" She turned to me, grinning devilishly. Then she pulled me to the corner of the bed facing the mirror and pressed herself to my back, her hands moving to the front of my shorts to pull the drawstring. Brooke hooked her thumbs in the waistband, her eyes finding mine in the mirror and after a silent questioning look, which I answered with a nod, she divested me of my last pieces of clothing.

Brooke knelt and helped me step out of my shorts and underwear. Then with hands and lips, she marked a path up the back of my thighs, over my ass and up my spine, seeming to delight in my shuddery, incoherent response. She took her time until she'd made her way back up to stand behind me. Her nipples were hard points on my back, her hips pushed against my ass.

I watched us in the mirror as her hands stroked my belly, up my ribs, lightly palmed my breasts. The whole time, she had her lips on me—my neck, my shoulders, sucking and licking and biting softly. I tilted my head for her, letting her take what she wanted.

My breasts felt tight and heavy with desire and I reached up to cup them, running my thumbs over erect nipples. Brooke's exhalation was audible and careful hands slipped under mine, deft fingers taking over the teasing motion. "Look at you. So fucking sexy," she murmured, kissing the back of my shoulder. Her fingers teased my nipples. "God, these are lovely."

"Really?"

She spun me around. "Mhmm. I mean, I know admiring physical attributes is kind of shallow, but...yum." She bent her head, slowly ran her tongue around a nipple, before gently biting.

The pressure of her teeth sent a spark through my belly and my hands came instinctively to the back of her head, holding her against my breast. "Not too small?" I asked softly, the echo of that exact sentiment from past, and very short-lived, lovers echoing in my head. Aside from the occasional body-confidence issues, I'd always been fairly comfortable with my appearance. Who gives a fuck what anyone else thinks, right? But now, I had a sudden desire to be what she wanted physically as well as all the other stuff.

Brooke shifted to peer up at me. "Are you kidding? They're perfect." She moved back, lips brushing over the other nipple.

Very slowly, I leaned down to suck her neck then held my hands under her jaw to raise her head so I could kiss her again. Her arms came around my waist. I was acutely aware of how her hands stayed above my waistline, and her sweet thoughtfulness at once pleased and frustrated me. I reached around and pulled her hands down until they were on my ass.

Brooke let out a little surprised squeak around our kiss. "I didn't want to presume."

"We're naked in my bedroom. Your hands and mouth have already been on my breasts. Presume you may put your hands and mouth anywhere you please."

She slapped my ass lightly then pulled me forward in what seemed an almost unconscious movement. "Are you sure?"

I took her hand and drew it between my thighs. She moaned when her fingers made contact with my wetness, her thumb straying dangerously close to my clit. We both said an almost simultaneous, "Oh, fuck."

I bit her earlobe lightly. "Feel that? That's what I want. That's what I feel. I'm sure."

When I rocked my hips forward into her hand, she groaned again and I smothered the sound with a deep kiss. Our tongues played lazily against each other, her fingers stroking languorously through my heat yet studiously staying away from where I most wanted her touch.

Brooke backed me toward my bed, lay me down and slid next to me. Legs intertwined, hands and lips on skin. We started slowly with whispered instructions and careful touches. Sweet kisses and words, until my stomach was tight with need.

"Do you have toys?" she murmured against my neck.

"I do." The statement registered and I frowned. "Was I supposed to display them so you can see and compare to yours or something? Shit, is that part of it that I didn't read about?"

Brooke's head fell back onto the bed, laughter shaking her whole body. Once she'd regained control, she shook her head. "No, of course not. I just thought it might make you feel more comfortable with the whole thing. More familiar?"

"Ohhh, oh, right." Leaning down I traced the smooth surface of her lower lip with my tongue before kissing her again. I wanted to kiss her forever, but there were other more pressing issues at hand. "No, I don't need that. Maybe some other time if you're into it but right now, I want to learn the *unfamiliar*, and something tells me you're an excellent instructor."

"That I am, and a good instructor teaches by example…" She rolled us over until she was on top, settling her hips between my thighs.

"I'm paying very close attention." Instinctively, I wrapped my legs around her ass, tilting my hips, trying to make contact with as much of her as possible.

Brooke groaned into the skin of my neck. "God that's so sexy." She rocked against me, a steady rhythm that was too slow to make me come, but so sensuous that I couldn't help but tighten my legs around her as my arousal began a steady climb.

Her hips thrust in an almost casual motion, matching her long, deep kisses, which reminded me of a lazy morning in bed. She kissed my lips, my chin, my jaw before making her way to my neck. I kept my fingers tangled in her hair, still rocking my clit against her skin until she moved back slightly, dragging a disappointed groan from my throat.

Brooke reassured me with a husky, "I'm not done with you yet." Pressing open-mouthed kisses to my skin, the silken softness of her hair gliding over my belly, she made her way down until she was nestled between my spread thighs. Nose brushing along the inside of my legs, her kisses grew light and sweet, almost ticklish. "Jana…" Her fingers swept over my stomach.

I raised my head to look down at her, blinking to clear the haziness of my vision. "Mmm?"

"I hate to be a temporary buzzkill, but is there anything I should, um, worry about? I'm clean and healthy, just so you know."

It took me a moment to connect the dots. "Oh!" I shook my head emphatically and answered truthfully, "No, *nothing*. But I think I have dams in that drawer if you want?" Despite the fact I always practiced safe sex, I still had regular sexual health testing. Having an overprotective older sister who was also a doctor guaranteed that from my first foray into the world of sex, safety in that regard had been practically beaten into me.

Brooke exhaled, warm breath caressing my thighs. "Oh no, I do not want. I'm absolutely dying to taste you."

I swallowed hard at the sensuous tone of her words, the thrill in my belly replaced by a sudden sensation that felt a lot like panic. "Yep, I even have an email confirming it's all good under the hood. And I take birth control, so you know…not that there's any chance, we um, never mind." The moment I'd finished my blurting, I bit my lip. "Shit, sorry. That was such a stupid thing to say. Maybe I'm still nervous? I'll stop blathering. Uh, go nuts down there."

Brooke's laughter was low and amused. "Shhh, it's okay, sweetheart." She gently kissed my thigh. "I adore your blathering. And we can stop at any time. Even now. Nothing you don't want, remember?" More soft kisses mapped the inside of my thighs, teasingly close to my wetness. "But if we keep going, I don't want you to be shy about telling me exactly what you want, exactly what you need."

I could barely think to answer her and had to force my brain to focus on something other than how desperately I wanted her to touch me again. "I will… And I don't want to stop."

From between my legs, Brooke raised her eyes to mine and at my slightly desperate nod, she finally took me in her mouth. When I felt the wet warmth of her tongue, I couldn't help myself, grasping a gentle handful of her thick hair as that tongue made slow, steady laps around my clit and slipped through my folds. I've always enjoyed receiving oral sex—even the mediocre has moments where it feels nice—but from the moment her tongue made contact, I knew this was going to be something different. Something incredible.

Used to having to give guidance from the get-go, I was surprised when all that came out of my mouth were soft moans and whimpers, and variations of, "Oh that's so good." She took her time exploring, tasting every part of me, adjusting to every sound and movement I made until it felt like every muscle in my body was quivering. Rather than just foreplay as necessity, or a fine-let's-get-it-out-of-the-way orgasm, Brooke's slow and patient worship promised to be unlike any I'd had before.

Worship was exactly right. I felt worshipped and desired but not in a seedy or objectified way. My orgasm was the star attraction, my pleasure her sole purpose, and she made sure I knew it. Her hands roamed my body as her mouth sent me higher and higher. There came a light touch at my entrance, a teasing swirl of pressure before a murmur of, "Oh, sweetheart, you are so, *so* wet and you taste so fucking good." That touch again, a promise of something more. Her voice was husky, hot breath against my even hotter flesh. "I want to be inside you, please. Can I?"

There were few things I would say no to, certainly not that, and certainly not to this woman who clearly knew what she was doing. "Yes, please. Anything, I trust you, *please* just fuck me until I come."

When she groaned, the vibration against my clit made my legs twitch. Her tongue didn't let up its knowing strokes, and I felt her then, deep inside pressing against the spot that makes my body tingle. I couldn't help but push against the pressure, frantic with the overwhelming sensations. "Oh, God. What are you doing to me?"

"What I said I would. I'm enjoying you." There was a hint of amusement under the lustful tone. "Very, very much."

I pushed her hair from her forehead so I could watch her expression as she licked me. "Please keep enjoying me. That feels so fucking good. Whatever you're doing, please don't stop…that's incredible… I'm close."

"I won't stop, sweetheart. Not until you've come for me," she whispered before the heat of her tongue moved slowly through my wetness again.

I'd caught glimpses of this side of her before, simmering below her flirtation, but I had no clue just how sexual she was. Carnal. With every passing moment it became clearer how much she'd hidden it.

It was unlike anything I'd ever experienced and I fucking *loved* it. I'd had men between my thighs. On top of me. Underneath. Behind. But nothing had ever come close to the raw sensuality of Brooke between my legs, murmuring how good I tasted, how sexy I was, how hot my pussy was and how much she wanted me to come in her mouth.

Her own sounds of pleasure as she pleasured me heightened my own need and added another level to arousal that was already running out of control. She knew what each twitch of my leg meant. When my hand tightened in her hair she repeated her movement, a slow soft swirl of her tongue around my clit. Then there was this incredible sucking thing that had me incoherent with pleasure. She adjusted to my involuntary cues and it wasn't long before I felt the first insistent swell of my climax. Her hands and lips and tongue worked with skillful coordination until that delicious heat bloomed low in my belly as she drove me closer and closer to the brink.

I lifted my head to watch her and in that first moment of eye contact, I felt so raw and exposed I was almost frozen. Her eyes were dark and wide with desire, and their undisguised need had me squirming even more underneath her intense gaze. Her free hand came to my stomach, stroking my skin gently in time with her tongue and the thrust of her fingers until the heat between my legs and rolling through my body grew to an unmistakable crescendo.

I glanced in the full-length mirror in the corner of my room and the sight made my breath catch. Brooke with spread legs, a knee cocked up to expose her to my view. The glistening of her arousal was exposed to my gaze and the reflected image sent a thrill down my spine.

I stared for as long as I dared, then it was all over. I threw my head back, arching up into her mouth. "Oh fuck, I'm going to come."

A low chuckle vibrated against my clit and I twitched again, balanced on the edge of climax. Brooke raised her head, grinning wickedly. "Yes, that's the whole point."

Inexplicably, that panic rose again. I didn't want to let go so early, didn't want this to be all I had. Squirming, I tried to push her away. "No no no, not yet. It's too soon."

"Too soon?" Her eyebrows rose. "Because you like being teased? You want me to draw things out?" She placed the lightest, softest kiss on my clit then rested her chin on my thigh, staring up at me.

"Yes, no. I mean I do. Sometimes. I just don't…I want more than this. I want it to last longer." I was so desperate that I almost felt like I was about to cry. Very sexy, Jana.

Brooke's voice dropped, the hand on my belly making soft, soothing strokes. "Sweetheart, I'm not going to run out of steam after you've had an orgasm. This isn't all there is tonight, or after if that's what you decide you want." She kissed my thigh, the warmth of her lips on my skin as sensual as any of her intimate kisses. "We're not done until both of us are so satisfied we can barely move."

It was such a stupid fear and I felt ridiculous for having even worried about it. "Are you sure?"

"Positive." The kisses moved higher. "I promise…" She paused a moment, then dropped her head to put her mouth back on me.

She walked me along the edge of the cliff and held me teetering there. She didn't shove me over and wave goodbye, but carried me over, staying with me the whole time. As I crested and began to cry out, her fingers slid back inside and with that perfectly placed pressure, I climaxed. Heat scorched along my nerve endings until my body felt as though it was on fire. It was a familiar sensation yet at the same time, wholly new. Deeper, longer like a lower frequency, and almost too much.

My words were a hoarse, unintelligible, endless stream of syllables crying out my pleasure. She reached up to take my hand, tangling our fingers together, grounding me as I bucked and shuddered. When my brain finally kicked in with something other than pleasure-pleasure-pleasure, I managed a very eloquent, "That was…holy shit. I, uh, incredible."

"Oh? I hadn't noticed," Brooke drawled.

I swatted at her. "Smug."

"Just a bit." She delicately wiped her mouth against the inside of my thigh and crawled back up beside me.

We lay quietly for a short while, fingers slowly stroking over skin until I recovered enough to suggest, "Maybe I could try being smug too?"

"I'd like that," she said, the slight huskiness in her voice lending the simple words a slightly desperate air.

I traced my fingers lightly over her breasts. "I'm going to need a little guidance. I, um looked up some stuff online but I *really* want to be able to please you, not just be a starfish."

Her eyebrows peaked. "Starfish?"

"You know." I spread my arms and legs. "Starfish. I'll just lie here, come get me."

"Ohhhh." Brooke laughed. "A pillow queen."

"So many new terms. Clearly I need to watch more videos, find a lesbian dictionary."

Brooke inhaled sharply when my lips brushed over an erect nipple. "You don't know the half of it. But I'll teach you all the important stuff." She turned her head to me, her breath catching again. "So you researched?"

The sound she'd made had my stomach twist with excitement. I backtracked to her nipple, this time gently rolling it between my thumb and forefinger as I talked. "A little…and I thought if I was up here the, uh, angle would be easier for me for my first try."

Brooke grinned. "You are so fucking sweet." She kissed me, long and slow. "And that's one of the sexiest things I've ever heard."

"You'll give me lots of feedback, right?"

"Absolutely." Her voice had dropped an octave and taken on a little rasp. "Kiss me. I love the way you kiss."

The kiss was slow and soft, a reconnection and reminder of what we were sharing. I was torn between pulling back to watch my hands on her skin and staying there to keep kissing her.

Brooke made the decision for me. "Jana, that feels incredible but I'm about to explode." She raised her head, her eyes slightly unfocused. "Please touch me."

Cautiously, I slid my hand down her belly. I'd touched her earlier, felt her against my thigh but this was completely different. I slipped my fingers through the neat patch of curls and into slippery heat. My stomach did a slow flip. "God you're wet."

"You did that," she murmured against the sweaty skin of my neck. "You coming in my mouth made me so fucking hot, Jana." She gasped. "I'm not going to last long."

She murmured encouragement as my tentative hands and mouth explored her. Touching her, feeling her heat and desire and listening to her soft pleas had my excitement rising until I thought I'd come apart. The softness of her skin, the gentleness of her caresses at once soothed some of my worries and ignited my need. I reveled in her, the wholly new sensation of being naked beside a woman.

After a careful exploration, I dragged my finger up through slick heat and pressed against her swollen clit. She jerked, her thigh coming up between mine. "Right there, that's it."

I kept up the motion, trying to match the movement of her hips. I could smell her, the musky scent of her arousal making my body tight with want. I wanted to taste. Licking my way down her neck I savored her, my throat tightening as I thought of how she'd taste if I were to slide down the bed and take her in my mouth. I could almost feel the heat and tang on my tongue. I'd tasted myself on someone else's mouth before, but this would be something new, exciting. Carefully, I brought my fingers to my mouth. She tasted incredible, sweet but musky, and that gentle but insistent throbbing set up residence between my legs again.

Brooke groaned, her hand tightening on my shoulder. "Oh, God. Jana. Watching you suck me off your fingers is so fucking sexy."

I lowered my face to within an inch of hers. "You taste incredible. I want to lick you but…" I finger-walked my way back down to her clit, finding her even wetter than before. Now I was more confident, sure

I could bring her to orgasm with my fingers. This time, our first time, more than anything, I wanted her to climax and I wanted it to be from me. Licking her could wait. But not much longer.

"Inside," she begged, lifting her hips and bucking up into my palm. "Fuck me please."

I slid a cautious finger into her depths and she let out a low moan. The sound caused a twitch between my thighs, another flutter of arousal and excitement filled my belly. I added a second finger and worked some joint magic to keep my thumb stroking her clit, delighting in her long, low sound of pleasure.

I'd never, *ever* experienced this before—this complete and utter overwhelming pleasure just from pleasuring someone else. I'd spent my whole life thinking one thing, and now I knew I'd barely scratched the surface of my desire.

That desire grew as I watched her, the curves of her body as she bucked and writhed against me, the way she pinched her nipples and grabbed my wrist whenever I slowed down. "I'm close, please don't tease," Brooke begged. "You're so good, you're going to make me come."

She was so unashamed and unrelenting in telling me exactly what she wanted that with every word, I felt myself grow wetter. I'd never been with someone as vocal before, and especially not someone who didn't make me feel like I wanted to giggle when they whispered dirty things in my ear.

Brooke chanted my name, over and over, the pitch of that single word growing until it was less encouragement and more wonder. She gripped a handful of the hair at the back of my neck, buried her face in the curve of my shoulder, biting as she climaxed. The addition of this small pain sent my arousal into overtime and I could do nothing but hold on to her as she writhed against my hand.

She was floppy, boneless in that way I recognized as post-orgasmic stupor. "Shit," she breathed, releasing her grip on my hair and smoothing her hand over my head. She kissed my shoulder where she'd bitten me. "Sorry. God that was good. I totally forgot myself. I didn't mean to hurt you."

I shifted so I could lie on her, more than a little pleased that it'd been *me* who'd done that to her. "You didn't. I liked it. And I loved how vocal you were. It was so unexpected and so fucking sexy."

"Ah, yeah." Her cheeks turned that delicious pink. "I may have dialed it up a couple of degrees for you. I wanted you to be sure you knew what you were doing felt really *really* good."

"Mm, it was a huge turn-on." I smoothed my palm over her ribs. "And I'm certain there's more vocabulary in there I haven't heard."

"There might be, but you're going to have to pull it out of me. You're such a good learner."

"Only because I've had the best teacher. And I intend to pay very close attention to further lessons." I rubbed my hand up and down the sweaty, slippery skin of her stomach. "Just so you know, I'm both a high achiever and a perfectionist."

She pulled me over until I lay on top of her. "I have a feeling I'm going to enjoy your learning process very much…"

CHAPTER TWENTY-FOUR

When I woke just after nine on Sunday morning, I was sprawled in my usual position with the unusual but very welcome feeling of a warm body against my back. I took a few moments to isolate the sensations—the light weight of her arm over my hip, warm breath on my neck, hair brushing my bare shoulders. Shuffling back, I pressed into her.

Brooke's arm tightened, pulling me even closer. "Morning," she mumbled into my hair.

"Hey." Carefully, I rolled over. "How'd you sleep?"

She stretched, muscles quivering. "Like a log. You totally wore me out. You?"

"Same. I haven't had a night like that in a *very* long time. Actually, not ever."

"I would hope not," she remarked dryly.

Laughing, I kissed her then extracted myself from her arms so I could use the bathroom. The image reflected back at me in the mirror was one of a woman who'd been up all night while someone reinvented her sexual wheel. Tired, but supremely satisfied. Come to think of it, satisfied didn't even begin to scratch the surface.

Speaking of scratches...

There were some very faint ones on top of my shoulders, and also a hickey on my left breast. The hickey was a teasing joke. The scratches were not. Around midnight, lying twined with her in that half-awake, half-asleep limbo I'd groggily suggested teeth brushing and bed—real bed as in sleeping. I'd offered her a toothbrush and she'd produced an adorable mini *just in case* toiletries bag.

We'd taken a shower to wash away sweat and sex, somehow managing to keep our hands mostly to ourselves. But when she kissed me goodnight, all bets were off. Once more we dissolved in a tangle of limbs, and the more things escalated the more I became aware of two overwhelming thoughts—I wanted her to come first, and I wanted her to come in my mouth.

She didn't push me, but as I made my way down her body I could feel the tightness of anticipation coiling in her body. The moment my tongue made contact with her wetness, Brooke exhaled a low moan. "Oh yes, that's good. Again, just like that...*please*."

In that instant I forgot all my shyness. All my worry and my clumsiness. Every sense honed in on the way she pushed up into my mouth, her hand fluttering over my neck and gently tugging my hair, her nails digging into my skin, those sounds she made. Her scent and taste were intoxicating and in that moment, I understood with perfect clarity that this wasn't about my insecurity. This was about her enjoyment, her pleasure. The only thing that mattered was her release.

She'd made me comfortable with that same calm confidence she'd shown during all of our lovemaking. Even though it took a little time for me to figure things out with some misplaced strokes, missed cues and clumsiness, she gently helped me adjust, offering soft instruction until her breathing grew ragged and her feet began to move restlessly against the sheets. She tensed, arching when I swirled my tongue a little faster, and her plea was a hoarse, "Just...a little harder...oh fuck, I'm coming."

And it was one of the sexiest, most gratifying things I'd ever experienced. As I'd fallen asleep, cuddled up to her, I'm pretty sure I mumbled, "I could definitely get used to you..."

And I swear she'd kissed my forehead and murmured, "Me too."

The reminder of the lovely naked woman in my bed snapped me out of my hazy, sex-satisfied memories. I paused in the bedroom doorway, just watching her. She lay on her back, body partially covered but her curves and swells were clear under the sheet. Oh boy.

Brooke stretched again, a little squeak escaping as she arched her back. She rolled over, propping her head on her hand. "I hate to be this person, but I really need to get home and bust ass on your gift for Sabine and Rebecca. *Someone* has been occupying my evenings and I haven't had as much time to work on it as I want."

I'd seen progress pictures of the work—a metal sculpture about a foot and a half long. Two women reclining, entwined so it seemed that they flowed into each another. They looked like they were one, yet separate. Awed, I'd tried to explain what I saw in it, using clumsy non-arty words, and Brooke had laughed and said that I'd pretty much nailed the concept. I couldn't wait to give it to Sabs and Bec, and tell them proudly that Brooke had made it.

I bent to kiss her, my hand on the bare skin of her belly. "Wow, *someone* sounds like a really demanding person."

"Oh she is. But I like it." She tilted her head back, grinning up at me. "I especially liked how many orgasms that same someone demanded last night."

"What can I say? I got a taste for it."

"So did I," she murmured. "For you…"

"Don't do that, don't be all sexy or I'll never let you go." I backed up, away from her enticing form. "Do you want coffee or breakfast?"

"I'm good, thanks, I'll just grab something on the way home." Her expression was pure innocence as she swung out of my bed and sauntered to the bathroom. I stared, noting with delight that staring at her ass was even more fabulous when it was bare. Things just kept getting better and better.

I dressed and picked up the clothing left on the floor when she'd undressed me in front of the mirror. The memory sent a low thrill coursing through my belly. On the back of the thrill came another, unexpected sensation. Relief. I *had* enjoyed it. It'd been pretty much everything I'd expected and then some incredible things I hadn't expected. I wanted more, a lot more. And perhaps most importantly, for my ego, I wasn't a complete girl-on-girl-sex idiot after all. Everybody wins.

Brooke came back, now dressed. She stared at the panties in my hands. "Oh that's just cruel."

"You're telling me. I just had a very pleasant flashback and now you're leaving."

Her expression was pure, devilish delight. "Mmm, good. And I guess we'll have to make more."

"I am very much looking forward to that."

She smiled a smile that was both promising and reluctant as she made her way into the living room to collect the rest of her belongings. "I really wish I didn't have to go."

"Me too, but there are plenty of days and nights to look forward to."

"True." She cleared her throat, swiped her tongue over her lower lip. "So, I was thinking, on weeknights, maybe for a few weeks or a month we shouldn't do the sleepover thing? I absolutely loved sleeping and waking up with you, don't get me wrong, but I'm just worried about pushing things too quickly."

"Sure, that makes sense." With my hand on her back, I guided her toward the door. "But just to clarify, we're only talking about sleeping and waking up, not sex?"

She grinned. "Definitely only talking about actual sleeping."

I sagged against her. "Phew."

"I don't have *that* much willpower, Jana." Still smiling, she paused in the entryway to pull on her shoes. "I'll call you tonight once I'm done working."

"Look forward to it. Is this the part where we spend an hour kissing goodbye?"

She answered me by gently grasping a handful of my top, pulling me the final step toward her, and kissing me all too briefly. "I wish, but then I'd be even more behind on this piece." Still lingering near my lips, she lowered her voice. "Maybe just ten minutes?"

"Done." I wound my arms around her neck and pressed my mouth to hers.

The sound of my front door unlocking pulled us out of the kiss but not each other's arms. A second later, the door swung open and was toed shut again. Brilliant timing, Sabine. Sabs stopped abruptly, her expression one of surprised excitement as she looked from me to Brooke. She didn't even bother to moderate her manic grin. "Hi, Jannie. Hey, Brooke. How's it going?"

Brooke raised a hand in greeting. "Fabulously. You?" She moved so we were side by side instead of pressed front on against one another in a way that was probably not polite in my sister's company.

Said sister's grin grew even wider. "Same."

I stepped in before she could escalate things into embarrassment territory. "Where's Bec?"

"She's meeting a friend for coffee this morning. Sends her sorry for not being here to help with the cards."

"Oh, no big deal. Brooke and I finished them last night. She's a lot less annoying than you at reading out names."

"I see. Good for you two." Sabs's eyes sparkled, her mouth twitched, and I could see the immense effort it was taking her to not ask or say something inappropriate.

I mouthed *don't you fucking dare* at her, and guided Brooke around her to the door. "Drive carefully. See you tomorrow morning."

"You bet." Our actual goodbye kiss was surprisingly tame considering what we'd been doing for most of the night. She leaned around me. "Catch you next time, Sabine."

"Mhmm, absolutely, yep. Look forward to it. Take care." Sabine smiled, waving cheerily at Brooke.

I closed the door with a final murmur of, "Bye."

Sabine's hand dropped, her mouth falling open with exaggerated slowness. "You did it, didn't you? You had sex with a woman. With her."

I threw my hands up. "Seriously? Am I wearing a sign? Exuding something only women who like women can pick up on? Is there some black light stamp on my forehead or something?" I slid past her and into the kitchen to start coffee.

Sabs followed me, her words practically tripping over each other. "Jannie! This is huge! Come on, come on, tell me everything! How was it?"

"It was very satisfying. And a little different. But good different. *Very* good different. Overall eight out of ten."

"Ohmyfuckinggod," she breathed. After a beat, Sabine queried, "Wait, why the drop of two points?"

"Because it was kind of confusing trying to figure some stuff out which made me feel a little awkward. But she was really sweet about the whole thing." I couldn't help my grin. "The second and third times were nine out of ten." Especially when Brooke found her *kinky sex game mask* that had been left at my place after the migraine incident.

"In-fucking-credible. God, I didn't even come my first time. Though, you know, I was only sixteen and we both had no fucking clue. And here you are rocking it on your first attempt." She held up a hand for a high five.

I slapped her hand as hard as I could, and as she had for the past thirty-something years, Sabine simply raised an eyebrow at my attempt to hurt her. I filled the coffee machine. "Well, I wouldn't say rocking it, Sabs. I'm still only on my learner's permit. Lesbian Learner." I snorted.

She huffed a laugh. "So, uh…everything go okay? Nothing you need to talk about?" She slid the coffee canister along the counter to me.

Sabs and I shared pretty much everything, including nonspecifics of our sex lives. But what I'd shared with Brooke felt almost *too* personal, too special and I felt suddenly weird about getting into details about it. So I offered a quick, "Yep, everything was fine." After a breath I added,

"It was great, and we talked a lot which was novel, and surprisingly sexy."

She pulled me in for a long, tight hug. "Good."

I relaxed into her embrace. "I'm still not sure what happens next?"

Sabs squeezed me, then released me. "More of the same, I'd think."

"Well, yeah obviously." More of the same over and over again if I had any say. I set the coffee machine to brew. "The sex is easy, well not easy but it will be when I'm more certain, but you know what I mean. It's everything else that I'm worried about. I want *more*, but you know me and relationships. All those from the past decade have lasted a month or two at most, and not at all serious. I think this could be."

"Shit…"

"Yeah. You're telling me. I don't know if it's just the excitement of her being the first woman I've slept with, and it was so crazy good that I want it all the time now even though it's only the morning after our first romp. Or if it's because I'm attracted to her mind and body and all that. I mean, we were great friends before *this* happened, and I think it's just made everything so much better."

"Does it really matter why you want her? And do you think that because you want to have sex with her constantly that it's just mindless lust? Come on, Jannie, when was the last time you slept with anyone just for the sake of having sex?"

"Never," I said immediately. "I've got a vibrator if I just want an orgasm."

"Right, exactly. I know you, I know how you operate and I know how high your standards are." Under her breath she mumbled, "Ridiculously so sometimes."

I stretched out a leg, intending to kick her, but she'd cleverly positioned herself out of my reach. Smiling smugly, Sabs continued, "You have a long and thorough checklist of pre-attraction and attraction before you even consider going to bed with someone. So why would you just be sleeping with Brooke for the sake of her making you come?"

"Well, I wouldn't." I let out a long breath. "I'm just paranoid about the whole thing I guess. Worried if I'm going too fast or too slow."

"Don't be. Just take it as it comes. She seems pretty easygoing."

"Yeah she is." Then I smiled, remembering how *not* easygoing she'd been while she'd been writhing underneath me, frantic with desire. Ahem. I shifted my thoughts away from the wonder of the night before. "Brooke accepted your unofficial wedding invitation, by the way."

"Oh, awesome."

"For the record, I still think it's way too early to expose her to the combined family crazy. Mom and Dad will probably scare her off. And it's making a pretty big declaration, don't you think?"

"No, I don't think. I think you should do whatever feels right." Sabs collected mugs and milk. "Speaking of Mom and Dad, when're you going to tell them?" she asked slyly.

Ahhh, fuck.

Mom beat me to it, phoning just after six p.m. as she prepared dinner—her favorite time to call—which usually meant I had to shout into the phone whenever she set hers on the counter so she could do something else. She was distant when she said, "Sabine said you were thinking of bringing a date to the ceremony."

"Yes, I've invited someone."

"That's unusual. You've never brought anyone to a family function before." My mother's voice was impressively neutral. I'd have given anything to see her face—she must be close to exploding with nosiness and excitement. "He must be special."

Buckle up, it's going to be a wild ride. "She, Mom," I corrected gently, not at all surprised that Sabs had left the gender unspecified so I'd have to tell my parents everything. Shithead.

"You're in a relationship with a woman and you didn't tell me and your father?" By the end of the sentence, her voice had risen four decibels and two octaves.

"Yes, I am and it's *very* new, like only just over a week new, and I'm not sure where it's going. But she's a very good friend aside from…all the other stuff."

Mom hmmed. "I see. Well, I must say I'm somewhat surprised. I didn't realize."

"Yes, I imagine you would be. As am I and pretty much everyone else."

The refrigerator opened, jars clinked. "So are you a bisexual?"

"I think it's just bisexual, Mom."

"Well that makes no sense. Sabine is *a* lesbian. Mitchell is *a* gay man. Why not *a* bisexual?"

Trust my mother to turn this into something bizarre. "I don't make the language rules, Mom but I'm pretty sure it's just bisexual. And I don't know what I'd call myself." Could you call yourself bisexual if you were only attracted to one woman? I smiled as I thought back to the whiskey-tinged memory of Sabs calling me *Brooke-sexual*. That summed it up perfectly.

"But you want to date women now too?" There was absolutely no accusation or sadness or disappointment, just curiosity. Mom was just momming, putting everything in its place.

"I don't think I want to date *women*, no. But I do want to date this one woman. Look, it's new and still a little confusing for me and I don't really know what's happening." Well I knew but telling my parents that at the moment Brooke and I were mostly just making out and screwing like rabbits and seeing where that led wasn't really appropriate.

"Hold on one moment." She called out to Dad, "Gerhardt! Come here! Jana is dating a woman."

After an eternity, during which I could hear my parents having a muffled conversation, my father came on the line. "A woman? What's she do? She worthy of dating one of my daughters?" Leave it to my father to ask that first. Of course, Dad was just dadding.

"Yes, Dad, of course she is. She's an architect for her father's property development company. Handles a lot of really important projects."

"Pah," he scoffed. "Stable but boring." Well, I guess I had to disappoint him some way. Bec ticked all the boxes. Despite how Bec and Sabine's relationship had started—by breaking Army rules—my Vietnam-vet father was predisposed to like Rebecca before even meeting her because she was not only military, but a high-ranking officer. To sweeten the deal, Bec loved discussing military strategy and history with him. And she loved Sabine with every cell in her body.

Would I ever be able to say that about Brooke and me? I knew with certainty that I wanted it, wanted her to feel that way about me and wanted her to fit into my family. "I really like her, Dad, and I think you guys will too."

Dad conceded with a grunt. "Well…all right then. Here's your mother back. I'll see you soon. Love you."

He was replaced by Mom who'd turned to full fretting mode during my short conversation with Dad. "What about my grandchildren now? You know Sabine and Rebecca will *not* have children, and you were my last hope. Oh, Jana, I just…"

I scrunched my eyes closed as she rambled until eventually, I couldn't stand it. "Mom! Listen very carefully. As far as I know, I'm not infertile and there's more than one way to make a baby, okay? Or to have a child. Like fostering or adoption."

That brought her down instantly. "Oh. Well all right then. So you still want children?"

"As much as I did before Brooke and I started seeing each other." I sighed. "Like I said, we've only been dating for a week, so kids haven't really been discussed but my stance hasn't changed." Brooke and I *had* talked briefly about kids, over coffee, when we'd confirmed we both wanted them. I added it to the list of things to discuss later. Much later.

My mother sighed too, but hers was relieved rather than exasperated. "You don't know how pleased I am to hear you say that. Children are precious, and it's not like anyone else can keep the Fleischer name going. You know Nancy Erikson is at me all the time about the fact I'm not a grandmother yet, like her daughter is better than my girls when that simply is not true. Jana Banana, you know I'm not the violent type but I could have slapped her right there in the street. But, rise above and all that. So I simply stared her down and laid out every single thing you and your sister and Rebecca have done to make us proud, and she skulked away with her tail firmly between her legs. But my love, grandchildren would just put the frosting on that cake of love and pride your father and I baked for you girls. Please remember that."

Fuuuuuuuuuuuck. I could not believe I was going to expose Brooke to this insanity. "Yes, Mom. I know, Mom. Great analogy and thanks for the pressure."

"Good. We love you, we're so *so* proud of you and we'll see you soon. And I'm very much looking forward to meeting this architect!"

In the background my father droned teasingly, "Borinnnng."

CHAPTER TWENTY-FIVE

Having a girlfriend, I discovered, was basically the same as having a really good friend but with the added bonus of snuggles and sex. Such a fabulous combination—why hadn't anyone ever told me how great it was? We'd laid out weeknight schedules for what nights would be spent at whose house, and Monday after work I drove straight to her place. I barely had time to slip out of my heels before she'd pulled me against her and kissed me. "Hey."

"Hey yourself."

Brooke took my hand and led me into the kitchen where she divested me of handbag, briefcase and laptop bag. "Tell me about your day."

"Condensed version? Long, stressful, not as successful as I wanted it to be."

Brooke frowned. "Why? Tell me." She bent low to kiss the base of my neck, lingering against my skin before kissing her way up to my ear where she gently nuzzled the sensitive skin under my jaw.

"Not sure. Grumpy judge, stars didn't align, maybe I came at things from the wrong angle? And my mediation meeting sucked. I'm pretty sure it'll go our way, but this woman's almost-ex-husband is *such* a lying fucking asshole. I was *this close* to throwing my water glass in his face. Professionalism is such a drag sometimes."

"You mean your water?" Brooke swapped to the other side of my jaw, paying it the same attention while her hand worked at the buttons of my blouse.

"No. The glass. Actually I wish I had two so I could have thrown one at his attorney too." Stupid Weisman.

"I'm sorry." Her kisses grew light along my jaw.

I shuddered as fingers brushed over my stomach. "I can't concentrate on what I'm trying to say when you do that," I said in a voice that was half-complaint, half-surrender. Despite my feeble protest, I angled my head to give her better access.

"That's the point. It's supposed to make you forget every shitty thing that happened today. It's supposed to make you forget about everything except us."

I shuddered, skin tightening to goose bumps as she undid the last button and parted the fabric. "It's working. Bad thoughts fading. Oh, and I forgot to mention it this morning, but I told my parents about you last night." Brilliant timing, Jana. Could you not have held on to that tidbit 'til after?

Brooke's mouth paused. "Yeah? Were they okay with it?" She straightened so she was at eye level.

"Of course, more than okay. They're both really excited to meet you. Mom's still worrying about the grandkids thing, despite my reminding her that there's nothing wrong with my reproductive organs or my suitability as an adoptive parent. Oh, and sorry but my dad thinks property development and architecture is, and I quote, borinnnng."

Brooke smiled. "He's right. It is."

"Mmm, just be prepared for him to rib you about it, but I promise it's all in good fun. My family is really goofy, and teasing is kind of a Fleischer love language for us. But if you don't like it then just tell me and I'll tell them to dial it down."

"I'm sure it'll be fine, and I look forward to it." Her eyebrow furrow was brief, but unmistakable. Also unmistakable was the raised pitch of panic in her voice. "So uh, kids?"

"Yeah. Remember how I'm a failure of a daughter because I'm not churning out grandkids?" My brain finally caught up to her reaction of moments earlier. "Shit, sorry. Hey, I'm not saying you and me right now, or even whenever or at all for kids. I was just trying to…look, my mother is great, but also weird and neurotic about me having kids, so I wanted to warn you. That's all."

She visibly relaxed. "Okay, sure. And um, phew? I admit you did have me mildly panicked for a moment there. But I'm looking forward to meeting your family. Weird neuroses and all."

"Great. Now, sorry, back to what we were doing before I decided I just *had* to impart that information."

Grinning, Brooke pulled my blouse off my shoulders and I shrugged out of it, letting the garment fall to the floor. She guided me backward, carefully directing me through her house. I pulled her top over her head, cupping her breasts, teasing her nipples through her bra. Brooke groaned quietly, yanked me roughly against her, and kissed me with more than a little desperation. We removed clothing as we kissed and fondled our way to the bedroom. Bras, skirts, pants, panties—all left wherever they fell.

"This is like a breadcrumb trail," I mumbled against her mouth. My hands slid down her back, cupped her ass.

"I don't need one." Brooke pressed me against the wall, teeth grazing the base of my neck. "I want to stay lost with you forever." She pulled my leg up, hitched it around her ass and pressed forward until her hip made contact with just the right spot.

If her words hadn't already sucked the breath from my chest, the contact against my clit certainly would have. Brooke reached between us and after slicking her fingers through my arousal, paused at my entrance and whispered, "Can I?"

I could only manage a strangled grunt, a desperate nod before she entered me with a smooth thrust. I clutched her back, her shoulders, anything I could grab as she slowly stroked. The grunt turned into an almost embarrassingly needy groan when she hit that perfect spot. I arched, my head hitting the wall behind me with a *thunk*.

Brooke froze. "Shit. Okay, time to move this to a safer location."

I tried to protest that right here was just fine and I wasn't hurt and please for the love of orgasms, don't stop now. But she carefully released me and led me the final few feet into her room. I'd never been in her bedroom but was too focused on other things to pay much attention at that moment.

A few vague details registered—scented candles, paintings of female nudes on the walls, a sculpture on the floor and the sensation of being immersed in a forest which I later realized was probably the color scheme of greens and earth tones and the laundry detergent she used on her sheets. I pulled her down to the bed and rolled us so she was on top of me.

More sensations, definitely not vague. The weight of her, the smoothness of the back of her thigh and the way she shuddered when I slid my fingers over it, the low hoarse groan when I pressed my thigh between her legs, and how her sweetly tormenting hands roamed my body with such infinite care. I sucked her earlobe, licked her neck, bit her. "God, I want your mouth on me."

"Okay." Brooke shifted slightly, opened her mouth wide and suctioned herself to the inside of my elbow.

I froze. "What…are you doing?"

Her eyes came up to my face. "Pufing mah moufon oo."

For a moment, I could do nothing but stare at her, stuck on my arm like a lamprey. Then I cracked up, laughing until my eyes teared. "Oh my God. Come here."

Brooke detached herself from my skin and climbed up. She kissed me, her lips still lifted in a smile. "I'm sorry, I couldn't help myself, and I totally broke the sexy mood. I'm such a weirdo." She shifted so we were lying side by side, facing one another. Her hand roamed until it found my ass.

"Yeah you are, must be why I like you so much. And trust me, the sexy mood is very much unbroken. In fact, I think it might have even amplified a little. I don't remember ever having *fun* in bed like this, or come to think of it, I could also say fun outside of bed the way we do."

"Stop, rewind. Go back to the part where you said you like me."

"Actually I said I like you so much. As in a lot." My hand trailed lazily down her stomach and slipped between her legs. "I'd like to try something, if you don't mind."

She lifted her hips, pressing into my hand. "Whatever you want, baby."

Baby…

For some reason that endearment sent a thrill through my core. "Lie down on your back," I murmured.

Brooke rolled over slowly, her eyes on me the whole time. "Whatever you're about to do, I think I'm going to enjoy it very much."

"As much as I will, I hope." I straddled her, tilting forward until I was pressed against the tense muscle of her stomach.

"Yep," she squeaked. "Definite enjoyment."

Slowly, I rocked, taking my time to enjoy the motion and accompanying waves of pleasure with every press of skin to skin. I exhaled a long breath, which turned to a gasp as the unmistakable stirring of an orgasm building rolled through my body.

She paused, swallowed visibly. "I, uh, that's—"

"What?" I breathed.

"I was just thinking about how I called you cowgirl."

"Oh? You like being…ridden like this?" I rolled my hips forward, grinding into her, drawing out the sensation.

"Yeah, kinda, a lot," she choked out. Brooke's legs came up, her feet flat on the bed and her thighs pressed into my ass, holding me in place. Her smirk was unmistakable. "You're totally topping me right now."

My voice came out a hoarse whisper. "Is that a bad thing?" I pulled her hands to my breasts, holding them against me.

"Not at all. But I had imagined I'd have to spend a bit more time showing you the ropes." Brooke's fingers kneaded, thumbs strafing over my nipples. Her eyes burned with desire, her undisguised need made me feel exposed, seen. Not an unpleasant sensation, but scary all the same. Scary to feel so needed, so desired, and scary to need her so much already.

My words came out clipped, stuttered around my sharp intakes of breath. "I think you've done an excellent job of giving me the basics but I want to move on to the advanced course." I ground down harder on her. "I'm sorry, this is selfish of me but you feel so good and this is one of my favorite positions."

Her eyes went wide. "No, baby, it's not selfish. It's hot. Watching you riding me is so fucking sexy." Slowly, she traced her hands down my chest, over my stomach until they came to rest on my hips. "A favorite hey?" Brooke rocked me forward, rolled me back, over and over again until my breathing was so erratic I was on the verge of hyperventilating.

"Mhmm."

Then she drew a hand down between my thighs until her thumb pressed firmly against my clit. "Mine too."

Warning jolts shot through me and I cautioned her, "That's going to make me come."

"Good," she murmured. "Do you want my fingers inside you again? Do you want me to fuck you?" Her thumb moved with sure, steady strokes, which made decision making impossible.

"I don't know, oh God," I groaned. All I knew was that I had to come.

"Or do you want me to get something else to fuck you with?" She slid further between my legs, teasing my entrance, slicking through my wetness before coming back to stroke my clit. "I have toys…" She drew her hands up to my hips, tracing lightly over my skin. "A harness."

I had to bite my lip to stop the scream that was threatening and all I could do was shake my head no. No, I didn't want anything other than what she was doing to me in that moment. Later, maybe, but now? Now was so fucking good. So good. For me. Wait. For *me*.

I forced myself to focus, to be still. "You keep talking about toys, am I missing a cue here? Is this toyless sex too vanilla?" I tried to be teasing, but I could hear the uncertain note in my question.

"Oh fuck no, not at all." Her stomach muscles clenched underneath me. "I think maybe I'm just overthinking it, worrying it's not good enough for you because it's, uh different to what you're used to."

"Oh, honey, it's plenty good enough. *Beyond* good enough." I rolled my hips forward and back again, slow and teasing. "For sure, we can do that soon. If you really want, then I want."

"I do. And not because of…you know. I want to, because fucking you like that would be so hot. And you fucking me will feel so, damned, good." She punctuated those last words with firm strokes. "But this is incredible."

"It is." I sat up, twisting around so I could reach between her thighs. With a hand braced behind myself on her knee, I could balance enough to slip my other hand…down…Christ, right there. "As is this."

She was so wet and hot, and the moment I found her clit, Brooke gasped, her legs jerking against my ass. "Oh fuck."

I loved the way her breathing hitched, the way her voice grew high and tight as I touched her, and barely managed to concentrate with the slow suffusion of pleasure rippling through my body to ask, "Can you come like this?"

Her words were clipped. "If you keep doing what you're doing, then yes."

I had no intention of stopping, not until she'd come. I let her set the rhythm, keeping pace with her as she slicked and teased and stroked my heat. She didn't enter me but kept up that knowing movement of fingers on my clit until I was on the brink of exploding.

Her hips bucked underneath me and she sat up abruptly, one arm coming around my waist, the other hand still pressed between my legs, expertly driving me toward climax. Then her hot mouth was on mine, her tongue surprisingly gentle considering how frantic our other movements were. The slipperiness of her, the chafe of nipples against mine, the wet warmth of her under my fingers combined with her skillful stroking tipped me over the edge. Not that there was any doubt, but I couldn't stop myself, muttering a helpless, "Fuck, I'm coming."

As the first tremor came over me, I moaned against her mouth and surrendered, trying desperately not to lose touch with her. Brooke shuddered, an indistinguishable sound rising to match mine as her hips jerked, pressing her clit firmly into my fingers.

I buried my face in her neck, trying to steady my breathing and ride out my climax. Brooke carefully eased her hand from between us, wrapping her arms around me, holding me close until I could feel my limbs again. Loosely slinging my arms around her shoulders, I held on, kept my face pressed to her neck, planting soft kisses on whatever skin I could reach. "How do you do that?" I mumbled.

"Do what?" she asked, breathless.

"That. Make me come like that? It's like an orgasm on crack, the best I've ever had. Complete and utter digit-tingling, toe-curling, stomach-clenching full body feeling."

It wasn't just the actual orgasm that made sex with her so fabulous. It was all the small details that seemed to coalesce during our lovemaking that took it from great to utterly incredible. Like the feeling of her hair on my skin, silken and soft as it trailed in the wake of Brooke's kisses— it was a sensation I'd never encountered and now never wanted to be without. Her words, sometimes sensual, sometimes filthy. The way she touched me, seeming to know exactly how and where I needed it. The sound she made when I touched her.

She grinned. "Naw, you're just saying that."

"Nuh-uh. Seriously." Shakily, I declared, "That was definitely a twelve out of ten."

After dinner, an episode of *Dexter* and five minutes of languorous goodbye kisses, I went home. Home to my empty house and cold bed. Get a grip, Jana. It's the same bed you've been sleeping in alone for how many years now?

But now, sleeping, waking up alone, going to the gym, eating breakfast, showering and dressing for work all felt kind of empty and stale without her. As I closed my front door to leave for work, I gave myself another mental shake. Just over a week of dating does not a lifetime commitment make. Well, no, but there was nothing wrong with not liking being apart from her. Nothing wrong with enjoying her company in and out of bed.

My day was mercifully uneventful. Drafting documents with Erin, teaching moments with Belinda, meeting with a client, court appearance with a very favorable outcome. As I walked back to the office, I realized *Jana Celebrates* was going to be a whole lot more exciting now that I had someone to share it with. Brooke's day was running long so we decided she should come home with me. She met me by my car, greeting me with a short hug and a long kiss…after she'd glanced quickly around the parking garage. She stared at the Porsche, in its usual spot, which included a few stolen inches of my spot, frowned and muttered, "God, my dad parks like an asshole."

There was no other response for that revelation except to laugh.

We decided that we'd take a walk to collect dinner, and when we stepped out of my apartment building the sky was slowly darkening into evening, twilight making everything seem warm and sensual. Without thinking I took her hand, entwining our fingers as we strolled along the sidewalk. An older guy walking toward us stared as he approached, his mouth set in a tight line. As he passed, he said something under his breath that I didn't quite catch and didn't care to turn around to figure out. Brooke's grip tightened, then eased almost as though she was about to pull her hand from mine.

I glanced down. "Is this not okay?"

It took her a few moments to answer, and when she did it seemed like she was forcing herself to sound casual. "Sure. I just haven't ever really done the whole public affection thing." She made a nervous gesture. "Just habit with my dad and stuff, and honestly I've never really dated someone who was into it."

"Oh. Well, I'm into it but if you're not, then…" I loosened my fingers and moved to disengage my hand but she gripped it tighter and pulled me to a stop.

Her smile was tight. "Really? Even with that asshole who clearly doesn't like *fuckin' dykes*, as he so helpfully told us on his way past."

"Yes, really. Babe, I don't give a shit what other people think. When it comes to you and me, the only person whose opinion I care about is yours. I'm not ashamed of being with you. Why would I be?"

She shifted uncomfortably and I realized I might have gone a little too far with my *who cares* attitude. I added, "I'm not saying you're ashamed of us."

"Good, because I'm not," she insisted quietly. "I'm just…wary. Worried about being safe."

"I know, I'm sorry." I drew her hands to my chest, held them tight. "I just really like you and I like being with you and I want to hold your hand when we're out in public. I guess I just want everyone to know I have a smart, funny, sexy, beautiful, and incredibly good in bed girlfriend."

"Well they're going to know that by the way you keep looking at me," she said dryly.

"And how's that?"

"Like I'm a piece of meat hanging in the window of that butcher's shop across the road."

I followed her gaze. "A butcher. *Fleischerei*. It's fate."

She lowered her voice. "Despite the fact you're talking about a person who cuts up meat for a living, you sound so fucking sexy. Do you speak German often?"

"Every few weeks when I talk to my grandparents. Sometimes with my dad, usually when there's a word or phrase that just doesn't work in English. And whenever Sabs gets an urge. She's so weird, like she can barely go a day without it. She says she loves the way German feels in her mouth." I grinned. "Take from that what you will."

"I see."

"Oma and Opa speak English just fine. It's more just that I like having this special thing with them, but it's not really a big deal. One set of grandparents are German, the other Californian, just the way it is."

Her left eyebrow twitched up. "Do you speak Valley Girl with the Californian grandparents?"

"Like totally oh my Godddd, like whatever Malibu and LA and, uh, shit."

Her answering laugh was loud and free.

I stepped in, leaning forward to talk quietly against her ear. "I know a whole lot more than just that one German word. Maybe later I'll give you a little language demonstration, teach you some of my favorite dirty phrases…"

She sucked in a quick breath and kissed me right there on the sidewalk with people slipping around us.

CHAPTER TWENTY-SIX

Brooke's grasp of the finer points of dirty German phrases was both quick and accurate. *Jana Celebrates* indeed. By the time we'd exhausted and satisfied one another it was past eleven p.m. Groaning, with regular frustration instead of sexual frustration, Brooke rolled over. "I should get going."

I squirmed my way across the bed, hugging her from behind. "Mmm. It's late." I couldn't help myself, kissing her neck and shoulders, breathing her in. I stroked the smooth skin of her stomach and added, "You could stay the night." The words had come out before I'd even registered what I was about to say.

It wouldn't be the first time we'd had a sleepover, but it would be the first time on a weeknight with the added logistics of work the morning after. She didn't answer and I hastened to add, "Or not, I mean, whatever. I know what we agreed." That things like weeknight sleepovers might move things forward too quickly. Too late. I was already moved.

"Yes, we did say that," she said carefully. "Honestly, I'm so tired and I'd love to stay but I'm just thinking about the morning and the fact I don't have any work clothes here. Boring stuff like that."

"I can take you in if you want, it's just a short detour to grab your clothes or whatever you need. We can go as early as you want." Short detour wasn't quite right. It'd be a drive in the opposite direction then back again and add at least forty minutes to my commute. But I didn't care.

"I'm not sure I trust your driving," she said, half-serious, half-teasing.

"Puh-leeease. Didn't you see that news piece last week about the bus crash? The driver went right through a red light. *I've* never done that. Never had an accident, just a couple of speeding tickets. A couple in almost twenty years of driving. Pretty good record, I must say." I kissed the edge of her ear. "Anyway, it's just a thought."

"Mmm." She rolled back over and snuggled against me. "I like your thought."

I decided to skip my morning gym session in favor of cuddling in bed with Brooke. Okay, cuddling with a little kissing thrown in for good measure. I made my usual breakfast, multiplied by two, and we ate while checking news and social media on our phones and talking about plans for the rest of the week. We decided I should pack a bag in case I ended up staying over at her place that night, and the relationship-ness of the whole situation was simultaneously weird, scary, and wonderful.

The moment I'd drained my last mouthful of coffee, Brooke insisted on cleaning up and shooed me off to shower, get dressed, and put a face on. I slid dresses and suits along my racks until I found something that said, "Hello, new client, why yes I am a very capable and compassionate divorce attorney." A dark gray dress with three-quarter sleeves and a boat neckline. I wandered back into my kitchen, doing up the clasp on a simple gold necklace. Brooke sat at the table, fiddling with one of the cooler bags that normally lived atop my fridge.

"What's that?" I asked.

"It's um, lunch." Her cheeks pinked as she pushed the cooler bag toward me. "I made it for you. Sorry it's nothing special, just leftovers from dinner and some other stuff I found in your fridge and pantry."

My brain was so stuck on the fact she'd used relaxing-with-coffee time to make me lunch that I couldn't make my hands move to grab the bag.

The pinkness turned to full-on embarrassed redness. "It's silly. Sorry, I should have asked. You've probably got a lunch meeting or something on today."

She grabbed for the bag but I snagged it before she could grasp it. "Mine," I mumbled like a cavewoman. Clutching the cooler bag to my chest, the only thing I could get out through a throat tight with emotion was, "You did this for me?"

"Yeahhhh…" She brought both hands to her cheeks, rubbing gently as though she wanted to rub the blush away. "I just remembered what you were saying that night we had drinks, about the things you wanted in a relationship. I thought it'd be something that you'd enjoy, and you being happy makes me happy."

I almost melted at her simple, unselfish reason. "You really are the sweetest thing. I'm going to fall in love with you if you're not careful."

Her eyes widened, she blinked a few times as though surprised by what I'd said. "Oh, Jana." After a long pause she murmured, almost to herself, "Then maybe I should stop being so careful."

As planned, we detoured to her place. As she walked to her bathroom, stripping off yesterday's clothes, she called over her shoulder that in case I had any reciprocal ideas, she actually did have a lunch meeting. Damn. Though, judging by the usual bare status of her fridge it would have been a struggle to cobble together lunch for her.

Brooke took twenty minutes and appeared just as I was finishing up an email. "Okay, let's go take the law and architecture worlds by storm." She wore one of her usual pencil skirts, paired with a low-cut blouse that exposed a lovely yet tasteful amount of cleavage. I stared. I enjoyed. Previously, another woman's cleavage had done nothing more than make me envious. Tracing the exposed swell of Brooke's breasts with my eyes, I felt an unexpected and exciting thrill of pleasure.

"What?" Brooke glanced down at herself, fingers twitching at the neckline of her blouse.

"I think I just discovered I like boobs. Specifically, yours."

She grinned. "I'm very glad." She collected her handbag and folio briefcase from their table near the door. "Come on, we're going to be late if you don't stop staring at my cleavage."

"I wouldn't mind…"

Traffic was its usual morning horror, and after some idiot in a Mazda slammed his brakes on then surged forward for the third time, I lost my temper. "You fucking idiot!" I laid into my horn, and for good measure, gave him the finger before zipping around him and zooming off.

Brooke shifted in the passenger seat, still gripping the handle above her head. "So uh, it's going to be a road rage day huh?"

"Hmm?" I glanced at her. "Oh no, that's not road rage. Just statement of fact."

"A statement. Uh-huh. It kind of seemed like the prelude to an accident."

"Nope," I said cheerfully. "Remember? I've never had an accident or even an incident."

"I see. But…how many accidents or incidents have you caused driving like this?"

The lift of her mouth gave her teasing away and I swatted at her legs. Then I carefully eased back, bringing the Mercedes to just above the speed limit. "Impudent wretch!"

"Oh, those are big words for such an early hour." Brooke turned her phone over, glanced at the screen then turned it facedown again. "What did you want to do tonight? I was thinking I might cook? Or we could order in."

"Either or sounds great." I rolled to a stop at a set of traffic lights. "Brooke?"

"Mhmm?"

The light changed, and I planted my foot down, waiting until I'd overtaken everyone else before I said, "You can read your book if you want to. You don't need to make car small talk."

"Are you sure? I mean, I don't want to be rude, but…it's kind of my pre-work relaxation thing."

"Absolutely." Without taking my eyes off the road, I reached over and rested my hand on her thigh. The idea of her sitting beside me going about her normal transit routine made my chest tighten. "Reading during your commute is your thing, and I'd kind of like it to be our thing. I'd like for us to evolve into more weeknight sleepovers at both our houses and more driving in to work together, and I'd like you to be comfortable and relaxed."

Brooke thumbed the phone screen. "Well you're a lot hotter than the bus drivers of D.C., that's for sure." She gasped, and again grabbed for the handle above her head with her free hand as I zipped around a tediously slow Prius. "But, if you want me to relax, Ms. Daytona, then maybe we need to talk about speed limit rules…"

Alone in the elevator up from the parking garage, she kissed me quickly before the car came to a stop in the lobby to collect passengers. As the doors slid open, Brooke dropped her hand from my back. Then she took a step sideways. She stepped *away* from me. I barely had time to register the movement before, along with a few other people,

Brooke's father slid into the elevator, taking up a position beside her. "You're in later than usual," he said by way of greeting.

"Mhmm. I didn't see your car in the garage?"

His expression flickered to confusion for a moment before he regained his neutral composure. "It's being detailed."

"Oh." She gestured with her folio. "Dad, you remember Jana Fleischer?"

"Of course. How's all that caviar, Ms. Fleischer?"

Still stuck on Brooke's initial response to her father's arrival, I scrambled for a response. "Wonderful, as is my new Aston Martin."

Richard Donnelly chuckled, the sound echoing in the enclosed space. Tension permeating from Brooke was like heat waves, and I almost touched her before I recalled her reaction less than thirty seconds earlier. Brooke's dad exited the elevator first, with a wave and a vague *nice to see you again* aimed at me, which I returned. Brooke was slower but made no move to say anything or touch me. I made no move toward her either, but broke the taut silence with, "See you downstairs for coffee? Ten minutes?"

Brooke's expression was one of complete and utter misery. "Mhmm." Then she was gone.

* * *

We didn't talk about the elevator incident during coffee. Or during our two other sneaky café meetups during the day. Or our drive home. Because she didn't bring it up, I'd decided that I wouldn't either—I already knew her dad was a sore topic and niggling her about it wasn't going to help. But that didn't mean I was particularly pleased about it.

Because of our unexpected sleepover and changed morning routine we decided to take a walk around Brooke's quiet neighborhood before dinner, which had the added bonus of Brooke in a tight tank and short shorts. I raised my face, watching the early evening sky darken. "Do I do anything that you really hate?"

"Now that is a question with no right answer, Jana. Have I done something specific to make you think about this?" Her question was quiet, almost cautious.

"Not really, no. Which, for Ms. Picky Me is a miracle. That's why I thought about it just now because I've always avoided any sort of outdoor workouts with other…uh, people because they never want to do the same things as me and they huff and snort and grunt. And not the good kinds of those sounds. Plus, no air-conditioning. But I like this. I like this with you."

"I like it too."

"Good. Now what about my question about stuff that I do to annoy you?"

She made a sound that was breath and harrumph in one, almost like a horse snorting. "Well, uh…it's not annoying really but the way you crunch ice cubes makes the back of my neck feel awful. Flicking through songs after listening to half of them drives me insane. You organize your herbs and spices weirdly."

"Weirdly how?"

"By name, not the ones you use the most."

Valid annoyances. "Hmm, fair enough."

"Also, your driving scares the living shit out of me."

That one tripped me up. "Really? Scares you?"

She nodded, absolutely serious. "Yes, and not just when I'm in the car. I'm utterly terrified you're going to lose control of that thing and have a serious crash. Or cut in front of someone and get clipped and crash. Or pick the wrong person to have a bout of road rage at."

"Oh." Over the years, Sabs and Bec and even my parents had all commented similarly about my driving, which I usually brushed off. "I'm just…impatient."

"I know."

"I hate bad drivers."

"Yep, I know that too."

"D.C. traffic sucks."

"Yeah, it does. But there's no D.C. traffic in my quiet suburban street," she reasoned.

I let out a long breath. "I guess I *could* try being a little less Daytona and a little more mom with kids in the car?"

Her shoulders dropped. "That would make me feel a whole lot better. Thank you."

I mentally catalogued the things I could try not to do around her— ice crunching and song skipping, as well as the driving thing. Strangely enough none of what she'd said brought up any annoyance, or any real feelings aside from a desire to make her happy.

Brooke's quiet question broke me from my thoughts. "Did you mean what you said this morning?"

"Mean what?"

"That you could fall in love with me."

226 E. J. Noyes

At the time, it was meant as nothing more than an offhand teasing kind of comment. But when I took a moment to actually think about it, I realized it went deeper than that. I didn't hesitate. "Yes. I meant it. Not like right now because, you know, so soon. But I kind of think I could, yes."

"Really? Jana Fleischer, self-confessed champion of casual believes in love?" she teased, but it seemed more like a deflection.

Trying not to frown, I answered, "Well, yes. With the right person, sure."

"I see. So based on previous statements, you think I might be the right person?" The question was almost too casual.

"It's possible." I tugged her hand to make her look at me. "Hey, is this too much? I just, you know…honesty."

She paused a few moments. "No it's not that. I'm uh…look, ignore me. I'm overthinking everything as usual," she added quickly. The tone was easy to recognize. Anxiety.

"Are things moving too fast?" I asked quietly, peering over at her.

Brooke's forehead was furrowed, teeth worrying at her lower lip. "No, not too fast. It's not so much the speed, Jana. It's the possible destination that I keep thinking about."

"Ah. The 'possibility of you and I in a monogamous committed relationship instead of this casual relationship' destination?"

"That's the one. The one that hasn't gone so great for me in the past…"

"Ah, of course. Well, if one of us gets there first then there's no rule saying we can't wait for the other one to catch up? Or if we decide we want to take another route, or detours then there's nothing saying we can't do that either." I could barely believe I was even having this conversation about commitment. Or more to the point, that despite the fact Brooke was being cautious, I was still totally on board. Talk about a role reversal.

She let out a breath, as though forcibly trying to relax. "Right. Exactly. I mean, I'm sure we're on the same road. I think I'm just… driving slower than you are."

"Nice analogy." Without breaking stride, I leaned over and pecked her quickly on the cheek, relieved when she dipped her head to receive my kiss.

We walked quietly for a few minutes more, my mind turning over and over. Given her dating history, everything she'd just said made perfect sense. If I had to wait for her, then I had to wait.

We crossed the road, and she guided me to one side to give an approaching guy in casual business wear room to pass by. He smiled at us and I smiled back at him, thinking that he was cute, and the moment I thought it, an unexpected wash of panic made my hands suddenly clammy. Tightening my grip around Brooke's waist, I pulled her closer. The guy's smile didn't waver, he just nodded at both of us as he passed and that was that.

Unconsciously, I slid my hand down to Brooke's ass and she made a little purr. "What's this about?"

"Nothing, just uh. Nothing." Goddammit, now I was blushing.

Brooke stared at me for a few seconds before she turned to stare at the guy. "Do you know him?"

"Nope. Not at all." My response was a touch on the squeaky side.

She stopped and pulled us off the sidewalk. Her expression was knowing, tender. "Jana, sweetheart, I don't care if you check other people out, even if it's a guy. I don't hate guys, I have male friends I adore and I find plenty of men pleasing to look at. I just don't want anything to do with them romantically."

"No, it's not that, I just thought—"

"About kissing him?" she finished teasingly.

"No!"

"Would you have before?"

"Maybe, probably. But the only person I want to kiss now is you."

"I see. So what's the problem?"

"I just thought he was cute-ish and…" I lowered my voice. "I wondered about his butt."

She grinned, yanking me toward her and burying her face in my neck. She lingered, kissing my skin softly before pulling back, but she didn't let me go. "Hmm, but you didn't look at his butt. You actually grabbed mine. And less than two minutes before that you told me that you could maybe fall in love with me."

I blew out a long breath. "Yeah. I guess I'm just confused. Like shouldn't I only be checking you out?"

"I don't think there's an off switch, like you've swapped your train to another track and that's that." Brooke held me close, kissed my neck, my earlobe. "There's nothing wrong with looking or thinking or wondering. So long as when you're *with* me, I'm the one you're thinking about that way."

"Believe me, you are. And when I'm not with you." I pulled her to a stop at the corner under the warm glow of the streetlights. "Come here." When she shuffled closer I kissed her, just a quick soft brush of lips but the familiar electricity still coursed down my spine. Layered on top of that was my excitement that Brooke had accepted another public display of affection. Maybe she'd tell her dad about me soon too. Baby steps.

Actually, screw it, let's try some adult steps. "I was thinking maybe we could invite your dad around to my place for dinner sometime?"

Her posture changed instantly, like someone had flipped her switch to *Tension*. It was basically the same stance she'd had that morning when her dad got into the elevator. "I don't think that's a good idea," she said flatly

"Why not? I'd like to get to know him better, and maybe he'd like to know me better too?" Or at least know who I am aside from The Attorney Who Works Upstairs.

Her eyes closed for the briefest flicker. There was no anger, no malice or disdain. She just looked sad. "No."

"But, maybe if we explained and he spent some time and—"

She cut me off. "Jana, look. I understand what you're saying, and I would love nothing more than to waltz into my father's office holding your hand and say 'Hi, Dad, this is my girlfriend!'. But it's not going to happen, and that's really shitty for many reasons, the least of which is that I want him to know you because you are a fucking amazing human. But he won't be able to get past that one concept. Girlfriend, as in his daughter is still gay."

"Brooke—"

"Please, just…let it go. Just, I, look I need you to let me have this one awful thing, Jana, please. Please let it go, because I have no idea how to change it."

CHAPTER TWENTY-SEVEN

Sabine was messing around with her vows, while I mentally tried to unpack my fledgling relationship and the weird discomfort that I hadn't been able to shake. A café was not the best place for either of those things, even during a quiet post-work lull.

I picked at my muffin and watched my sister's face, contorted with her *oh shit, fuck, help* expression. Clearly, despite all her earlier bravado about letting things happen as they happened and trusting us, and her temporarily increased medication, her anxiety was slowly creeping up. I could either let her be overwhelmed and leave Bec to deal with it later on her own, or I could try to stop it in its tracks. Reassurance and/or distraction were my tried-and-true methods.

"Do you think Brooke is why I've never been able to find the right guy? Because this whole time, the right person for me has actually been a gal?"

"Maybe," Sabine said distractedly, crossing out a few words.

"I spilled ink on my dress and it's fucked."

Frowning she replaced *love* with *LOVE*. Wow, that's a big and worthwhile edit, Sabs. "Mhmm, your dress is wonderful."

"Sabine?"

"Mmm?"

"Listen to me, like really listen."

"I am listening," she protested.

"No you're not." I took the notepad from her but left it open and within her reach. "Sabbie, you're just editing the shit out of the vows you've already perfected to hell. Remember how we went over them on the phone every day this week?"

She nodded.

"Remember how they made me cry?"

"Yeah," she said sheepishly. "Sorry."

"Don't be, it means they were amazing. But there's such a thing as ruining a good thing. Trust what you've written."

She exhaled a long breath. "You're right. Sorry. So, what's new?"

"Nothing much, just questioning my new relationship."

She must have picked up on the desperation, because she set the pen down and turned her full, laser-like focus on me. "What's going on, Jannie? Why do you look like you're going into a test you haven't studied for?" Sabs asked cautiously.

Here goes. The kicker. "I know it sounds really weird but I think I might be in a relationship with a homophobic, commitment-phobic lesbian."

"Okay, back up. You're going to have to explain this one to me. Maybe start with the homophobic part."

"It's like she genuinely loves women and being a lesbian. But because of her family, I think she also doesn't like it?"

Sabs shrugged. "I get that and unfortunately, I don't think it's unusual. We're lucky, Jannie, *seriously* lucky to have the family we do. Even with years of the Army ramming *being gay is wrong* down my throat, I still never felt like I was doing the wrong thing by living my life, because I always had such a super supportive family. But there's still the undercurrent, and if you don't have support, it eats at you."

"What undercurrent?"

"The people who look at you when you're holding hands with your girlfriend. The ones who make disgusted sounds if you kiss your partner in public. Hate speech from people in the public eye or strangers on the 'net. All that shit permeates your soul even if you don't realize it. And Brooke, me and Bec, Mitch and Mike? We've had a lifetime of it, of being chipped away at and everything it does to wear you down and make you question yourself."

"Oh."

Her eyes went soft. "I'm not saying this to make you feel bad or excluded, Jannie but you've popped up in the middle of it without any of that shit behind you. You don't have that inbuilt defensiveness yet. You need to be kind to her, that's all I'm saying. As well as everything else we deal with, she doesn't have a family like ours to support her." Sabs grinned. "But she can."

"Yeah, she can." I spun my cappuccino around and around, needing to fiddle. "I guess I just imagined, stupidly, that the natural progression was to go on and introduce your new partner to your parents. And I was excited about that. But even though her dad knows she's gay, he doesn't accept it, so I'm basically just *a friend* which makes me feel kind of excluded and minimalized. And yes, I know it's fucking idiotic to feel like that because she shows me in so many other ways that she cares about me."

"You've had excellent same-sex attraction role models." Smugly, she buffed her nails against her chest. "And seen nothing but full family support the whole time for me, and now you." Sabs's voice dropped. "And now you're unfortunately realizing that not everyone has the same great experience."

"I know all that. But knowing that it's true for others, and suddenly being in the middle of someone else's unpleasant truth are two totally different things. When I decided I wanted to jump into this thing with her I imagined that would mean I'd get the whole experience. I was excited for that and it's not happening, and I kind of feel like it won't."

"Have you told her how you're feeling and why it's an important thing for you?"

"Sort of. I've brought it up a few times and been shut down. I just don't want to push her and have it all go fucked up. She explained why she doesn't want to be open with her dad, and then I kind of left it alone because she gets upset. But, is it going to screw things up for us if she's not able to work things out with her dad?" The thought of something external like that coming between us was so overwhelmingly upsetting that I had to stop talking and rein in my thoughts. Brooke and I were still a thing, an item or a couple or whatever. We were still us. This was just a small roadblock, and it was up to us to keep it from becoming a huge roadblock.

Sabs hmm'd. "Fear can be a huge thing, even with certainty that your family and friends will support you. Is she fearful for a reason, or just 'cause of the unknown?"

"It's real. She had a really hard time with it as a kid. As well as her dad not accepting her sexuality, her mom doesn't speak to her at all because of it. How can I ask her to set aside twenty plus years of family stuff for me?"

"Maybe you can't. Maybe you have to accept things as they are. But it's early days yet." She swallowed a mouthful of coffee. "Just step back for a minute. You know how hard it was for me and Bec with Don't Ask, Don't Tell, right? The Army wanted everything from us, but they didn't want to know who we really were. It was soul-crushing, Jannie. And that was just our employer. Just a job really."

"Mhmm."

"Can you imagine what it must feel like for Brooke, to feel that way but instead of an employer it's her *parents*. How fucking devastating it must be for her?"

"I know," I whispered. "She hurt herself when she was younger because of it, Sabs, like *hurt herself*…you know, physically."

Sabine's expression changed instantly to intense concern and her voice dropped to the low, protective tone I knew so well. "Self harm?"

"Yeah." It was all I could say around the lump in my throat and stinging tears.

"Fuck," Sabs breathed. "Poor Brooke. That's really shitty." Her hand came to my back, rubbing small comforting circles. "How is she now?"

"She says she's okay, and I think she is. But all that childhood stuff is obviously still in there, coloring how she's approaching *us*. I just don't think I have any right to ask her to do something she's not happy with, or that's only going to cause issues for her and put her relationship with her dad on shaky ground. Especially given *my* history and shit. I mean, I'm not exactly the poster girl for relationships. And we've only just started dating. What if I push her to do this, and it goes really badly, and then later down the track I figure out I really can't do this whole long-term thing? Right now, I feel like I can, but who really knows?"

Sabs let out a breath, her cheeks puffing up. "Valid points. This is a tough one." She smiled her lopsided smile. "But, you always did have to do shit the hard way and I guess discovering you're not as straight as you thought you were would be no different."

We sat quietly for a minute, working on our coffees and me picking at my blueberry muffin. Sabs eventually pulled the plate away with a, "Stop massacring that." She rescued a blueberry out of the rubble. "You know, when you said you were questioning your relationship, I honestly thought it was going to be you saying you were bailing for some random reason like Brooke blows her nose oddly. Not that she's cautious about being open with her family and doesn't want to U-Haul with you just yet."

"Believe me, the irony is not lost on me. My first *yes I can do this* response to a person, and the person I'm falling in love with is the one who's relationship-phobic." I gave Sabs a bare-bones outline of Brooke's dating history and some of our conversations about it, and the issues I thought were stemming from that.

Sabine laughed long and loud. "Oh this is *so* great. How's it feel, Jannie, now that the shoe's on the other foot, hmmm?"

"Oh fuck you. For the record, it feels like shit. And you know what? This is way different. I've always been upfront about my feelings and intentions."

"Upfront the way Brooke's been with you? She never said she doesn't want a long-term thing, Jannie. Just that she's cautious about it, and with good reason. She's being honest with you about her fears."

"Yeah, upfront. But then she goes and does something like making my lunch for me or staying over when we'd said we weren't going to do that just yet. Total mixed signals."

Sabs leaned forward. "Doesn't sound like mixed signals to me. Sounds to me like she wants a relationship with you and she's afraid of that. She tries something, and likes it but then remembers it's scary so she pulls away a little. Rinse and repeat."

"Sure, fine. That makes sense. But how much longer is this going to go on?"

"I can't answer that. Maybe until she knows you're solid…" My sister's gaze was penetrating. "And here's where *you* get the tough love—given your dating history, I don't think it's unreasonable that she's worried you're going to bail on her like previous girlfriends have."

There was nothing to say to that except agreement. "True. Fuck." I pushed muffin rubble into a pile. "You know what, she actually does blow her nose funny."

"Oh?"

"Mhmm. She also puts her milk in the main part of the fridge, not the door, because she thinks leaving it in the door makes it go sour faster because of the door opening and closing and it getting warm and cool again. She hums off tune *all* the time. After she eats ice cream, she coughs for like five minutes. When she sneezes, she does at least four or five in a row, and I once counted *seven* sneezes. And the way she pronounces assume like *azz-youm* is so fucking weird and I don't like it."

Sabs groaned. "Oh, for…fucking…shit. So those are the deal breakers you're going to hoard so you can throw them out as excuses in case you change your mind and run for the hills." She pinched my thigh. "Goddammit, Jana. I actually like Brooke. This is bullshit, grow up!"

I shoved her hand away. "Actually, no. And thanks for the vote of confidence. Those things? They bug me a little, and other things too, but they don't bug me enough to want to not be with her. They aren't deal breakers, nowhere near it." With anyone else, I'd likely have run a mile for that sort of thing. And had in the past. But with Brooke, they barely rated which was why I hadn't bothered mentioning them when she'd asked.

Sabs gaped, her mouth working open and then closed before she spluttered, "Who the fuck are you, and what have you done with my sister? My sister who once pretended to have food poisoning to leave a first date because she didn't like the way the guy used his knife and fork."

"Not a clue. Is this *it*, Sabs? Is this the forgetting about all the little things that you'd usually hate, the things you'd use as reasons to say no, but you still say yes because you're in love?"

She blinked. "Shit. Love?"

"I think so? It's definitely more than liking and there's lust and stuff there too. I hate not being with her, I think about her pretty much most of the day whenever my brain isn't doing something else, the sex is…mind bogglingly incredible. I've had great sex but this is next-next level stuff. She's hot, funny, sweet and caring, she's as weird as me and has all these adorable anxious quirks and stuff. She even likes my bizarre jumping around from point A to F to L and back to A blathering."

"Sounds like love to me."

"Yeah…maybe. But is that enough to overcome the other stuff? Especially if I'm ready to commit to something more, and she's not?"

Sabine stared at me, utterly silent. After a shrug, she said seriously, "That's something only you can figure out, Jannie. And I really hope you do soon."

So did I.

* * *

Unfortunately the next night turned into a last-minute-having-to-work-from-home evening because of an inconsiderate attorney who'd been screwing around with an annulment asset-division proposal I'd been asking for all week. Given we had a meeting the following day,

I had no choice but to suck it up and take work home after the draft arrived late that afternoon.

Brooke, bless her, showed no hint of annoyance at having to cancel our evening's plans. And they'd been fabulous plans. We'd decided that we'd go straight from work for a sunset walk along the Potomac, spend some time watching the night sky and boats cruising the river and then find somewhere for a nice quiet dinner before coming back to my place.

Instead, Brooke had ducked out to pick up dinner while I sat with papers spread over my kitchen table and my laptop while I wondered if my opposing counsel was completely out of her mind and had actually attended law school, or even read the pre-nup. Brooke ate her dinner at the coffee table and I distractedly picked at some very good Chinese takeout with one hand and picked apart the proposal with the other. Romantic. At least my apartment was open plan so I could see her and have a conversation, albeit a disjointed and distracted one.

"For fuck's sake," I mumbled to myself. "You must think I'm a real fucking idiot, Mary Elvins, if you think I'm going to agree to this bullshit. Nope, nope, hell nope," I said, drawing a line diagonally through a paragraph and making a note about how I wanted the clause updated.

"What was that?" Brooke asked from the kitchen where she was putting leftovers in the fridge.

"Nothing, babe. Just me throttling someone in my head."

I didn't realize she'd moved until I felt the heat of her behind me. She kissed my neck, slipped a hand through the neck of my baggy tee and gently cupped my breast. "God you're hot when you're pissed off like this."

I turned the document facedown and leaned my head back to look up at her. "Then I must be the sexiest thing you've seen, because I am *mightily* pissed off."

"That you are. Sexiest thing, that is," she said against my skin, her thumb stroking my nipple, which hardened under her knowing touch. "Why don't you have an office at home?"

She pinched my nipple and I inhaled sharply at the sensation. "Because I like being out here where I have a nice view, am right near the kitchen, and can stick my feet up on the other chairs. Plus if I had an office here, I'd be tempted to bring work home more often."

"Mm, makes sense." Gentle teeth on my neck accompanied a pleasing pinch of my other nipple.

I stifled a groan. "Brooke, I can't right now. Sorry, I really have to get this done." Even as I said it, I sighed inwardly, waiting for the irritation and passive aggression or even pushiness that would accompany my *no*. I was already preparing my conciliatory speech, the one I'd always used when declining sex, and wondering what sweetener or compensation I'd have to offer to placate her.

Mix and match a genuine excuse with a reward as needed.

I'm: too busy/too tired/crampy/plain not in the mood now, but if you can wait a bit I'll reward you with: a striptease/role play or dress up/any fantasy you want/a whole lot of really good oral sex.

But the expected response never eventuated. Instead she carefully withdrew her hand, kissed my temple and took a step back. "Oh, sorry to distract you. Can I make you some tea? Water? Do you want some dessert now or later?"

I turned around on the chair. "You're not mad?"

"About what?"

"That I don't want to go to bed with you. Actually that's wrong, I do want to go to bed with you but I've got so much to do and I don't think billing a client for a *sexy recreation break* will endear me to the Bar Association. Nor will fucking this up because I'm not focused."

Brooke's eyebrows scrunched together, her expression utterly perplexed. "Of course I'm not mad." The brows crinkled even more. "Really? You thought…I'm not, we…Jana, there's no obligation here. You never need to give me a reason for not wanting sex."

"Are you sure?"

"Of course I'm sure. If you suddenly decided you don't want to have sex for the rest of the time we're together, then that's your prerogative and okay too. I mean, personally devastating, but okay."

"Well that's never going to happen. I enjoy you far too much."

"Phewww…" She slumped, shoulders sagging. "I know I just acted cavalier just then, but I'd probably have curled into a ball and cried for days. I enjoy you very much too."

"I'm glad we're in agreement. And thank you," I added quietly.

"No problem. But just so you know, I'm going to masturbate right now to the image of my sexy, pissed-off attorney girlfriend."

I threw a pen at her and missed by a mile.

Brooke grinned and wandered over to retrieve it from up the hallway. "Kidding. What I am going to do is get you whatever you need to help you work, then I'm going to sit on the couch and read and sneak peeks at you being hot and angry." She kissed the edge of my mouth. "So what'll it be?"

"Tea please."

She saluted. "Coming right up."

I turned the proposal over again, spinning the pen in my fingers. But I couldn't concentrate. Was this the sort of amazing, happy-making stuff that would balance the not-so-great stuff? Had I finally made it to real relationship territory? Was this how it felt to be with someone where I could just be me, and enjoy her being her, and be comfortable with being honest and knowing she understood?

I twisted around on my chair again, watching her collecting my favorite tea mug and fussing around my kitchen like she'd lived in my apartment for years. "Brooke?"

"Yeah?" she said, not turning around.

The words fell out before I could police them. "I think my *could fall in love with you* is turning to I might be falling in love with you."

She went utterly still. "Oh." Slowly she spun to face me, the canister of teabags gripped tightly in both hands. "You can't say that now."

Fuck. Too soon. Waaaaay too soon. So stupid, Jana. But she didn't seem annoyed or upset, just a bit like a deer in the headlights. "Why not?" I asked tentatively, trying to ignore the anxiety that'd made me feel suddenly queasy.

"Because you're working and we can't talk about it. And you look so adorable right now that I kind of want to drag you off to bed." It came out almost casually, as if her reasoning were the most obvious thing in the world.

The anxiety fell away again, replaced by a swell of relief and predictable excitement. "Oh. Well all right then."

"You could take it back." It was said teasingly, without accusation or fear. "Wait until another time when you're not working."

"I can't."

She grinned. "Sure you can."

"No I can't, because I mean it."

The kettle clicked loudly. She didn't say anything, just poured water into my mug and added milk. Brooke kissed me lightly. "Different driving speeds," she reminded me. Then she took a long slow breath. "But I think…I might be getting pretty close to where you are. Maybe just pump the brakes a few times and let me catch up?"

It was almost ten thirty by the time I finished. I'd even managed to make my responses to Mary Elvins eighty percent polite and professional. Score a point for me, though I might lower the polite and professional down somewhat when I saw her face-to-face.

I stood, stretching my arms above my head. Oh God, bliss. Was there anything better than stretching? I smiled as a decidedly naughty thought popped into my head. Actually, I could think of a few things.

A quick glance into my living room confirmed the object of my thoughts was still reading on the couch. Every so often, I'd glanced over at her for no other reason than the simple pleasure of looking at her. Sometimes she'd noticed and raised her head to meet my gaze before smiling and returning to her book.

Brooke's smile started tentatively, then grew as I approached her. "This looks awfully like you being done working for the night."

"It does, doesn't it." I reached back to pull the tie from my ponytail, fluffing my hair out and massaging my scalp to release the tension from hours of being hunched over at the table. "Whatcha been reading?"

She closed the leather case and set the Kindle aside. "Re-reading a lesrom."

It took me a few moments to translate the portmanteau, and I added *lesrom is lesbian romance* to my fast-growing WLW—women loving women—dictionary. "You're reading a romance novel?"

"Yep. My favorite kind."

I raised an eyebrow. "Any sexy bits?"

"Mhmmmm. It's given me plenty of ideas on top of all the ones I've already been having about you tonight." Brooke dropped her feet from the coffee table.

"I see. Why do you like romances so much? You've always struck me as more like the fantasy or nonfiction type." I'd read the odd romance novel myself but reading just didn't form much of my leisure time.

"I like all books." She tilted her head back until it rested against the couch. "But everything in romance always feels so much better and more fantastical than real life. And it always works out in the end, people always have their happily ever afters." Now her smile was slow, contented. "It makes me feel all squishy inside."

"Fantastical, hmm. Yeah that sounds right with everyone's perfect body and face and hair and job."

Brooke snorted out a laugh. "Yeah. But I happen to think your body and face and hair and job is pretty perfect."

"Very good answer." I leaned down and kissed her. "I kind of think our little piece of reality is pretty nice at the moment."

"I kind of think it is too, and I feel like it's only going to get better." Carefully she placed her feet outside mine with her legs slightly parted. "And our sexy bits are way better than anything in fiction."

"I think I'd have to agree with you." I knelt between her legs, pushing her knees even farther apart. "So it only makes you feel *squishy*?" I asked innocently, trailing my index finger up the inside of her thigh.

"Among other things…" Brooke lightly cradled my face. "Other things I've been feeling all night whenever I looked at you."

"Mmm." I carefully unfastened her jeans. "Lift your butt."

She braced a hand on my shoulder and raised up an inch so I could slide her jeans off. She wasn't lying about her *other feelings*. The crotch of her panties showed evidence of her enjoyment of whatever she'd been reading. I couldn't help myself. I leaned in, burying my face between her thighs and inhaling her. "I've never been like this before." I kissed the junction at the top of her thigh. "I love the way you smell. I'm like a fucking addict."

"Just the way I smell?" she asked coyly, the hand now massaging my shoulder.

I drew her underwear aside, and after indulging myself further in her intoxicating scent, slowly ran my tongue through her heat. The hand on my shoulder tightened until her fingertips dug in as I swirled my tongue around her clit. I sucked lightly, the now-familiar excitement tightening my gut and making my own clit tingle. "Not just the way you smell. Everything about you. The way you touch me, the sounds you make. Your taste."

Brooke let out a long, low groan when I sucked her again and suddenly all I wanted was her naked on top of me. My fingers deep inside her. Her mouth on me. Abruptly, I stood and my voice was rough with lust. "Bedroom, now, please so I can thank you for tonight." At her blank expression, I elaborated, "For being so chill about it, for not pushing, for being generally amazing."

"Jana, you really don't need to do that. I don't expect it."

"I know. And that's why I want to. Well, part of the reason why…"

CHAPTER TWENTY-EIGHT

It took until almost midnight for me to thoroughly express my appreciation to Brooke for being such a wonderful, sweet and understanding girlfriend. In the morning, she left at the same time as me, but not to go to work. She'd declared she was taking a mental health day, citing both wanting to put the final touches on the commission for Sabs and Bec, and that she was so drained after a drawn-out argument with both a builder and her father yesterday that she couldn't stomach going in to the office. I'd been sent off with the lunch she'd made, a kiss, and an almost shy promise that she'd miss me.

Mary Elvins was appropriately contrite at both the lateness of her document and the shit she'd tried to pull, and I managed to keep my polite and professional above the eighty percent. A winning morning all around. I busted my butt for the rest of the day, managing to keep my head in the game, except at lunch when I saw the adorable note wedged in beside a sandwich bag and a container of dip, carrot and celery sticks.

I'll be thinking about you every minute. Hope you're having a good day. See you after work xo

"Oh, Brooke," I murmured. Pretty soon my *I'm falling in love with you* was going to tumble into *I'm hopelessly in love with you*. The thought was both thrilling and terrifying. She said she was close, but what if she changed her mind? What if something set her on another course? What if she never caught up to me? Could I keep going as we were, just hanging out, enjoying spending time with her and sleeping together? I mused over the question every free moment and couldn't find a firm answer, though my gut said no—I couldn't keep going, not feeling the way I did about her, if she never found the courage to be with me fully.

When I was done for the day, I drove directly to her place. Navigating around the side, I was greeted by the grind and clang of her working in the shed. The sound triggered a strange sensation almost like a reverse déjà vu—instead of having done this before, it was something I would be doing over and over in the future. I hung back for a minute, simply enjoying the sight of her, the easy confidence with which she worked until my need to be near her overwhelmed my enjoyment of watching her.

The moment I appeared in the open shed door, Brooke shut off her power tool and held it away at arm's length. When it'd stopped whirring enough for her to be heard, she greeted me with an enthusiastic, "Hello, gorgeous."

"Hello yourself." I stepped carefully around assorted metal and workshop things to kiss her, careful not to get too close to the tool. "This is looking really good." She'd been working on the Amazonian sculpture and had added more steel, shaped the curves of thighs and breasts.

Brooke set down her power tool, and pulled off her protective goggles and earmuffs. "Thanks. I finished that piece for Sabine and Rebecca, and my brain went straight back to this one. Did you want to see your commission? It's in the house ready to be packed up."

"Sure. When we go in." I gestured to the freestanding sculpture. "What are you planning for this one? Someone would pay ten grand easy for a sculpture like this."

Brooke studied her project, eyebrows drawn together. Her mouth was lifted in a barely perceptible smile. "Probably, yeah. But I can't sell this one. She's too special."

"What are you going to do with it then?"

"Not sure. Might rustproof her and put her out on the front lawn." She flashed a wicked grin. "Cause a neighborhood scandal with the nudity. Or move her inside. I really don't know."

I touched a section of smooth metal. "It just seems wasteful, almost like the whole world should see her. But I'm not an artist person, so you know, opinions and grain of salt and all that."

Brooke caught my wrist, pulling gently until I faced her. "You dope. Remember how I said I *tripped* over the inspiration for this piece? *You're* my inspiration, Jana. I told you, I've wanted you from the instant I saw you. After I'd bumped into you, as the elevator doors were closing, I saw you standing there with a hand on your hip and your chin up and that sexy as hell take no bullshit expression." Brooke fanned herself. "Holy shit, I nearly melted right there. I'll never get rid of this work, I love her too much."

"Oh. It's me?" I squinted, trying to see myself in the curved lines, full breasts and soft shaping of the figure.

"Inspired by you, yes. I've had a lot of inspiration since we met…"

"Oh, well in that case I need to revise my estimate upward by about a hundred grand." I pulled off her leather work gloves and set them down. "I have an overwhelming urge to kiss you right now."

"I think you should listen to that urge."

"Well, I think we've already established that when it comes to you, I've given up trying to control myself." I wrapped an arm around her waist to pull her closer, but she resisted. "What?" I asked.

She smiled self-consciously. "I'm sweaty and dirty, and you're wearing very nice clothes."

"I don't care about any of those things. I like you every way including sweaty and dirty. Plus, you may have heard of this thing called a dry cleaner?"

She laughed and acquiesced, but when I kissed her, she still carefully kept everything except her mouth and hands away from me. The heat of her mouth was enough to scorch me but I wanted more. I unbuttoned her coveralls to the waist, noted with pleasure that all she had on was a crop top, then slipped my hands inside to clutch her waist. I pressed myself against her. "Your argument about cleanliness is now moot."

Her response was a muffled sound of agreement.

I trailed my fingers down until I encountered the waistband of underwear, and nothing else. I brushed my lips against hers, lingered close. "Ms. Donnelly, are you practically naked under these coveralls?"

"It gets hot in here," she mumbled.

"Well now I feel overdressed." Very gently, I bit her lower lip.

Brooke groaned softly. "Not for long…" She knelt and reached under my skirt to brush her fingertips up my thighs before she carefully pulled my panties down, slipped them off one heel-clad foot at a time and placed them in her pocket. She caressed my calf, palm gliding over my skin, gently kneading the muscle as the other hand pushed my skirt up. Her lips joined in to place open-mouthed kisses on one thigh then the other as she kept up her massage of my calves. "Mmm, I love your legs," she said against my thigh. "Heels are a crime against comfort, but the way you wear them is so fucking hot."

Her careful attention had made my libido sit up and take notice, and it was all I could do to answer. "Likewise."

She stood, gripped my hips and pressed into me for a bruising kiss. As our tongues danced, Brooke maneuvered us around the sculpture, scrap metal and all the neatly ordered piles. She paused, her eyes wild as they swept the space, then dragged me over to a bench in the corner and pressed me back against it. She didn't unzip my skirt, simply pushed it up further and helped me up onto the waist-high bench. Despite my earlier reassurance and demonstration that I didn't care about her being work-dirty, she still stepped back and shucked her arms out of the coveralls, shoving the garment down so it hung at her waist.

Then she went incredibly still, staring at me with lust and awe. Her expression quickly turned to one of scrutiny so intense I almost felt as though she'd already stripped me naked and spread me open.

I gripped the edge of the table. "What?"

"You. I, uh…give me a minute?" She reached around me for a draft pad and pencil. After flipping quickly through the pages, she got straight to work, her hand flying over the page. Without stilling her frantic sketching, she explained, "You look so fucking hot, I want to paint this."

I stayed as still as I could, watching her intensity, the swift and skillful movement of hand over paper. Her concentration was so sexy that instead of cooling from the interruption, my desire heated to boiling point.

Brooke glanced up for a second. "I swear you've turned into my muse." She dropped the pad and pencil onto the table behind me and stepped between my thighs again. "Sorry, where were we?"

I hooked a finger in the crop top, pulled her closer and bent my head until our lips were a breath away. "I think somewhere about here?"

Brooke groaned before taking my mouth in a deep, lingering kiss. Her hands roamed to delicious places, exploring and teasing until I was almost melting with desperation. When she moved to suck the skin along my collarbone, I licked the salty skin of her neck. "I'm pretty sure I had a fantasy about this."

"What? Getting fucked in a hot, dirty shed by an equally dirty woman?" Her hand made a quick sweep up the inside of my thigh, heading straight for my arousal.

"Yes. And you forgot the second hot." I gasped when her fingers slipped over my clit, the touch featherlight and maddeningly teasing.

"I did? What do you mean?" She repeated the movement, but slower and firmer this time.

"Hot dirty shed, hot dirty woman. And the fantasy was *you*, fucking me just like this. Do that harder please."

"Do what?" she asked, all innocence.

"You know what." I spread my legs wider, trying to draw her in.

But she ignored my plea and kept up her sweet torture. Despite the growing pressure and undeniable arousal, I wasn't in the mood for light and easy. I wanted her to take me rough and hard. I barely suppressed a frustrated groan. "I swear, I'm going to jump down off this bench, go inside and finish this myself in a minute."

"I doubt it. Now be quiet," she murmured against my neck.

"Make me be quiet," I said, fully intending for her to kiss me to shut me up. Which she did. Her tongue played over mine, teeth grazing my lower lip as her fingers maintained their teasing between my legs until I was squirming. Okay, maybe the light touch was also effective.

By the time Brooke let me come up for air, I'd changed my mind. "Actually scratch that." I sucked her lower lip. "Make me scream…"

Brooke curled an arm around my waist, holding me in place and with a knowing smirk, entered me so slowly that I nearly went into orbit. She thrust gently, turning her fingers to stroke my favorite spot. "Tell me about this fantasy you had."

"Pretty much this," I managed to say around a sharp intake of breath. "Except you licked me until I came in your mouth."

"Oh. I think I like the sound of that," she said, her voice thick with lust.

"Me too."

With a devilish grin, Brooke backed up, bent her head and put her mouth on me. She took me skillfully, and it was barely two minutes before I spiraled into release with one hand in her hair and the other gripping the table so tightly I thought I might leave dents in the wood. When I could finally breathe again, I mumbled, "God you know how to press my buttons."

Brooke laughed as she straightened up again. "Just the one that matters." She let out a long contented sigh, kissing my neck softly. "I love fucking you. You're so controlling and bossy, demanding that I do this and that and touch you here and with this exact amount of pressure and at this precise speed and rhythm, and it's *so* goddamned hot. Then all of a sudden it's like you just surrender and you make this little whimper, like a desperate please and yes that feels so good all in one. And you turn from a lioness into a kitten."

"A kitten?" I arched an eyebrow, trying my best harsh school mistress face on her. It was less than effective, probably because my whole body felt boneless.

"Mhmm." Carefully, she helped me from the worktable and pulled my skirt down. But she didn't return my underwear.

I took her hand, and led her out of the shed. "Let's go inside so I can *surrender* some more. And if you're lucky, I'll show you just how kittenish I can be."

After we'd taken a long, hot shower together—made longer by our slow, sensual lovemaking—Brooke and I cooked dinner, then curled up on the couch. She leaned into me, an arm wrapped around my waist while the other hand worked the remote. Once she'd settled on a *Grey's Anatomy* rerun, she pulled me even closer.

She talked quietly during the show the way she always did, but she seemed distant, as if her mind were elsewhere. I stroked her arm. "You okay?"

"Oh. Yeah, just thinking about stuff." In the next breath she elaborated, "Today was pretty much perfect. Waking up with you this morning, then me staying home to work on those pieces all day, doing something I love and that I wanted to do. No work stress or anything. Then you being here after work and we've had the hottest *missed you all day* sex. I mean, it sucked not seeing you for sneaky coffee breaks during the day, but I knew I'd have you after work." Brooke shrugged. "It was amazing, and I guess it's kind of bumming me out because I know tomorrow I have to go back into the office and have a miserable workday."

"True, and that part of the day will be shit. But I'll be beside you all night in bed, wake up with you, then we'll drive in and see each other again for coffee before work and during the day. When all the work stuff is done, we'll leave together and do pretty much what we're doing now." I reached out and brushed her hair behind an ear. "Maybe you could talk to your dad about changing your work hours so you can focus more on your art?" Her professional relationship with her father seemed a safer topic than their personal one but I still held my breath.

Brooke snorted derisively. "No. I wouldn't waste my time."

"Even if it's something that'd make you happy? Not to mention your insane talent. Why wouldn't he come on board with something like that?"

"Because he just *won't*, Jana. He doesn't get it, just like he doesn't get the *other thing*, and thinking about having to talk to him about how much I despise my job makes me feel sick. How am I supposed to tell my dad that I don't like working with him, working *for* him." Though her posture was relaxed, the clipped tone made it clear she wasn't. "Can we please drop this? I'm not in the mood to talk about it and I really don't want to have an argument."

"Sure, of course." I brought her hand to my mouth and kissed her palm. "I'm sorry, really I am. I know I have no right to push you about this. It's just that I'm a pushy bitch."

She curled her fingers to lightly cup my face. "Yeah, you are. But I like having such a badass on my side. I like knowing that you care about me enough to want me to be happy, but it's utterly pointless to try to make him see my point of view with both work and personal life."

Her personal life was a whole other issue that I couldn't even begin to unpack. But as for her job, it was just a job. I had no idea what held her to her father's side this way, why she was so afraid of moving away from his company when she could start her own firm, work for another company, or even do something else entirely. The only explanation I could come up with was based loosely on watching my sister join the military when I knew she didn't want to.

Expectation.

No matter which way I turned the puzzle to examine it, I still couldn't understand how Brooke could give up so much of herself for a father who didn't even accept her. And I wondered if I'd ever know. Or if anything would ever change.

CHAPTER TWENTY-NINE

As well as being a Monday, which meant it was duty-bound to be crap, I'd been chewed out by a client, denigrated by a judge *and* lost an earring on my walk back from the courthouse. The day officially sucked. Plus Brooke had something urgent to take care of at work and told me she'd just meet me at my place when she was done, so I didn't even have the comfort of her presence on the drive home.

But when I opened my door to her, greeted her with a long hug and a soft kiss, my irritation melted away. She held on to me, arms hooked around my shoulders and her face against my neck. I felt her quiet inhalation of breath before she spoke. "Sorry I missed you this afternoon. Today has been crazy."

"Same. But I feel better now you're here." We disengaged, and she followed me to the kitchen. "I was talking to my parents today, and Dad confirmed he'll pick us up from the airport on Friday. Oh, and a heads-up, I'm sure at some stage he will want to show off his herd of cows and his pride and joy, The Bull, so it might not be a bad idea to pack some clothes and shoes to wander around the fields. I already have the hotel booked, so another heads-up—Mom's going to get all whiny about the fact we're not staying there, specifically in my childhood bedroom. Do you want a drink?"

"Jana, wait."

"No?"

"No, I do want a drink. I, uh—"

I paused, turned around and noted right away her misery. Her hands twisted together nervously and for a few terrifying moments I thought she was about to tell me she wanted to break up. I had to lean against the table to steady myself. "What's up?"

What she said was awful, but thankfully not *that* awful. "I'm not going to be able to make the wedding. I am so sorry."

My already slightly panicked stomach lurched. "Oh. Why?"

She pushed a hand through her hair, the gesture rushed and jerky. "My father has called an urgent *meeting* this Saturday."

"A meeting. On a Saturday..." A tiny, hateful part of me wondered if she was bailing, running away because I'd been too forward by declaring I was falling in love with her. I dismissed the idea right away, and mentally chastised myself for being such an untrusting bitch.

She dropped her hand, which clenched to a fist, and gestured angrily. "Yes, on a fucking Saturday. To discuss the future of Donnelly and Donnelly, which translates to let's start making a timeline for me to take over."

"Oh. Did you tell him you had something planned?" *With your girlfriend*, I added in my head, though even as I thought it, I was certain it wouldn't have had any bearing on her father's decision. Actually, him knowing that probably would have just made things worse.

She paced across the living room, twisting her fingers together. "Of course I damned well did! And I tried to get him to reschedule it, but he's adamant it can't be during the week because he doesn't want the staff to know about it." She was tearful. "And it *has* to be this weekend. He kept going on and on about getting the ball rolling and having meetings with lawyers scheduled for next week."

"Oh," I said again. Apparently my intellect had disappeared. I blurted the first thing that came to mind. "Well we all know how inflexible lawyers are with their schedules." Shut up, Jana. Being passive-aggressive isn't going to help.

But either she didn't catch my tone or chose to ignore it. "I'm really sorry, but I have to go to this meeting, and I need to prep for it on Friday. I don't have a choice." Her jaw was rigid, the words ground out as though it hurt her to say them. "I know bailing days before the party and wedding is such a shitty thing to do. I tried to get out of it, I really did. I'm so sorry."

I was *this close* to telling her that no she didn't have to go to the meeting. That she didn't have to come running every time her father called, especially for something she was so against. And if she didn't want to take over her father's company, then she didn't have to do that either. But it wasn't for me to say what we both already knew. And there was even less point in me rehashing something we'd already had small disagreements about.

I almost suggested that maybe she could just fly in on Friday after work and doing her preparation stuff to attend the party, meet my family and then fly back to D.C. early Saturday for the meeting. But not only was it unfair and pointless to ask her to screw around so much, the idea of having her be there and then leave again before the main event almost felt worse than her not coming at all. Brooke paused a few feet away, looking so completely devastated that I set aside some of my upset.

I forced cheer into my voice. "Well, yeah, it sucks but if that's what has to happen then it's what has to happen." Smiling, I added, "Pity, you won't get to see me do my MC Hammer dance."

She didn't take my bait. Instead, her jaw muscles bunched. "I was looking forward to it so much, and meeting your parents and everything."

I drew my hands up and down her biceps, hoping my touch might soothe her when words clearly weren't. "I know, sweetheart but there'll be another time, and probably not before long. Trust me, Mom won't be able to help herself if she doesn't meet you soon and will probably come here specifically."

"Are you sure?"

"Positive."

"Mm, okay then." She rubbed her hands over her face. "I'll call Sabine and Rebecca and tell them I can't make it."

"It's fine, I can do it." I rummaged in the fridge for the bottle of sauvignon.

Her shoulders dropped. "No, Jana. I should be the one to tell them. I want to explain and apologize myself."

"Sure, whatever you want to do is fine with me."

"Are you mad?"

"No, I'm not mad." And I wasn't, not if I used the traditional definition of mad. "Can you grab some wineglasses please?"

Her response was slightly muffled as she turned her back on me to reach into the cabinet. "You seem like it."

"Brooke, I'm not mad."

"Well you're *something*."

Even though I knew it would hurt her, I told her the truth. But not before I'd poured us each a glass of wine and taken a large mouthful to help my dry mouth. "Okay, what I am is really upset."

"I get that, and I own it," she said evenly. Then the evenness of her tone faded for a tremulous, unhappy one. "Like I said, I really want to go."

"No, Brooke. It's not about you not being able to make the wedding or the party even though yeah, that fucking sucks. I know you want to come. I'm upset because your dad is running your life when he doesn't even *accept* your life. You're keeping a major part of yourself hidden from him and that's not fair of him to make you do that. You're not living authentically."

"He's not making me do anything," she said, voice icy calm. "I keep this from him because I don't want to deal with his disappointment and his anger and everything that's going to follow on from that. Don't tell me you never did things just to please your parents, or to make things more comfortable for them?"

"No, because they would never ask that of us," I said immediately. "I mean, Sabine's just Sabine and she joined the Army because of her own sense of duty to the family and to her it was the right thing. But my family loves unconditionally, and not just people who they share genetic material with."

"Well, I'm sorry but *my* family isn't accepting of things like this the way yours is. It must be *so* nice to have that but I don't, Jana, and there's nothing I can do about it and having you holding it up as a beacon of inclusivity honestly just makes me feel like shit."

My snap came out before I could rein my tongue in. "Well I'm sorry my family's the poster child for love and inclusivity." I rubbed my eyes, well aware I'd gone too far. "Fuck, I'm sorry I said that, it was mean and hurtful and so unnecessary. I'm sorry I'm being a bitch. It's just…this isn't quite how I imagined things going with us, and even if you set aside the whole *let's hide Jana* thing, it's really hard for me to see you struggling with this."

"How do you see things going with us?" she asked hoarsely.

The response came out without thought. "A long way. I see a relationship with you, but I want all of it. Like the part where we spend some holidays with my family, and some with yours even if we're sitting there uncomfortable as heck listening to childhood stories, eating food we hate and family is bickering. I want you to tell your dad I'm your girlfriend." I tightened my hold on the wineglass, willing my hands not to shake. "You want me to change everything about myself, commit to this thing that's new and scary, but you won't even introduce me to your family?"

"I've told you multiple times why it's not really an option to tell him," she said, the calmness in her voice forced and tight at the edges. "And I haven't asked you to change a thing. You came to me."

"Yes we have discussed it, and yes I did come to you. But I didn't realize the full picture then. All I'm saying is, what happens later, Brooke, if this thing goes long term? Am I going to be something that you keep hidden away at Thanksgiving or birthdays? Will you have to go running to your father every time he wants you to do something, even if it interferes with our plans? Will we have to hide my stuff in *our* house and send me away every time your dad comes around?"

"I don't know how we'll handle things like that in the future because I've never considered it before with any other woman."

The whole argument was like a revolving door with no exit. "Being…diminished like this makes me feel really shitty."

"Diminished? Are you fucking serious? I'm literally considering putting years of hurt and fucking mental bullshit about my past relationships aside to be with you. All I'm asking is for some goddamned time, which I don't think is unreasonable. I can't do everything at once and frankly, I don't have the mental stamina to deal with my dad right now."

"Okay, I'm hearing that, I accept it. I want to move forward with you when you're ready. But your dad thing is a real issue for me. Later when *regular* couples would take the next step and do the introduction thing…that's not going to happen and maybe it never will." I let out a breath. "I guess I would have liked to have known this before, well, all of this."

She went utterly still. "Would it have changed your decision about moving forward with us?"

Immediately I realized my mistake, my poor wording. "No! Fuck, no. Sorry, I meant I could have prepared for this scenario a little better, had more time to get used to taking myself out of the closet and then putting myself half back in. Making it easier for you. You're asking me to hover in limbo here and I don't know how to do that."

"I guess I didn't think it would bother you, or honestly that we'd end up here so soon, staring down the barrel of an actual committed, possible long-term relationship." She paused, nervously licked her lower lip. "You said it yourself, that sort of thing isn't you, and your self-confessed reputation for casual made me think it *wouldn't* be an issue." Ouch. But not entirely unfair. She raised both hands helplessly. "And I'm not asking you for a goddamned thing except a little, I don't know…trust? Faith? Effort? Patience? What's the damned hurry?"

"Faith? Trust? Jesus, Brooke, this is my first relationship with a woman. Hell, possibly my first real relationship ever. If that's not having faith in you then what the fuck is?" I sucked in a quick breath. "Honestly…you're confusing me. Sometimes you seem like you're totally into being with me, like the excitement about meeting my parents just as a quick example. To me, that's a couple's thing. But then I feel like the next minute you've panicked and changed your mind again. And I don't know if it's because of your dad or your past relationships stuff, or all of it. Or…if the issue is actually me."

"I don't know what it is," she whispered. "But I do know it's not you."

I exhaled a relieved breath. "Good, okay then. Look, I'm just being honest and open about my feelings, which I'm sure you've already gathered is kind of my thing. And I feel like now that I'm not saying what you like to hear, saying things that make you uncomfortable, you don't want to hear it."

"Jana, it's not that I don't want to hear it, but it's that what you're saying is utterly pointless. The thing with my dad is flogging a dead horse, a dead and practically decomposed horse." She took a few steps backward, keeping the kitchen counter between us, swiping her hand under both eyes. "Do you think I haven't been through this over and over in my head millions of times for the last, I don't know…twenty or more years and even more so since we got together? Do you think I'm just being a little bit stubborn for the hell of it? That I'm playing around because I want to toy with you? Believe me, I'm not. My family isn't like yours, Jana. And no matter where you and I end up, there is absolutely nothing I can do about that." By the time she'd finished, her color was high and despite her tears, her voice remained steely.

So I made a decision then, something that would affect how we progressed. Or didn't. "Okay," I said quietly, raising both hands. "You know what, I'm not going push you any more about this. Because clearly it's not something you're willing to change, not even for me. That's not to say I agree, or I'm happy about you being constantly upset and making yourself sick about your job and your relationship with your dad. It's your life. But at some point, it could be *our* life and I just want you to remember that."

The anger faded, and her voice went eerily flat. "Okay, thank you." She kept backing away from me, in the direction of the front door. "I might go home. I don't think it's a good idea to be sitting here with this hanging over our heads and both of us getting even more upset." She gathered her things and was in the entryway before I'd even moved from the kitchen.

"Brooke, wait a moment. Please don't go home. We'll drop it and forget about it, I promise."

"I can't just drop it, Jana. Don't you get it? This thing with my dad is *everywhere*, fucking up everything. Just like my exes are still in my head, fucking up everything. Please, I just can't do more of this right now." Now instead of flat, her voice had turned tight and tearful. She shrugged into her coat and slipped out the front door with a mumbled, "I'll call you, bye." The door closed behind her with a soft *snick*.

I stared at the closed door. Well. Goddammit. I let myself slump forward until my forehead rested against the cool wood. "Fuck. Fuckity fuck fucking. Shit."

Excellent coping mechanism you've got there, Jana. Maybe add a *boo hoo poor me* for good measure. I stayed there for a minute or so, pressed against the door, hoping answers would be transplanted into my head somehow. They weren't. Right, time to try another coping mechanism. Finish that bottle of wine and eat an unhealthy amount of chocolate.

I'd just opened my fridge when the doorbell rang. I so did not feel like talking to the building maintenance or security, or the woman a floor below who regularly received my mail by accident. I considered just ignoring it, until a second, longer ring came on the back of the first.

As I peered through the peephole, my irritation evaporated. Brooke stood crying in the hall, nervously turning her keys in her fingers. Relief and fear meshed as I pulled the door open and stepped back so she could come inside.

But she just stood there. "I wasn't sure you'd want to let me in again," she said, voice so quiet I thought I'd misheard.

"Of course I do." Instead of waiting for her I made the decision, gently taking her hand and leading her inside.

"Good. I wasn't sure after...what just happened." The words were cracked, and Brooke's mouth twisted like she was trying to regain control of her speech. "I was riding down in the elevator just now, and I kept thinking how upset I was that we'd just argued, and how much I wanted a hug. No big deal right? Like go see someone I know and get hugged. But it only took me two floors to realize that the hug I wanted was back upstairs. You're the comfort and the support and everything I need." She shrugged, her hands flopping helplessly to her sides. "I'm sorry. You're right about my dad, I'm letting him control my life when he doesn't support it, but I'm so fucking afraid of being honest with him about my personal life, and how much I hate my job that whenever I think about it I want to puke or cry. Or both. I just don't know what to do. I'm petrified."

I hugged her close, held her tightly against me. I didn't say anything, just held her and let my fingers drift slowly around her back. Brooke gripped the back of my sweatshirt, and her tears were wet against my neck. "I didn't mean to run out like that but you made me so fucking scared and I just didn't know what to do."

"Why I did I scare you, sweetheart?"

She sniffed, palmed her eyes. "Because I've never had anyone on my side like this. I've never had anyone loving me like this and it's terrifying because I don't want to lose it. I don't want to screw this up and all I can see are these things with my past relationships and my issues with my father pushing you away."

"Then I guess we're even. I'm scared too, by my appalling track record, extreme pickiness, bossiness, bitchiness and thousands of other dreadful traits that might drive you away." I took a chance. "We can deal with the relationship stuff as it comes. And yeah, this thing with your dad is a bit of an issue, but there's always going to be an issue for us to work through together, right? I mean, my family is pretty intense, especially for someone who doesn't like crowds. I think maybe we just need to accept that this is how things are now and figure out how we can work with it so we're both getting what we need."

"I think what I need is you. I mean, I need to sort this out before it gets…bad, but I really just need you."

"Likewise. Come to bed with me," I murmured.

She smiled shakily. "I'm totally wrecked, and to make things even better, I'm pretty sure I just got my period. I don't think—"

I took her hand, pulled her until she stepped forward. Slowly she met my eyes. I framed her face in my hands and kissed her softly. "No, come to bed and let's just lie there for while. I just want to hold you. I just want to be with you." I just wanted to love her.

CHAPTER THIRTY

Friday morning, the phone calls started at five thirty a.m. Inconvenient at the best of times, but even more so when Brooke and I were engaging in a little *won't see each other for two days* morning nookie. Sabine and Bec had flown to Ohio the night before, and my job was to bring the dresses with me on my lunchtime flight. When I told Brooke that the calls were probably about that or some other inane ceremony thing, she laughed. I growled and pulled her back down on top of me.

I managed to ignore seven calls up until half-past six. Then Sabine started calling my landline, and I caved and answered. Even after assurances that I'd packed all three dresses and I was fine with details, she kept calling me to remind me that Dad would meet me at the airport at two thirty, don't forget to pack shoes—no shit—and the party dress, and and and…

In the end, I sent her photos of me with my two suitcases, the clearly identifiable dress bags and my shoes, and a screenshot of the email from the airline confirming that I would be allocated space to hang all three ceremony dresses in the onboard closet. Then I texted Bec with a single *Help!* which did the trick. I received nothing more than a *Hope you and the dresses have a good flight* from Sabine as I was getting ready to board. Did she have a hidden cam following me and reporting my every move?

As I settled in my seat, I was acutely aware of the empty one beside me that should have held my girlfriend. Girlfriend. No matter how many times I thought it or said it, that word still sent a little thrill through me and I realized how quickly I'd become accustomed to it. Even with everything of the last few days, the slight uneasiness between us, my feelings for her hadn't changed.

We'd carefully avoided poking at still-raw wounds. Brooke had wrapped and boxed her sculpture and it rested in the overhead compartment, along with her card. All I could think was how I'd already written out a card and had left a space for her to write something too. I'd never done that before, never been in a relationship where I'd had the need, or want, to give a shared gift. I inhaled slowly, let it out even slower. There was no point in dwelling on the upset of being by myself. We hadn't broken up, just…had differing schedules, which would probably happen again. All couples had things like that.

The flight was quick, helped by a few glasses of wine and a book. Me, not working on a flight, a novel concept. The moment we started taxiing, I turned my phone back on and was assaulted by the expected barrage of texts, alerts and email notifications. Four texts from Sabine—who knew my schedule down to the minute—all with variations of "Hurry up, I'm so excited I might explode" as if I were capable of making the flight go faster. Two from Mom with basically the same vibe as Sabine. One from Bec, warning me that conditions in my parents' house had reached peak excitement, and I should prepare myself. Geez, Bec, I hadn't noticed.

There were also the expected work emails and missed calls from Sabs, Sabs, Brooke. Only one voice mail. Brooke.

"Hey, I'm just about to go into a client meeting and uh, I knew you'd be in the air but I'm lame and just wanted to hear your voice, even if it's only a recorded message." Laughter. *"So I guess this is pretty much a pointless message. Hope your flight was okay. Talk soon, bye."*

I listened to it one more time, then hit call back. It went right to her voice mail as I'd expected. "Hey, just landed and I know you're probably with your client so this is also pointless, but…I just wanted to say hi. And to tell you I read a book during the flight instead of working. Please be appropriately impressed. Um. I miss you. Give me a call when you're finished at work? Bye. Love you." Those last two words had come out without thought. As I ended the call, I wondered when and if I'd ever hear her say them back to me.

* * *

Once the party crowd had dispersed, I shirked cleanup duties to take Oma and Opa home. I was desperate for some quiet time, time away from having to pretend everything was fine and that I wasn't miserable without Brooke. I'd spoken to her for fifteen minutes or so before our ceremony rehearsal thing, we'd texted back and forth while I was getting ready for the party and I'd told her I'd try to call once everything was done. Truth be told, I didn't think I could face talking to her feeling as lonely as I did.

Sabine found me leaning my forearms against the porch railing, staring out into the night and slowly working on a bottle of red. She leaned in and gave me a one-armed hug. "When did you get back?"

"About twenty minutes ago. I was going to stay for coffee but Oma shoved me out the door and said I needed to go home and rest so I'd look my best tomorrow."

"Shit, I didn't even hear you drive in. Usually it sounds like a NASCAR rally."

"Ha-ha. Hard to go fast in your parents' fifteen-year-old car. Aaand...Brooke mentioned that my driving bothered her, scared her. She's worried I'm going to write myself off. So I'm trying to be a little more suburban housewife when I drive."

"Scares us too. I guess we owe her big time for finally making you listen to what we've been trying to get through your head since you got your license." Sabs laughed quietly, nudging me with her shoulder. "She's good for you, in more ways than one."

"She is," I agreed. "But I'm not sure I'm good for her," I added quietly.

"What do you mean?"

I let out a long breath. "We had a pretty big fight earlier this week. Who the fuck fights two weeks after agreeing to be in a relationship?"

"Only two weeks hey? Shit, I got snippy at Bec after two days because of how she stacked the dishwasher."

"Did you throw around insults and mean words designed to hurt each other?"

"Well...no. But we've had some pretty rough arguments since. It doesn't mean we love each other any less."

The last thing I felt like doing was selfishly digging in to the issues I was having with my girlfriend the night before my sister's not-wedding. "Mmm. Where is everyone?"

"The M 'n' Ms went back to the hotel. Mom's on the phone talking to Aunt Tracey about something for tomorrow and Bec is having a drink with Dad and talking about carrier pigeons in World War One." She grinned. "Did you know they used to parachute them in?"

I smiled into my glass of wine. "I did, which always seemed so stupid. Why parachute something that can fly?"

"Beats me." My sister held out her hand for my wineglass, took an appreciative swallow and passed it back to me. "Party went well. Mom's still over the moon that Barbara Hopeshaw noticed the new vase we gave her for her birthday."

"Always thinking of the important stuff." Sabs and I shared a laugh, and I topped up my glass. "How're you feeling? Nervous?"

"No," Sabine said seriously. "I've been waiting my whole life for tomorrow. Are you?"

"Me? Course not. All I have to do is stand around and look fabulous, pass you a ring, then drink and dance my ass off."

"True, and we both know those are things you excel at."

I saluted her with my wineglass. "We all have our talents."

She bumped me with her shoulder. "So…what's going on?"

I swallowed a mouthful of wine, shaking my head. "Nothing."

"Come on. You can pull that shit with everyone else but you don't fool me. Never have." Sabs slid her arm around my waist and pulled me close, resting her cheek against my hair.

"Just a little tired with work, that's all."

"Nuh-uh. Try again."

"Worried I'm going to trip walking up the aisle tomorrow."

She let me go. "You won't, and if you stumble at all, you've got Mitch to hold you up. So why don't you quit screwing around and tell me why you're upset with Brooke."

"I'm not upset with her," I said instantly.

"Yes you are."

"No, I'm just upset she can't make it."

Sabine said carefully, "Mmm, I'm sure she is too. She seemed it when she called me to tell me she couldn't attend after all."

"Yeah well, her dad called and she had to go running." Under my breath I muttered, "Of *course* it's her dad that's in the way."

"Hey, that's not fair."

"What? It's the truth."

"Grow up." It wasn't said unkindly, but there was a definite edge that told me I was going too far. "Sometimes that's just how things work out. No matter how hard you try you can't always make schedules line up, or something comes up last minute. And it sucks, but that's a relationship. And you can either sulk and bitch and whine and make her feel even worse about it. Or you suck it up and support her with something that's clearly hard for her."

"I *know* it's hard for her, I know she doesn't like it, and I know I'm being a whiny baby. But that doesn't change how I feel. I really wanted her to be here, Sabs, and for stupid selfish reasons which just makes me feel like an even bigger shithead."

"What selfish reasons?"

"So she could meet everyone, so I could show her off, and show everyone that I can be a grown up and in a relationship. And I'm upset because I'm being a bitch about the whole thing, like yeah her family is her family. But they give her nothing in the way of support and I cannot understand why she keeps throwing herself at this brick wall of bigotry."

"Because he's her dad," she said, as though that statement explained everything.

"Well yeah, but it's hurting her."

"Jannie, you know I'm *always* here to talk to about stuff, but this is the sort of thing you need to talk about with her."

"I tried."

Sabine's eyes narrowed. "Did you really? Or did you do that thing where you throw your opinions at someone then walk away?"

Ever so slowly, I extended a middle finger at her. "I'll have you know I stayed after throwing my opinion at her. She doesn't think she can be honest without him completely losing his shit, and I don't want to be a thing hidden away or made to leave our hypothetical shared house in the future whenever he comes around."

"A good old-fashioned impasse, eh?"

"You could say that." I covered my face with both hands. "Fuck. The irony really is hysterical. My job is to negotiate issues like this. But now it's my own life, I'm completely fucking stuck." I dropped my hands, looked up at her pleadingly. "I'm sorry to throw this at you like eighteen hours before you're getting not-married. I know you've got other shit on your plate right now."

Sabs shrugged. "Eh, it's what I'm here for." Her gaze grew intense. "Be honest with me. Is this because she's a woman? Are you having second thoughts about it?"

"No. I think it's because she might be *the* woman."

"Wow. You didn't even hesitate. Shit."

"I know. You must be rubbing off on me."

Sabine came out officially to me when she was twelve, half an hour before telling our parents. She didn't mince words or dance around it, just declared, "I'm gay, Jannie. I like girls," she'd added quickly, like she thought I wouldn't know exactly what gay meant. Not I think, but *I am*. Clear and succinct, typical Sabine. And that was it. She'd never seemed to display any self-doubt about any aspect of her life. I'm gay. I'm going to be a surgeon. I'm in love with my superior officer and it's a huge big secret deal but she's leaving the Army and we're going to be together. I'm marrying Bec.

Me on the other hand? Wishy-washy to the extreme. But not now. I knew one thing. I loved Brooke. But was love enough? Especially if it was one-sided? I drank a slow mouthful of pinot. "So I love her, but what about all the other stuff? I told her I loved her and basically got an 'okay, great, maybe I might love you one day too soon-ish.' I feel like I'm not important to her. Not important enough that she'd tell her dad about me. Not important enough for her to get over past dating shit."

Sabs blew out a breath. "I hear you, and I understand what you're saying, and I know it's valid. But you're also being a bit of a dick."

"Hey!"

She held up a hand. "Just listen. This has nothing to do with you, and you need to get over it and get over yourself. This is Brooke's battle and at the moment, you kind of seem like you're not even on her side. You're standing on the sideline yelling 'You're doing great! Let me know when you've slain the dragon and I can come reap the benefits.'"

"I am on her side," I rebutted.

"Okay then. Good. Show her." Sabs ran a hand through my hair, curled it into a loose bun at the back of my neck. "Now spit it all out. I know there's more."

"I hate the way you always know stuff," I grumbled.

Her grin was slow and smug. "Big sister intuition. Come on."

I took a few moments to sort my thoughts. Eventually, all I came out with was, "How do I know it's right, Sabs? That's she's The One and I can do it? All this uncertainty is just ramping up my paranoia that I'm not cut out for this. Especially when it feels like I'm waaaaay more invested than she is right now."

"You don't know. But you do it anyway. If there's even the *tiniest* feeling that she's the one for you, you jump in with everything you've got. You give her all the love you can and you let her do the same for you." She released my hair, let it tumble around my neck.

"But what if loving someone, wanting them isn't enough? What if she can't change? What if I can't change enough to be what she needs?"

"Bullshit. I don't believe that."

"Well yeah, you wouldn't, Sabine." I waved my arm toward the house. "The love of your life is in there getting ready to commit to you. You've got everything you ever wanted."

"That's a little unfair," she said softly. "You know it hasn't just fallen in our laps. We've worked and waited and compromised and sacrificed too. That's what you do when someone…when something means everything to you." She was right. Bec left her Army career to be with Sabine. They'd fought war and bureaucracy trying to keep them apart, Sabine finishing another deployment, her PTSD and Bec's guilt over having been the one who sent Sabine on the mission that almost killed her. And still they were together. Better. Stronger.

I groaned. "I'm sorrrrryy. God, I suck."

"Yep, sometimes you do," Sabine agreed, but she was grinning. "So, call her and talk to her, then get over yourself for a few days. Having you moping in all our photos is going to ruin the whole thing."

She stepped away from my arm punch as Bec called from the porch door, "Sabine?"

"Yep, we're here, baby."

Light footsteps came around the corner. "I thought you might have raced off for a sneaky, last-minute hen's night." She kissed Sabine quickly and leaned into her, a head against her shoulder and an arm around her waist.

"I thought about it," I said breezily. "But you'd have been invited anyway."

Bec smiled. "Good." She turned her attention to my sister. "Sweetheart, your mom wants to talk to you about something."

Sabine sighed, raising her eyes skyward. "The flowers are fine, the caterers are triple confirmed, our dresses still fit, the DJ called to double check everything and yes, Mike has calculated cupcake numbers perfectly. What could she possibly want?" She took Bec's face in both hands, kissed her then stomped away.

"I think she's maybe a little more worked up than she's admitting," I said dryly.

"You think?" Bec drawled, the ice in her glass clinking as she raised her tumbler of scotch to her lips.

I pulled my almost sister-in-law close for a hug. "She just wants it to be perfect."

"It will be," Bec said seriously. "But not because of the food or the music or what we're wearing. It's perfect because we're declaring how much we love each other in front of other people we love."

I had to swallow hard. "How're you doing? Nervous?"

"Not at all." She turned sideways to face me, lifting her elbow onto the railing. "I've been waiting for this my whole life. Even when I thought it was impossible, there was still part of me clinging to the notion that one day I would marry the woman of my dreams, the one who completed me. And it's happening tomorrow." Bec laughed quietly. "Well, not legally for a few more days, but close enough."

"Yes, it is. And I for one, cannot wait." I tipped my wineglass to her and she gently clinked her crystal tumbler against it.

"Neither can I." Bec's gaze was calm, measured, and just a little shrewd. "I'm sorry Brooke couldn't be here."

"Me too." I realized where she was leading. "You heard some of that conversation just now, didn't you?"

Her cheeky dimples confirmed my suspicion. "A little. You know, sweetheart, just because things don't go exactly to plan, or exactly the way you want them to doesn't mean you have to give up on your ideas of happiness." She set her drink on the railing. "Do you remember when Sabine was away on her last deployment and we talked about why I chose to leave the Army?"

"Mhmm." I knew how they'd danced around unspoken attraction to each other for years while working together. Then Rebecca, sneaky thing that she was, sent Sabine home on leave to get her head together after a rough breakup, and arranged for herself to be back in the USA at the same time. After what I gathered to be a very sexy and enlightening night and day together, they ran into a major stumbling block about how they would actually be together, given Don't Ask, Don't Tell was still in play and Bec was Sabs's commanding officer. Big no-no.

Bec's eyebrows drew together. "You know, despite everything I felt for her, and how desperately I wanted us to be together I still couldn't quite accept making such big change to my life."

"Which one?"

"Leaving my job," she said instantly. "Even when I knew it was the easiest and most logical solution for us. It was my security, the thing I'd clung to the last time I'd been afraid to commit to someone. I didn't know how I would leave that behind. What if I was making a mistake, what if I was confusing lust for love? All those fears were so overwhelming, and I would have had nowhere to go if I left the Army."

"It was The Incident that changed your mind, wasn't it?"

"Yes," Bec said simply. "One fear overrode another. It was as simple as that." She drank a slow mouthful of scotch, the edges of her mouth curled up in enjoyment. "Some things are too big to ignore, some things you have to take a chance on. Love is one of those things."

I fiddled with my wineglass, turning it in slow circles on the railing. "But what if I'm not brave enough? Or what if I'm just not enough for her, if I can't be what she needs or wants? What if I ask her to change her life for me and that completely fucks up her relationship with her dad, and then I fuck things up with her and she's left with nothing?"

"I can't answer that, Jana, because nobody knows how things will happen until they happen. But I do know you're brave enough, you are *enough* for her and I'm sure Brooke knows that too."

"Maybe." I hoped she knew it. "I guess I still thought that maybe she'd say fuck it, fuck the stuff with her dad and tell him exactly how she feels about her job, and about me and come charging back to me saying she's ready to throw herself fully into Us. This whole thing has basically hit all my insecurity buttons, because I feel like what she's actually saying by not being here is that I'm not important enough to her."

"Or…maybe what she's saying is that she's in an incredibly difficult position, and she needs something big that's going to show her the way, something or someone to help her. You need to be that thing."

But hadn't I already done that? Hadn't I told her I loved her? Hadn't I said that I'd wait until she was comfortable with moving from a dating relationship to a real, committed long-term one? Hadn't I said that I would stand by her even if she didn't tell her dad about me? Surely that was enough? Yes I had, but maybe not in a particularly convincing way. More an *Okay, whatever, I don't want to argue about this anymore* sort of agreement.

Bec leaned close, eyes twinkling. "In case you're not sure, what I'm saying is maybe you need to evaluate exactly what's important to you, and if you can compromise what you want right now so you two can move forward."

We were quiet for a while and I turned the problem over in my head like a Rubik's Cube. Eventually I conceded, "You're right. I think it has to be me because honestly, I can't see her changing this part of her life. Not any time soon, and maybe not even for me." The thought still hurt, but at the same time, the thought of losing her over the issue with her dad hurt even more. "I don't want to lose this because I can't let go of something that, in the scheme of things, isn't really that important." If I had Brooke and my family, and she had my family too, then what did anything else matter?

Bec mused quietly. "Mhmm. If you love her then you need to show her, even when things aren't happening as you want them to. She needs to know you're there, no matter what. Don't waste the moment."

"She needs to know…especially from someone who's used to jumping out the window and sprinting away the moment things aren't the way she wants them to be?" I asked wryly.

Bec, who knew my history and teased me about it as much as Sabine, laughed. "Yes, exactly. But I don't think that's what you're going to do."

"What makes you so sure?"

Bec cupped my face gently in her hand. "Because you're in love with her."

CHAPTER THIRTY-ONE

Mom's wedding day breakfast was scheduled for *seven a.m. sharp and don't any of you dare be late.* I caught a ride from the hotel with the M 'n' Ms, relaxing in the backseat while Mitch, who had obviously caught Sabine's excitement bug, chattered incessantly for the whole twenty-minute trip. Mike and I engaged with him whenever he took a breath and the rest of the time, I stared at my phone. Not wanting to wake Brooke up early on a Saturday, I hadn't texted her yet, but then I worried that not texting her might make her think I was upset with her.

So I typed and deleted a dozen messages, trying to find the right tone between telling her I missed her and not making her feel guilty that she wasn't here. In the end I just wrote *Morning, beautiful xo* as we pulled into my parents' long, packed-dirt driveway.

The moment Mitch cut the engine, it was full steam ahead with family stuff. Mom had gone all out with breakfast, putting on a hotel buffet-style spread. Sabine, normally the master of unconscious stress fasting, actually ate a full breakfast and Bec and I shared a look of relief across the table. Game on.

After we'd finished, I snuck outside. I made my way across the freshly cut lawn to the far corner of the post-and-rail fence enclosing the backyard. I gave silent thanks that the weather was near perfect—cool and promising to remain rain-free, with the sun trying to break through light clouds. The ceremony was scheduled for three p.m., hair and makeup crew were to arrive at midday and I wanted to have a quick shower before they got to work. Given it was only eight thirty I had plenty of time to call Brooke before things got hectic. Even more hectic. Thankfully, with everything moving so quickly and so much happening, Mom and Dad hadn't pushed about her absence.

Brooke answered on the second ring, the sound of high heels moving quickly on the sidewalk coming though the phone. Her voice was low and intimate. "Hey. I was just thinking about you guys."

"Hey yourself. Sorry, I would have called earlier but Mom insists meals are phone-free zones. Is this a bad time?"

"Not at all. I'm just walking to the bus stop."

"How're you feeling?"

"Nervous, but okay. I spent most of yesterday afternoon and last night working out some strategies and whatnot." She cleared her throat. "So, how're things there?"

I turned back to the house. "Quietly insane. We just finished breakfast and I'm trying to chill before the preparations start. But everything seems to be going as it should, if Sabine's lists are anything to go by."

"Sounds great. I wish I were there," she said quietly.

"Me too," I responded before I could help myself. After a quick pause to collect my thoughts, I dove in. "Brooke, listen. I've been thinking, and getting my ass kicked by Sabs and Bec about my behavior. There has to be compromise here. And it's me. I yield."

"You…yield?"

"Yes. I know I've already said it, but honestly, I don't think I was fully committed to leaving it alone." I took a deep breath. "But I am now, I swear. I'm not going to push you about your relationship with your dad. I'm not going to niggle or nag about your job. I'm not going to pout if you're driving more slowly than me to our relationship destination. I'm just going to support however you live your life, for as long as you'll let me."

"Why?" That one word came out so hoarsely it took me a moment to realize what it was. "I know you care about it."

"Because me being stubborn about this isn't good for us. Because I'm sticking on it for all the wrong reasons, selfish reasons that in the scheme of *us* don't even matter. So, I'm surrendering."

"Damn, I love it when you surrender," she said huskily.

"Me too…" I swallowed hard. "What I'm saying is I'm with you, no matter what. I just want you to live the life that makes you comfortable and happy, and I want to be by your side while you do that. I love you." I let out a long breath, feeling the tension ease along with it. That feeling of peace was all the confirmation I needed to know I'd made the right choice. "And my family will always be there for you too, if you need them, because I'm sure that they'll love you too."

"Jana Banana!" Mom hollered from the back porch. "Where the heck are you?"

I moved the phone away from my mouth, and yelled back, "Right here!" as I waved at her from my very visible and obvious position. Then I raised the phone to my ear again. "Did you hear that?"

Brooke laughed. "I did."

"Mmm, well based on that, whether you love my family back is questionable."

"I'm absolutely certain I will," she murmured. "Now go help your sister get married, and I'll talk to you after."

The rest of the morning was spent putting final touches on decorations and checking the lighting strung around the marquee and exterior of the house for later that evening. Once the hair and makeup crew arrived, Bec was installed in my childhood bedroom while Sabine stayed sequestered in hers. I was sent downstairs to be done at the kitchen table while I watched caterers carrying trays of deliciousness moving in and out of Mom's kitchen. Unfair.

There was nothing from Brooke to let me know how her meeting had gone, and part of me wondered if she was somewhere, alone and upset about what had transpired and thinking I was uncontactable. I sent her a heart emoji text and left it at that. There was no response, and I had to set aside my worry about her to concentrate on the rest of my day. I could call Brooke later that evening to talk about her meeting. Right now, I had to help my sister get married.

Once I'd been made up, and my hair done in a fabulous half-up and half-down style with loose front bits and some complicated braid woven into it that I knew I'd never be able to replicate, I slipped into the bathroom to dress. When I checked on Sabs, she seemed excited but stable as Mitch and Mom helped her into her dress, so I left them alone and went to help Rebecca. Guests were arriving, and the sound of laughter and talking carried through the house.

Bec, in a silk robe, sat at my childhood dresser with her hands resting in her lap. She'd chosen to have her hair mostly down, and the stylist had pulled parts of it back to form a sort of half-crown, and the rest fell in loose curls down her back. Bec glanced up as I closed the door. "Wow. You look incredible."

"Not as incredible as you're going to look once I help you into that dress."

She stood, her grin huge and infectious. "Let's do it."

Bec's gown was a lacy off-the-shoulder sweetheart neckline with a short, lace-detailed tulle train and pearl buttons up her spine hiding the zip. The bodice hugged her curves and then fell away from her body in elegant lines. I'd just finished zipping her in when I heard Mom yelling, "Gerhardt! You'd better be getting into that suit right now!"

Bec and I caught each other's glance and burst into laughter. I shook my head and gestured at the wall that divided the two bedrooms. "Sure you want to legally tie yourself to this insanity?"

"Never surer."

A knock preceded Mitch's question, "Y'all decent?"

I made a quick check. "Yes."

"Jana, swapsies. Sabine needs you." He lowered his voice. "And I need a goddamned drink. Did you happen to smuggle a hip flask, darlin'? This best man stuff is hella stressful."

"Sorry, no hidden booze." I reached up and unnecessarily brushed down the shoulders of his suit jacket before carefully straightening his tie and fluffing his pocket square. The same tie and pocket square that Brooke had chosen. The sudden surge of missing her was so strong that I had to pause before answering, "Where exactly did you think I'd put a hip flask?"

"Strap it to the inside of your thigh or shove it down that cleavage you've suddenly grown."

I smiled sweetly and punched his pec. "It's called a push-up bra, and thanks for the reminder about my rack, you ass."

"You look amazin' and you know it."

"Yeah, I do, and I do."

Bec chuckled. "That's my line."

"I'm glad you remember. And *you* look so damned beautiful I could cry. I'll see you out there in a few minutes?"

Her smile was brilliant and full-dimpled. She paused for the briefest moment then pulled me in for a hug. Hair and makeup be damned. "Love you."

"Love you too."

I left Bec with Mitch and raced out the door, down the hall into Sabine's room. She was already dressed and carefully slipping into her heels. My sister's hair was up in a complex chignon, complete with a diamond hairpiece woven into the back and loose pieces tucked behind her ears. Her gown clung to her long lithe body, an ethereal mix of lace-cutout bodice and an airy chiffon skirt. A lace racerback partially covered the large, irregular scar next to her right shoulder blade.

Immediately I noticed a conspicuous motherly absence. "Where's Mom?"

"Hovering around Dad." She stared at her partially open window. "Sounds busy down there."

"It does. I think we're almost set." I moved to stand behind her, staring at our reflections in the mirror. "Do you need help with something?"

"How's Bec?"

"She's fine, absolutely fucking gorgeous." I narrowed my eyes at her. "Did you drag me in here just to give you an update when you're about to see her?"

She shrugged and turned to face me. "Maybe."

"Sneaky bitch." Carefully, I hugged her then stepped back and smoothed her dress down. "I still can't believe today is finally here. My big sister, getting almost-married."

"I can't believe it either. I'm so glad you're here, Jannie." Her eyes went wide. "There's nobody else I would want to stand by my side. Seriously, every time I think about it I could cry."

"Sabs, stop. You can-*not* do this, not now." I raised my eyes to the ceiling, willing the brimming tears away.

"I can't help it, I love you so much and my whole life whenever I've thought about getting married, you've always been right there standing beside me."

Desperate to shift away from the sappiness before I totally lost my shit, I blurted, "Did you know bridesmaids were originally just decoy brides to confuse evil spirits so the bride wouldn't be eaten by a demon on her wedding day. So that's how much I love you. I'm willing to step in front of a demon for you."

"And I'd step in front of a demon for you too." Sabine reached down to grab my hands. As she spoke, she swung them side to side. "Do you remember when you stayed with me after The Incident?"

"Yes. Why are we talking about this now?"

"Because it's important, Jana."

"Okay." Sure, fine, if she wanted to talk about those awful weeks of rehabilitation minutes before she was due to walk down the aisle then that was her choice.

"I know I was taking pain meds and some things were hazy, but I remember we were watching *The Notebook* and you were laughing that nothing was ever that perfect, and movies made us want unrealistic things." Sabine's eyes bored into mine.

I laughed. "Yeah, I remember that."

"And what did I say?"

"You said movies reminded us of how things should be. How they could be." I grinned. "And yeah, I thought that maybe you were taking too many pain pills."

Sabine tossed her head back and laughed. "Maybe I was, but I was *very* poetic at the time." She sobered, squeezing my hands firmly. "You asked me how I knew she was worth it. Worth the fear and all the issues trying to keep us apart. And what did I tell you?"

"You told me…you told me that the only time you felt whole was when she was with you." I bit my lower lip, willing it not to tremble.

"Yes," she said quietly. Her steady hands grasped my shoulders and held me tight. "Do you understand what I'm saying? Don't be dumb and don't wait until it's too late. This is it. This is the moment where it all comes together, or where you let it fall apart."

"Bec told you about our conversation last night, didn't she."

"She did."

"I called Brooke this morning," I offered. "And told her I didn't care if she never tells her dad about me. I just want her to be happy and I just want to be with her, whenever she's ready."

"Did you mean it, or were you just saying it?" This was so Sabine to try and fix my problems when she should be focusing on herself.

"I meant it. I love her, and like I told Brooke my family is big enough for her too."

"Clever Jana. Look at you, acting like a grown up in a relationship. Only took how many years?" She smirked then instinctively stepped back.

I didn't aim a kick or a punch or a flick at her. What I did do was launch myself at her, hugging her tightly but carefully because, you know—hair and makeup and delicate dresses and stuff. "I love you so much."

"Love you too," she whispered against my ear.

Dad's voice came from somewhere on the landing, his voice tight with emotion. "Sabine? Rebecca? Are you ready? All the guests are seated, and everything is ready to start whenever you are."

I inhaled deeply. "Are you ready to go?"

Sabine took my hand. "Absolutely."

"Right, then let's do it."

Sabs and I left her room hand in hand, and on our way past my bedroom door, I knocked. "Bec? It's time."

"Coming," she called. A few seconds later, Mitch emerged, his tall muscular form blocking the doorway. He was on the verge of crying and as he stepped to the side to let Bec out, I passed him one of the tissues I had hidden in my bra.

"Thanks," he muttered. After a pause he added, "So that's what's pushing them up?"

"Screw you," I laughed.

"You going to get through this, Mitch?" Sabine deadpanned. "Do you need a Valium? Shot of tequila?"

"Both. Y'all just look so goddamned beautiful and I love you so much."

Bec stepped out of my room, spotted Sabine, and they reacted at pretty much the same moment and in pretty much the same way.

Sabine's mouth worked open and closed like a fish tossed onto land. "Ohmygod."

Bec's eyes went wide as she reached for my sister. "Darling…"

Sabs rushed forward, and I inserted myself between them, arms out to keep them apart. "No kissing. Not yet."

Dad made a noise that sounded like a cross between a sob and a squeal. Jesus it was about to become a tear factory at any moment. I leaned over the second-floor railing, waving to catch the DJ's attention. I gave him an *okay* symbol and he flashed me a thumbs-up in response. Thirty seconds later the music started and I heard the sound of fifty-something people standing.

I cleared my throat. "Well, let's get you two fake-hitched."

CHAPTER THIRTY-TWO

Walking up the aisle with my arm looped in Mitch's I looked straight ahead, beyond the post-and-rail yard fence, knowing that if I looked at the crowd and saw my mom's or grandparents' faces, I'd totally lose it. In the flat pasture behind the yard, the huge white marquee and dance floor waited. Everything looked wonderful, the lighting was set up, weather still fabulous, yep, don't cry, don't cry.

"You okay, darlin'?" Mitch mumbled.

Judging by the roughness of his voice, he was seconds away from tears himself. I squeezed his forearm. "Mhmm. You?"

"No I'm not," he choked out. "I need more tissues."

Laughing quietly, I leaned into him as we made our way to the celebrant, Donna—an old Army friend of Bec's who wore a fabulous navy three-piece suit and tie, with killer heels. Mitch and I leaned in close with arms still looped as we turned to watch Sabine and Rebecca make their way up the polished wood aisle runner. The moment I heard the first strains of that damned wedding march, I had to tamp down my tears. My waterproof mascara could do only so much and I had a feeling I'd need it at full effectiveness when my sister and her fiancée exchanged vows.

Dad walked both Sabs and Bec down the aisle, one of them on each elbow, his chest so puffed with pride he seemed to have expanded a foot out and upward. Sabine kept trying to glance around him at Bec and eventually Dad nudged her until she faced forward again. According to Sabine's diagram and the rehearsal the day before, Dad left the brides in the right place. He hugged both of them, then hugged me and Mitch—none of which was listed in Sabine's minute-by-minute schedule—uh-oh—before taking his place in the front row beside Mom.

Donna indicated that everyone should sit. "Thank you everyone for being here to witness the joining of Rebecca Anne Keane and Sabine Ingrid Fleischer…"

I held my bouquet, watched Donna, tried hard to absorb the words and mostly succeeded. Thankfully, Sabs and Bec had opted for a short ceremony but five minutes in, I was already antsy. Sabs, Bec, and Mitch were Army stiffs and used to standing still for ages. I got fidgety easily—unless I was with clients, or arguing with other attorneys, or paying attention to something I could turn to my client's advantage. Midway through a heartwarming spiel about love and commitment, my control on my attention faltered and I let my eyes wander.

Hmm, Mom and Dad, Oma and Opa, Grandma and Grandpa—all crying. Family members, close friends of the brides who made the trip from D.C., great hair, family, friends, family, nice dress, family, squirming child of cousin, Mike behind them on the aisle, Brooke beside him.

Wait.

I let out a surprised squeak, cringing at my maid-of-honor faux pas. Sabine leaned close and winked at me, and though I'd never have thought it possible, Rebecca's smile had grown even wider. With immense effort I managed to stop myself from simultaneously bursting into tears and throwing myself at them for hugs. But I couldn't stop staring at Brooke, whose smile probably matched my own. Still smiling, she indicated with a tilt of her head that I should return my attention to the task at hand, which I did, but not without effort.

As expected, my mascara was put to the test during the vows. Bec held Sabine's hands, her thumbs sliding up and down the backs of her knuckles. Bec's usually calm, confident tone held an edge of tears as she spoke. "Sabine, you have given me everything I could ever have dreamed of. More than just yourself, you've given me a family…"

When it was her turn, Sabine, as she was prone to do when nervous and put on the spot, laughed. She clamped her mouth closed and shook her head as Bec leaned close and murmured something to her that I couldn't quite hear. Sabine swallowed, nodded and wrangled her tears. "Rebecca, Bec. Thank you for giving me a safe place to rest…"

Rings and kisses were exchanged, and Donna declared Sabs and Bec joined for all intents and purposes until they were legally married in a few days back in D.C. We all wandered back down the aisle, and as I walked past Brooke I held out my hand, stretching past Mike, and felt the faintest brush of her fingers. Soft as it was, I'd never felt as connected to anyone as I did in that moment.

As soon as Sabs and Bec moved past the final row, I nabbed them. It was clear from their expressions that they'd had a hand in Brooke's last-minute attendance, and I needed to make this quick before they were engulfed by family and well-wishers. I went for an easy question. "What have you guys done?"

"What needed to be done," Bec explained. She looked like a naughty kid who'd orchestrated a day off school to go to an amusement park.

Sabine nodded her agreement. "Just made a phone call, that's all. Meddled a bit, you know, like I do."

There were no words I could find to express myself, so I launched at them and hugged them both, first Bec and then Sabine. "Thank you for sharing your happy day with me, Sabs," I murmured near her ear. I could feel Bec's hand on my shoulder, connecting the three of us.

Sabine squeezed me, her voice tight with emotion. "Don't you get it by now? Your happiness is my happiness." She let me go and wiped under her eyes. "Goddammit, stupid happy tears."

I blew them each a kiss then slipped away, weaving in and out of guests, pausing to exchange a brief word before promising each person I'd be back for a longer chat. Brooke stood clustered with Mitch and Mike, the three of them already with champagne glasses in hand. Mitch looked like he was being poisoned. I stopped a waiter, silently exchanged Mitch's champagne for a beer then turned to Brooke. I could barely get the words out. "You came."

Even if her smile hadn't been splitting her face, the expression in her eyes gave her away. I saw everything I'd been looking for, all her love and her trust. "I did. Surprise?"

Apologizing to the boys, I pulled Brooke to the side and unable to think of anything else to say, hugged her then drew back to kiss her lightly. "You look amazing."

"Thanks." She laughed, indicating up and down herself. "I wore this on the plane, touched up my makeup in the airport bathroom then drove here at speeds you'd be proud of. I feel like a mess, especially standing next to you, who looks so incredible that I can't even describe it."

"Thank you." I gently thumbed the edge of her mouth. "Brooke, this is going to sound wrong no matter how I say it, but what are you doing here? What about the meeting with your dad?"

"I had it, well I had an abbreviated version of it. On the phone as I drove to the airport." She let out a breath, smiling uneasily. "While I was waiting for the bus, I texted Sabine to wish her well and she called me pretty much right away and reminded me that I'd RSVP'd to the wedding, and if I wanted to attend I was still more than welcome." Her smile relaxed a little. "Something about already adjusting the catering numbers to accommodate me and the fact that she hadn't seen you moping this much since you found out Milli Vanilli lip-synced all their songs."

I couldn't help laughing. "Very true."

"Mmm." Brooke touched my cheek, leaned in for a quick kiss. "Apparently Sabine just *happened* to be looking at flights for this morning and just *happened* to notice there were seats free from D.C. to Dayton. She said if there was any way I could make the ceremony to let her know and she'd have a new plane ticket booked for me by the time I got to the airport, and a rental car waiting at this end."

I rolled my eyes, though my stomach felt like it was doing excited backflips. "Sounds like her, bossy to the very end."

Brooke grinned. "Yeah well, seems it's a shared trait."

"Smartass."

The grin turned shaky. "She also said I shouldn't be afraid or stay away because I was worried you were upset with me. Which I was because there's been that weird underlying awkwardness ever since our argument. But there was always the promise of champagne and food to make it worth the flight."

I let out a breath, opted for the truth. "Honestly, I was upset. But not with you, not at all. Just at what was happening. I'm sorry, I should have made that clear. But I meant what I said on the phone this morning, Brooke. Every word." Sabine's frantic waving interrupted my very important conversation. "Ugh, they want photos now." RIGHT NOW if the hand signals Sabine was giving me were any indication. "Sorry. Will you be okay for a little while?"

"Of course." Brooke shooed me gently in the direction of the brides. "Go, look gorgeous. I'll be right here."

Bec and Sabs had decided they mostly wanted a roaming photographer to capture candids, and shots of them with everyone rather than spending hours posing and waiting around post-ceremony.

We spent fifteen minutes taking a few official photos of the wedding party under the huge sycamore tree shading a corner of the yard, then some with parents and grandparents before dispersing back to the marquee.

I beelined for Brooke who stood at the edge of the crowd with a champagne flute in one hand and a canapé in the other. I snuck a sip of her champagne. "Can we talk about what happened?" Clearly something big if she was here, not there.

"Of course but don't you have to circulate?"

"That can wait a few minutes." I grabbed her hand and pulled her away from the crowd, toward the barn where we could talk in peace. "Follow me."

Mom intercepted us at the edge of the marquee. "Jana Banana? I've convinced Sabs and Rebecca that there should be one quick speech after all. Can you speak on behalf of the family? Twenty minutes?"

"Yep, sure, fine, whatever."

My mother stared pointedly at me. Then Brooke. Then our joined hands. Oh yeah, that's right. Oops. "Mom, this is Brooke Donnelly." I straightened and added, "My girlfriend. Brooke, this is my mom, Carolyn Fleischer."

Mom's carefully cultivated veneer of neutrality broke. Under my breath, as Mom's expression changed, I murmured to Brooke, "Here comes the hug, move if you don't want it, seriously, she's going in."

But Brooke didn't move.

Mom barely wasted time with a, "Wonderful to meet you" before she let out an excited squeal and enveloped Brooke in an embrace. "Oh, sweetie, I'm so glad you made it."

My girlfriend didn't hesitate, hugging my mom right back. She looked part-dazed, part-pleased and part like she was about to cry. I had the feeling I might cry myself. When Mom was finally done with her overly familiar greeting, Brooke dabbed under her eyes and turned on a brilliant smile. "Jana mentioned that you're responsible for most of this decorating, Carolyn? It's absolutely beautiful. The fairy lights look amazing."

"Thank you. I did have some help from the ladies in my craft circle. Everyone took on an aspect to work on, and the theme was so easy that they simply…"

I tuned Mom out, knowing she'd blather for ten minutes about it and other stuff like someone stealing her special scissors and that they'd gotten xyz material on sale and wasn't it beautiful how something matched something else? Brooke indulged my mother, prompting and actually genuinely engaging with her as they debated light and color and a bunch of other boring decorating shit.

Once Mom finally let us go, Brooke left her empty glass on a passing tray and we wove through the crowd. I raised a hand to Sabine, then pointed to the barn. Sabs grinned and nodded, then made eye contact with Brooke and gave her another cheeky *I'm watching you* gesture. Brooke laughed and intertwined our fingers as we walked away from the marquee and up the hill toward the old barn.

In our heels, we picked our way through the ankle-length grass, silent for the short walk. Bales of hay were stacked high along the far wall, the sweet smell of grass filling the space. It'd been years since I'd come into the barn, but it was exactly the same as I remembered. Brooke looked around, walking slowly across the old, cracked concrete floor. She peered over the half-door of one of the stables while I fiddled with the latch on the stable door.

"So, what's going on?" I asked.

Brooke's answer was to pull me close and kiss me, long and lingering. "What's going on is that I think my could fall in love with you has turned into an I love you."

My voice squeaked up. "Oh? You've…arrived?"

"I have." Her hands slid to my waist. "I…after you called, I stood on the side of the road and just burst into tears. And I just kept thinking that I'd made the wrong choice by not being with you, and that I was about to make one of the biggest mistakes of my life if I didn't tell my dad that I don't want to take over his business. Then Sabine called, and everything just escalated from there. So I called him and told him I wasn't coming to the meeting because I was going to my girlfriend's sister's wedding."

My voice squeaked even higher. "Really?"

"Mhmm. I also told him there was no point in having his meeting because I didn't want to take the reins of Donnelly and Donnelly. Not in a year, or two or even ten. It was the world's quickest life-changing conversation."

"I…shit." There were so many questions, worries, statements in my head but the only one that mattered was, "Are you okay? Are you and your dad okay?"

"I think we will be, eventually. He's a little upset and I think more than a little mad, but with some time and communication and a better explanation I hope he'll understand why I did it. Or did both things really."

"Why did you do it?" I asked softly.

278 E. J. Noyes

"Because I realized you were right. I wasn't living honestly. And, Jana, fuck…I want to be with you. And I can't do that if I'm hiding. I've been out most of my life, but I feel like I've always been hiding a part of myself. You grabbed and dragged that part of me into the light where it should be." She exhaled a long breath. "You're *It*, Jana. You're the one. I know that's heavy and in your face, but it's true. I can't keep you in the shadows when you're my light."

"Oh."

She took my face in her hands, her gaze so intense that I felt completely exposed. "I love you. I want to be with you. I want to be part of your family. I mean, I haven't even been here for two hours and I already feel so welcomed."

"I want that too," I managed to choke out.

Brooke kissed my forehead then released my face to take my hands. "I'm sorry, but you shouldn't expect any family outings or anything including my dad for a while, if ever. I don't know if he'll ever come around and accept it. I mean I don't think he'll be rude or anything like that if he sees you," she added hastily, her grip on my hands tightening briefly. "He's not that kind of guy. He's the head in the sand kind."

"Okay, well I guess we'll deal with his behavior as it comes. I really didn't want to cause issues with your family, Brooke. I just couldn't stand to see you hurting that way. Like we established, I'm a pushy bitch."

She laughed. "Yeah, sometimes. But I know that it's because you love and care about me. And honestly, now that I've told him and I no longer feel like I'm going to hurl, I'm kind of relieved. Sad, but relieved at the same time."

"What will you do now? Are you going to keep working for your dad?" I asked cautiously.

"Honestly, I'm not sure. If I stay, then I need to step down from my team leadership role. Maybe I'll contract myself to the company so I can work part-time and really get into my art. Sell that. Eat into my savings a bit if I need to." She stood up straighter. "Maybe I'll start up my own small firm and take on private clients, people who want beautiful unique houses. Just to make sure the bills get paid in case the art thing goes bust. I really don't know until I talk to him next week." Brooke put her hand on her stomach, suggesting the thought was nauseating.

"Your art thing won't go bust," I said, meaning it. "You're so fucking talented, you're going to have more buyers than you can cope with."

"You really think so?"

"I know so. And if you need help with bills, we can just move in together and share them." The offer came without me thinking about it, but the moment I realized what I'd just said I knew it was the absolute truth. "Obviously not now," I hastened to add. "For one thing, neither of us has a closet big enough for all our shoes."

"So, we'd have to buy a bigger house then?"

"Way bigger. I think you should design it. Our own beautiful, unique home."

Brooke laughed, then paused, seemed to sort through her thoughts. "Do you remember that day I stayed home from work to finish Sabine and Rebecca's gift?"

"Mhmm."

"I told you that it was a perfect day, that you'd gone off to work in the morning, we'd talked through the day, I'd worked at home and then you came back to me." She blew out a breath. "I left some things out. I left out the part where all I could think about for most of the day was how I wanted that to be our life and how it turned into this runaway fantasy. Dinner on the table when you got home, you telling me about helping a family and me showing you what I'd been doing all day. Going to bed together, waking up together and then doing it again the next day and the next and the next. I want us to get a dog or cat or bunch of fish or a fucking chinchilla or whatever. I want kids with you. And whether all of this happens in a year or three, or whenever, I don't care. But I want it, and I want it with you."

My mouth was suddenly dry. "Oh? You're really sure?"

"Yeah, I am. I'm sure, because thinking about all that scared the shit out of me. And I've been fixated on that, on how terrifying it was to want to settle down with you, to move on from everything I've been holding on to. And I realized the reason I'm so afraid is because it's important, it means something to me. *You* mean something to me." She sucked in a quick breath. "I've been so focused on my own issues and my fear of you leaving me that I haven't been focusing on all the ways you're showing me you want to stay. Like your call this morning. You've been there waiting patiently for me, reminding me— sometimes gently, sometimes more…forcefully—of our destination."

"It's a really wonderful destination. Magnificent views. I'm so glad you made it."

"Same. Sorry it took me a little longer." She grinned. "I told you I'm a slow driver. But I'm here now so we can drive on together."

I couldn't think of anything to say, because the feeling was so strong that a simple *me too* wouldn't suffice. So I did the only thing I could do. I pressed myself against her, pushing her until her back hit the stable wall and she let out a little squeak. Then I kissed her. I kissed her like I'd missed her so much it felt physical. And I kissed her like she'd just told me she basically wanted us to spend the rest of our lives together, make a family, together.

So all in all, it was a rather nice kiss.

I leaned my forehead against hers, lightly kissed her nose. "I love you. And fair warning, when, or if all of this happens, my mom is going to freak out."

"I look forward to it."

"Uh, let's revisit that idea once you've seen what her freaking out looks like." I laughed. "We're totally going to U-Haul, right? This is a massive toaster oven moment."

"Have you been on lesbian dictionary dot com again, babe?"

"Well how else will I learn?"

"I'll teach you, the way I have with everything else."

"Jana! Brooke!" Mike called through the open barn door. "Fair warning to um, get dressed or whatever."

"We're dressed!" I shot back.

"Phew." His head appeared around the door. "That could have been weird. Sorry to interrupt…whatever important thing that seems to be happening here but your mom is looking for you for that speech. She's…you know."

Yeah, I did know. "I'll be there in a minute."

Brooke took my hand. "Come on, I'm very much looking forward to hearing this speech."

"We'll talk more later?"

"You bet." She kissed me lightly. Not an earth-shattering, go weak at the knees kiss. But it was the sweetest kiss for what it promised. The future.

The dance floor had cleared, with everyone in a semicircle around the raised stage, glasses in their hands. The DJ handed me champagne and a microphone. Serious business. I stepped up, glanced around and just started talking. "Hi, sorry I haven't prepared anything. Because this is technically a casual not-wedding, everyone told me there would be no speeches." I stared pointedly at Sabine, who raised both hands and shrugged, then shifted my attention away from her to peer around the marquee filled with people. "In case any of you don't know who I am—in which case I'm offended—I'm Jana, Sabine's younger, smarter, better-looking sister."

"Lies!" Sabine called.

The crowed tittered.

"Okay, maybe not smarter. But definitely the other two." I cleared my throat, desperately trying to think of what to say. "When I was five, a girl in my grade asked me if I wanted to be her best friend. She had the best dolls, prettiest hair ribbons and really great lunches that she said she'd share with me. But I told her I couldn't be her best friend because I already had a best friend and I'd had her from when I, and I quote, got borned."

Everyone laughed and I waited until they'd settled before continuing, "Sabine, I'm so blessed, so...*honored* to have you as my sister. My best friend. My champion. I love you so much. You've taught me so many things, but I think the greatest lesson I've learned from you is about love."

My voice cracked and I had to clamp my back teeth together and pause a moment before I could continue. "I used to think having a sister, *my* sister was one of the best things in the world. I recently realized that wasn't exactly true. Having my sister give me another sister is one of the best things in the world. Bec, I love you. Thank you for being the second sister I never knew I wanted, but now know that I need. When I first saw the way Sabs looked at you, like she could finally breathe again, I knew that everything would be okay. I'm not going to do the welcome to the family speech, because you've been part of it from the moment you took my sister's hand."

"Hear hear!" whooped Dad, and again I had to wait for the applause to die down.

"So all I'll say is congratulations and may your lives together be eternally fulfilling. To Sabine and Rebecca." I raised my glass, finding Brooke in the crowd. Eyes locked with hers, I finished my toast. "To love."

Brooke raised her champagne flute, mouthed *I love you* and drank.

The crowd split as Steve Winwood's "Higher Love" began to play, and I caught Sabs's nose wrinkle before Bec laughed and pulled her onto the dance floor. They'd mutually agreed on this eighties flashback song for their official couple dance, though Sabine had grumbled, "Do we have to dance by ourselves for the whole song, with people just staring at us? That's always so awkward at weddings and I've only been the starer, not the staree."

So I stared at Sabine, mostly because I knew how annoyed it would make her. She managed to discreetly give me the finger without moving her hand from Bec's back. When they reached the point in the song where the DJ announced that people should join the happy couple on the dance floor, I slipped through the crowd to find Brooke. On my way I was accosted in turn by my maternal grandparents, a friend of Bec's, one of the guys Sabine had been in the car with during The Incident and his wife, and what felt like a hundred people wanting to tell me how lovely my speech was.

By the time I'd finished talking, Brooke had moved on and was sitting with Oma at one of the small tables. I collected some wedding cupcakes, a fork and a half glass of white wine. I could hear Oma talking very, very slowly in German and caught part of the conversation about babies. I groaned inwardly—not you too, Oma.

I bent down and kissed my grandmother's forehead, then set the plate with two cupcakes on the table in front of her. "English please, Oma. And enough with the great-grandkids talk, please. You're as bad as Mom."

Oma raised a forefinger in protest, but as asked, switched to English. "Your Brooke was talking to me in German. I was being polite by doing the same."

"Mmm." I handed her the glass of wine. "And I'm sure Brooke was being polite speaking German to you." Brooke knowing German was a fact she had somehow avoided mentioning.

Brooke laughed. "I think *speaking German* is a generous term. I'm really not very good."

Oma leaned forward and cupped Brooke's chin the way she did with all of us when she was pleased. "You are excellent." She leaned close to kiss Brooke's temple then settled back and asked me, "Where is your Opa?"

"Dancing with Sabine." I glanced at Brooke who'd lowered her head and was blinking rapidly. Bless her.

"Wonderful. He will be out of my hair for at least fifteen minutes so I can enjoy my cake and wine in peace." Oma made a small shooing motion. "You two, you should dance also."

I knew my scheming Oma well enough to know she wasn't being rude, nor did she really want to sit alone and eat her cake. She wanted Brooke and me to enjoy time together. I held out my hand to Brooke. "Care to dance?"

"Yes." She stood, then leaned close to Oma. "May I come back to talk with you again, Mrs. Fleischer?"

Oma reached up to squeeze Brooke's wrist. "I already told you, please call me Johanna. And yes, I would enjoy that very much." Oma winked at me. "*Auf Deutsch.*"

I mock scowled at her as she smiled cheekily at me, speared some cupcake and waved at us with it.

Brooke smiled, shaking her head almost in disbelief. "Your family is so great."

"So great at pushing my buttons you mean." I held her close as we moved around the dance floor. "You didn't tell me you spoke German."

"I don't really." She grinned. "Mostly it's what I remember from high school, but I started an online brush-up course." She twirled me expertly.

"Why?"

"Because even though you minimized it, German seemed important to you and to your family," she said seriously.

It kind of was, because everything family was important to me. "You did that for me? For my grandparents?" Even though I'd told her that both my paternal grandparents spoke English as well as any native speaker, she'd still done it.

"Mhmm."

"You're amazing. Don't tell Sabs, she'll never leave you alone."

Brooke burst into laughter, looking so beautiful and vibrant that I didn't care that we were in the middle of a crowd of my relatives and Sabine and Bec's friends, or that we might create an obstacle. I pulled her closer, and with my arms around her neck gave her a long slow kiss. "Why are you so amazing? Sabs and Bec think you're wonderful. My parents are completely smitten. You've won over Oma and Opa. Grandma and Grandpa nabbed me before to tell me how sweet you are and how you talked about rescue cats and golf with them. How'd you do all that?" She'd taken everything I'd told her about my family and almost turned it into a personal interaction project. She'd done all that, despite the fact I knew it would have made her anxious.

"Just my natural, effortless charm." She grinned. "Worked on you, didn't it?"

"It sure did. Thank you, seriously. Thank you for wanting to be part of my family. They're important to me and I know how hard being with new people can be for you."

She kissed my nose. "I know, sweetheart. And you don't need to thank me, everyone is so great and welcoming. I want to fit in with your family, with your life."

For what felt like the hundredth time that day, I felt tears threatening. My voice was tight when I asked, "Is all lesbian stuff such a cliché?"

She laughed. "Jana, I think love is one great big cliché."

My father's deep voice came from over my shoulder, slightly gruff as it always was when he was emotional. Welcome to the club, Dad. "Excuse me, may I cut in?"

Brooke released her hold, though she kept a hand on the small of my back. "Absolutely. You'll have to save a dance for me, Mr. Fleischer. Jana told me you're an expert foxtrotter."

Dad straightened, a hand resting flat on his belt buckle, his chest puffed out. "Why yes I am. And please call me Gerhardt."

"All right, then. Gerhardt. I took dance classes while studying in Paris and you know I just haven't been able to find myself a decent partner back here." She side-eyed me, barely restraining her teasing smile.

"Well I'd be delighted to take you for a twirl, if Jana can organize some music."

"I look forward to it, and I'm certain she can." Brooke softly kissed the edge of my mouth and with a final *charm the socks off* smile at my dad, let us be.

Dad offered his hand. "Ready to make your old man look good?"

"Always." I settled my hand on his shoulder. "Still think she's boring?" I asked sweetly.

"I never said that, Jana," he rebutted, barely managing to withhold his manic grin. "I said her job was boring."

"That's not the way I recall the conversation." With our joined hands, I nudged him in the ribs until he grunted.

"Hush, you." Dad pulled me in for a hug, managing to keep us moving around the dance floor as he did so. After an extravagant twirl, he pulled back, his eyes brimming with tears. "I'm so proud of you and your sister, you know that right? You've always made such good choices, Jana. You're smart and caring and compassionate, and now you've found someone who sees all the things your mom and I have known your entire life."

"Dad, stop, please. You're going to make me cry."

He sniffed. "Good. Then I won't be the only one."

We talked quietly as Dad guided me around the floor and as the music finished, he relinquished his hold and led me to the edge where Brooke waited, talking to one of my cousins. Dad opened his arms to her and she stepped in for a hug. Keeping his hands on her shoulders, he warned, "I'll find you later for that foxtrot. I'm not going to forget."

She laughed with genuine pleasure. "I look forward to it."

He thumbed her cheek, grinned his naughty-little-kid grin at her, then left us.

Brooke took my hand. "Shall we?"

We danced for another twenty minutes, rotating through rock, pop, and a slow ballad where we held each other and moved slowly around the floor. We didn't talk, just enjoyed each other. Around us, couples were doing the same, including Sabs and Bec who were talking quietly, both of their faces so bright they could have lit Earth in the sun's place.

Brooke broke first, leaning in to ask, "Can we take a break for a few minutes? I need a drink and to rest my feet."

We sat under the sycamore, provisioned with champagne, water and a bunch of cupcakes. A few people passed by and said hello, greeting Brooke by name and I felt a little warm glow. Once we were satisfactorily fed, hydrated and champagned, I asked, "Ready to get back out there and show them how it's done?"

Brooke's answer was to kiss me swiftly, but not softly, then lead me to the dance floor. As I stepped up onto the wooden platform, my foot caught and turned over, followed by the unmistakable sensation of my heel breaking. "Oh you are fucking kidding me. Again?" Grasping Brooke's hand tightly for balance, I tried to bend down to take the shoe off and only succeeded in nearly pulling us both over.

Laughing, Brooke told me to, "Stand still." Once I'd stopped doing an impersonation of someone on hot coals, she crouched in front of me and carefully angled the broken heel off. "Why, Cinderella, I feel like this is becoming a habit." She slipped the non-broken heel from my other foot then stood with both shoes dangling from her fingertips. "Are you going to blame me for this one too?" she asked dryly.

"What's that saying? If the shoe fits..." Aware of the height difference that matched our first meeting, I rested a hand on her waist and stretched up to murmur in her ear, "I *am* going to blame you for making me the happiest, most in-love girl at the ball."

"Jana, we're at your sister's wedding. Do you think maybe Sabine and Rebecca get dibs on being the happiest gals at the ball?" Brooke slipped out of her heels so we were level, and placed both pairs on the grass at the edge of the dance floor.

Pulling her onto the dance floor, I quietly disagreed, "Nope, because I get you. Cinderella has her very own princess."

Bella Books, Inc.

Women. Books. Even Better Together.

P.O. Box 10543
Tallahassee, FL 32302

Phone: 800-729-4992
www.bellabooks.com

CPSIA information can be obtained
at www.ICGtesting.com
Printed in the USA
LVHW021309051021
699588LV00001B/1

9 781642 470567